The Iron Shadow

Book Ten of the Iron Soul Series

J.M. Briggs

J.M. Briggs

Contents

For everyone who has a nickname that no one remembers the origin of.

1

Life Slipping

Magic slipped out of Alex's hands as she turned her palms up. Lingering in the air, it left faint trails of a dark gray color in its wake. Not for the first time, Alex wondered why the color of her magic was so... dull. Aiden's was a bright fiery red, Nicki's a soothing blue, and Bran's a cheerful yellow. Morgana had silver and Merlin had leaf green. Hers could be considered the color of worked iron, but it seemed too dark to her. Too similar to Arthur's black magic.

She was overthinking it. Alex was sure of that much. Merlin and Morgana had never indicated that the color of magic was important at all. But Alex was still an English major, and she couldn't shake the need to be on the lookout for symbolism. It was easy enough to think that Nicki's blue was related to water being the first kind of magic she used. The same could be said for Aiden with his red magic and fire. Yellow was a bit harder to pin down. Merlin used the earth, but not a lot of plants so his green didn't seem a great match, while silver could relate to Morgana's use of light.

Sighing, Alex ordered the dancing sparks of dark gray to form an orb. She was sitting cross-legged on her bed with Mjǫllnir and Cathanáil on their mounts behind her. The soft hum reassured her that they were both still there. Her bedroom door was shut, but she could still hear muffled sounds coming from the others' rooms: at least the sound of the newscast wasn't echoing up the stairs.

It had taken two weeks for the media to lose interest in the bombing, but the FBI had yet to leave. The reporters who had all but surrounded the campus and pulled any student they could find over to say a few words were gone, but Alex knew that the questions of the bombing wouldn't be answered for a long time. A few organizations and causes had tried to claim responsibility for the bombing, but Arthur wasn't among them. None of them had an explanation for the clear perimeter of the bomb. One area of the Student Union was completely destroyed and there was a clear line between it and the intact area.

The answer was magic, and Merlin and Morgana were paranoid that something was going to reveal it to the government. Collapsing back on her bed, Alex waved her right hand and let the orb of magic disperse. Her eyes traced her bookshelf. There were several novels that she hadn't read in a long time and a couple from her last trip to Aiden's family bookstore that she still hadn't touched. Yet, she had no interest in them. This was what her life as a mage had come to. Practicing the bare basics and staring at the ceiling while she obsessed about her enemy's next move.

Arthur had killed his mother. The ancient Queen of the Sídhe that Arto had fought against was finally dead, but it wasn't a victory for them. Arthur had grown tired of her or frustrated with Scáthbás' concern for the Sídhe outside of Earth. Alex's magic had shown her fragments of their relationship, but not the final conclusion itself. It was like she'd missed a chapter in a book and could now only guess what had happened based on what information she had.

A knock on her door stalled Alex's groan and she sat up on her elbows. The door swung open a moment later. "Hey." Nicki poked her head in. "Whatcha doing?"

"Nothing," Alex said. "I should be working on homework, but...." she fell back against her bed once more. "Eh."

"I know the feeling," Nicki said. "Timothy and Aiden are making dinner; it'll be ready soon."

"I could eat," Alex agreed. "What are they making? Pasta?"

"No actually, a stir-fry."

"Okay." Alex nodded, her head moving awkwardly against her comforter. "Call me when it's ready."

"I will." Nicki paused after she started to close the door. "You okay, honey?"

"You shouldn't be calling me honey," Alex replied. She sat up and smiled. "After all, you finally have that date with Avani."

"Please, I wouldn't look at you twice," Nicki scoffed. "You're pretty and all, but very dramatic. Too dramatic."

"Dramatic, huh?" Alex's smile morphed into something more real. "Well, that solves the mystery, doesn't it?"

"What happened wasn't your fault," Nicki said sternly. "Arthur is just crazy."

"No," Alex said. "He's never been crazy before. The bombing had to have a purpose."

"It's not in his favor for the Feds to figure out that magic is real," Nicki reminded her. They'd been telling themselves that for the last two weeks while the investigation had been going on. "We'll stop him. But classes resume tomorrow and you need to eat, not sulk."

Nicki started to leave, but Alex asked, "Do you think it's going to be weird? Tomorrow, I mean. Being back on campus?"

"Yes," Nicki said. Turning back to Alex, she grimaced a little. "I know that a good chunk of the freshman population left. No one in administration is admitting to how many transfers there have been. The Feds are still sniffing around and the teachers are rattled. There was an actual bombing without a threat. At least no one died."

Nodding, Alex reminded herself of that. Bran's vision had given them time to pull the fire alarm. Thankfully, none of Jenny's fingerprints had been recovered. Nicki walked into the room and leaned over Alex. The redhead kissed her forehead quickly and gave her a soft look.

"We'll get him, Alex. The only question is who gets him first."

With that Nicki swept out, and Alex snorted. Arthur had better pray it wasn't Nicki who got to him first. Her anger toward him putting Aiden in a coma burned as brightly as ever. Alex turned her head and looked at the photos of her family hung up on the wall. Her heart tightened and she struggled against a wave of tears. It was hard. Taking a slow breath, Alex reached up to her pillow and picked up her stuffed dog Galahad. Hugging him to her chest, she waited for the fresh pain to ease.

It was becoming easier. That was one of the worst parts. The knowledge and realization that the pain really did start to fade away. It wouldn't ever be gone. Arthur had killed her parents and pushed her into the position of sending her brothers away. If she had the chance, Alex would kill him in a heartbeat for it. But it just didn't hurt as bad now. Kissing Galahad, Alex closed her eyes to stop the tears gathering and inhaled slowly. It only took another moment for her to regain control.

Setting down Galahad, Alex swung her legs off her bed and pulled on her waiting socks and shoes. Her backpack was on the chair of her desk, ready with her tablet and books for the morning. It was all very normal. Standing up, she went to her dresser and quickly brushed out her long blonde hair before securing it with a headband. Alex noted the bags under her eyes with a grimace. It was amazing that Nicki hadn't started hounding her about getting more sleep yet.

Then again, none of them had been sleeping well since the bombing. They'd all been there for lunch together and may very well have been the targets. Or Arthur may have figured they'd escape. Shaking her head, Alex tried to push away thoughts about the incident, at least for the time being. They'd gone over what had happened a dozen times already.

When she opened her door and stepped out into the hallway, the smell of cooking meat and sharp spices hit her nose. Alex's stomach rumbled and she suddenly realized that she was starving. It wouldn't matter what kind of stir fry it was at this point. Jumping into the bathroom, she quickly washed her hands before going into the dining room. The table was already being set by Bran, who gave her a warm smile.

"Hi," he greeted. "How did today go?"

"Got some more iron enchanted," Alex replied. "I'm a bit sore, but it went well." She gestured towards the plates. "Anything I can help with?"

"No," Bran said. "I don't think so. The rice will be done in a few seconds and Aiden and Timothy are wrapping up the stir-fry." Bran leaned back so he could look in the kitchen. "They put some extra stuff in it, but I think it'll be good."

Everyone else had things well in hand and Alex just had to stay out of the way. Heading to the front door, she double checked the locks, chain, and deadbolt, and wondered if they were a little silly. Arthur had magic of his own, and the locks wouldn't stop him. Shaking her head, Alex gathered up the jackets and bags scattered on the bench by the door and started hanging them up in the small closet just around the corner. It was a tight fit, but she got all the jackets hung up and then pushed the various shoes under the bench. They hadn't been in the house that long and already they were making a mess of it.

"Dinner!" Aiden called.

Footfalls overhead told Alex that the rest of the house had heard. Lance came down the stairs first and gave her a warm smile. Jenny was right behind him, checking something on her cell phone. At the bottom of the stairs, Lance paused and waited until his girlfriend had her feet firmly on the ground before moving towards the dining room. Catching his eye, Alex shrugged and smiled. At least Jenny was good at navigating even while on her phone.

Morgana had furnished the house with a long heavy wooden dining table that looked far too nice to be in the home of a bunch of college kids. Alex took a spot at the head of the table as Aiden and Bran each put down large steaming bowls of stir-fry. Additional bowls of fresh white rice were scattered around the table in easy reach of everyone. Nicki sat down at her right with Avani beside her. Bran sat to her left with Aiden beside him. Lance and Jenny sat across from each other at the far end and Timothy jumped up to sit opposite of Alex at the other end. The Brownie waved to her and Alex smiled and gave him a small wave in return.

Alex dished up a good portion, very aware of how hungry she was. The first few minutes at the table were silent as everyone ate quickly to take the edge off their hunger. Timothy finished first and bounced away from the table. Watching him go, Alex wished she knew how to make him more comfortable staying around them for long periods of time, but the Brownie always seemed to have something he was working on.

"So," Nicki said. "Anyone do anything interesting today?"

"I was at the bookstore," Aiden replied quickly. He took another large bite and Nicki clicked her tongue at him.

"Not really," Lance said. "Jenny and I worked on homework at the library."

"Did you see anything at the Student Union?" Alex asked.

"No." Jenny shook her head. "They still have the building blocked off, but it does seem like they are actually working on clean up now."

"Let's hope that's a good sign," Alex said. She looked down at her plate, urging her appetite to stay strong. "I was just at Merlin's today. We got some more iron enchanted and stashed."

"Have any luck with Merlin about the Tree of Reality?" Bran asked cautiously.

"No," Alex snorted. "The whole time we were in the forge today, he wouldn't talk much about it."

"Well, we know how they got their information," Aiden said. "I just don't get it. They don't seem to be taking the threat seriously."

"Stubborn old coots," Nicki muttered. She speared a piece of meat and used it to scoop up some rice onto the fork. "They don't always know best."

"They're set in their ways," Bran said gently. "That's all."

Lance shook his head. "If Alex is right and there's something destroying outer worlds then sooner or later, it's going to get here. It explains a lot."

"It explains the Sídhe and the Demons," Nicki agreed. "But the Old Ones... we know very little about that world."

"No new Old Ones have been sent here for a long time," Jenny said. "Even when the gates were failing and the Sídhe were pushing through. That world might not even be there anymore."

"We know that the first Sídhe world has fallen and that the Demons are running from something," Aiden said between bites of food. "Their world could be right next door for all we know. We have no idea how many worlds they're spread across."

"We've been through all of this," Alex said. The others looked at her and she sighed. "We're just beating around the bush, making the same statements we've been making for two weeks." Shaking her head, she forced a smile. "Come on, let's talk about something else tonight."

They all looked at each other, waiting for someone to offer up a topic. Alex almost started laughing. It was sad, almost pathetic that they had so little in their lives beyond magic. Aiden cleared his throat and offered an update on his sister Aisling. It was crazy to think that the kid was in high school now, but they were juniors. Officially, they were approaching their final hurdles for their degrees.

Avani took over when Aiden stopped talking, telling them a bit more about her family. Alex paid close attention and could almost feel Lokpal soaking up the information. Of them all, Avani had been the most poised through the recent ordeal. She had been just as shocked and nervous as them, but reassuring when it came to their fears about magic being exposed. Her family had been using magic for centuries without anyone ever becoming the wiser.

Aiden, Bran, and Nicki started talking about some game and Lance joined in, much to their delight. Jenny watched with an affectionate smile and caught Alex's eye for a moment. Avani seemed as confused as she felt, but the change in topic was wonderful.

After dinner, they crashed in the living room, slumping into the armchairs and sofas that Morgana had furnished the place with. Lance and Jenny snuggled up close on the loveseat and Avani sat next to Nicki with a small smile. Aiden turned on the television and they argued briefly about what to watch before letting Aiden just pick a random film from the streaming list. Alex's mind whirled. There were things to do. Things she should be doing. She could go back to the forge or go and speak with Morgana again. Classes resumed tomorrow and she needed to double check that she had everything. After losing two weeks, teachers were sure to be under pressure to not only catch up but provide a sense of normalcy that would make things a bit more intense than usual.

But she didn't move. Alex flexed her fingers, feeling her magic leap to attention and roll down to her hands. She didn't summon the sparks into the world, but held the magic there, letting it fill her up. Then she pushed it out gently, ordered it to ripple around the house. As the film started, Alex closed her eyes and checked the area. Her magic washed over everything around them, illuminating the lines of the furniture, her fellow mages, the house and beyond. The symbols around the foundation that helped ward the house glowed brighter in response, and Alex pushed a little more magic into them just to be on the safe side.

Upstairs, the mounted Sword and Hammer thrummed in response to her gentle prod. In the heavy leather bag that Merlin had given her, the Iron Chalice glowed at the brush of her magic. Ever since the bombing, Alex had been keeping the Chalice close at hand rather than in Merlin's safe. She searched the yard quickly, but there was nothing out of place. Reaching into the woods, Alex let her magic outline every tree and fern and checked it over carefully. There was nothing there. No Fae with Arthur's damned medallions waiting to attack and no Red Caps lurking in the shadows.

Pulling back her magic, Alex swallowed and blinked to clear her vision. The back of her neck was hot and she could feel a little sweat gathering. Bran came into the living room and sat down next to her, his hand still a little damp from doing the dishes. They were all here and they were safe. While that reassurance did nothing to stop her irritation with Merlin and Morgana, it did give her enough peace of mind to settle down to watch the movie. She honestly couldn't remember the last time she'd done something so normal.

2

Lone Attacker

Climbing out of the car, Alex looked around with a critical eye. Everything seemed normal enough, but she didn't want to assume anything. The parking lot wasn't full, but there was a decent number of cars present. Nearby, a line of trees was now turning colors for the start of autumn, though a few across the street were still green. Students were following the pathways towards the various classroom buildings like normal.

Yet a sense of unease hung over the campus. Alex noted that students were traveling in packs more than usual, and instead of looking down at their phones, many were looking around with alert eyes. There were police officers and campus security patrolling around the buildings, watching everyone carefully.

She couldn't see the Student Union building from here, but Alex was sure that there were extra guards around it just to be sure. While parts of campus such as the library had been open to students, this was the first proper day back to classes and she was ready for trouble.

Cathanáil hung on her back, unseen by nonmages, and the weight was comforting. The Iron Chalice was tucked away in her backpack along with a textbook and her tablet. In theory, she was ready for the day. The other door of the car closed and she looked over at Nicki who had driven them here.

"Ready for this?" Nicki asked.

"I think so," Alex said. She scanned the parking lot again. "I wish we had more classes together."

"Me too," Nicki admitted. "Look, keep to the plan. We text each other every hour just to be sure. If he has a vision, Bran will alert us, but I don't think Arthur is going to try anything. He was lucky that no security footage caught him last time."

Alex settled on nodding. There wasn't much more to talk about there. She still wasn't convinced that Arthur cared about whether he exposed himself or magic. Nicki grabbed her stuff and they headed up the main walk together. They didn't have far to go together before Nicki broke off with a smile and a wave, leaving Alex on her own. Ignoring a look from a nearby guard, Alex fought the urge to tighten her grip on her bag and hurried toward her 19th Century Russian Masterpieces class. Thankfully, no one stopped her for a search. She wasn't sure how she'd explain an iron cup in her bag. They didn't exactly do show and tell in college.

The classroom wasn't as empty as Alex had feared. Apparently, upperclassmen were a little harder to scare off, if for no other reason than they had more to lose. Walking to the back of the small classroom, Alex set her bag down and pulled up the folding desktop attached to the seat. A couple of people waved at her and she smiled in return. At least the old issues with the football team over Arthur were starting to fade from memory. Her fingers tapped against the desk nervously as she set up her tablet and put her feet around her bag protectively.

It was a few minutes later when Professor Gruben walked in. The pile of papers in his arms threatened to go flying, but he kept them under control until he reached the front. One of the students jumped up to help him put them down safely on the table next to the front podium. The professor was one of the longest serving on campus, with a completely bald head, a slight hunch, and beady little eyes. Thankfully he could still talk loud enough for the classroom.

"Welcome back everyone," the professor said. His voice was softer than normal, and he looked at all of them for a moment in turn. "As this is a 9 a.m. course, I'm going to assume that it is your first class back in session. I know that the incident was a shock to us all, and that some of you were even nearby." His eyes jumped to Alex and she tried not to move. "The University is still in shock, still looking for answers. I fear that we may never properly understand what happened and why someone would inflict such fear and pain on our students. I am grateful to see all of you here, grateful that you have not given up on your educations and the pursuit of your futures." Folding his hands on the top of the podium, Professor Gruben gave them the warmest smile Alex had ever seen from a professor in class. "I am proud of you." He paused to let the words sink in and then chuckled and reached for a book. "But that doesn't mean that I'm not still going to teach you."

Gruben pointed at the student who had helped him earlier and gestured for him to come up. Handing him the pile of papers he'd brought in, Gruben patted his shoulder. "Take those around. These are your new syllabus. As we lost two weeks, I adjusted things slightly. You'll note that I've adjusted the amount of time we'll have for *War and Peace*. Instead of you needing to read the whole work, we'll be focusing on specific sections."

There was an audible sigh of relief. Alex's own shoulders relaxed a little. She'd never read *War and Peace*: she'd always been too afraid of the length and how people talked about it. Taking her new copy of the syllabus, Alex glanced over it. The professor had shorted not only *War and Peace* a lot but cut a day out of other books here and there. At least the amount of time they had for essays hadn't changed.

Class was a nice distraction. Gruben didn't hold back and continued his lecture on Russian culture in the early 19th century after only a quick recap of where they'd been two weeks ago. Letting herself fall into the lesson, Alex smiled as her brain managed to connect some of the cultural points to the parts of what she'd already read. It had been a while since something had connected properly. She'd forgotten how nice it could be.

When class was over, Alex packed her things up slowly and let the other students leave ahead of her. Professor Gruben glanced her way and gave her a quick nod before he headed out the door. Swinging her bag over her shoulder, Alex headed out into the hallway. It was crowded, but the crush of bodies didn't seem as bad. Once again, she wondered how the bombing had affected the student population. Alex pushed the thought away. She was dancing at the edge of a good mood and wanted to hold onto it.

Pulling out her phone, she sent her check in text. Nicki responded back first with a smiley face and her location. She and Nicki's next class was one of Merlin's. Glancing around, Alex tried to remember which building was the Hamilton Building. She was pretty sure that Nicki's last class was one that had been in the Student Union Building.

"Iron Soul."

Alex reached up for the hilt of Cathanáil, drawing the Sword without concern for how strange she might look to bystanders. Her mind spun. Someone had called her by her title. Turning around, she easily spotted the one who had called her that. It was a Fae, leaning against the side of the building in the shadows. The crowd was moving off to other locations and classes, leaving them largely alone. The Fae pushed itself off the wall and nodded to the right before it started walking that direction. Alex hesitated, but slowly followed them around the wall of the Meier Building.

They stopped around the corner where the building cast a long shadow and blocked out the sun. The Fae's hood hid much of their face, but Alex recognized the shimmering pale skin. Lowering her right hand, Alex called on her magic. The spark in her chest burst to life and her skin tingled as energy rushed down her arms to her fingertips. The Fae didn't move and Alex told herself to wait. It might not be an enemy. Those who meant no harm could enter Ravenslake without the blood protection spell activating, but thanks to Arthur's magic enemies could too now. Slowly, the Fae moved towards Alex and she tensed, wanting it to say something.

"Do you have information?" she asked. "We can arrange a meeting with the other mages."

"Quietly," the Fae said. "Quietly."

Frowning, Alex kept her eyes fixed on the Fae. Its face was downcast to avoid the sun so she couldn't see much of their expression. Her hand moved up to the hilt of Cathanáil and she wrapped her fingers around it tightly.

"Stay there," Alex ordered. "Arthur has been sending troops into Ravenslake using magic. We can't tell friend from enemy now. So, give me some space and say what you need to."

The Fae stopped and Alex's chest eased in relief. They reached into the pocket of their hoodie and she thought they were pulling out a note. There was a small glint of light off metal and Alex jumped back, barely dodging the knife that was slashed towards her. Swinging Cathanáil forward, Alex drove it into the Fae's gut. The hood fell back and she stared into shock filled eyes. Anger rose in them and it glared at her. Then there was a weak gurgle and the Fae's body dissolved into dust.

Alex eyed the clothing that dropped to the ground. Sheathing Cathanáil, she glanced around to make sure that she was still alone. With her foot, she shifted around the hoodie and grumbled when she found the medallion. The small disk was much the same as the others that Arthur had made. Alex knew that if she used her own magic to examine it, she would find traces of Arthur's magic knotted up around the metal.

Tightening her jaw and resisting the urge to scream or curse, Alex bent over and picked up the medallion. She hesitated for a moment before putting it in the pocket of her jeans. The Iron Chalice might currently be in a bag with school books, but she wasn't going to sully it by putting Arthur's medallion in there. She wrapped the dagger up in the t-shirt on the ground and put that in a side pocket of her backpack for disposal. The pile of remaining clothes was still a problem, but Alex didn't have room in her bag for the jeans, hoodie, and shoes. With any luck, people wouldn't notice the slice in the hoodie and assume it was a prank or a streaker. Thank magic for disappearing bodies.

She heard people coming towards her. That cry would surely draw attention on a campus already on the edge. Walking quickly to the left, Alex tightened her grip on her bag and tried to act casual. Heart pounding, Alex licked her lips and pulled out her phone. She lacked Jenny's perfect skill with texting but managed to send off a warning that Fae with medallions were in the area. She followed up with a text telling the others that she was alright.

Alex frowned, watching the tiny vibrations in her hands as they trembled. That was odd. The fight had been next to nothing. One Fae was hardly a problem. It had been a weak assassination attempt. Flexing her fingers, Alex kept moving and waiting for her heart to calm down. It hadn't been that bad, but she'd given it a chance to get close. Maybe that was the point. Arthur was playing on her not wanting to kill first and ask questions later. That Fae had gotten her alone and gotten her to hesitate.

"Alex!"

Nicki was approaching her at a rapid pace, a fake smile on her face with her cell phone clutched in her hand. They stared at each other a moment and Alex stayed still as Nicki quickly checked her over for injuries. More students were moving around them and Alex stepped to the side to get out of traffic. Smiling, Nicki followed and then threw her arms around her in a tight hug.

"You okay?"

"I'm fine," Alex said quickly. "It was one Fae."

"But it's the first attack since..." Nicki trailed off and squeezed Alex's shoulder. "I'm glad you're okay."

"I had the Sword," Alex reminded her. Giving Nicki a smile, she shrugged her shoulders which shifted the Sword. "It has much better reach than a dagger."

Nicki gave her a look but didn't seem interested in having an argument about Alex's insistence that she was fine. "So, medallion?"

"It was tucked under its clothing," Alex explained. "I couldn't see it and thought it might be a messenger. It didn't try to backstab me or anything. I found the medallion after it was dead."

"Well... luring you away might be a sign that Arthur really isn't interested in exposing magic." Nicki was frowning thoughtfully, making her brows furrow. She tugged Alex's hand gently so they could start walking. They kept to the path, but stayed away from the other students. "Or he may be hoping that one of the Fae will get a lucky shot if you're at ease."

"Maybe." Alex shrugged. "But it does make me think that we need to contact the Fae again. Things have changed with the Queen's death, but they may not be aware."

"Do we think they're more likely to help Arthur or not?" Nicki asked.

"I'm hoping less," Alex said. "He seems very happy to throw them at us. Almost like suicide squads. I get the impression that while the Queen didn't like the Fae, she did at least recognize them as Sídhe descendants and cared a little. Arthur... I really don't think he cares at all."

"But he's charismatic and very convincing," Nicki said. "A dangerous combo." Then the redhead sighed and looked around. "We're not going to fix this here. And you look too wound up to sit still in a classroom. Let's get some food."

"Only the normal cafeteria is available," Alex reminded her. "Unless you want to go off campus."

"Off-campus then," Nicki said. With a shudder, she linked her arm with Alex's. "I'm not paying cash to go into the dorm cafeteria. I'm a junior living off campus!" The look of exaggerated disgust on Nicki's face drew a laugh from Alex.

Her phone beeped with new messages and Alex pulled it out quickly. There were responses from Merlin, Aiden, and Bran. She was a touch surprised that Jenny and Lance hadn't checked in yet and that Morgana hadn't demanded her position. Then a text message came from Jenny, letting Alex know that she was with Lance at Central Diner and they were fine.

"Hey," Alex said. "Feel like power walking to Central Diner for lunch?"

Nicki groaned, but changed the direction they were walking, almost making Alex trip. "There are other places in town," she said. "Seriously, they just opened a new Greek place on 2nd."

"I was just attacked," Alex said. "Lance and Jenny are there and I want comfort food."

"There's that 'Mom's Cooking' place on 3rd," Nicki offered. "Big vats of mac and cheese."

"If it's in big vats, it's not home cooking," Alex corrected. Her thumb moved across her phone screen. "And too late. Jenny and Lance are expecting us. I need food before another class and an interrogation."

"Fine," Nicki conceded. "I suppose you deserve it. Tell Jenny to order me a cheeseburger with everything."

Alex nodded, trying to keep on smiling, but it was tough. After sending Jenny their meal requests, Alex sent a message to Merlin that she was skipping class with Nicki and smiled as he texted back that he forgave them. Putting her phone away, Alex inhaled slowly and focused more on keeping up with Nicki. Her eyes scanned the people around them as she and Nicki headed to the edge of campus. Arthur had given them the two weeks after the bombings to stew in their anger, but now he was back. Yet once again, Alex couldn't put her finger on what he was trying to accomplish beyond killing her. There had to be more to his plan, but what, she wasn't sure.

3

Into the West

1 502 C.E. Rhineland

Morgana hated what had become of the world. Things might have been looking up in a few small ways, but she missed the less complicated world of her childhood. She longed for simpler days without so many vicious power hierarchies interfering with each other and being dismissed because she was a woman. In her day, they'd acknowledged division of labor, but the disrespect that this era showed would have been unthinkable.

"Stop glaring," Merlin said. "You'll draw too much attention."

She turned her glare on Merlin as the cart jostled once again. Merlin kept a tight hold of the reins of the horse pulling their cart, but it wasn't enough to smooth out the trip. The roads were a disgrace.

"You're in a foul mood," Merlin said.

"I was comfortable," Morgana replied. "As much as I could be at least. Now we're moving back into the ugly land of feudalism."

"Morgana," Merlin sighed. "Give it a chance. Besides, it was your scrying that sent us here."

She grumbled again and Merlin chuckled. His amusement was misplaced. She distrusted the modern European system, no matter Merlin's insistence that things were showing signs of improving. All the wars, the diseases, and disorder had been bad enough to make even the Fae and Old Ones fear trying anything.

"It won't be all bad," Merlin assured her. "Really, I'm confident of it."

"We've been on the road for over a month," Morgana said. "How can you still be optimistic?"

"I've missed this," Merlin admitted. "Having a purpose." His voice softened and Morgana looked at him in confusion. "It's been very easy to feel old recently. Ever since the Byzantine Empire fell, it's been difficult to feel at home anywhere." Looking around the rolling hills of fertile fields along the massive river, Merlin sighed. "I know you've felt it too."

"Yes," Morgana admitted. "The Fall of Constantinople was... unpleasant."

"Agreed."

"But now we're in the land of horrible medicine and hygiene," Morgana complained. "Why couldn't they have at least held onto Norse grooming habits?"

Merlin laughed at her. "I recall you rolling your eyes frequently at Thor's habits."

"They seemed excessive, but if I'd known that the rest of Europe would turn into a cesspool, I wouldn't have teased him!"

"Somehow I doubt that," Merlin replied.

They kept moving and Morgana took in the landscape. It really wasn't as bad as she'd feared. She had to admit that part of her hesitation was about the stories that circulated Constantinople about the west, usually about their ridiculous medicine. This area was at least supposed to have a strong culture, and thanks to the river it was less prone to famine. Maybe it wouldn't be so bad.

"It will be fine," Merlin said. Morgana knew that he hadn't read her mind, but it felt like he had. "You can stop frowning. Mage or not, it will give you wrinkles."

"Perhaps then we would raise fewer questions, old man."

Merlin huffed, holding back a laugh, but thankfully he didn't say anything more on the subject of her wrinkles. Time moved slowly for them, but there could be no doubt that it did move. Over the past century she'd started finding the occasional gray hair, and Merlin's lines were much deeper than they had been when she'd first met him as a child.

"We're close," Morgana said. She straightened up and looked around the landscape carefully. They were in the heart of the Rhineland, and the area was filled with farms and small villages that supported nearby larger cities. There weren't really any landmarks to help her, but a flare of magic in her chest reassured Morgana that they were on the right track. "Close by is where trouble will start soon."

"And you thought it was the Sídhe descendants?"

"That's what I saw in the mirror," Morgana replied. "But... there's been no sign of them."

"Not of the Fae," Merlin agreed. "But there were many of the smaller creatures in the forests. Most of them seemed peaceful enough."

"Yes, well, you know that scrying is limited," Morgana said. "The vision was unexpected as it was."

That was true. The only reason Morgana had even been scrying at all was a long-standing promise to Merlin. For over a hundred years, things had been peaceful. At least when it came to the beings from other worlds. Shiva was watching over the Far East as he'd promised Lokpal, and the Sídhe creatures had been keeping their heads down. Morgana scanned the area once more, her eyes lingering on the river and some distant buildings. Why here and now was an utter mystery to her.

"I do wish I had your talent with scrying," Merlin said. "Pity I've never been able to get it to work for me."

"You have your own gifts, Merlin," Morgana replied. She did smile at the reminder that there were things she was better at than the ancient mage. The gap in their ages mattered little at this point, but a small spark of awe still remained in Morgana from when she was a child. "Besides, it's unlikely that magic would have shown you anything different than what it showed me."

The cart jostled again and Morgana turned around to check on their luggage. Everything they owned was wrapped up and boxed in the back of the cart. What they still owned at least. Leaving the East had meant selling off much of her possessions. After a century of peace, she'd gained an alarming amount of material goods. Holding back a sigh, Morgana reminded herself that this was her duty.

A threat was gathering once more. Perhaps not a new invader. The magic of the Iron Gates was still holding strong, but the Sídhe creatures had been reproducing steadily for years. Sometimes she wondered if the decision not to hunt them down right after Arto's death had been the right one or not.

"Any thoughts on where to go now?" Merlin asked. "We're in the right area."

"My vision was detailed enough to bring us here," Morgana snapped. "Hundreds of miles away and you want a specific ending point?"

"It would be helpful," Merlin replied. He smiled at her and Morgana glared. "I jest, Morgana. Your gift has done very well. I just wish I knew if we are going to keep traveling or if we need to build new lives here."

Morgana paused. That was a valid concern. She did not have the answer. Licking her lower lip, she tried to remember everything from the wild flash of images. There had been Fae causing trouble, and a long sweeping vision west from her home to where they were now. But what happened next, she didn't know. It was never that easy.

"I am not sure," Morgana admitted. "Magic led us here, but what we should do next, I do not know."

"Let's start with putting a roof over our heads tonight," Merlin said. "I'd rather not suffer another bumbling attempt at theft."

Morgana laughed at the reminder of two nights ago. An older man and woman with a full cart on the road were a tempting target. But there was enough magic in the world that they'd made quick work of their attackers. Of course, in a land dominated by the Catholic Church, they had to be careful not to draw unwanted attention to themselves.

The sun was sinking lower in the sky by the time they decided to stop. There was a small farming village near the road with a tavern that looked like it had potential. Carts with farm goods were leaving the village in a hurry. It had likely been a market day, Morgana decided. Merlin brought the horses to a halt and Morgana curled her nose. The stink of animals filled the village and she glanced towards the stable. It was, of course, right next to the building. She'd be smelling horses all night.

Merlin climbed down and went inside. Morgana stayed with the wagon and glanced around quickly. Everyone nearby seemed human and no one was paying them any mind. Travelers would be common enough along this road. The nearby cities required food and resources from the outside after all. Still, she was uneasy. Things had been peaceful for a long time and now magic was pushing her and Merlin here.

A young man came out of the stables. "Your husband wants the horse in the stable tonight," he said.

"Of course," Morgana agreed. She climbed out of the cart quickly. "Did he say anything about the wagon?" she asked.

"I'm going to lead the horse over there," the young man said. He pointed to an empty spot by the stable. "It'll be out of the way."

Nodding, Morgana followed the cart and kept a close eye on the young man. He was short, but strongly built and paid her no mind. She supposed that this was just another night to him. Once the cart was in place, he unhooked their horse and led it to the stables. Looking around quickly, Morgana checked to make sure that no one was watching her. She was alone and the humans were all tending to other things.

Touching the side of the cart, Morgana pushed a spark of magic into the wood to reactivate the spell she and Merlin had crafted after one too many theft attempts. Underneath the heavy cloth pulled over the boxes, there was a faint flash of light. Satisfied, Morgana stepped away from the cart, content to know that the back would seem empty and hold no interest for potential thieves. It was a pity that they didn't have enough magic to keep it active while on the road. That would have simplified things greatly. The front door of the tavern swung open in front of her and Morgana blinked as she nearly collided with Merlin.

"Everything secure?" Merlin asked softly.

"Yes," she answered quickly. "I trust you made arrangements."

"A room and dinner," he said. "They believe us to be married."

"For the best," Morgana agreed. She fell into step alongside Merlin as they entered the main room of the tavern.

It was surprisingly clean and Morgana relaxed a little in relief. Regular bathing might not be in style in the west, but it seemed that they did at least place some value on cleanliness. The room had hunting trophies mounted on the walls and tables scattered in front of the fireplace. Patrons were in varying states of exhaustion and drunkenness and a couple of people were moving between tables with food and drink. Yet there was a sense of order even amongst the chaos. The owner of the establishment clearly knew how to do their job.

There was a section that everyone was avoiding in the tavern. Tables were left empty near the left corner furthest from the door. One person was there, a man sitting alone and drinking. The man was at least forty years old but looked much older. He carried a weight of experience on his shoulders that was so heavy it made him slouch over. In front of him were an untouched meal and a large empty mug. One side of his face was badly scarred and his left eye was glassy with blindness. Morgana couldn't see his legs but rather suspected from the crutch propped up next to him that they were in poor shape. Then he turned as if he sensed her gaze. Instinct warned Morgana to look away, but she held fast and met his eyes.

It was the smell of decay that hit her first. She was standing on an open plain, but there were corpses strewn around her. Broken weapons were cast to the side and the carnage stretched on for a mile. Ravens and crows were singing and plucking out their favorite parts of a meal. A laugh to the right caught her attention. A man in chainmail was walking away from the battle hand in hand with a woman who had long brown hair. Morgana couldn't see their faces, but their happy laughter blended with the caws of the crows.

She came back to herself and swallowed. "Oh no," Morgana whispered.

The man was looking at her with one wide eye. He wasn't panicking at least, but one hand was creeping towards something beneath the table. Swallowing, Morgana pointedly looked away from him and scanned the tavern once more.

"Morgana?"

"I just had a Connection," Morgana said softly. "The man alone at the table. Old soldier or knight by the looks of him."

"I see." Merlin didn't look his way. "Just another mage or...?"

"During the Connection... I think I saw a memory," Morgana said. "There was a man and a woman walking away from a field of battle. A strong sense of betrayal and grief."

"If that was part of the Connection then it could mean that memory defines him," Merlin said softly. He hummed thoughtfully. "Betrayal by a man and a woman, potentially at a critical moment. It could be the Iron Soul."

"Yes," Morgana said. "But he's in bad shape, Merlin. If we had the Iron Chalice then maybe we could heal him, but without it..."

"Let's stay calm," Merlin said quickly. "If he is the Iron Soul then I'm certain it will be alright."

Morgana wrinkled her nose. "You may not think that after you have a Connection with him." Holding back a shiver, Morgana corrected her posture and exhaled slowly. "That Connection was rough, Merlin. I don't like this."

She was aware that Merlin was watching her now and picked up her wine. The sweet taste did nothing to calm her. Morgana didn't know what to think. Even after all that they had seen, her and Merlin's Connections were still peaceful. She knew that the man would have seen the tor near her home village and smelled the ocean. That fundamental part of her had never changed.

Then Merlin turned and he stilled for a moment. A soft grunt escaped him a moment later and he turned back to his meal. Silence filled the space between them as Morgana tried to think of the best way to approach the man. Clearly, something was going to happen in this area. Her vision had directed them here and now they found another mage.

But he was not what she would have chosen. Maybe ten years ago when he was younger, but not now.

"So," Morgana said. "What do you think?"

"It was unusual," Merlin said diplomatically. "I can feel him watching us and he hasn't called for a priest yet, so at least he isn't easily shaken."

"I suppose."

"We'll speak with him after we eat," Merlin said. "No reason to draw attention to ourselves. If he leaves, we'll follow him out."

Morgana nodded in agreement and told herself to calm down. Nothing had been decided yet. They didn't know what the threat was. Perhaps this man was exactly what the Iron Soul needed to be at this time.

Morgana turned her attention to her food. It was poor quality and the spices were remarkably bland given how desperately they were trying to cover up the taste of old meat. Sternly, she reminded herself of her duty. If fulfilling it meant being here then she would be here and deal with the food. Still, an uncomfortable worry about this new mage had taken hold at the bottom of her stomach, which only made the food worse.

4

Talking in Whispers

The descendants of the original Sídhe warriors who had been trapped on Earth after the war lived in the shadows of the modern world. Now they were known as the Fae, and Alex was grateful to have another name to call them. She reached up and grabbed hold of the handle alongside the vehicle door while Merlin pulled off the main road and onto the small bumpy road.

Tree branches scraped the side of the SUV and Alex braced herself for the next bump. In the past month the Fae had formed a small temporary settlement using their trailers in the hills around Ravenslake. It moved every two weeks or so to keep the authorities from harassing them, but it was always nearby.

Alex leaned forward and scanned their surroundings as they came around a curve. Up ahead in a flat area were six trailers in a horseshoe shape. They were shaded by tall trees growing alongside a nearby stream and all of them had awnings rolled down to form protected patches. In the middle of the horseshoe was a large canopy tent with a cooking area set up. Some folding chairs were tucked up under one of the trees and a guitar was nestled on one of them. If Alex hadn't known that the people living here weren't human, she would have assumed it was just another camp.

There were no children. There never seemed to be. Deep down, Alex knew that this settlement was only here to communicate with the mages and keep an eye on them. They wouldn't risk children here. Despite it being the daytime, there were Fae outside in the dark shade of the trees. Three of them looked up sharply as the SUV rolled in, and Alex noticed clothing they were mending in their hands. One jumped to its feet and rushed over to one of the trailers, knocking loudly on it.

"Are you sure you want to talk with them?" Merlin asked. "I'm glad to-"

"We need to know if they've heard anything," Alex said. She chuckled darkly. "And you and Morgana terrify all of them."

Climbing out of the vehicle, Alex moved slowly and kept her hands where the Fae could see them. She wasn't sure if they had enough magic innately to see Cathanáil on her back, but she made a point of not reaching for the Sword. Flexing her fingers, Alex inhaled slowly and held the breath in for a few long seconds. Her heart slowed slightly and she exhaled, calming herself down. This was not the time to be on edge.

She suddenly wished that the others were here. True, all the mages arriving might have frightened the Fae, but she was now feeling very alone. Merlin climbed out of the SUV but lingered alongside it, his hands in his pockets. Alex was grateful that he was at least obeying her wishes.

One of the doors of a trailer opened. Alex didn't move any closer and waited patiently. The figure that came out was tall, and in a change of pace wasn't bothering with a hat or a hood. His long white hair was pulled back into a braid. At least, Alex thought it was a him, based on the height. On his forehead were the two small nubs that were all that remained of the Sídhe's horns. The Fae had suffered many changes over their long residency in the Iron Realm.

"I am Randall," the Fae said softly. It was the first time any of them had ever introduced themselves by name. "The others have agreed to let me speak for them."

"Thank you," Alex replied. She nodded respectfully for good measure. "That simplifies things. I hope that you are well."

"We are managing, as we always have."

"Good, good," Alex said lamely. Nodding again, she licked her very dry lips. "Uh, I'm Alex."

"The Iron Soul," Randall added. "I am aware. There are three female mages, and only one is blonde."

Alex blinked at the statement. She'd never thought of it that way, but they were all rather visually distinct from each other. Blonde, brunette, and a redhead. Like the start of a joke. "Right," she said.

"What can I do for you, Alex?" Randall sounded almost amused using her name.

"I had a vision of the death of Queen Scáthbás," Alex said. There was no point in beating around the bush. "Have you heard anything to that effect?"

"Yes. It's difficult to confirm for certain," Randall said. "But the rumors are certainly saying that she is dead and that Arthur killed her. He is presenting himself as a friend to the creatures trapped in this world. He speaks of taking over Earth for those that live here, not for the Sídhe Empire." Randall was watching Alex closely as he spoke. "He claims that he is part Sídhe like the Grand Mages, but will use his powers to ensure the freedom of the Fae in this world."

"And people are believing it?"

"It's what they want to hear," Randall said. "Letters from Arthur have been circulating in the cities and hidden communities. There are those who have already joined him, but this new campaign is winning him support."

Bile slipped up into Alex's mouth and she tightened her jaw. Mind reeling, she tried to think of what she could say. Randall didn't seem violent and seemed willing to talk. Alex could work with that. The memory of the latest attack, the young Fae who had taken Arthur's medallion and attacked her, made her insides turn and her stomach drop.

"I see," she finally said. "That's unfortunate. Arthur... he's not a leader. Not really. This is just a ploy to get bodies he can throw at us."

"Yes," Randall agreed. "I believe that. He murdered his own mother, his creator and his partner. I do not think that his loyalty can be trusted at all."

Nodding, Alex hoped that her raw relief wasn't too apparent on her face. The knowledge, the confirmation that some of them saw through Arthur's pretty words was making her light headed. "But they don't trust you either," Randall added.

"Mages have allowed the Fae to live in peace on Earth for centuries."

"Live in the shadows," Randall said. "This resentment does not grow from nothing. We live on the edge of society. We can join in on some aspects of human culture, but our ability to take part is limited. Some of us find success in small ways through the internet, but we cannot live amongst you. The human rejection of magic and other species has made that impossible."

"I know," Alex admitted. "It's not a perfect system, but that's not the fault of the mages. If humans knew about you, about us, then they'd be terrified. I'm sure it would turn violent."

"You're probably right," Randall said. He nodded to her, but his violet eyes glinted with calculations. "But to a young Fae who is frustrated, Arthur's words sound sweet."

"Even if it means wars and suicide missions?"

"I do not think you mages have ever considered what life is like for us," Randall returned. His voice was sharp now, and Alex flinched. "Your loyalty is to humans. To the Iron Realm's natural residents, not those of us who do not belong here."

"I want peace," Alex said. "I don't want anyone, of any species, to be hurt."

"I'm not sure that is possible," Randall said. Resigned, he glanced towards one of the nearby trailers. Alex saw the curtain in the window move and a face duck away from her view. "As I said, there is a great deal of frustration."

"Have you heard anything about what Arthur might be planning?" Alex asked. The question felt dangerous on her tongue. Randall quirked his head slightly, looking surprised that she'd asked so directly. Holding back a sigh, Alex swallowed. "Any targets or plans? Anything that might help us counter him?"

"No," Randall said. "I'm not sure if he truly has a plan. He strikes me as insane."

"Strikes you.... Was he here?" Alex asked softly. "Did he come here?"

"After the bombing, yes."

"So, it wasn't just recruiting posters then." Alex guarded her voice, not wanting to yell. Her jaw tightened and her stomach turned. Suddenly, she was concerned about throwing up or hitting something.

"He left some," Randall replied. "Two Fae left with him to help 'spread the news.'"

"And you didn't tell me this before why?"

"I owe you nothing," Randall said evenly. "You came to me for information. I wanted some in return. You lack an understanding of your enemy. That much is clear."

"Arthur was... charming and controlled when he was in Ravenslake," Alex said. "Always smiling and understanding. We thought he was the Iron Soul." Randall scoffed a little and Alex wondered if the Fae would have known he wasn't. "Since then, he seems to have become more erratic. I thought he and the Queen would keep working together without problems until recently."

"I suspect that you know more about their relationship than I do," Randall said.

"More than I'd like."

They fell silent. Alex tried to think of what to ask. Everything she'd learned was ugly and yet if she was honest, to be expected. Arthur was... he'd always had a presence. And he'd been raised by his mother to be a consort or a king. None of this should be a surprise, but somehow it still was. Her stomach turned.

"You said he was insane," Alex finally said. "Why do you think that?"

Randall looked surprised at the question, his violet eyes staring at her. "He talked to himself. In low whispers when he moved away from those he was speaking with. His whole body twitched when he did it. And the look in his eye..." Randall trailed off and shivered.

"That's.... new," Alex said. Her jaw was a bit slack and she searched Randall's face for any sign of a lie. It was almost impossible. His cheekbones were sharper than a human's and his skin was pale and almost shimmered. The usual tells weren't worth much. "Thank you for telling me." Swallowing, she straightened her shoulders. "If you learn anything more..."

"We have your phone numbers," Randall said. Then he paused and studied her for another moment. "I apologize for not telling you that Arthur was here. Given the bombing and the news coming from Ravenslake, it didn't seem important."

Alex didn't believe that, but Randall wasn't going to do anything more than play nice with the mages. Still, she pretended that she believed him and nodded. Randall pretended that he didn't know her mixed feelings and nodded in return. They backed away from each other, neither turning their backs. When they were a few feet apart, Alex turned and strode back to the SUV.

Merlin stood up straight, looking between Alex and the departing Randall with a frown. Alex held her tongue. Starting to curse or scream now wouldn't help. Randall had a point which she hated. Giving her information might make them targets of Arthur and Alex wasn't oblivious to the bad history between the Fae and mages. For all she knew, Randall just didn't want to give them a reason to kill all of the Fae. Pulling open the passenger side door, Alex inhaled slowly, counted to ten, and climbed inside.

The air in the cabin was already a bit stale, but it distracted Alex. There was a hint of pine from Merlin's air freshener and she sat perfectly still as the older mage climbed in behind the wheel. Cathanáil dug into her back as she pushed herself against the back of the seat as Merlin settled.

"Well?" Merlin asked.

"They don't know much more than us," Alex said. Reaching behind her, she adjusted Cathanáil and pulled her seatbelt over her shoulder and around the sword. "They've heard the Queen is dead and believe it. Arthur is apparently recruiting from the Fae settlements."

"Recruiting?" Merlin began to back them out of the camping area and Alex saw a few Fae look out the windows of the trailers towards them.

"Yeah, with flyers and everything!" Alex huffed and curled her hands into fists. "He's playing on their frustrations." She exhaled slowly to gather her self-control. "He was here. After the bombing, he swung by and gave a pitch. He left with two Fae who agreed with him."

"Playing on a person's frustration is an easy tactic," Merlin said sadly. "It's common enough. Humans are not the only ones easily swayed by their frustration and fear. It overwhelms compassion and common sense." He reached over and gently touched her arm. "We already knew he was in the area. This shouldn't be a surprise."

"So, what do we do?" Alex asked. She stubbornly looked ahead as they turned around and drove towards the main road back to town. "We still don't have any details about what he's planning, and I don't think we'll be able to convince any of the Fae to spy for us."

"I'm not sure," Merlin admitted. "Arthur isn't seeking a simple objective. He is taunting us and making noise like he wishes to take over the world, but we lack details on how he means to do it."

"Terrorism is effective," Alex said. "He already proved that with the school."

"Yes, but we're the only ones who know the truth of who is behind that bombing."

"Merlin, there was something else," Alex said.

"What?"

"Randall, the Fae I was talking to, said that Arthur was talking to himself."

Merlin glanced at her, but quickly returned his eyes to the road. "Talking to himself?"

"Yeah, and by the sound of it, he wasn't just remembering something or talking something through. Randall said that he was twitching."

"That... that isn't like anything we observed when he was here," Merlin said. "Have you seen anything like that when watching him?"

Alex really hated how that sounded. Spying would have been better, even as sinister as it sounded; watching made her sound obsessed or something. Still, she thought back. Before he killed his mother, she'd noted that Arthur seemed frustrated with her, but there hadn't been anything like this.

"No," she finally said. Shaking her head, Alex looked out at the trees as they swept past. "Nothing like that at all. He's always been very controlled."

"Randall may have it wrong," Merlin said.

"I don't know," Alex said. "I don't think so. He seemed concerned that I didn't know enough about Arthur. I've seen his childhood... and other things." Alex shivered at the uncomfortable memories of watching Arthur make out with his mother. "But this seems different."

"We'll keep an eye out for it," Merlin said. "Morgana and I have been discussing ways to track him down discreetly. We're considering if an investigator might not be a good option. I don't think Arthur will be keeping an eye out for anyone but a mage."

"Maybe." Alex sighed: she didn't like the idea of sending some normal human to follow Arthur, but Merlin might have a point. "But this talking to himself thing... that bothers me. I don't like it at all."

"Arthur may just finally be showing the signs of insanity from his childhood," Merlin offered. "Being raised by the Queen... well, you know Morgana; it leaves a mark." Merlin's fingers tightened around the wheel. "Or it could be related to his nature. Scáthbás made him and now she's dead. I wonder if he damaged his own magical existence in doing so." A low laugh escaped Merlin. "That would be justice. Or the destruction of the Iron Chain might have started eroding his magic. There are many things to consider that could have affected him."

"So, you think it's important."

"Certainly," Merlin agreed. He nodded sharply. "I will speak with Morgana about it. She and I are half Sídhe but bound to the Iron Realm. Arthur may finally be feeling the effects of being a half breed who is in opposition to the Iron Realm."

Alex didn't think so. That didn't sound right to her. Arthur had been made by her magic, the power of the Iron Soul and the Iron Realm through an Iron Artifact. It didn't seem likely that the death of Scáthbás would destroy that connection. Tapping her fingers on the armrest, she licked her lips and tried to think.

It meant something. Alex believed Randall when he said that Arthur was talking to himself. That was important. It absolutely meant something. There'd been a change. Something in Arthur had changed that had turned him from going along with the Queen's plan to wanting to strike out on his own. She didn't remember Medraut completely, but he was a user. He liked power and being important, but he was a coward. Back then he'd needed an offer from the Queen to turn on Arto and the rest of his people. So, what has changed now? Or, who had made him a better offer?

5

Spark of Inspiration

Aiden loved books. He always had. When your family owned a bookstore, it was almost a given that you learned to love books, or else go mad. Even as a child, if he hadn't been reading in the store, he'd been at a small play table in the back room with a coloring book or some toys surrounded by the smell of books. At home, his father's office had enough textbooks that, when added to the fiction paperbacks in the living room, ensured that the house was thick with the fine scent of books as well.

All of his happiest memories were wrapped up in that smell. Well, except for the happy memories of that Disneyland trip they'd made when Aisling beat her cancer. Burger smells and fried food featured in a lot of those memories.

Yet, Aiden was beginning to find books frustrating. Nowadays, they didn't have the answers that he needed. They had clues, fragments of myth, legend, and history that teased at something, but they couldn't provide answers. It was beginning to feel like he'd been betrayed by his first love. Not that he'd admit that books had let him down to his mother. The only things she loved more than books was her family, and that was just barely.

Sighing, Aiden sat up straight in the armchair and rolled his shoulders. They cracked slightly and he glanced around their living room. Alex was in the other armchair, all but curled up with her legs tucked beneath her and awkwardly holding a massive old book on Celtic mythology. Bran had his tablet and was browsing the web for any odd news that could indicate activity from Arthur while stretched out on the sofa. Nicki was sprawled out on the floor with a pillow and was scribbling in a notebook with a far-off look in her eyes. She was slipping into the zone again and he could only hope that the results would be good.

He closed the book on Germanic stories in his lap and reached forward to pick up his glass of water from the coffee table. Taking a sip, he looked towards the stairs. The faint sound of instrumental music was drifting down from Avani's room. Their nonmage housemates were apparently in the midst of an intense magic practice session. Thus far, Avani was very pleased with their progress. They all just had to hope that it would be useful soon.

"I don't get it," Alex said. She closed her book with a heavy thud and tossed it onto the coffee table. Aiden flinched at the rough treatment. "I don't even know what I should be looking for! The Celts had stories about other worlds. The Norse knew a bit about the Tree of Reality, but no one seems to have any stories about this Darkness!"

"These myths are reflections of things on Earth," Bran said. He calmly swung his legs off the sofa and turned towards Alex. "They wouldn't have been concerned with a distant danger."

"Then what am I supposed to do?" Alex snapped. "We're not getting anything done! Arthur is out there, swaying more Fae to his cause and I don't know what I'm looking for." Groaning, Alex put her face into her hand and leaned against the armrest.

"We're protecting the Iron Artifacts," Bran said gently. "That's important, Alex. Arthur may not want to open the Iron Gates, but I don't want to see what he'd do with Cathanáil or Mjǫllnir or the Iron Chalice."

"Or the pieces of the Iron Chain," Nicki added. She still didn't look up from her notebook and kept scribbling frantically. "The magic is weakened, but he was made with it so I bet he'd come up with something nasty."

"I just…" Alex made a sound of frustration. Aiden glanced at Bran, but he didn't seem to know what to say either. "I hate this."

"That's fair," Nicki said. She finally looked up and her eyes gleamed with eagerness. "But I have some ideas for magical items that could help us. If we work together, I bet we could pull off some good stuff!"

"Nicki, you just made a magical sheath that is invisible to nonmages," Aiden said. It was hard not to laugh at her excitement. "I think you've already proven very impressive."

"But I could do more," Nicki said. "We could do more!" Rolling onto her side, she looked up at him and smiled. Her eyes were a bit wild. "Alex is worried about what Arthur is doing and we can't scry for him all the time. It would exhaust us."

"So, what are you thinking?" Alex asked. She was leaning forward and trying to read Nicki's notebook. "Thoughts?"

"Well… our current concern is what he's doing, right?" Nicki pushed herself into a seated position and crossed her legs. Seeing her sitting on the rug like that made Aiden remember make-believe games on a magic carpet. "So, what if we create something to help us track his movements, or at least the major things he does?"

"That sounds like scrying," Bran said slowly.

"No no no." Nicki held up her notebook in her right hand and waved her left hand around. "No. I've been poking at the internet. Looking at fictional items in more modern magical shows and books for inspiration, and I've found a couple of things that look like they might just be possible."

"What are you thinking?" Alex asked.

"A book, or maybe a scroll, on a table," Nicki said. "Magically set to Arthur's magic, his being, and powered by a battery like the house's wards. With enough focus on the spell, I bet we could make an item that would be able to record what he does."

"Are you serious?" Alex asked. Her voice went a bit higher than normal. "That sounds.... I can't-"

"Think about it," Nicki said. Her eyes were still a little crazy, but she was reigning in her manic energy. "Arthur is a distinct being. There are only three half-Sídhe in the world, and he's one of them. We know we can scry for him, though his defenses can be a bit difficult, and we know we can make batteries."

"Automated scrying," Bran said slowly. A smile bloomed on his face. "It wouldn't track him all the time, but it would boost the likelihood that we'd get through his defenses."

"But we wouldn't be able to see anything," Alex protested.

"Maybe not," Nicki said. Then she frowned thoughtfully, pressing her lips together. "At least not at first... maybe with a later version we could use the camera of a laptop as the eye of the scrying... no, nope, not yet." Nicki shook her head. "But that's the problem, right? We keep trying to find Arthur, but his defenses are solid. And we do have lives that we're trying to live. Still, if we could even get something set up that let us know when he was moving between cities or talking to a specific person-"

"We might be able to piece together what he's doing," Bran said. "Do you really think you can make something like that?"

"Well, I'm envisioning a leather-bound book," Nicki said. "I'd like to figure out how to do it with my tech, but I could put symbols into the leather to hold the spell and maybe iron in the spine, or hell an iron symbol fixed onto the cover, to power the spell."

"Would it need ink or something like that?" Aiden asked. The idea was starting to form in his mind, but he didn't think he was on the same wavelength as Nicki. Bran seemed to be though. "To write with, I mean?"

"No," Nicki said. She was frowning a little again and scribbling in her notebook. "No, the magic itself could just leave a mark on the page, that way we wouldn't have to worry about smudging or it running out of ink. If it is a bound book alone then it can be moved much more easily. So that's at least one more spell... they'd need to be linked together..." Biting her lip, Nicki crossed something out frantically. "I wish there was an actual magical language. Something that I knew I could use to carry the magic with clear instructions."

"Maybe you do just write it out," Bran suggested. Nicki looked up at him sharply. "Within the cover I mean. You write out in English exactly what you want the book to do while pushing your magic in. It isn't visualization exactly, but it should tell the magic what you want." He nodded towards Alex. "Unless you want to come up with symbols again like you did for Cathanáil's sheath."

"That did work," Nicki said. "But you might be right. Maybe I am making it too complicated. But could it really be that simple? Writing out what I want?"

"If it's filled with magic and connected to a battery, I don't know why it wouldn't," Bran said. "I hate to say it, but it might help if we made all the parts of the book ourselves. Even the paper. It won't hold magic as well as iron-"

"But it would make it easier for the magic to move through the whole book," Nicki finished. "We've got something here, I think. I haven't made paper in years, but I do know how to. I've got lots of leather. Bran, it might be best if you wrote the spell since you actually have a knack for scrying." Nicki tapped her pen on her chin. "The issue I'm still seeing is how to make sure that it can reach Arthur."

"Maybe we use part of the Iron Chain," Alex said. Everyone looked at her. "It's broken, but like Nicki said, there is still some magic in the iron and he was made with it, so there's a connection there."

"Do you have the pieces?" Aiden asked. His eyes went to the ceiling as if he could see into Alex's room. "Here?"

"No, they're in a box at Morgana's house," Alex answered. "I didn't want to just throw them out, and melting it down seemed... dangerous. Nothing's happened around them so we've just sort of been able to forget them."

"Yes," Nicki said. "If we take a thin piece of that and put it into the spine, that might be able to help focus the item's magic on Arthur."

"And an iron triskelion on the front," Alex said. "To power the thing."

"Yes!" Nicki jumped up, her body vibrating. "I like this idea, guys. It has potential!"

"It does," Alex agreed. She held up her hand. "But let's not assume victory yet. There's a lot of pieces to this."

"Which is why Merlin and Morgana have never done it," Nicki said. Aiden recognized her stubborn pout coming into play. "They aren't so good at nondirect magic."

"You're not wrong," Alex allowed. Then she smiled. "Well, let's try it. If it works then as you said we might finally get a read on what Arthur is up to. Any idea how detailed it will be?"

"No," Nicki admitted. "I doubt we'll get a novel describing his motivations and emotional states, but I'm going to live in hope that we can pick up some useful things." Then she was gone in a swish of red hair as she rushed up the stairs.

"Do you think it'll work?" Alex asked him.

Aiden blinked. Alex was slumped over with a far-off look in her eyes. He had to wonder if her earlier energy had been an act for Nicki. How much of what they saw from Alex nowadays was an act or just going through the motions?

"I think that magic can do more than we've tried," Aiden said gently. "I mean, magic made you. A spark of power and consciousness that is reborn shortly before it's needed somewhere. That seems like a force that should be doing more than simply making fireballs or ice spears. Merlin and Morgana are very good battle mages, but Nicki brings something new to the table." He couldn't help but smile with pride. "You remember that she wanted to make items since day one?"

"I remember," Alex agreed. A slight smile appeared on her face. "And now she's getting the chance."

"She's confident in her basic skills," Aiden said. "It's harder to cast weird and complex spells in battles. We all always seem to default to what we're best at. That's not a bad thing, but it won't push us forward. If Arthur is trying new things, like those medallions of his, then we need to innovate as well."

"Alex!" Nicki called from upstairs. "What size do you think would be best?"

A soft smile appeared on Alex's face that instantly made Aiden feel better. Shaking her head, she stood up and headed for the staircase. Bran watched her go, his eyes a bit worried. Aiden held back a smile or maybe a sigh. Then his friend nodded to him and stood up, putting his things to the side.

"I'm going to go and keep an eye on them," he said. "Just to be safe."

"Probably a good idea. Nicki doesn't tend to stop when I tell her to," Aiden agreed.

Aiden stayed where he was. The sounds of the others going through the house was comforting, and yet it left him listless. Nicki's idea was mad, good, but mad. Yet for him, it underlined how much things had changed. Nicki used to make little art projects, but now her energy was geared towards finding a way to stop Arthur.

Their innocence was gone. They'd lost some of it that first night when the Hounds had attacked, and it had eroded since then. At first, the knowledge that magic was real had carried him through the fear. Death had been like a distant idea, something that couldn't really happen to one of the heroes, until he'd found Alex bleeding out on the shore.

That had killed the last spark of innocence. Betrayal from Arthur and realizing after being woken by the Iron Chalice from a coma that he'd almost traded his life for another. All the secrets, all the brushes with danger had just worn them down. Nowadays they barely thought about it. Alex's parents had been killed and yet... sometimes it barely registered.

Once upon a time, they'd been told that magic made them physically more resilient. It was the only reason they had survived being slammed into buildings and cars and all the other horrible things that had happened to them. Now he had to wonder if it went deeper than that. Did magic change them emotionally, spiritually? Or was this really just human?

Picking up his phone, Aiden sighed and opened his contacts. Without thinking about it, he scrolled down to Sara's contact. There was no reason for his ex-girlfriend's number to be in here anymore. They were over. They'd been over for a long time now. Distance and secrets had eroded what he'd once thought was a strong relationship.

But he'd been younger then. After high school, he'd thought he and Sara still stood a chance despite going to separate schools. Another loss of innocence. Shaking his head, Aiden quickly deleted the number from his phone and gently tossed it onto the coffee table. Footfalls above him made him look up. By the sounds of it, his fellow mages were already gathering supplies.

Aiden gripped the armrests and slowly leveraged himself out of the chair. Inhaling slowly, he expanded his lungs all the way and reached for the ember of power in his chest. At the first brush of his consciousness, it burst to life and warmed his body. Maybe it was more than fire: it could be anything, but it always felt like liquid heat pumping through his veins.

A loud bang made him flinch. He heard Jenny's voice even if he couldn't understand what she was saying. Hopefully, Avani had finished whatever exercise she had Jenny and Lance working on before Nicki's manic energy disturbed them. His eyes landed on his phone and he chuckled. There were only a few phone numbers that he truly knew. Sara's was still one of them. Picking up his phone, he shoved it in his back pocket and headed for the stairs.

This was his life now. Lost innocence or not, this was what he had now. Awkward nervous dinners with his family as they tried not to worry. Guilt over not telling them everything. Worry about what happened next. But it was just the life now. His life. Climbing the stairs, Aiden pushed away the dark ideas and went to join the others.

6

Disappointment

1 502 C.E. Rhineland

The rain pounding down on the roof fit Morgana's mood. Everything had been shut up to keep out the water, but the scent of wet earth and straw was still filling the tavern. Their small room was becoming claustrophobic and all Morgana could do was pace the narrow six-foot space in front of the doorway.

Sitting down on the bed, Morgana stopped pacing and tapped her fingers against the small table alongside the bed. She missed her home in the east. When her scrying had picked up the growing levels of magic here, she'd been certain that moving wouldn't bother her. She'd been wrong. Morgana found herself missing dozens of small things that made life in Constantinople much more comfortable than it was here. Then again, it wasn't like things hadn't changed in the east over the years as well.

The door opened and Merlin stepped into the room, shrugging off his wet cloak. There was a small hook by the door for him to hang it on, but nothing to stop the water dripping off of it. Green sparks burst from Merlin's fingertips as soon as the door was closed and swirled around his body, drying him off.

"It is pleasant to have magic for cheap tricks once again," Merlin said. "Remarkable how much you get used to having to be mindful of how much you use."

"Is the wagon still secure?" Morgana asked.

"Yes, the spells are holding," Merlin said. He walked towards the closed-up window and tapped on the shutter thoughtfully. "A truly ugly day. I'm glad we arrived when we did. The autumn rains are beginning to set in."

"We can't stay here forever," Morgana said. "It'll attract attention. Our best option is to move to the city and start establishing ourselves. I'd like to have that done by winter."

"I'm aware," Merlin said. "I've actually already sent some letters into Strasbourg. Our best option is probably to set up a shop. That would help explain any traveling that we need to do."

"Strasbourg," Morgana repeated thoughtfully. "What have you learned about it?"

"It is a large city for this area, and one of the self-governing cities of the Holy Roman Empire. Guilds are very important and we'll have to be mindful of local politics. I'm afraid that it is a bit harsh towards the Jews. They aren't allowed inside the city walls at night and there are other restrictions, but it has been some time since the city had any major violent events. Oh, and it is the city where that new moveable type press was created, so innovation is welcome there."

"That's something, I suppose," Morgana said. "I dislike needing to adjust to a new culture, but it seems we don't really have a choice in the matter."

"I'm afraid not. As you said, we can't live above a tavern until whatever's coming is resolved."

"That still leaves us with the issue of Nikolaus," Morgana said. "Even using my magic to probe the locals, I've only learned very little about him."

"And?"

"And I'm sure he is the Iron Soul," Morgana said resignedly. Shaking her head, she looked towards the shutters again. Maybe she should open them to get some air. "He was a highly regarded soldier who fought in many battles. Happily married, at least it seemed that way until he was injured and his wife vanished with his best friend and second-in-command. Apparently, her departure played a part in his wound becoming infected and his right leg being amputated. A betrayal with great consequences." She gave Merlin a pointed look.

"We need help," Merlin said firmly. Yet his tone had a slight shake to it that Morgana caught in an instant. "We don't know what is coming, and Nikolaus is a mage."

"He won't help us," Morgana hissed. Standing up, she shook her head and paced across the small room twice. "Nikolaus might have been a warrior once, but he is determined to die in that bar! You've spoken with him Merlin, same as I have." She stepped closer to her partner, meeting his stubborn gaze. "Can you look me in the eye and honestly tell me that you have faith that Nikolaus will help us?"

Merlin lowered his eyes, but there was no thrill of victory. They were stuck. Magic was building up in the area and they had yet to figure out the source. So far there were no tunnels, no cracks in any of the Iron Gate defenses, and even the Old Ones seemed to be behaving. Yet, something was coming, and their only help was an old man who was determined to drink himself to death.

"We have no options," Merlin said. "At least he hasn't tried to accuse us of witchcraft."

"The local church doesn't seem to like him any more than us," Morgana scoffed. "He's probably protecting himself as well."

"Must you be so negative?"

"I've traveled hundreds of miles on bad roads only to find that the current incarnation of the Iron Soul is an old drunk with no interest in helping anyone." Morgana raised an eyebrow and gave Merlin a nasty look. "I'm not happy, Merlin, so yes I will be negative."

"I think you just don't like being in the west again," Merlin said. "This was once home."

"Not this area," Morgana replied. "And you know very well that home has changed just as much. Our world is long gone."

"At least they remember us," Merlin said gently. "Even if the stories are wrong, they remember Arto and his struggles."

"To an extent," Morgana said. Shuddering, she remembered the latest version of the story that she'd heard. "But what they get wrong is rather insulting."

Merlin shook his head at her with a disapproving frown, but Morgana knew him well enough to spot the amusement in his eyes. He could posture all he wanted; at this point they could easily read each other, and he was worried too. It was a gnawing worry that bored into the bones and guts and wasn't easily shaken.

"So, what next?" Morgana asked. "Do we stay in this little village where we'll attract far too much attention or move on?"

"The city is the better place for us," Merlin agreed. "People aren't used to strange newcomers here. But we still need to address what to do about Nikolaus."

Neither of them spoke. Morgana didn't have any ideas. All attempts at conversation had been firmly struck down by the man. He didn't want to talk and he didn't want to listen. Bitterness radiated off of him and when drunk, he'd chant his wife's name and curse his former friend. There was none of the forgiveness and compassion that Arto had carried in him. Morgana doubted that she'd ever truly forgive Gwenyvar or Luegáed for what their flight had started, but at least she could recognize that maybe Arto had been right to let go his anger.

All the locals knew about Lorenz and Clare, but even they made a point of never talking about the runaway pair near Nikolaus. Merlin was staring at the shutters in silent thought. They had few options: they could remain here and risk bringing too much attention on themselves, they could leave Nikolaus behind and risk him using magic on accident while in a drunken stupor, or they could use magic to change his mind, but then they'd have to be constantly keeping him under control.

"What if he were to die?" Morgana asked carefully.

"Die?" Merlin repeated, his eyebrows raising.

"You've never really considered the mechanics of what happens," Morgana said. "Not properly, but then again, we usually like or at least respect the incarnations of the Iron Soul. But when they die, they are reborn."

"That takes time," Merlin said.

"Does it?" Morgana pressed. "Or do we just not find them for a while? Let's be honest, Merlin. In times of peace, we don't go looking for the Iron Soul. We leave them to their life."

"We don't even know for certain that they are born outside of times of need," Merlin said.

"I'm confident they are," Morgana said firmly. "I've always been sure that Arto's soul is out there in the world somewhere. Which brings us back to my original question. What happens if Nikolaus dies? How quickly will he be reborn? We know that magic is growing in this area, but that doesn't mean the threat is upon us now. It simply means that what magic is in the world wants us here."

"Morgana, I'm not sure where you are taking the conversation," Merlin said.

"Just... bear with me for a moment," Morgana said. She held up her hands nervously. In her chest, her heart was beginning to race a little. "What if Nikolaus dies and we use our magic to give the Iron Soul a push? Urge it to be reborn nearby into a child that we can raise as a mage, like you did Arto?"

The memory of Merlin disappearing with her little brother pushed to the front of her mind, but Morgana did her best to focus on Merlin's face. His expression was one of both horror and consideration. That was more than she'd hoped for. He hadn't immediately shouted the idea down.

"We can't just wait for him to come around," Morgana said. "And you and I know that mages shouldn't drink. If he connects with his power, as unlikely as it might be, while drunk, he could do a lot of damage. He has a temper and little self-control. Europe doesn't need anything triggering another witch hunt craze. And neither of us wants to enslave him using magic." Merlin flinched at the idea, and Morgana was certain that he'd considered and dismissed the idea. Probably before she'd even thought of it. "So, what do you suggest?"

"Right now? A drink," Merlin said. "This room is too small."

Pulling open the door, he looked her way and nodded into the hallway. This was running away from the problem, but Morgana decided to allow it. A drink sounded right. Pity that she hadn't gotten properly drunk ever in her life. Sometimes it looked like fun. Staying a few steps behind Merlin, they walked to the narrow staircase connecting the rooms with the main tavern.

There was a sudden shout just as they reached the top of the stairs. Tensing up, Morgana flexed her fingers but remembered where she was in time to still the urge to call her magic. Following Merlin down, Morgana flinched at another shout and a crash. A fight had broken out with tables being shoved to the side. It was chaos, and the screaming was growing louder and louder. She would have sighed and gone back upstairs, but then she spotted Nikolaus.

He was screaming at a barmaid, standing up using his cane and looming over her. The girl was barely past childhood. Around them the fighting and arguing continued, with spilled wine covering patches of floor. Merlin made a sound of disapproval, and a stout man that Morgana recognized as the owner slammed something down on a table to get attention.

The barmaid hit a nearby wall. Nikolaus kept shouting for another minute as the girl threw her arms over her head to protect herself. Things suddenly went very quiet, leaving a moment for Nikolaus' last vicious words about the girl's virtue and her mother to carry through the tavern. Sucking in a sharp breath, Morgana braced herself, but no one moved.

Nikolaus stumbled back to his seat, swaying dangerously even with his cane thanks to the drink. The barmaid was crying as another patron helped her to her feet. Morgana's eyes jumped to the tavern owner who was glaring at Nikolaus but making no move to throw him out. What arrangement they had, she didn't want to know. Merlin was frowning disapprovingly at Nikolaus, but the old soldier paid them no mind.

"He's not going to save anyone," Morgana said softly. "Merlin, we don't know what is coming. We have to prepare."

"Your plan is dangerous," Merlin whispered. "So much could go wrong."

"We need the Iron Soul," Morgana protested. "There's no sign of any other mages thus far."

Nikolaus took a long drink from his mug, spilling some of the reinforced wine on himself. As he put down the mug a moment later, Morgana saw something in his eyes. A flash of regret as he glanced towards the barmaid. But he said nothing, and the softness vanished. Whatever had happened with his wife and his friend had broken him. An ugly hacking cough escaped the man, reminding Morgana once more of his age and the damage that had been done to his body.

"Merlin," she said much more softly. "I don't think he can help us protect anyone."

There was a sigh of defeat from Merlin, and she knew that he'd seen the regret as well. But they had a world to protect. Already, her mind was spinning, trying to figure out exactly how the magic would need to be channeled to ensure that they could make the soul be reborn right away. Nervous excitement built in her chest. This was dangerous: potentially they'd lose the soul completely and it would be reborn somewhere else.

Yet, this was new magic. Something completely untried, and they'd have the Iron Soul as a child once again. Young and innocent, someone they could raise and teach and train. Someone who could be a real hero and the mage that the world needed. Merlin put a hand on her shoulder and squeezed it in silent solidarity. Hopefully, this would be the only time such a step was necessary.

Touching Merlin's arm, Morgana tilted her head back upstairs. The owner and the poor girl were trying to clean up the main hall and didn't need more people down there. Turning around, she quickly returned to their room and pushed open the shutters. At least the rain had begun to ease and the air was now fresh.

"So," Merlin said. He closed the door to the room. "I trust you have a plan?"

"We'll need some preparation," Morgana whispered. In her chest, her heart tightened. They were really talking about this. "We don't... we don't really know much about what the soul is. I know the Christians have their version and we had ours, but surely we can use our magic to catch it when Nikolaus dies."

"Catch it," Merlin repeated. He laughed. A brittle, heartbroken laugh. He collapsed into the small chair in one corner, which creaked beneath him. "I can't believe..." Another weak, broken sound escaped him. "By all the ancestors, Morgana."

"What would you have us do?" Morgana asked. "Something is coming, Merlin. Magic wanted us here."

"I know, I know, I'm just... I hope we're right about this," Merlin replied. "I think... I haven't used a circle to focus magic in a long time, but that might be the best way to go. Use our blood to make a circle around Nikolaus. But surely, we can't just hold onto the soul. Too much could go wrong there."

"Agreed," Morgana said. "No, we use our magic to push it into the village. Maybe use a little magic beforehand on a couple."

Merlin groaned again, and Morgana found herself silently agreeing with him. Leaning against the window frame, she looked out across the small village. There were many families in the area who could be considered. Somehow it had come to this: plotting the death of an Iron Soul incarnation because he wasn't what they wanted or needed. It should have shocked her, it should have horrified her, and yet there was a small part of her that was surprised it had taken this long for things to come to this.

7

Poisonous Thoughts

Alex wasn't a fan of postmodernism. Her class on Contemporary American Fiction had solidified that view. There were some good short stories certainly, but most of it was too depressing. Yes, there were issues that literature could explore better than other mediums, but given the state of her life, she really preferred stories with simple "good triumphs over evil" plots without hard questions or choices. She had enough of those in her own life.

Closing the latest assigned book, Alex slumped back in her chair and tossed the book onto the bed. It almost knocked Galahad off, and Alex grimaced in sympathy for the stuffed dog. Still, she didn't get up. Cathanáil was leaning up against her desk, secure in its sheath, Mjǫllnir rested in its stand and the Iron Chalice was still in her bag near the doorway. Everything was as it should be.

Yet there was a distinct feeling that she had forgotten something. Picking up her phone, Alex scrolled down her calendar. There was nothing there. Her social life was pretty restricted to the people who lived in this house. Jenny's birthday was coming up fast on October 7th and she needed to talk with Lance about if he had any plans or ideas. Otherwise there were no projects due, and her one paper that was due next week already had a first draft done.

It didn't take her long to pinpoint what was bothering her. The Darkness was still out there to worry about, but closer to home there was a question of the poison Merlin had brought back from England and the leftovers from the potion she'd used. They'd discussed weaponizing it, but thus far nothing had come from it. She'd almost forgotten it in the wake of the Queen's death, but she couldn't afford to forget big details like that.

The poison was a problem. Just the knowledge of it bothered Alex. She could understand why Merlin had kept it a secret for so long. It was creepy, a thick black liquid that clung to whatever it was in. Something about how the light interacted with it didn't seem right. Maybe it was all in her head, but just thinking about it put Alex on edge. She wondered if that was some sort of instinct as a mage. Surely it was reasonable for a magical human to fear something that destroyed magic.

Merlin was right that it could be an impressive weapon, but what would Arthur do with it if he managed to steal some? At least the recipe of the potion that created it was lost. Arthur did not need a stronger connection to the Iron Realm and a cauldron full of poison. Tapping her fingers on her desk, Alex glanced around her room. It was Sunday and her things were ready for class the next day. There was time to go and check in with Merlin.

Standing up, she toed off her slippers and grabbed her sneakers before she could change her mind. She strapped Cathanáil on her back but hesitated about taking the Chalice. It only took her a moment to dismiss it. She was only going to Merlin's. It wasn't far, and as full of iron as the place was, it seemed unlikely that anything would attack her there.

Alex grabbed her bag and headed downstairs, keeping an ear out for the others. Jenny and Lance were in the living room, snuggled close together. At first Alex didn't see their soft smiles. A twinge of something flared in her chest and Alex's fingers tightened around the banister. Hot and oily inside, she struggled to catch her breath and lowered her eyes from them. There were no whispers from the others, no indications that it came from them.

"Alex?" Lance called. His voice was gruff and Alex held back a sigh.

"Hey," Alex called. Lance and Jenny had shifted apart on the sofa, making her a little amused. It wasn't like they all didn't know what happened in their bedroom. It wasn't like they didn't occasionally hear more than they wanted. "Uh, sorry. I'm heading over to Merlin's."

"Everything okay?" Jenny asked, tucking a strand of hair behind her ear. Her eyes were lowered, signaling her embarrassment.

"Yeah," Alex said. "Just... done with school work. A bit restless and I want to try and talk with him about something."

"You sure everything is okay?" Lance asked. "You could just call."

"I don't want to talk about it over the phone," Alex explained. "I'll be back at some point."

Jenny was frowning slightly, but she nodded her understanding. Next to her, Lance relaxed and put his arm back around Jenny's shoulder. There was another poke of something hot in Alex's chest. Since she was ready for it, the sensation wasn't as bad this time. Rushing for the door, she said a quick goodbye and headed for her car.

Jealousy, she realized with a grimace. That flare of emotion had been jealousy. Not for Jenny or Lance exactly, but for what they had. Shaking her head, Alex stomped to her car. There was no point in being lonely. She had friends, Merlin, and Morgana. Her family was gone, but she wasn't alone. Groaning softly to herself, Alex unlocked her car and slumped into the driver's seat. Maybe she was lonely. The last time she'd been jealous had been over Arthur, and that wasn't something she wanted to return to.

For a moment she just sat there, torn between examining the feeling and dismissing it. The heat faded away and tears pricked at Alex's eyes. Again, she wondered what would happen if they ever finished this war. Nicki was completely head over heels for Avani, so hopefully they'd stay together, Lance and Jenny had each other, Aiden and Bran had their families, but she was on her own. Like Merlin and Morgana. Shaking her head, Alex started the car and used the small turn they'd created in the driveway to pull out. She was fine. Besides, this war would never be over. Sooner or later, she'd probably just be killed and reborn again.

Alex's thoughts were unsettled as she drove towards Merlin's. Her urge to cry was gone, but the tightness in her chest wasn't. It was there, brewing beneath the surface. Just to be on the safe side, she decided it would be a good night to put on a crying movie and just get it out tonight. That was something she could do easily enough in the living room or in the privacy of her own bedroom.

Nicki's car was parked along the curb, making Alex frown. She didn't remember Nicki mentioning that she was coming to Merlin's today. Then again, she'd been late down for breakfast so maybe she'd just missed that announcement. Parking her own car, Alex checked her phone before securing it back in her bag.

Slamming the door of her car, Alex ignored the front porch of Merlin's home completely and walked around to the side gate. As she drew closer, she could hear muffled sounds from the workshop. At least that meant that Merlin was home. She scanned the yard for any sign of Nicki, but she wasn't outside. Grumbling to herself, Alex reconsidered if she really wanted to try and talk about the poison in front of Nicki. The book needed to be the priority. Still, secrets were always a problem in books. Heroes kept things secret and it went bad at the worst moment. She'd made enough mistakes without making that one.

The inside of the forge was beyond hot. Sweat sprang to the top of Alex's skin almost instantly as she opened the door and stepped inside. One of the furnaces was filled with glowing coals and Merlin was standing in front of it, tongs at the ready. He looked over and smiled at her in welcome. Nicki was across the room, leather spread across one of the worktables, her mouth moving as she traced something out.

Merlin gestured for her to wait and quickly secured whatever he was working on. At the moment it was just a long bar of iron, but there was a soft shimmer of green magic beneath the surface. Leaning against the doorframe, Alex's eyes were drawn towards the safe secured a few feet away. Now that the Chalice was staying near them in case of an attack, was that where Merlin was keeping the poison?

"Alex, good to see you," Merlin greeted. He picked up a cloth and cleaned the sweat from his face. "What brings you here?"

"I just... I wanted to talk to you about the poison," Alex said. She lowered her voice as if Arthur was right outside listening.

"The poison," Merlin repeated. His smile vanished and Nicki looked up from her project in surprise. "What is it that you want to know?"

"You were talking about weaponizing it," Alex said. "You haven't spoken of it in a while. Have you had any ideas?"

"Nothing that worked," Merlin admitted. He tossed his work gloves to the side and pulled off his apron. "I had high hopes that it might be useful. I've been experimenting with it," Merlin admitted. "Trying to find ways to use it safely."

"Really?" Nicki's eyes were wide with excitement, but her expression was tempered with a healthy dose of fear. She gave Merlin plenty of space as she came over to join them. "Have you learned anything?

"A bit," Merlin said. He looked away from them and Alex had the distinct impression that he was embarrassed. "It works for twenty seconds before becoming inert, but can do a great deal of damage in that time."

"It eats everything, right?" Nicki asked. "Dissolves it down like an acid."

"Yes," Merlin said. "I knew it was dangerous. That's why I buried it for so long. In the old tunnel, it destroyed a few Fae and ate through the wall. At the time... at the time I was so scared that it wouldn't stop. When it did, I was beyond relieved, but the stone that was still intact..." Merlin trailed off and shook his head. "I don't know. I want to use it against Arthur, but I'm worried about it backfiring."

"I've been trying to figure out how to use it too," Nicki said. "When I was making Cathanáil's scabbard, I kept thinking about it." She shrugged when Alex looked at her. "It seems like it could be useful, but we wouldn't want Arthur to get ahold of it, so a lot of the basic ways to turn something into a weapon just wouldn't work."

"You have a real gift," Merlin said warmly. "If anyone could figure it out, it would be you."

Nicki blushed a little but shrugged. "Well, don't get excited because I've still got nothing."

"Maybe not with the poison, but your new project is certainly interesting," Merlin said. "I'm not sure it will work, but the theory is sound, and if you can find a way to keep tabs on Arthur it would be a triumph of magic."

"I'd like a look at one of the jars," Alex said.

"Why?"

Alex shrugged. She didn't know how to explain her reason and 'just because' sounded too childish. Merlin frowned. The corner of his mouth twitched and Alex just knew that he was considering arguing with her, but he seemed to realize that there really was no point. Alex knew that the poison was here somewhere and had seen it briefly once before. Nodding, he turned and moved over the safe. Nicki shifted out of his way, her fingers flexing with contained excitement. Sometimes, Alex wondered about her.

He did indeed go to the safe. It wasn't hidden, the lines in the concrete floor making it perfectly obvious, but there was a small handle that Merlin had to free and pull up on to swing the slab up. Beneath it was the safe door, aligned so that its door opened the other way. Merlin pulled open the safe door with a soft huff, gently setting it against the side of the floor with a metallic tap.

The safe was a few inches lower, the thick iron walls strong enough to repel the Fae. Alex noted that it looked like Merlin had added a new layer of protection to the safe as a new triskelion symbol on the inside of the door was gleaming with stored magic. There was a layer of foam that Merlin quickly pulled down to reveal the top of a wooden crate box. Once he freed that, Alex could see thick cotton wrap and a few blankets for good measure. Nicki chuckled softly, but Alex appreciated the caution. Reaching down, Merlin slowly pulled a mason jar free from the soft prison.

Alex stepped forward and carefully took the jar when Merlin held it up. The most dangerous substance in the world was in mason jars. She hadn't properly appreciated the humor of that before. Mason jars were for paintbrushes in Nicki's room, sweet tea down south, canned goods, and other decorative things that people could come up with. Yet, the poison was secured in clear mason jars.

Taking the first jar carefully, Alex held it up towards the window. No light managed to pass through the thick black liquid. The purple sheen that she'd noted last time was still there, but it did little to alter the thick blackness of the poison. As she shifted the jar, Alex noted that the liquid wasn't very fluid. It wasn't like water, but was much thicker, almost like some sort of batter. Yet, from Merlin's description of the tunnel, it could splatter well enough.

Merlin and Nicki were silent and stayed still as she examined the jar and slowly turned it. That was a good thing. Alex did not want to be startled and drop it. A strange stray thought occurred to her. As the Iron Soul, a being with a core of magic, what would happen to her if she interacted with the poison? Would it destroy her extra quickly or would it be slow, or would something else completely different happen? What if more than a few drops were released? How far could it spread? It was a dark thought, and Alex grimaced internally at having even thought it. She'd thought about the poison in the past since learning about it, but nothing had ever stuck. No ideas, no moments of understanding. Just confusion over why the Iron Realm would allow it to exist and a fear of using it.

Something bothered her. A half-formed thought that she couldn't remember. Shifting the jar, Alex waited for a moment of inspiration. For a helpful eureka moment. The thick liquid only churned in the jar like a dark cloud carrying storm. Dark. The word stuck and Alex frowned, turning the jar again. The pitch black was intense and knowing what it was, what it could do made her skin chill.

Yet, that stray thought planted another one in her head. Trying to see some light through the poison, Alex couldn't help but think that it was like liquid darkness. The hint of purple reminded her a touch of a dark night sky, but there were no stars here. No relief of any kind. Lowering the jar, she gently set it on the nearest work table. A frown took over her face and her brows knit together. Slowly, she pulled her hand back from the jar and risked a glance towards the safe where the others were still secure. She could just see the top of two more jars.

"Merlin, do you think the poison and the Darkness could be connected?" Alex asked. She studied the small sealed jars with a deep frown. They all contained the same dark fluid. "That maybe that's what the Darkness is?" She glanced over and saw his doubtful expression. "On a larger scale," she added in a rush. "Maybe in another world, someone tried something and released a lot of the stuff. If it ate through a whole world then maybe it wouldn't be restricted by time anymore and could keep eating through more worlds, following the lines of magic between worlds!"

The words fell easily from her before Alex could fully form the thought, but it seemed to fit. Something in her chest shifted and for a moment the voices went quiet, all of them, in a shared horror. Merlin looked thoughtful, but then he started to shake his head.

"No," he answered. Even Nicki gave him an irritated look now. "No, I don't think so. The potion opens a connection to the Iron Realm, this poison is just a left over. There'd be no reason for it to be created in another world."

It was Nicki who spoke up. "But other worlds have different rules," she said.

"It's an interesting theory, but I don't think so," Merlin said. His voice took on a hard hint. Standing up, he picked up the jar and wrapped it in a length of cotton wrap. It wouldn't' really protect the jar if he dropped it, but Alex supposed it made him feel better. "As I said, the poison only works for a short time." His brown eyes were sharp as he looked at her. "You're still convinced that there's something going on."

Nicki's eyes widened and she back stepped away from Alex and Merlin. Alex almost laughed at the retreat, but her frustration with Merlin won out. "Yes." She raised her chin and met his gaze. "I do. Merlin, I've seen that dead world, and I know you and Morgana don't believe it, but the Queen really was worried about something."

"She was trying to get your sympathy."

"To what end?" Alex pressed. "Arthur had killed her. Surely she didn't think that I needed to be convinced that he was my enemy." Throwing her arms up, Alex laughed bitterly. "Seriously, Merlin, she reached out to me with all the magic she had left."

"She was a very manipulative person."

"Okay, yes, fine, that's very true, but seriously she was dying. She didn't try to muster allies or save herself, she just made a plea to me!"

"Alex," Merlin sighed. Then he shook his head and knelt down to return the jar of poison to the safe. "Alex, when you're as old as I am, you focus on the threat in front of you. The future is impossible to predict. Believe me, I've been listening to people's predictions for centuries and they never get it right. We have to focus on what we know, on the present threat." He reached out and placed a hand on her shoulder. "I understand that you're worried, but truly, Arthur is the threat we have to worry about."

Holding back a growl, Alex folded her arms over her chest. She glared at the safe. The idea that had been planted in her head wasn't going to vanish. Alex knew that, but thanks to the voices at the back of her head she also knew that trying to convince Merlin wasn't going to go anywhere. As kind and intelligent as the old mage was, he was stubborn and set in his ways. With that, Alex turned and headed for the door. She didn't bother to say goodbye to Merlin but did call back a quick 'see you tonight' to Nicki.

8

Robin

Aiden wasn't writing anything important. Sometimes it was just easier to put a pencil to paper and see what came out. There were a few notes at the top for upcoming projects, little thoughts on how to improve the basic robot they were supposed to make, but it dissolved into a list of thoughts about magical items for Nicki. Maybe someday they'd cross over, but as much as he liked the idea of weaving a magical spell into a computer or cell phone, he had no idea where to start.

It was a pity really. When they'd first started learning magic, Aiden had hoped that they'd be further along by now. The problem was that while you could cause an effect using magic, you couldn't be sure of everything you'd get. A fireball to burn a Fae was easy enough, and with practice an ice spear to stop Shadows was doable. But he couldn't put his finger on how to control magic in something like technology. If writing down what they wanted worked for the book then it would open a lot of new possibilities. Aiden almost drooled at the idea of experimenting with inserting magical spells into tech. Nicki would help him, that much he was sure about, and they'd scare the others by playing mad scientists. It was something to look forward to.

Closing the notebook, Aiden looked back at his tablet. He really did need to get some work done. Sometimes it was hard to work at home. Bran was a great roommate, but sometimes that was the problem. He just wanted to talk science with his friend or brainstorm ideas rather than do the planning he actually needed to focus on.

The library was open for students, thankfully. Tables at the north-western corner by the windows tended to fill up as people had a strange fascination with looking at the ruins of the Student Union building. At least there wasn't much they could see that hadn't already been whispered about. Clean up efforts and exposure had already helped wear away the distinct line that Alex's shield had created during the explosion. Fascination with the horror remained though, and people would creep to those windows to get a better view. Aiden was at the table in the south-east corner instead.

Someone set a textbook on the table a few seats down from him. Looking up, Aiden frowned a little. There were lots of empty tables and even a few empty study rooms, so he didn't know why they'd be sitting here. It was a young woman, about his own age with smooth dark skin, high cheekbones, and long natural curls that surrounded her heart-shaped face like a halo. Dressed in a Ravenslake t-shirt and jeans with a backpack over her shoulder, she didn't look at all like a Fae, so Aiden relaxed.

"Hi," the young woman greeted with a bright smile. There was a spark of nervousness in her eyes that confused Aiden. "I'm Robin."

"Aiden," he answered automatically. Studying her face, he tried to place it. "Uh, do we have a class together? You look familiar?"

"Yes, we're in Microcontrollers together," she said. "Though, I don't think we've ever spoken."

"Oh, right!" Aiden grinned and shook his head. "Sorry, I didn't mean- I just- I'm bad with faces."

"You must be," Robin said. "Most people remember the only girl in class."

"You're not the only girl in class," Aiden protested. "There's the... I think she's blond? And that Hispanic girl."

"Fine, one of the three," Robin replied. She rolled her eyes a bit but was still smiling. "Electrical engineering isn't the most popular subject for women."

"No, it isn't," Aiden admitted. It was hard not to tap his feet. "So, uh, can I help you with something?"

"Oh, I was just saying hi," Robin said. She smiled again, that hint of nervousness back. "I just transferred here and I'm trying to meet people." Shrugging, Robin's fingers tightened around the strap of her backpack. "It's a bit harder to meet people without freshman orientation."

"You transferred in?" Aiden blinked at her in surprise. "And you didn't leave after the, uh, the bombing?" He lowered his voice on the last word, half afraid to say it out loud and potentially cause a panic.

"That was terrible," Robin agreed. "But no one was hurt, which was a miracle. I took that as a good sign. Even if bad things happen here, it's like there is a guardian angel looking over the campus. That's reassuring. Besides, there's nothing in the history of the campus or town to indicate something like that would happen again."

"Yeah... I suppose not." Aiden struggled with what to say before realizing that she was still standing. Gesturing to the chair across from him, he smiled. "Well, please have a seat if you have time."

"Thank you." Robin pulled out the chair and gracefully eased herself into it, swinging off her backpack in the same movement. "How are you enjoying this year so far?"

"It's more interesting," Aiden answered. "I like the greater focus on projects, but it is a lot more stressful. My roommate is probably going to kill me by the end of the year. Half of our place has been taken over."

"What's he studying?"

"Physics; he's got his own stuff, but it doesn't take up as much room as mine."

"It's nice that you're living with friends," Robin said. Her smile was a bit wistful, and Aiden wondered just why she chose to transfer. "That's gotta be easier than living with strangers."

"It is in a lot of ways," Aiden agreed. "Though, the commute to campus is a bit annoying. I used to live a lot closer."

"I can see that," Robin agreed. She nodded, making her hair bounce. "Probably going to be more of a pain in the winter."

"Yeah, I suspect I'll be spending a lot more time in the library then," Aiden agreed. "Easier to just camp out rather than drive back and forth across the river."

"So, what are you working on now?" Robin asked. She finally sat down and rested her chin on her hand, still giving him a soft smile.

"Oh, just trying to brainstorm," Aiden replied. "I'm a junior so I've got some bigger projects for this semester."

"Good on you for starting so early," Robin complimented. "At least we haven't got anything too bad for Microcontrollers, just the final from Hell."

"Yeah," Aiden snorted. "I've heard it's bad too."

"How's the lab going for you so far?"

"Uh, good I think," Aiden replied. "I'm feeling good about my assignments so far. I just have to keep myself from overthinking it."

Robin's answering smile was pretty and understanding. She nodded a little and Aiden found himself relaxing a bit more. The knot of tension that lived between his shoulder blades nowadays loosened. How long had it been since he talked with someone outside his family or circle of friends?

"Well, good luck with your work," Robin said. "Just tell me if I disturb you."

They settled into silence, and Aiden found himself quietly glancing at Robin. Her tablet was set up and she'd put an earbud into her right ear. While she wasn't humming, her head was moving a little and she had a small smile on her face as she listened to music and worked on whatever she'd brought with her. It was a nice smile. Aiden had to make an effort not to stare. There was something about her. Robin seemed nice and friendly so far, and he knew that she had to be smart to reach an upper-level electrical engineering class. His mind was already trying to figure out the best way to ask her to lunch or something before he caught himself.

He didn't have time for that. Sure, he sort of missed dating and missed talking to people about something other than magic, other worlds, or threats, but he'd only just talked to her for the first time. Aiden could feel his cheeks heating up. It was a pity that his father's Italian complexion hadn't done more to cancel out his mother's pale Irish skin. Keeping himself focused on his tablet, Aiden read the same sentence for the third time and shook himself. His mind finally started working again and he typed up the official lab report he needed to turn in next Tuesday.

Then his phone beeped softly and Aiden quickly pulled it out. There was a text message from Lance, reporting figures that looked like Fae in the university arboretum. A reply from Alex popped up, saying she was on her way and cautioning Lance to pull back. Swallowing, Aiden put his phone away and stood up. Robin looked up as he started to pack up his things.

"You're leaving already?"

"Afraid so," he said. "Something's come up. Uh, sorry. It was nice to meet you, Robin."

"Nice to meet you too," Robin replied. Then she smiled at him again. "Don't worry, next time I'll ask you out properly rather than just sneaking up on you."

Aiden froze, staring at her as he tried to decide if she was serious. Still smiling, Robin turned her attention back to her tablet. His phone beeped again with another message and Robin frowned a little.

"You'd better get going," she said, much more gently this time. "See you in class."

"Right."

Aiden moved to the staircase, his brain still whirling. He was more than a little surprised but tried not to read too much into Robin's comment. She might just have been teasing. Better to not get himself all confused and fixated on it. He managed not to fall down the stairs and made it to the first floor before checking his phone again. Nicki was on her way to the arboretum as well. Inhaling slowly, Aiden stepped outside and quickened his pace down the long sidewalk heading towards the lake.

Around him, the street lamps were starting to turn on. His stomach growled, reminding him that he'd only eaten an apple since lunch. Campus wasn't too crowded, even the lawns by the dorms were mostly empty. Fog was rolling up the slope by the lake. A few students stopped to look at it in surprise before moving on. Aiden hesitated for a moment, but then held out his hands and stepped into the fog.

It brushed across his skin. A puff of air escaped him as Aiden realized that it was magical. Of course, it was magical. He should have figured that out sooner. There was another heartbeat of hesitation before he reminded himself that most likely it had been created by Alex or Nicki to hide the fight. The Fae didn't have magic anymore, not really. Not most of them anyway.

There were only two Fae left when Aiden made his way through the fog. It opened into an oval space where Alex and Nicki were standing at the ready and glaring at the pair of enemies. All around them, fog churned and chilled the air, but it stayed back so it didn't disrupt their sight. He was both impressed and irritated. They could have handled this and he could have kept working in the library.

The Fae hadn't noticed him yet. They were watching Nicki and Alex and waiting for them to make a move. Bringing up his hand, Aiden spread his fingers and tugged on the spark of magic in his chest. The air around his hand burst into flames, casting a fierce light around him. The Fae looked at him in alarm. That was all the opening Alex and Nicki needed. Lightning flashed. A Fae threw itself to the right, barely avoiding the bolt of lightning that ripped into its partner.

Throwing the fireball, Aiden didn't really have to put any force into it. The magic carried it exactly where he wanted it to. Which was a good thing, given that it hadn't rained much lately and they were amongst trees. The Fae shrieked and collapsed to the ground as the magical fire consumed its body. Watching the Fae stop moving and its body begin to crumble, Aiden grimaced and shook his head. He was getting far too used to this. With a wave of her hand, Nicki sent a little jet of water over the area just to be sure there were no embers left.

"Hi," Alex greeted. She turned to him with a weary smile. "Thanks for coming."

"Lance get away safely?" He didn't really need to ask. Alex wouldn't have been so calm if he didn't.

"He's fine," Alex said. Then she looked at Nicki. "You okay? No injuries?"

"Never touched me," Nicki assured her. Then she smiled at Aiden, her eyes checking him over despite him arriving at the last second. "I'm starving."

Alex waved her hands and the fog started to lift. Slowly, but it was lifting. Aiden supposed that was for the best. They didn't need people panicking because the fog just vanished. Moving forward, Alex nudged the piles of clothing with her foot. Well, pile; one of the Fae's clothing had been burned up. She knelt down and dug out two medallions.

The last of the fog was gone now and Alex put the medallions into her pockets. Falling into step with the girls, Aiden tightened his grip on his backpack strap. He briefly considered heading back to the library, but that felt awkward. Alex was on his left and Nicki was on his right, both relaxed and calm even after the attack. Then, Nicki's stomach growled loudly and he looked at her, raising an eyebrow.

"I'm hungry," Nicki said with a sharp hint of defensiveness.

"You're hungry," Aiden repeated. "That's a shock. Is that an 'I want to go out to dinner' or 'I want to go home and raid the fridge'?"

"Well, we do have a very good lasagna at home now," Nicki said approvingly. "Timothy did a good job."

"Yeah, he did." Aiden glanced around as they slowly started climbing up the hill towards the dorms. Alex had her phone out and was texting the others.

"What's with you?" Nicki asked. She tilted her head quizzically and studied him. Now that she and Avani were an item, or at least nearly there, she'd returned to being frighteningly aware of him. "Something is up?"

"Nothing is up!"

Something in his voice must have betrayed him because Nicki started to smile. It wasn't a nice smile. It was the smile that when you saw it on your best friend you either ran and hid or were grateful that they were on your side if someone else was the target. There was no in between. Right now, he was the target. Glee filled her eyes, and he knew that she had put something together. Yet, there was also a slight tightness in her features. She was trying to restrain herself, trying to behave. That made him feel a bit better.

"Go ahead," he sighed. "Get it out of your system."

"Is she pretty? I bet she has a nice smile." Nicki grabbed his arm tightly, excitement pouring off of her. "You've always been a sucker for a nice smile! When can I meet her? I promise not to bring out any embarrassing stories for at least a month!"

"I just talked to her for the first time," Aiden protested. "Apparently we have a class together. She just introduced herself at the library. We talked, but only for a short time."

"But you're thinking of asking her out," Nicki observed sagely. She nodded in approval. "It's been a while."

Sighing, Aiden nodded in resignation. "She does have a nice smile, but I'm not planning to ask her out," he said firmly.

"Oh, come on!" Nicki cooed. Her smile was horrible again.

"Leave him be," Alex said. She sounded near to laughter. Nicki pouted and turned to look at Alex. Aiden mouthed 'thank you' to her. "Home, then?" Alex asked.

Aiden nodded, aware of Nicki still watching them. She wasn't going to let this go anytime soon. Strangely, that made him happy. At least as much as things changed, Nicki would still be an annoying best friend. Smiling, he put his arms over the shoulders of both of his fellow mages, feeling oddly happy with the state of the world.

9

A New Home

1 504 C.E. Rhineland

It had taken time, but it had all worked. Morgana smiled down at the small being in her arms, rocking him gently and resisting the urge to coo at him. Merlin was across the room and she could already feel the weight of his eyes. It was a miracle. In their centuries of using magic, they'd never done anything such as this. They'd almost changed their minds, the parts of them that protected the Iron Soul rebelling against the idea of ever harming one. Yet Nikolaus' disregard and continued refusal to help had made the choice for them.

"I'm a bit surprised that his parents just agreed to let us take him," Merlin said softly.

"Caring for a child is expensive," Morgana said. "I'm not surprised that they took the purse of gold and were happy."

"Still, it seems a bit cruel," Merlin said sternly.

"It was necessary. We went to a lot of trouble to help him be born," Morgana said, keeping her voice light. "Besides, he's old enough to eat mashed up foods now. We won't need a wet nurse so he's old enough to leave his mother." She shifted the baby in her arms as he grew a little too heavy. "He's growing quickly."

At six months old, the young boy was about ten pounds, had quickly growing brown curls, bright, curious brown eyes, and was healthy. Thankfully, he was adjusting quickly to them, something Morgana was grateful for. Merlin stood up and walked to the window of their small house. It wasn't anything fancy, but it was above the small store they ran. For now, it could be home. The child only added to the impression that they were husband and wife.

"Are you sure he'll be alright with the solids?" Merlin asked. He was frowning deeply. "I've never spent much time around such young children."

"We'll give it a try," Morgana answered. His eyelids were dropping. "And Strasbourg is large enough that if there are issues, we can find a wet nurse." Standing up, she lifted the small child and took him over to the wooden box filled with blankets that served as his bed. "We have him now, Merlin; stop worrying so much."

"He needs a name," Merlin said. He looked over at the child, smiling sadly. "Not Arto."

"No," Morgana agreed. "Not Arto. Something that will fit in better here. We'll monitor the situation with magic, but I believe whatever crisis is coming is a few years off. He'll have some time to grow and play with other children." Merlin looked surprised, and Morgana resisted the urge to glare at him. "I have cared for children before, Merlin."

"So you have told me," Merlin replied. He was smiling again. "It is just strange every time I think about it."

She left that alone. Morgana wasn't sure she wanted to explore why Merlin would assume such a thing about her. Over the years, she'd let a few details about her childhood in the Sídhe realm slip. Holding back a shiver, Morgana tried not to think about that land so far away. She'd never wanted for anything, but she'd come to understand that her life there had been wrong. The fear still clung to her. Fear that she never wanted this child to understand, but knew that someday he would.

Looking out the window, Morgana took in the stone street. There was at least an effort here in Strasbourg to be civilized. Somewhat. It wasn't the cleanest street and bathing daily was still a rather foreign idea to the population. If they knew that she and Merlin bathed daily they'd be shocked. Still, they were here now, and there was no need to worry about the Iron Soul beyond caring for him. Morgana, to her surprise, didn't even feel guilty for it. The torment in Nikolaus' head was gone now; his pain was over, and there was a happy child that could be trained in the ways of magic in his place.

Things were going smoothly. After Nikolaus' death they'd managed to push the Iron Soul towards a married woman who already had three children. Over the next month Merlin had made trips to the city to make arrangements while Morgana watched. When the woman started to show, Morgana had made excuses to get close to her. There had been a hint of magic around the woman that put Morgana's worries to rest. She wouldn't be able to confirm with certainty until the child was born, but it had been enough to make Merlin optimistic.

The child had been born while Merlin was in Strasbourg, but Morgana had gone over with some offerings of food. Maria's husband hadn't been keen on it, but he was grateful enough for the help even if he'd been a touch suspicious. Maria herself had been too tired to care, with three other children already demanding her attention and her body weakened. In a moment of pity, Morgana had used some of her magic to ease the woman's recovery. There would be no promises for the next time she gave birth, but given what Morgana was planning, it seemed the least she could do. Soon after, she'd made her offer of taking the child and the deal had been struck.

Upon locking eyes with the child, Morgana had been certain the plan had worked. His Connection was weak, barely formed, with only intense emotions washing over Morgana. Yet it was there, curious and trusting. Morgana almost went over to pick up the child in hopes of feeling that again. That sweet innocence was soothing.

"At least things are going according to plan," Morgana said softly.

"Indeed, I'm a bit surprised that your plan worked." Merlin's tone shifted to one heavy with guilt. "I still... what we had to do was most unpleasant."

"Nikolaus got to pass in his sleep," Morgana said. "It was a much more peaceful death than I think awaited him otherwise. His mind was going and the locals were losing patience with him."

"Yes, but still..." Merlin trailed off. "Still, he was the Iron Soul. We've never raised a hand against the Iron Soul before."

"He was a lost soul," Morgana corrected. Then she exhaled and reminded herself that she couldn't aggravate Merlin; not now. They were stuck together for several years at least again. "It was necessary, Merlin. Unpleasant, but necessary. And it worked perfectly. Surely that means that the magic understood that it was necessary."

"I suppose so," Merlin conceded. He was clearly unhappy, but it would pass, or at least he would bury it. "He seems a strong boy. I'm sure that we'll be able to raise him to be a good mage. Then again... Arto was much older when I... adopted him." Holding back a snort at his choice of words, Morgana turned to look at Merlin and raised an eyebrow. He smiled, but his cheeks did color at her look. "I hardly had a choice, Morgana," Merlin reminded her. "Your foster mother was far too curious about the Iron Soul, and you hadn't found your way yet."

Nodding, Morgana couldn't argue. She wanted to, but the words were true. It was a topic that rarely came up in conversation between them. In the great span of her life, those years of confusion and childish devotion were but a droplet of water. Though, they now had a child to care for. He didn't look like Arto, but the knowledge that it was the soul of her brother was sure to catch her off guard from time to time.

"I hope we raise him well," Morgana said softly. "Given what we did to create him."

"We both care for him already," Merlin said gently. "I have faith that we will manage."

"I hope so." Morgana's stomach twisted with new worries; ones she'd never thought she'd need to consider.

"How about Michel?" Merlin suggested.

"Pardon?"

"His name," Merlin said. "I want something to call him properly. I know his parents didn't bother, but we both know that he'll survive to grow up. We won't allow anything else to happen, so he should have a name."

"Why Michel?"

Shrugging, Merlin moved over and looked down at the infant. "It's a name in this part of the world. Rather popular. Besides, I think he looks like a Michel."

Walking over to join Merlin, Morgana peered down at the slumbering baby. She didn't understand how he looked like a Michel, but Merlin looked happy. Peaceful. Smiling, she shrugged a little and nodded.

"Michel then," she agreed. "I suppose that will work. What name have you decided to use again?"

"Ambrose," he answered. "There's too many stories of Merlin now."

"Ambrose," Morgana said, testing the name. "Isn't that Latin for immortal?" Merlin's smile told her all she needed to know. Raising an eyebrow, Morgana fixed him with a stern stare. "That's not a local name, Merlin."

"No, it isn't," he agreed. "But I'm a foreign trader settling here from the east. I think an exotic name will help in our new trade. Besides, I can always say that my name was chosen in memory of Aurelius Ambrosius."

"I rather doubt that the common man knows the history of a man in the 4th century." He just smiled. "Just so we have our stories straight, how long have we been married?"

"Five years," Merlin answered. "I know we both look a touch older, but only having an infant after a long marriage seems a bad idea. You were a widow," he added, is voice a touch gentler now. "We came here to take advantage of the growing economy, and will be taking some trips for goods. That'll give us cover for taking Michel out of the city if need be."

"It will be needed when he starts showing magic," Morgana said. "Anything else I need to be aware of?"

"The locals don't love our accents," Merlin said. He shrugged a little. "I suspect we'll adjust to the language quickly. I'd rather not have to use so much magic in day-to-day life."

"We'll be fine, I'm sure," Morgana said. "I'll stay with Michel. Alert me if you need my assistance."

"I will." Merlin paused on his way to the door. "Uh, thank you, Morgana. For taking care of the boy. I know it isn't your preferred activity."

"We must blend in," Morgana said. "Though I will expect you to pull your weight in the evenings."

Merlin nodded in agreement. He was about to head downstairs to open the store when magic sparked at the edge of her senses and Morgana gasped softly. Merlin had straightened up and as one they moved to the window. Peering down onto the street, Morgana frowned and scanned the people going about their mornings. Some clouds were rolling in overhead, signaling rain, but there was nothing else.

"What was that?" Morgana asked. Merlin didn't have an answer. "It's gone…"

"Maybe," Merlin said. His eyes narrowed and swept the street again before he twisted around to check on Michel. "An Old One, maybe?"

"I didn't get that impression when scrying," Morgana replied. "I think it is the Fae."

"Still, there may be an Old One in the area," Merlin said. "They've never been very active in this region, but times change."

"That's all we need," Morgana growled.

"We'll keep an eye out," Merlin said reasonably. "Try not to worry." Coughing to clear his throat, Merlin left the window. "I'll be downstairs."

"Make money."

Her remark made Merlin laugh all the way down the stairs, but that didn't change that she meant it. Surrounded by people, they'd need to be careful about using their magic. It was tempting to use their powers to improve their lives. Something was brewing here, and the amount of magic available was growing. Morgana suspected that the Fae population had grown too large, perhaps too concentrated in one spot. Last night when she'd arrived with Michel, she thought she'd spotted a Fae in the streets.

Her lips twisted into a frown. Morgana wished she knew what to expect. Magic had sent them here early, far earlier than normal it seemed. Usually, they arrived when trouble had already started. Looking over at the infant, Morgana wondered if them spurring on a reincarnation had been part of what was supposed to happen. Even after all these years, she still did not fully understand the mysteries of magic.

A soft cry came across the room from Michel. Pushing aside her thoughts, Morgana swept over to the infant. His eyes were open, the soft brown color meeting her own green. This time there was no half-formed Connection, but Morgana certainly felt something. A smile tugged at her lips and she picked up the boy who instantly quieted.

"This is all very new to you," Morgana said gently. "I know that this is a new place, Michel, and you were stuck traveling all day yesterday, but things will settle now. Merlin and I are determined to take care of you. We will keep you safe and educate you." Scoffing a little, Morgana smiled superiorly. "Bluntly, you will have a better education than any of your peers. What we teach you will open so many doorways and give you insight into the truth of our world. It will be very exciting, but difficult. You'll need to be strong and good. I have faith that we can help you become that."

Michel just shifted in her arms, bringing chubby little hands up to touch her face. Morgana didn't pull away as the child made soft gurgling sounds. Long dismissed memories of her mother telling her about caring for infants flooded back. She'd helped a bit with Arto, or at least her human half had when he was born, and Eigyr had expected her to have children when she left to get married. Michel stirred in her arms, becoming impatient with the silence.

"Airril would have been a good father," Morgana said softly. Taking Michel's little hand in one of her own, she rocked the boy. "He was patient and loving. Honestly, he deserved better than me. Merlin and I are half Sídhe, so we cannot have children. I'm not sure Merlin ever wanted any, but there was a time... it was a long time ago. I've changed a great deal since then. Perhaps someday when you are older, I will tell you the whole story so that you understand where Merlin and I came from. We don't always explain it. In fact, we usually don't."

Michel was slipping off again. Morgana wished she remembered her mother's words more exactly on how much infants slept. Surely it was a great deal as they were constantly growing. Her memories of the infant Arto were largely being annoyed. She'd loved him, but Arto had been a fussy baby.

"Not like you," she cooed. Michel's eyes slid closed. "I have a feeling that you are going to be a very easy and calm baby. That will make everything easier on Merlin and I. While protecting and training you is important, we will have to be ready for any magical threat that comes in case you're too young to help."

Putting Michel back into his little bed, Morgana debated how tightly she was supposed to wrap him up. The box had high sides, but if he moved the wrong way, it might rock. She carefully lifted it off the table and set it on the ground by the wall. Michel didn't stir. Watching him for another long moment, Morgana waited until she was sure that he'd be alright before she stepped away.

Turning her attention to the packages of their things that Merlin hadn't unpacked, Morgana busied herself finishing the task of putting things away. Downstairs, she could hear voices and hoped that the goods they'd brought with them from the east would be enough to get them off to a good start. Morgana went to the top of the staircase and listened. It sounded like it was going well. She hoped it would. While small, their new two-story home would be comfortable. The shop filled much of the bottom floor and had a fireplace along one wall to help heat the space. Above that was a small room with another fireplace that would serve as the kitchen. There were two additional rooms that for now would allow Merlin and Morgana some privacy if they traded off who took care of Michel. When the boy grew up that might change, but it would do.

To her own surprise, Morgana found herself humming softly as she opened the windows and set about properly setting up their new home. Michel slept peacefully for about an hour before his crying drew Morgana back to his side. While cleaning up after the child's bodily functions didn't thrill her, Morgana didn't mind it too much. They could do this. Michel would be safe and would become a great mage under their care.

10

Reaching Out to Silence

They were all in the living room with the curtains closed and the blinds down. The chandelier cast a warm glow through the room, but it did nothing against the nervous energy building up around the mages. Alex was on the floor, her back against the sofa, and one knee up. Her fingers tapped against the floor, suddenly wishing they had hardwood floors in here. That would have at least made it more satisfying.

There were more signs that the house was properly lived in now. Movie cases were stacked around the television and a basket for the remotes had been added to the coffee table by Jenny. A crochet bag was tucked by the armrest that Nicki favored for watching TV. A half empty glass of water was on the end table and someone's phone was plugged into a corner outlet. Warm chocolate smells were coming from the kitchen and Alex almost canceled what she was planning in order to go and get one. A fresh baked brownie with some ice cream sounded really good and she knew for a fact that there was a tub of chocolate in the freezer. That would be her reward.

Nicki came downstairs, pausing in the doorway to look at her. Alex met her gaze and gestured to Nicki's armchair. The redhead frowned and glanced around at the covered windows. For a moment, Alex was afraid that Nicki would just head back upstairs and refuse to help her. Footfalls from the lower stairs reassured Alex that the boys were coming as she'd requested. Everyone assembled around her, looking down at her with hints of confusion. Alex suddenly wished they had a cat she could stroke.

"So," Bran said. "What is it that you want to try?"

"I want to combine our powers and look at the Tree of Reality," Alex answered. Leaning her head back against the cushion, she did her best to appear calm. "I need a look at it as a whole."

"What?" Aiden blinked at her. "Are you serious?"

"Yes," Alex answered. "Very sure. I've been thinking about it for a while now and it's time."

"Are you sure you want to try this?" Nicki asked. "We don't know what could happen."

"No," Alex said. "We don't. Because Merlin and Morgana aren't sharing that information." The words came out sharper than Alex wanted, and Nicki flinched a little. "I need to take a look, Nicki. You heard how quickly Merlin dismissed my theory."

"About the Darkness," Bran mused. He was tapping his fingers nervously against his knee. "That's a terrifying thought, that it could be the same thing."

"Maybe not exactly the same," Alex said. "But- but looking at it, I mean really looking at it, I just couldn't help but notice how it looked, and thinking about the damage it could do if there was enough of it."

"I understand your thought process," Bran said quickly. "But still, given that, do you really think trying to look at it is a good idea?"

"My instincts say I should," Alex replied. Shrugging a little, she managed a small smile. "I know that isn't the best answer, but I'm not thousands of years old. I'm not used to living with mysteries and things I can't answer. Merlin and Morgana are, and right now, that's a problem. Who knows how long it has been since they bothered to worry about anything outside of Earth."

"Fair point," Aiden said. He sat down next to Bran, looking as nervous as she felt. "But, do you really know how to do this? I mean, isn't your magic tied to the Iron Realm?"

"We've scryed before," Alex said. "And I managed to see the dying Sídhe world. While the magic is... different between worlds, there is something that connects them as part of the Tree of Reality. Some link of energy. So, it should be possible for me to see something outside of the Iron Realm."

"But you weren't trying to see that," Nicki said. When Alex looked at her, Nicki sighed. "Sorry, we're not trying to doubt you, Alex. This is just very different from anything we've tried before. I'm just worried that maybe Merlin and Morgana have a reason for not looking. I mean, a real reason, not the little excuses they gave."

"They did seem to think it was dangerous," Bran reminded her.

"That's why I don't want to do this alone," Alex said. Sweeping her eyes through the room, she stopped and met the gaze of the other mages in turn. "I want you to help me, to ground me in case there is trouble. But come on, at some point someone had to try this for the first time. Maybe it was Merlin or Morgana, or an earlier mage, or even maybe it was some being on a completely different world."

She could see Aiden and Bran's eyes brightening. That did make her smile. Trust in the science mages to be curious about the scope of everything. Taking a deep breath, Alex rolled her shoulders and relaxed her posture.

"Something is happening out there," Alex said gently. "The Sídhe homeworld is dead, and they became a major enemy of our world. The

Demons were terrified by new developments and came crashing into our world the first chance they got. We need to figure out what threat is on the horizon."

"But we could wait," Nicki offered. "We've all been a bit stressed with classes and the book."

"The book is almost done." Alex raised an eyebrow at her friend. "And finding out what Arthur's doing is important, but so is this. I don't want to wait too long and be facing another enemy."

"You're not going to let this go, are you?" Bran asked.

"No." Alex shook her head and let her smile fade. "The poison… I need to see if I can glimpse this darkness. I need an answer, because if we're fighting the wrong war then the sooner, we find that out the better."

"I'm not sure, Alex," Nicki said. "I mean, yes the poison is dark, but that's still a big jump to make."

"Maybe, but that's why I want to try this and see what I can learn."

Worry radiated off of the others, but slowly Bran sat on the floor to her right. Their knees bumped and Alex smiled at him. He still didn't look convinced, but neither was she. The past three nights her dreams had been dominated by a thick blackness that consumed everything it touched. It wasn't a magical dream, just a plain old nightmare brought on by her fears.

Something must have shown on her face because Nicki and Aiden sat down, completing their little circle. Alex didn't want to know what her expression had betrayed and touched her knee against Aiden's. Nicki was across from her and they all joined hands. All they needed was to fast-forward to Halloween and have a spirit board.

"You're in charge, Alex," Aiden said. "What do you want us to do?"

"I'm going to convert your magic," Alex said.

Closing her eyes, she focused on the sensation of Aiden and Bran's skin. A faint pulse traveled through her skin. It quickly grew. All the hairs on her arms stood on end. Her skin started to tingle as more magic built up around the other mages. Exhaling slowly, Alex pushed her own magic out. Just a little; enough of a glimmer to illuminate her fellow mages behind her closed eyes. Nicki glowed blue and her magic was traveling across the red outline of Aiden and the yellow outline of Bran towards her. Alex pulled, coaxing the magic closer to her. It gathered at her hands, the bright colors of the other mages' magic dulling to a dark gray color.

Pulling the magic back, Alex allowed it to gather in her chest. It built and built, a raw burning sensation spreading across her body. The magic hummed in warning and Alex tightened her grip on the hands of her friends.

"Show me the Tree of Reality," she whispered. Alex didn't know how to visualize what she wanted, what she needed. Instead, she pushed her curiosity, her fear and her desire into the pulsing core of the magic. "Help me."

Her heart beat loudly in the heavy silence of the room. Sounds grew more and more muted. The faint noise of Timothy in the kitchen disappeared. Alex's head was fuzzy, full of that strange half awareness when you're about to drift off and know it. Her skin thrummed with power as her fellow mages kept feeding it to her and Alex instinctively pulled it into herself. In her chest, the magic didn't flare. It condensed, twisting tighter and tighter around itself. Fear burst through Alex, but it wasn't enough to pull from her the fog. Then something shifted. It was a faint pop and the tight coil of magic released, flooding her body and head.

Everything was dark. Her eyelids were heavy and Alex internally groaned. She'd been knocked out and was probably going to wake up in Morgana's guest room...again. The lecture they'd get for trying to see the Tree of Reality was an unpleasant thought. Alex kept her eyes closed, wondering if there was any chance the others had just taken her upstairs and kept it a secret.

Except... she didn't hear anything. There were no muffled sounds of other people and no birds singing outside the window. Magic was still pulsing in her chest, but slipping away with more magic coming in to replace it. She reached out, pushing the magic and trying to figure out where she was. There was no outline of the others, no brilliant glow of their magical colors, and yet she could feel their magic.

Reassured that she was still connected to her friends, Alex turned her attention back to her own magic. It was stretching out, slipping out of her body in an unfamiliar way. Rolling off of her like droplets of water. There was a soft tug from it that made her dizzy. Like she was moving, being pulled somewhere. Focusing on her thoughts, on the Tree of Reality, Alex repeated her wish to see it and urged the magic on.

Magic stretched out behind her, thinning and tightening until it was only a thread. Yet, it kept her tied to the Iron Realm. Alex's eyes were closed. Everything was dark. She needed to look, but fear reverberated down her spine. What was here? What would she find?

Opening her eyes, she gasped in surprise and alarm. This void, this in-between spread out around her, was like the photographs of space. But there were no stars here. Instead, flickers of light in every color zipped around, erupting like tiny lightning bolts in unseen storm clouds before vanishing back into darkness. Then panic hit. This wasn't Earth. She couldn't breathe. Yet, air entered her lungs and her heart kept beating.

Her eyes were drawn to a shining blue and green world that was very familiar. Staring at it, Alex grinned like an idiot. It was stunning and she was here... beyond it, looking at it. Earth hung in the nothing as if suspended by hidden wires. A shimmering shell surrounded it, highlighted by tiny wisps of clouds on the light side and spider webs of city lights on the dark side. Below it was a well of light that pulsed in time with her heartbeat. Tiny sparks flew from the well, zipping up into Earth or flying off into the darkness. Thin streams of light stretched out from the Earth and reached to the other worlds, connecting with them in the shimmering branches of the Tree of Reality.

Alex couldn't move her feet, but she turned her head enough to survey the other worlds. They were a variety of colors, one was a gleaming red with purplish clouds billowing around it, another a softer blue than the Earth but with similar green masses of land. Craning her neck, Alex fought to see as much as she could and realized with a jolt of panic, that she couldn't even feel her legs. She was just... there, hanging in emptiness with a clear view of the Earth.

Telling herself to calm down, Alex watched the Earth. It was turning slowly, very slowly, but revealing more of the dark side to her. Lights twinkled up at her as the night time cities of Europe and Asia came into view. She could identify some of the cities, and the exercise in memory calmed her enough for Alex to turn her attention to the more unfamiliar and magical elements around her.

Her eyes went to the nearest branch leading off of the Earth towards a dark green world with hints of red clouds. The branch flickered against the dark background with flashes of brilliant white, light blue, and hints of other colors. While it formed a solid line, it wasn't static. Instead, it was a constant flow, like a stream or river. Examining it carefully, Alex noted that the flow was away from Earth, carrying something towards the next world and then the worlds beyond that. Turning her face up, Alex gazed up further into the Tree. Seven shimmering branches lead away from Earth and stretched out further with small colorful orbs hanging delicately in them. Above her head, the streams of light overlapped in different layers and she got lost trying to follow them.

She looked down, searching below Earth. From Merlin and Morgana's first explanation, she vaguely remembered that there had been a world or two down there. Yet, she found no orbs, just pulsing wells of light that kept feeding up into Earth. Frowning, she filed that away, unsure of what to make of it. Had the older mages been wrong about the structure of the tree? In Norse Mythology, Earth was the trunk, the middle world, but here it was something different.

Reaching out her hand, Alex almost touched one of the streams moving away from Earth before instinct made her wrench her hand back. The glow of the stream was stunning and yet... she didn't know. The thought that tried to form was gone in an instant, and staring at the flow of energy did nothing to restore it. Swallowing, Alex turned her eyes away from the stream and looked around, staring into the vast space beyond.

More small lights glittered around her. But the light moved strangely: it was warped, as if bouncing between mirrors. Her eyes tried to pin something down, but the flickers were impossible to follow. Logic didn't seem to play a role. She tried to count the worlds, but the distortion of light and the overlapping streams of energy made it difficult to see them all. There were at least twenty, spread amongst the branches, but the glow of the streams was weaker the further they were from Earth.

Alex's eyes scanned what she could see. She was certain there should be more worlds, but it was too dark far away. Wrestling with her magic, Alex tried to move, but it kept her close to Earth. Close to home. Looking up, Alex tried to see into the nothing. There was a patch of blackness where no light flickered. Was that it? Or was it just a naturally darker section? She had no context. She understood the Tree, but the wells of light were confusing. The branches were understandable, but what they were moving between worlds confused her.

Alex tried to move again, but it didn't work and her chest tightened. Her eye lids were growing heavy. Taking a deep breath, Alex tried to shake herself, but her body was growing sluggish. The air tasted stale and her original concern over there being nothing to breathe returned sharply. Was she physically here? What was happening? Her heart beat increased. There was a subtle tug in her chest. Her magic flared. It felt like a warning. Like an alarm going off after the snooze button had been hit too many times.

"Alex?" The voice was soft, muted, and distant, but it was there. Echoing around her. "Alex, come on. Focus. Focus on us. You need to come back." It was growing more worried with every word. "Alex?"

Looking back at the branches, Alex looked up again, pushing past the growing ache in her chest. The air was too thin now, but she had to look. She had to check and see if there was anything like the Darkness. Her eyes searched the highest branches of the trees, desperately trying to make sense of the glowing branches. There were dim worlds, but she couldn't reach them and she couldn't see what was beyond them. It was darker, but was it distance or something much worse? Panting for air, Alex swayed on her unmoving feet.

"Alex!" This time the voice was frantic. It was Bran. Suddenly her hand ached. Alex looked down at it but didn't see anything. Then another sharp pain: someone was squeezing her hand. "Alex!"

Shaking her head, Alex closed her eyes and told herself to let go of the Tree of Reality. Her magic pulsed and hummed in her chest. The dizziness eased just before the air all escaped her lungs. It hurt. Her chest was squeezed. The pressure built and the magic fluttered uncomfortably through her limbs.

Then she tasted air with a hint of a floral scent. Inhaling deeply, Alex suddenly became aware that she was quivering. The grip on her hand loosened. Opening her eyes, Alex grimaced at the sudden brightness. Her hands were cold and shaking. Aiden released her hand as she twitched and gasped for air, still a bit faint. Bran's warm hands went to her shoulder, leaning her back against the bottom of the sofa before he took her hand again. Nicki scrambled to her knees and crawled towards her.

"Give her some space," Aiden said.

"Are you okay?" Nicki asked urgently.

"You started convulsing," Bran said. He looked moments away from crying. "And your hands went really cold."

"I'm okay," Alex croaked. Her voice sounded broken and she swallowed. "Sorry about that... I think I stayed too long. It was fine at first." Closing her eyes, Alex did her best to center herself and straightened up. "How long was it?"

"Almost two hours," Nicki answered. "Glad you're okay. We were worried about running out of magic." Alex opened her eyes to find the redhead shifting back to give her space, but frowning thoughtfully. "Did you see the Darkness?"

"I don't know," Alex said. "It was... I was stuck by Earth so I couldn't see the furthest parts of the tree. There were a bunch of worlds." Alex frowned, trying to remember the image that Merlin and Morgana had made when they'd first explained things. "It didn't seem like enough though. But I saw the connections, the branches. Something is moving from Earth into the other worlds, like a stream." Biting her lip, Alex focused on the sharp pain to keep herself from drifting off. "And below the Earth, there were these bright points of light. Wells of light that fed up into the Earth."

"What does that mean?" Aiden asked, looking at Bran.

"I'm not sure," Bran said. He kept his grip on Alex. "But that's enough for today. Come on, Alex, up onto the couch and then we'll order pizza."

He and Aiden helped Alex onto her quivering feet and then lowered her down onto the sofa. Alex tried to smile, tried to relax, but her heart was still racing. She'd done it: she'd gone beyond the Iron Realm on purpose. Now they just had to figure out what it all meant. At least she was getting pizza tonight.

11

Pencil to Paper

It was strange to see Merlin at the front of the classroom. Sure, Alex knew that she'd first met the ancient man while he was merely a professor to her, but nowadays watching him give a lecture about literature was... odd. He didn't focus on her though and instead made a point of meeting the eyes of every student in the small classroom at least once per lesson. Professor Yates, as she reminded herself to think of him, moved a great deal while lecturing rather than staying at the desk. The whiteboard behind him had lines of notes that he or his teaching assistant had put up before class.

This class was larger than most upper-level literature courses. Then again, a class titled God: A Literary and Cultural Analysis was the sort of thing that stood out amongst the usual offerings of Shakespeare, Austen, and other western literature. Merlin was only allowed to teach it every three years or so to keep grumblings from more conservative-leaning professors and local residents down.

Leaning her chin on her hand, Alex scanned the notes. She should be paying attention. *Dante's Inferno* was far from boring, but rather than imagining hellfire, Alex's mind kept slipping back to that vast blackness. Rather than loud with screaming as Hell was described in the epic poem,

Alex's thoughts were on the absolute silence that surrounded the Tree of Reality. The words washed over her, with a few sparking in her mind from time to time. A sense that she'd forgotten something poked at her. At the back of her skull, a slight pain was beginning to build.

Blinking her eyes, Alex lowered them and leaned forward a little to shift out from directly under the bright fluorescent lights. It didn't help much, but Alex made another effort to listen to Merlin. If she'd known that her brain would be so flighty today, she would have just stayed home. Her fingers started tapping softly on the table before she caught herself and held back a groan. She checked the clock; class was only half over. Everyone else seemed fixed on the board as Merlin wrote more about the first circle of Hell.

Was Hell real in some form? She knew that Demons were real, but they were in India and aligned more with Hindu mythology than any of the Judeo-Christian myths. Was there a world that some mage seer had seen once which inspired these sorts of stories? They knew from the existence of certain myths and legends that occasionally someone had a vision and wrote it down. That was the basis for the story of Lancelot and Guinevere, and the Welsh story about a blonde-haired person entering a mountain to the sound of a bell. It was so confusing.

She looked at the clock again. She'd burned through a minute thinking about all the things she'd never get a straight answer on. At least those were mysteries to Merlin and Morgana as well. Checking on Merlin again, Alex found him still talking with a small smile on his face. He looked younger in moments like this. He was animated, moving his hands and pacing around the front of the room. In his heart, Merlin was a teacher. It was hard to imagine him as anything else, even if she had a very strong sense that he'd, of course, had other professions. That was probably memories poking through.

Tapping on the desk again, Alex scanned the other students. A few others were starting to look dazed so at least she wasn't alone. Shifting in her seat, Alex's eyes jumped to the doorway. The building was fairly quiet right now. Everyone was in classrooms and trying not to disrupt any other classes that were in session.

Closing her eyes, Alex sighed, letting the air out of her lungs slowly. Then she got an idea. She hadn't checked campus in a while, and they shouldn't rely on Bran having visions to check for trouble. With a soft exhale, Alex pulled on her magic. It flared in her chest and her feet thrummed as more magic pulsed up into her body from the Iron Realm.

The magic spread out easily, rippling beyond Alex to outline the people around her. Nothing was out of place: everyone registered with faint brownish outlines, except for Merlin, whose was bright green. Pushing the magic further, Alex gripped the edges of her desk to stay upright. The magic swirled around everything, allowing Alex to see it all as her power swept her through the building. Her stomach churned a little, but she didn't stop. Urging the magic on, Alex held her breath as the school was covered. She found Bran in the library, Aiden and Nicki at the coffee shop with a faint, goldish outline that she realized was Avani. Lance and Jenny didn't catch her attention immediately, but after a moment she noticed faint glittering outlines of indistinct color that she thought were them. There were no Sídhe, no knots of black magic, and no Arthur.

Alex was almost disappointed, but caught the growing irritation and squashed it. Letting the magic dissipate, she swayed in her seat and kept her eyes shut. Anyone looking would think she was trying to fall asleep. Opening her eyes, Alex checked the clock again. There was still another half an hour. She barely held back a groan.

Giving up on class, Alex reached into her bag and pulled out the small black notebook that she kept there. It was an old and odd habit in the digital age and one that she could blame on her mother. Still, she found a pencil and flipped it open. A blank, empty page was waiting for her. Putting the pencil down, Alex glanced up to check on the professor again. He wasn't paying attention to her and was talking about the history of Dante's choice to have Virgil as a guide in Hell.

Her hand started moving almost by itself, drawing a sphere as best she could. Alex tilted her head and added a rough shape of Europe to it and a few clouds. Then she drew several thick lines leading away from the sphere to smaller spheres. The page was a bit small, but Alex quickly added what she could remember. It wasn't much. The branches had been long and split at different points. She just couldn't remember how many worlds there had been or where. No wonder mythology had gotten so confused.

Straining her brain, Alex tried to remember the tree of light that Merlin and Morgana had made. Did they really know where the worlds were, or was that only a guess? Was it from their own experience or had Merlin been taught about the tree by Cyrridven? Looking up at him, Alex held back the question even as it burned her tongue.

Yet that didn't really matter. She wanted to know, but that information could be centuries old if not older. If the Darkness was really slowly consuming planets then a lot could change slowly. At least, Alex assumed it was a slow process, since the Sídhe's invasion and takeover of their branch of the Tree of Reality had been going on for more than 3,000 years.

Alex kept drawing, filling in odd little details here and there. There wasn't a true memory of it: the whole event was more a series of vivid images now rather than an understandable whole. Yet, she filled in a few more worlds on the crowded page. In total there were twenty-two, and once again, that seemed like far too few.

Where that certainty was coming from, she didn't know. A soft and unfamiliar voice was whispering to her that there should be more, but Alex didn't understand the context. Other voices chimed in with their own thoughts, but no one was helpful and they drowned out the first voice quickly.

Her pencil kept moving, shading in the space around the worlds. Near the upper branches, she made it much darker, and wondered again if maybe she had seen the Darkness. Surely, she would have known. It would have been different enough to stand out. Then again, the poison was black with only the barest hint of purple when you looked at it right. And the space beyond the Tree of Reality was black with only flickers of light.

"Alex?" It was Merlin's voice.

Snapping her head up, Alex was prepared for a stern look from the professor and maybe a few dismissive glances from the other students, but they were alone in the room. She was still at her desk, and Merlin was leaning slightly on the desk in front of her with a worried expression. Outside in the hallway she could hear the other students moving and chatting loudly.

"Sorry," she apologized quickly. Nervously, she set down the pencil and tried not to look at the page. "I guess my brain just wasn't on class today."

"That much was apparent," Merlin said dryly.

"I'm sorry," Alex apologized. "I did do the reading. My mind just couldn't settle."

"I trust you on that," Merlin said kindly. "But your mind was elsewhere." Dropping his gaze, he looked at the drawing again, his brown eyes darkening with worry. "Alex, is there something I should be worried about?"

"No more than usual," Alex replied.

"Have you been dreaming?"

"I dream all the time," Alex sighed. The pencil moved around the paper again and she avoided Merlin's gaze. "I just don't always remember."

"It's not getting better?" Merlin pressed.

"I don't know." Alex shrugged and glanced towards the door. "It's... it's like trying to remember what it was like when you were a few inches shorter. You know it happened, you know that you experienced it, but you're so used to the new status quo that real understanding of what you were like before eludes you."

"Well, I'm glad to see that you haven't lost your ability to articulate," Merlin said. His tone was a little too light and Alex's fingers tightened around the bottom of her seat. There was probably gum down there, but she didn't care. "I take it that you're still worrying about the Darkness and the Tree of Reality?"

"Yes." Giving up, Alex looked up at Merlin and nodded. "I know that you don't believe it, Merlin."

"The poison was created on Earth," Merlin said gently. "You know that each world is different, Alex. The chances of something like it existing on another world alone is small, but then for it to exist on the scale that you're afraid of... it just doesn't seem possible."

"The worlds may be different," Alex agreed. "But lots of things between them are similar. I mean, yes, the Old Ones are beings of pure energy and only look human because they want to, but the Demons and the Sídhe are very humanoid. They breathe the same air we do to an extent."

"You're not wrong, but the poison-"

"Maybe the poison itself was a warning." Alex blinked at the words that suddenly spilled out of her mouth. She hadn't really thought about them, hadn't considered them. They'd just been a random thought that sprang into her head. "A warning about the Darkness…" she trailed off as the thought vaporized.

"A warning?" Merlin repeated. He was frowning again and staring at her. "Alex?"

"I don't know," she admitted. "Stream of thought. Sorry."

"Don't apologize." Sighing, Merlin held up a hand but then hesitated for a moment and lowered it again. "I'm sorry as well. I don't want you to feel that I'm ignoring your concerns. You are a mage and a bright young woman, in addition to being the Iron Soul. Your worries and views matter just as much as Morgana's or my own." Merlin rubbed his chin and glanced at the door which was still slightly ajar. "I know that Morgana and I can be a bit stubborn. A bit stuck in our ways."

Somehow Alex managed not to snort. Merlin chuckled and shook his head fondly, telling Alex that even if she didn't snort, her face must have shown her agreement. Then his eyes went back to the drawing. Suddenly very concerned about it, Alex closed up the book and started packing up her things. Merlin made no move to stop her.

"Please try not to worry about it too much," Merlin said kindly, breaking the silence. "There is enough to be worried about with Arthur. Speaking of which, how is Nicole doing on the book?"

"We're almost there," Alex said. "She wrote several variations of the spell she wanted, but she finally has one that she's happy with." Smiling a little, Alex stood up and pulled on her backpack. "It rhymes."

"Rhymes?" Merlin repeated.

"Yeah, she ended up going for a rhyming couplet. She said that her brain just kept trying to make it rhyme and she gave in."

"I suppose that spells do rhyme frequently in the media," Merlin conceded. His amusement was returning. "And if it helps her stay focused then it will help the magic stay focused on what she wants."

"That's true. She was going to have Bran put it into the book this afternoon after classes." Alex pulled out her phone and double checked the time. "Uh, I should really be there too, in case more magic is needed."

"Tonight then?" Merlin's eyebrows went up. "I thought-"

"Nicki decided it this morning," Alex said. "We're just going along with her. So, it will probably be done tonight, but there's no guarantee that it will get anything right away."

"Of course." Merlin shifted back further to let Alex head for the door. "I hope you have a good evening. If you need Morgana or I for finishing the book, you need only call. Do let me know if there are any developments. We are here to help."

The way he said it made Alex grimace. He knew. He had to know what they did. Even if the others didn't tell on her, Merlin had to know. Was there some kind of ripple effect from her pushing outward? Worse, had she messed with the magic of the Iron Gates? That was a horrible thought, and she almost reached out with her magic again to check on them. In her bag, the little notebook was suddenly very heavy.

"Merlin, do you ever feel like you've forgotten something?" Alex asked.

"Often. It comes with age," Merlin replied dryly.

"No, not- not little things, not like something you had to do, but something big." Alex bit her lower lip and tried to rein in the wriggling thought. "A big piece of information, a clue that you need for something."

"Occasionally," Merlin said. He closed up his satchel and then stepped closer, putting his hand on Alex's head. The familiar gesture made her freeze. "Alex, my dear girl, you have so many memories inside your head now. I'll be honest, sometimes I fear for you. I wake up at night worried about how you'll manage all those different thoughts, memories, and glimpses of knowledge without the proper context. Given all of that, feeling occasionally that you've forgotten something seems very natural to me."

"Oh." Alex tightened her fingers around the strap of her backpack. Words were trying to form on the tip of her tongue, and yet nothing came forth. Her thoughts wouldn't organize, and she had a strong desire to use her magic to check on the Tree of Reality again. There had to be something. "Okay then." She reached for the door.

"Alex, why don't I organize a dinner with Morgana," Merlin offered abruptly. "We'll tell you everything we know about the Tree of Reality and how we came by that knowledge."

"Really?"

"If it's bothering you this much then maybe you do need to know." Merlin shook his head and smiled at her. "It isn't us trying to keep secrets, Alex, please understand that. It's just that after three thousand years, you gather a lot of knowledge and there isn't time to share it all." Then he nodded towards the door. "I have an advisor meeting to get to." Joining her at the door, he put his hand on her shoulder. "Remember, you can talk to us."

With that, Merlin left the classroom, and Alex joined the crowd of students moving through the building. She raced for the stairs, weaving between bodies and made her way to one of the side doors. Stepping outside, Alex inhaled the fresh air deeply and rolled her head back to look up into the sky. It was a bright blue shade with only small wisps of clouds scattered throughout. She shivered a little at the temperature. Soon, she'd have to concede that it was well and truly time to start carrying a coat.

Nearby trees were beginning to turn colors. Samhain would be upon them soon, and they'd need to start making plans just in case Arthur tried something. At least the book was almost done and they could learn what was going on. She needed to know what Arthur was after, and needed to solve the mystery of the Tree of Reality.

12

Childhood Innocence

1 516 C.E. Rhineland

Michel was bored. There was only so much that a boy could do in a wagon as they bumped along the road towards home. He'd long since given up counting trees and farms. Yet he knew better than to say that he was bored to Merlin and Morgana. One of them would launch into another history lesson, or worse, make him name all the trees and vegetation they passed. He'd gotten all that memorized last year.

Shifting against the box he was propped up against, Michel tapped his foot impatiently. They were almost home. Not today, but hopefully to-morrow night he'd be home again where there were things to do. Going on this trip had seemed so exciting at first. Normally he and Morgana stayed home while Merlin went off, but this time they'd agreed that he could go. Of course, that meant that Morgana had come along rather than staying behind in the shop.

"I hope that Lorenz has kept the shop in good order," Merlin said. He didn't really sound worried.

"I'm sure he has," Morgana replied. She just sounded bored. That made Michel feel a little better. "Though, I am not joining you the next time you take Michel out of town."

"Really?" Merlin laughed, tossing his head back a little. "I'm surprised to hear that."

"It is easy to forget how dull the road can be," Morgana replied. "You get tired of staying in one place but then are reminded of the hours of nothing."

Rolling his eyes, Michel agreed wholeheartedly with his aunt. If he'd known it was going to be like this, he wouldn't have been so eager. Granted, finally being allowed to use some of his magic in the forest had been great. Normally he was only allowed to use small sparks and spells in closed up rooms.

"Can we stop for a while?" Michel asked. He gripped the wall of the wagon and hoisted himself up a little. "To stretch and maybe... use magic," he added the last two words as a whisper.

"Maybe tomorrow," Morgana said. "I want us to make good distance today."

"But I'm bored!" The words slipped out.

"Michel," Morgana scolded softly. "Behave yourself."

"Morgana, he's only eight," Merlin chuckled. "Of course, he has been bored." Twisting in the driver's seat, Merlin looked over his shoulder at Michel. "But he's learned a great deal from his playtime, I imagine."

"I suppose," Morgana agreed. She turned and gave him a soft look. "But I also think that we could all do with getting home and sleeping in our own beds."

Pressing his lips together, Michel slumped back against the boxes. That did sound good, but so did getting out of the wagon. Morgana gave him a knowing look and a soft smile before righting herself in the front of the wagon. It would be nice, he supposed, to get home soon.

"Why don't I teach you more about the history of mages," Merlin said. He sounded far too happy with the idea and Michel held back a groan.

"You should be happy, Michel. You know far more about your previous lives than any other Iron Soul before you. Normally there isn't time to teach them."

"I suppose."

Then suddenly the whole wagon shook and slid to the right. The pair of brown horses at the front made startled sounds. Merlin was calm and used the reins to guide them to a stop. Michel realized that the front of the wagon was slumping. Instinctively, he started moving to see what was happening.

"Michel, move to the back," Morgana ordered. "The corner."

He obeyed quickly and they came to a stop alongside the road. Merlin leapt off the front bench to calm the horses. Morgana lowered herself gracefully and gave him a reassuring smile. Michel smiled; this was nothing they couldn't handle.

"Broken wheel," Morgana announced. There was a hint of a growl in her voice. "Not too bad, but it will be easiest to fix if we gather the pieces."

"As many as possible at least," Merlin agreed walking over. Patting the neck of one of the horses, his expression softened. "I know we wanted to push, but I think the horses deserve a rest."

"Very well." Morgana nodded. "Not too long though."

"May I stretch my legs?" Michel asked. He jumped out of the back and widened his eyes eagerly. Preparing himself to pout, Michel waited to see if it was necessary. "Please?"

"Don't go too far," Merlin said sternly. He was already checking the surrounding area for anyone who might see them use magic. "This won't take long to fix, and the horses don't need too long of a rest."

"I won't," he promised. "Thank you."

"Well, you've been behaving yourself," Merlin teased. His eyes were bright with fondness.

Michel didn't wait for them to change their minds. Magic wasn't that interesting to watch, not anymore at least. Merlin and Morgana never did big things like affect the weather, but there were enough small spells used in the privacy of their home that he was used to it. The nearby hill full of trees looked much more interesting.

His legs stretched out and ached gloriously, pulling a happy groan from Michel as he walked further up onto the hill. Beneath his feet the fallen autumn leaves crackled and snapped satisfyingly. Kicking a small pile, Michel grinned as they went flying into the air. All the energy that had been coiling up inside of him suddenly sprang free and he started running. The trees swept by and the slight breeze suddenly felt like a gust of wind through his hair.

A laugh escaped him and Michel threw his arms up, stretching them out. He was never going to ask to go on a trip again! Then he spotted movement. His heart jumped. It could be a bear, or worse, a wolf. Freezing in his tracks, he blinked in surprise as it turned out to be a person about his height. They were carrying a bag over one shoulder and seemed just as surprised as Michel to have found someone here.

Frowning, Michel inspected the boy in front of him. He looked very normal, with a round face and a slightly upturned nose. His curly brown hair had dirt clumped in a few places that matched the smudges of mud on his cheeks. Yet, the young man glowed slightly to him. It was a faint flicker beneath the skin, and it was all he could do not to grab the other boy's arm to examine it.

"Who are you?" he finally asked.

"Puck," the boy said.

"Puck?" Michel repeated. "That's an odd name."

"Maybe," the boy said. He just shrugged and didn't seem all that concerned. "What's your name?"

"I'm Michel," he answered. The glow beneath the boy's skin was still taunting him. "What are you?"

Puck grinned widely, his eyes lighting up with glee before he started laughing. "You don't think I'm human?"

"No," Michel said. A hint of fear crept into his heart. "My Aunt Morgana has told me that there are lots of other beings in our world. She says that sometimes you notice them because they're a bit different."

"I don't look different," Puck pouted.

"Your skin," Michel said. He pointed to Puck's hands and struggled with how to explain it while the other boy looked at his skin in confusion. "There's...light beneath your skin."

"Oh." Puck blinked and frowned as he closely inspected his hand. "I can't see it. My mother says that I look like this because it's how I want to look. I'm an Old One."

"Really?"

"Yeah, she says that we're really pure light." Puck grinned and then paused. "She says not to tell people that though. Says people get scared."

"My Aunt says things like that too," Michel said. Scraping his foot in the dirt, he glanced back towards the road. They'd be leaving soon. "I won't tell. I don't care."

"You don't?" Puck looked surprised and pleased, making Michel smile in response.

"As long as you don't hurt anyone." Inspecting the bag again, he asked, "What are you doing?"

"Collecting some plants."

"Do Old Ones eat?" Michel asked. He couldn't remember Merlin or Morgana ever saying before.

"We can if we want to," Puck answered. He shrugged, not seeming to understand just how amazing that was. "Mother says it can help us if we start being 'worn too thin' whatever that means, but usually no."

"So why do you need plants?"

"My mother uses them to help humans." Puck pointed off towards the west. "She's a medicine woman for a village about a mile that way. I came out here to gather some things for her."

"Really, I didn't know that Old Ones did things like that!" Michel was suddenly very curious, but sort of wanted to go back to Morgana to tell her what he had just learned. "Do you like it?"

"I don't do it!" Puck curled his nose. "But it gets Mother money and people leave us alone since she helps them." Setting his bag down next to the nearest tree, Puck looked up into the branches and smiled. "I like being out here. It's much more interesting."

Eyes wide, Michel watched the strange boy scramble up the tree. He knew people did this of course, but he'd never seen it up close. Even when traveling, the people in orchards picking fruit usually had ladders or he was too far to see it in detail. Puck moved with quick and fluid movements, almost swinging himself up into the tree. A grin took over his face. It was really neat and impressive.

"Aren't you coming?" Puck called down.

"Uh..." Michel eyed the nearest branches and the ground. He didn't imagine that Morgana would want him climbing trees.

"Haven't you ever climbed a tree before?" Puck seemed very surprised.

"No," Michel said. He studied the tree cautiously. It had a lot of thick branches that looked solid, and the lower branches weren't too bad either. His hands itched to try. "There aren't a lot of big trees in Strasbourg."

"You live in Strasbourg?' Puck said. "Really? What's it like around all those people?"

"Nothing special. It smells a lot." Michel inhaled the earthy smells around him. "I think I like how it smells here more."

"Bet there's more to do, though," Puck said.

"Not for me." Michel pouted and eyed the lowest branch again. "My guardians keep me close."

"They aren't close now." Puck leaned over the branch, peering at him with excitement. "You didn't run away, did you?"

"No! We were on a trip. A wagon wheel broke. They said I could stretch my legs while they fixed it."

"Oh." Puck didn't sound interested now and Michel frowned. Making up his mind, he threw his arms around the trunk and started shimmying up to the lowest branch. "Alright!" Puck laughed. "It's not hard! You can do it!"

Grabbing the lowest branch, Michel eased himself onto it. The branch quaked under his weight so he kept moving, grabbing the next branch and then the next one. Michel laughed and pulled himself further up into the tree. Heart racing, he reached for the next branch and grinned. Above him, Puck was laughing and cheering him on. He could do this. He'd never done anything like this before, and suddenly he couldn't remember why.

"Good job," Puck said as Michel joined him up near the top of the trunk. Two thick branches gave them plenty of room to sit. "Told you it was easy."

Michel nodded but stayed quiet. His lungs ached a little and his arms were throbbing. It had been exciting, but not as easy as Puck made it look. Still, the world was very different from up here. He could see into the upper branches of all the nearby trees and maybe, just maybe, see a little bit of a village to the west. But that might have just been more trees.

"So, what now?" Michel asked once he'd recovered.

"Nothing," Puck sighed. "It's better when there's more fruit on the trees. Then you climb them and eat your fill." Puck grinned happily. "Sometimes, I get into trouble with people in our village because I climb their trees and eat the fruit."

"That sounds fun."

"It is, but it gets me in trouble. Mother says that she has to repay them for the food I steal." Puck twisted his lips, pouting a little. "It's not that much."

"Aunt Morgana says that normal humans worry about starving a lot," Michel said. "And sickness."

"That's Morgana the Grand Mage?" Puck's eyes were wide again. He shifted back a bit on his branch.

"I guess so," Michel answered, unsure of if he'd upset Puck. "She and Merlin have looked after me since I was born."

"Oh, I- I didn't really... you just said your aunt earlier."

"Why does it matter?"

"She is a mage, isn't she?" Puck pressed. "Morgana of the Fae?"

"Maybe." Michel shrugged and glared at Puck. "She's my aunt."

"You live with Merlin and Morgana, the Grand Mages," Puck said. There was something in his tone that put Michel on edge. The other suddenly leaned forward. "Who are you?"

Michel shifted back. Puck's face was too close and the expression was worried and wrong. The sudden movement threw him off balance. Michel started to grab for the branch, but his limbs froze in terror. It was odd, the sense of falling and yet not being able to stop it. He willed his hands to move, but it wasn't fast enough. He hit a lower branch, grabbing it just enough to slow his fall. His grip wasn't strong enough and he struck the leaf covered ground a moment later. Staring up into the sky, he heard someone shouting his name and there was a blur of movement in the tree branches. Then Puck was leaning over him.

"Michel! Are you okay?" Puck held out his hand with three fingers up. "How many fingers do you see?'

"Three," Michel groaned. His head hurt and his back ached. "I see three. Why?"

"Just checking. My mother does that when people hit their heads." Puck's expression crumbled with guilt. "I'm sorry. I wasn't trying to upset you."

"Michel!" That was Morgana's voice. He started to raise his head to sit up, but Puck put a hand on his shoulder to hold him still. "Michel!" The voice was more panicked now. She was going to be mad.

"Over here," Puck called. His voice was shaky and Michel frowned, looking at his new friend in confusion. "He's over here." Then Morgana was next to him and Puck made a small sound of alarm. "I didn't hurt him!" Puck shouted, backing away quickly.

Michel wanted to assure Morgana that he was fine and that Puck hadn't hurt him. She was leaning over him protectively and glaring at Puck. Silver sparks swirled around her hand. Puck gasped and backed away further.

"He didn't," Michel said. "He caught me."

"Mostly," Puck said sadly.

The sparks remained around Morgana and she was eying Puck carefully. "You're an Old One."

"Not really," Puck said with a shrug. "I'm not that old."

Merlin walked over and knelt next to Michel and Morgana. The old mage set a gentle hand on his head. "There's a slight bump," Merlin said.

"He'll be feeling it tomorrow, but he seems alright, Morgana. I'll use a bit of magic to ease the pain." The back of his head tingled and the haze started lifting. "No harm done."

"And we're supposed to believe that this Old One was just here? We're supposed to trust that coincidence?"

"Morgana," Merlin scolded softly. "Look at him. He's barely in control of his form. He's young. I doubt he's any kind of a trap."

"The magic is gathering in this area."

"And we know that there is a colony of Sídhe descendants nearby." Merlin ran his fingers through Michel's hair and the boy relaxed at the soothing gesture. "This was an accident, nothing more." Merlin fixed Puck with a stern look and Michel wanted to protest. "I suggest that you return to your parents. Tell them that we expect trouble in the area and encourage them to move on."

"That's not fair," Michel said. He pouted up at Merlin, but the mage simply smiled at him.

"It is for the best, my boy. The Fae are becoming restless here. Old Ones in the mix would not help anyone."

"I wasn't trying to hurt him," Puck said. His voice was soft and sad now. "We were just playing."

"I believe that," Merlin said. At least he sounded calm. "But I think it's time that we took Michel back home."

Merlin picked him up as if he weighed nothing. Michel thought he felt a hint of magic tickling his skin and smiled despite the slight pain still lingering in his head. Resting his chin on Merlin's shoulder, he looked back at Puck. The other boy was watching them go, a scowl on his face. Michel raised his hand and gave his friend a small wave. He was very sorry that he'd fallen. They'd been having fun and it would have been nice to have a friend that he could talk to about magic. It was always a secret.

Their wagon was right where they'd left it, but the wheel had been repaired. Morgana opened the back and Merlin set him down amongst the bolts of cloth. He barely had time to relax before a blanket was tucked around him.

"I'm fine," he said. "I'm healed."

"Yes, your injury is gone," Merlin agreed. "But head wounds are tricky, Michel. Just rest and behave yourself."

"It really wasn't Puck's fault," Michel said. "I was the one who slipped."

"I know," Merlin said. "But you frightened us." Chuckling softly, Merlin stretched forward and touched Michel's arm gently. "We don't want to lose you."

"I've never met an Old One before," Michel said, changing the subject.

"Most of the ones who are friendly with mages are asleep now," Merlin said. "I was surprised to see a young one. Most of the Old Ones don't breed anymore."

"Why not?"

"They don't want to create children who are trapped in our world," Merlin said gently. He and Morgana climbed up onto the front bench again. "They don't belong here, Michel. The Iron Realm is for humans, not Old Ones. It fights them. Our world itself tries to tear them apart."

Frowning, Michel thought back to Puck's comment about being worn too thin. Maybe it had to do with that. He still really didn't understand, but as they started moving, it was clear from Morgana's body language that now wasn't the time to ask. Sitting up a little, he looked towards the hill and caught sight of Puck up in another tree watching them. He raised his hand and waved again, hoping that the other boy could see him.

13

The Book

The book didn't look very special, even with the triskelion set into the cover. Nicki had done a nice job binding it, but it still looked like a journal that you'd find at a big bookstore. All of the symbols that Nicki had burned into the leather were hidden inside, and the long spell or request of magic that Bran had written out using his own blood was beneath another layer of paper. The book was heavier than one would expect thanks to the narrow bar of iron in the spine created from a link of the Iron Chain. It was propped up on the coffee table, open to the first soft cream-colored page. Even that had been made by Nicki using some stuff at her grandmother's shop.

Everything involved had passed through the hands of the mages, and the book shimmered slightly to Alex without her even trying to see the magic. While not as powerful as Cathanáil or Mjǫllnir, the amount of magic bound up in the book was staggering. Even though she wasn't the biggest fan of fantasy, Alex found that she was still excited just by the idea of having helped make this.

"Well," Alex said. She drummed her fingers on her knees, barely managing to stay in her armchair. "It's done."

"How hard was it to rework the Chain?" Aiden asked. "You think it's still connected to Arthur?"

"I didn't do much with it," Alex admitted. "I didn't use any magic on it, just heated it up a little and then flattened it out. No magic involved, and I could still see a lot of magic in the link." She shuddered, remembering just what the magic had been put there for. "I think it's going to work."

"It'll work," Nicki said confidently. She was pacing nervously. "My biggest concern is if the magic is going to be able to form the words properly or if that'll take too much magic." Biting her thumb, Nicki's expression shifted to worry as she looked nervously at the book.

Avani stood up and gently caught Nicki's hand, giving the redhead a soft smile. "It will be fine. Even if it requires a bit of alteration, it is an amazing piece of magic." Grinning, Avani looked around the room at all of them. "You should all be proud."

"Nicki did most of the work," Aiden said. His eyes were bright as he watched the new couple. At least, Alex thought they were a couple after the recent late-night stargazing picnic. "I barely helped at all."

"You did some of the binding," Nicki said. "Thank god your mother knows as much about books as she does. And the internet." Nicki looked at Avani, her body still almost quivering. "The internet is so helpful. How did anyone ever get things done before the internet?"

"That's probably why the magic of the Iron Realm made the two Grand Mages," Avani replied. She was smiling like she was holding back a laugh. "To pass on information."

"That..." Nicki tilted her head quizzically. "That's a really really solid theory." Tapping her chin, Nicki hummed thoughtfully. "And to protect the Iron Soul." Then she shrugged. "Anyway, I'm just as happy living in this era with the information superhighway that is the internet."

"Aren't we all," Avani said. She was studying the book with a slight smile. "I really hope this works. It would be a great achievement in spell work."

And yet the book was still empty on the dining room table. They were all gathered around and Alex considered calling Merlin and Morgana. She knew that the older mages would be curious, but so far nothing had happened. Holding back the urge to pace, Alex kept watching the book, praying that everything worked how they wanted.

"There's no guarantee that the book will pick anything up tonight," Nicki said. She tucked a loose strand of hair behind her ear. "We're going to have to be patient to find out if it works."

"I have a good feeling about it," Bran said. He was smiling, and was by far the most relaxed of them all. "The magic is in it, even I can feel it. And your spell was perfect, Nicki."

"We'll see." Nicki licked her lips but then smiled. "I'm pleased with it as a first attempt. If it doesn't work then we can try again."

But Alex agreed with Bran. There was magic wrapped up tightly in the book. It was seeping into the leather cover and the pages from the small triskelion symbol they'd fixed on the front. Alex was confident that if she pushed her magic outward, that she'd see the glowing letters of Nicki's spell beneath the leather.

Time ticked by and the others peeled off for other activities. Jenny and Lance put on a movie while Aiden went in search of a snack. Bran settled nearby with a handheld game and glanced up from time to time. Alex kept watching, tracing the small flickers of magic she could see within the thick paper pages from time to time. Magic filled the book, but it was contained. Bound up and directed with purpose towards Arthur. It had to work.

Alex stared at the blank page, silently urging it to find something. Anything to do with Arthur. She'd even take him going through a drive-thru somewhere just for the confirmation that the book worked. Her fingers itched to turn through all of the pages and check to see if there was something on the other pages. After all, there was no guarantee that the book would start filling in from the front.

"Alex," Nicki called. "Take a break. We'll keep checking it."

"I just... I really want this to work."

"We all do," Nicki said. Her exhaustion was clear. "I'd like all that work validated."

"And I'd like the loss of blood validated," Bran added. "But stop staring. A watched kettle never boils."

"I know," Alex groaned. "I know."

Managing to turn around, she glanced at her friends. They all looked tired, and Alex wondered what time it was. She'd have to move to see into the kitchen and her phone was upstairs charging. Their lack of clocks was suddenly very apparent. Looking back at the book, Alex sighed and considered that maybe it was time to step away.

Arthur is using his magic to see the Tree of Reality.

The words appeared on the page suddenly, and Alex gaped at them. It was there. Some words telling her what Arthur was doing. Fisting her hands, Alex tried to contain her glee and jumped twice, but then the words finally came together in her head. Dropping her hands, Alex leaned forward over the book and read the words again.

"Tree of Reality," she whispered. "So, he can do that too, but why?"

"Alex?" It was Nicki's voice. "What's wrong?"

"The book," Alex said. She opened her mouth, but couldn't find the right words. Instead, she stepped to the side and gestured to it. "It found something." Turning to look at her friend, Alex shifted between her feet, nervous energy filling up her chest.

"Oh my god!" Nicki's whole face lit up and she rushed forward. "What? What did it find?" Then Nicki froze, her expression falling as she read the words. "Uh…"

"Yeah," Alex said. "I'm not sure what to think about that?"

"Do you think… no, Arthur doesn't know about the poison."

"He doesn't," Alex agreed. "But his mother knew about the dying worlds."

"I thought Arthur didn't care about that?"

"He doesn't. Or least he doesn't care about saving them," Alex said slowly. "If he thinks that it might be a weapon of some kind then maybe he'd want to learn more."

Bran came over to see for himself. "That's not much to go on, but the book works." Grinning, he gave Nicki a one-armed hug. "Good job!"

"It works!" Nicki cheered. Throwing her hands up, she started smiling. "I mean, that's not a lot to go on, but we know more than we did five minutes ago!"

"I wonder if it'll get more," Bran said. He leaned around Nicki and tentatively touched the page. Nothing happened and he lifted it to check the other side of the next page. "Or how much it'll write on each page."

"Oh!" Nicki snapped her fingers, scowling. "I should have done something so it would date and say the time of everything!" She was studying the book. "Do you think writing a note next to it would be a good idea or a bad one?"

"I'm not sure," Bran answered. He removed his hand. "That would be introducing real ink into the mix, but I don't see how that would interrupt the magic."

"I'm going to tell Avani," Nicki declared. She twisted around Alex and Bran to rush for the stairs." I'll tell the others too!"

Smiling, Alex drummed her fingers on the table and watched the page. Whispers filled her head, encouraging and supportive. It made her smile wider. They were just as impressed with the book. It was too bad that Nicki would never become immortalized in mythology. For this, it was deserved. She heard words being exchanged through the house, but no one came rushing. Alex waited, hoping for more. If the book could just give her another clue it could change everything.

The stillness and her concentration were broken by a ringing sound in the living room. Gritting her teeth, Alex wanted to yell at whoever had left their phone out before she recognized the ringing. It was the alarm. She didn't move away from the book but knew that if she was in the living room, she'd be able to see the triskelion symbol flashing.

She didn't look up from the book, but let her magic expand through the house. Right outside Fae creatures with knots of black on their chests were gathering, along with a few Red Caps. Gritting her teeth, Alex clenched her fists. She wanted to move, but... the book was still open and the words were still there. But what if they vanished? What if they missed something?

"Alex?" Bran called. He stepped up next to her.

"Four Fae," she said tightly. "Three Red Caps, by my count."

"Lovely," Bran grumbled. Nonetheless, he moved towards the front door. "Any out back?"

Frowning, Alex pushed her magic that direction, letting it sweep out away from the house for a good mile. Her eyes slipped closed as the signals and sights all became too much. Inhaling slowly, she eased the flow of information and then shook her head.

"No, all of them are near the front right corner of the house. They're preparing something."

"Right!"

Bran was gone. There was a commotion by the front door. Alex started to move, but she looked at the words again. No change.

"Alex!" Nicki shouted. "Come on!"

Her eyes traced the words again. There had to be more. What was Arthur doing? Did he have plans for the Tree of Reality? Was he simply curious or was he trying to verify his mother's fears? He'd already killed her, so why bother?

A crash outside pulled a gasp from her. Whirling around, Alex ran for the front door. Three Fae and a few Red Caps. It shouldn't have been a problem. They finally had a chance of finding Arthur, of learning what he was doing. Did he know about the book? Was this attack meant to distract them? The sound of gunfire exploded. Her heart jumped and Alex rushed outside.

The cool night air hit Alex's face, washing over her skin and pulling her firmly into the moment. She eyed the nearby battle. Nicki had a wall of ice up with her, Aiden, and Bran crouched behind it. The Fae line were all holding very large firearms, and one had something even larger. Alex had no idea what it was, but she wasn't going to wait to find out.

Sound exploded through the yard. Rounds were being fired into the ice wall and Nicki's hands were glowing, making the defensive wall grow with each moment. The Red Caps were already gone, but the others were pinned down.

Bran tossed a yellow orb of magic up and over the wall. It burst into small orbs and zinged through the air. The Fae jumped out of the way. One amulet flashed brightly and then sucked the small attack into it.

Gasping, Alex stared in shock, trying to understand what she was seeing. One of the Fae looked in her direction and hissed.

"There!"

They all turned towards her, moving their weapons. Throwing up her hands, Alex pulled on all the magic she could reach and threw it forward. A shimmering wall formed just as the bullets exploded towards her. For a moment, fear gripped her heart, squeezing it tightly. The bullets stopped, crumbling on impact with the wall.

Aiden used the distraction, jumping up and shouting. A wave of fire washed forward, swirling towards the Fae. It swallowed them in small twisters of flame. Brief, muffled screams made Alex flinch, but she didn't lower the barrier. There was still one Fae standing, stumbling back and charred. Nicki touched her ice wall and a spear burst forth and impaled it.

No one moved as the Fae gurgled and tried to pull itself off the spear. Its gun fell to the ground with a heavy thud. Alex watched the ashes and dust of the Fae bodies blow away. Keeping her hand up, she released a wave of magic. It spread out slowly like dripping syrup but found nothing. A knot of black magic with a hint of something else drew her eyes back towards where the Fae had died.

"That was weird," Nicki said slowly. Shaking her head, she took a tentative step forward and waved her hand. The ice wall melted away in a shimmer of blue sparks. "Really weird." Kneeling down, she was digging through the ashes. "Something messed with our magic!"

"Careful," Aiden cautioned. "Might still be hot!"

"I'm fine," Nicki huffed. "But I wasn't the only one who saw the magic not working, right?"

"Yes and no," Bran said. "The smaller attacks were sucked into the amulet or something like that, but Aiden's large area of effect spell didn't have a problem. And neither did your spear. The amulet clearly has limits." Bran glanced towards Alex, who still hadn't moved. "And it might have been only one amulet. It was hard to see, and when they pulled out the guns, I was worrying more about blocking bullets."

"I hate that Arthur is making stuff too," Nicki growled. Her hands were covered with dark gray soot. "Got it!"

She held up an amulet. There wasn't anything special about it at first glance. It was made of bronze like the other ones and the magic tangled around it, connected to the metal, but not able to properly set into it like it did with iron. Unlike the other amulets, this one had a small glass looking gem set into it.

"This looks like one of those stones you put into vases or aquariums," Nicki said. Frowning, she stood up and hurried over to the porch. Alex stepped off the porch to let her past. "Need a closer look!"

Aiden went after her, but Bran waved his hand, sending sparks of yellow magic around to poke at the piles of ash and dust. The smoldering remains of some jeans and hoodies were pushed to the side. He reached down to collect three more amulets that lacked the gem addition. Alex ground her foot down on an ember, grateful once again that they didn't have any super close neighbors. If anyone did call the police, they could blame a movie that was turned up way too loud.

"Alex, are you okay?" Bran asked. "You were a bit... distracted."

"Sorry," Alex said. She shook her head and didn't look at him. "I was hoping that the book would reveal more. I...I don't know. I'm sorry, I figured that number of Fae wouldn't be a problem."

"Well, in the past it wouldn't have been," Bran said. His expression was calm. He wasn't angry, and Alex relaxed. "As for the book, we can't watch it all the time," Bran reminded her. "Besides, when you went under you were gone for hours. This attack was probably set up before Arthur even used his magic."

"Still… something isn't right," Alex said. Looking back into the house, she could almost track the movement of the amulet. It's knot of black magic was different than the others. "There's something else."

"We'll figure it out," Bran promised. Taking her right hand, he squeezed it and snapped the fingers of his left hand. The remains of the clothing vanished in a rush of yellow sparks. "At least Merlin and Morgana will have to take your concerns about the Tree of Reality seriously if Arthur is poking at it."

That wasn't comforting, but Alex went with him into the house. Nicki had the amulet on the coffee table in the living room, kneeling by it and carefully examining it with Avani peering over her shoulder. Lance and Jenny were checking out the windows nervously despite the fact that the alarm had gone silent. Bran released her hand, locked up the house and then joined the others. Alex watched her friends for a moment, but then she went back to the dining room and looked at the book.

The words were still there. They hadn't faded and nothing had been added. Yet it was clear that Arthur knew something they didn't. Staring at the book, Alex reached out and gently touched the page, willing it to tell her what he knew. Why was he suddenly interested in the Tree of Reality? But no new words appeared.

14

Dinner Meeting

One nice thing about being attacked by a Fae carrying a strange, magic dampening amulet was that it absolutely got Merlin and Morgana's attention. The bad thing was that Alex and her friends were now hosting dinner at their house that night since everyone was curious. Classes were actually a welcome distraction for Alex, who did her best to hang onto every word all of her professors said. She'd left the book at home that morning, but missed it all day long. Nothing new had appeared that morning, but they had exchanged promises to alert each other if anything else did appear in the book.

Bran was done with classes first and had volunteered for grocery shopping duty. Timothy had been all aflutter with excitement over making a large meal. It would have been cute if Alex hadn't been hung up on the serious topics they needed to cover tonight. She'd gotten home, gone to the kitchen to see if she could help and then promptly been banished. Apparently, Bran and Aiden were the best kitchen helpers.

Nicki and Avani had the book open on the coffee table in the living room and Alex stopped with them to check that nothing new had appeared. It hadn't. Unsure of what to do with herself, but knowing better than to reach into the Tree of Reality without help, Alex went up to her room and pounded out 500 words for an upcoming paper. It took longer than it should have.

At exactly 6 p.m. the front doorbell rang. Absentmindedly, Alex imagined her family dog, Anne, running for the door and barking. But Anne was with her brothers, and as much as she missed having a dog, the last thing they needed was an easy target for Red Caps. Shaking herself, Alex pushed the ugly thought aside. She ran a brush through her hair and pulled her long blonde locks back. Catching sight of her reflection, Alex stared at it. She looked older than the last time she'd really thought about it.

Her gray eyes were beginning to look like Morgana's, carrying a darkness and weight to them that wasn't normal for a college student. Small worry lines were already beginning to appear faintly on her forehead. Magic apparently didn't keep normal mages young. At this rate, she'd start finding gray hairs by the age of thirty. If she made it that long.

But it wasn't just that. As sad as those thoughts were, Alex simply struggled to recognize the girl in the mirror emotionally. There were too many other images that tried to spring to mind. Different eyes, different hair colors, and different skin tones that crept in at the wrong times. Things that left her surprised when she caught sight of her own reflection. Sometimes, it made her wonder. Maybe she was going crazy. Maybe the voices were too loud, too many, and influencing her more than she realized. Maybe she was already crazy and in a hospital, somewhere. Maybe this was all already a delusion, a nightmare she couldn't wake up from.

A loud call from Nicki got Alex moving. The whispers were louder now, responding to her nervous thoughts. Being reassured by the voices in her head wasn't really helping. Morgana and Merlin were already in the living room when she arrived. Holding the book, Merlin was studying the page with writing thoughtfully, his fingers tracing the leather cover of the book. Morgana's expression was carefully neutral.

"Alex," Merlin greeted cheerfully. Alex didn't believe it. Arto whispered that he was worried. "Good to see you."

"Hi, thanks for coming to see us," Alex said. Nodding towards the book, she fisted her hands at her side to keep from reaching for it. "As you can see... our reasons to be interested in the Tree of Reality have increased." The understatement was a bit much, but she was at a loss.

"Yes," Morgana agreed. "I can understand your concern much more now, but I think the more urgent concern is this new amulet you recovered."

"It's on the dining room table," Nicki offered. Her eyes were jumping between Merlin and the book. "Uh, what do you think, Merlin?

"An excellent piece of magic. I hope that Arthur will lower his guard again soon. I'd like to learn more about what he is doing." Morgana made an impatient noise and Merlin gently set the book back down on the coffee table, leaving it open. "You should be very proud, Nicole."

Nicki didn't seem to know how to respond to that. The compliment was nice, but Merlin's continued use of her full name still annoyed Nicki. Giving her a warm smile, Merlin nodded to her and moved to join Morgana in the dining room. Nicki sighed and shook her head.

"They're going to make dinner wait, aren't they?"

"Most likely," Alex agreed. "Come on."

The amulet was wrapped up in a small towel, pushed off to one side of the dining room table. The others were already in the dining room. Bran had a stack of plates in hand and a handful of flatware. When Morgana headed to the table and sat down beside the bundle, his eyes widened. Aiden was in the doorway into the kitchen and shrugged helplessly. Both of them vanished into the kitchen for a moment before they came in and sat down. Movement behind her made Alex turn around. She found Avani, Lance, and Jenny waiting, most likely ready for dinner. Shrugging, Alex stayed silent and took a seat near Morgana.

Morgana pulled on a pair of gloves before picking up the amulet. Out of the corner of her eye, Alex saw Nicki both blush and roll her eyes. It was a valid concern, Alex reminded herself. If she'd been Arthur, she'd have tried to make the amulets a trap. They couldn't be careless. He was clearly altering his methods already.

"Interesting," Morgana said softly. "And you say it interfered with your magic?"

"Yes," Bran replied. He glanced at the others as everyone found a seat. "When we first went outside and I saw the firearms, I tried to use my magic to disarm them, but my magic just sort of... fizzled out. It almost looked like it was pulled into the stone, but I'm not completely sure of that."

"I threw up an ice wall," Nicki explained, "when it became clear that they still had their guns. We bunkered down behind that. Aiden tried a fireball and I tried a basic magic bolt. Neither connected. I didn't keep my head above the wall long enough to see why."

"Then Alex came out and distracted them," Bran said. "She used a shield to block the bullets which worked like Nicki's ice wall."

"I released a big wave of fire," Aiden finished. "That worked and killed them. We're not sure if it was the fact that the fire wasn't targeted on the Fae directly or if the amulet can only do so much."

"I see," Morgana said slowly. She gently ran a gloved thumb over the odd jewel. "This doesn't look like anything special." Raising her eyes to Alex, she asked, "What do you see?"

"It's a tangled black knot," Alex answered. "Like the others, but there is something different about it. The feel of it." Struggling with the words,

Alex released a thin stream of magic towards the amulet. "Sticky," she finally said. "My magic kind of sticks to it."

"Curiouser and curiouser," Merlin said. His fingers were steepled together as he frowned at the amulet. "I dislike this new development. Such a thing is a massive jump in Arthur's understanding of using magic. The amulets were bad enough, but this does seem like something more."

"The question is how does it work," Morgana said. "This stone doesn't look like anything special, but it works. Sticky, that's an odd description."

"Sorry," Alex said. "It's all I've got."

"Fair enough," Morgana said. She wrapped the amulet up again and pushed it to the side. "I suppose we won't find an answer so easily. I will scry this evening and see if I have any luck."

"If we're lucky, Nicole's book might reveal something," Merlin added. He rubbed his eyes, looking very tired, and his earlier cheer gone. "I was hoping that there would be some sign of how Arthur created that amulet, but it still seems that he doesn't use marks like we do."

"He knows they'll fall into our hands," Bran said. "He really doesn't need to worry about his amulets' magic staying strong. Have you checked the old ones?"

"No," Alex said. Blinking in surprise, she glanced at Merlin. "I didn't think of it."

"I have," Merlin answered. "And you are correct, the magic, that tangle that Alex sees, fades quickly. The amulets are one-time use. I suspect he doesn't really think any of his Fae forces will actually return but is willing to try his luck."

"Speaking of trying his luck," Nicki said. "You've seen the book, the recent entry, Merlin. What do you think?"

"I'm not sure," Merlin said. Frowning, he glanced at Alex. "Are you sure-"

"Arthur is looking into the Tree of Reality," Alex said firmly. "We don't know why, but he is."

"You said that he didn't share his mother's fears," Merlin said. Deep furrows on his forehead shadowed his eyes.

"He wasn't interested in helping the Sídhe," Alex said. Pausing, she licked her lips nervously and tried to voice the strange thoughts building up. "But... I also only saw their conversations. Arthur might have been lying to her. He might have already been planning his betrayal. I know he was frustrated with her trying to open the gates and help the Sídhe. But if he thought the Darkness could make him more powerful, then I think he'd go looking for it."

"So, Arthur thinks something is out there," Morgana sighed. "Or at least, he wants information on the Tree of Reality."

Bran shifted in his seat, folding his hands on the table. "How did you two learn about it?"

"Cyrridven taught me," Merlin said. "She guided me out of the Iron Realm when I was training with her." He shivered and his gaze turned distant. "It was stunning. I could barely believe it. Years later, she and I helped Arto see the Tree of Reality."

Alex glanced at Morgana who shrugged. "I was taught about it by the Queen. She had... there was this massive tapestry of it hanging in one of the libraries, and everything they knew was recorded in their archives, but it wasn't much. I've only ever seen it once myself with Merlin's help centuries ago."

"And we caught a glimpse of it once," Merlin added quickly. "When Thor was alive and the Sídhe pushing through caused some portals to other worlds. That was a very unusual circumstance."

"So, you really don't know much about the other worlds," Aiden said. Both Merlin and Morgana looked at him. "Not really anyway. It's mostly second-hand information."

"We've learned a great deal about certain branches from others from those branches," Merlin explained. "But yes, I suppose, you are correct. Morgana and I have never left this world, well, except for Morgana's childhood in the Sídhe palace. We don't have firsthand experience in other worlds."

"What about the trunk?" Alex asked.

"The trunk?" Merlin repeated.

"When... when you first showed us the tree, it looked like there were other worlds below Earth in the trunk," Alex said. "Were they worlds or something else?"

"I assume they were worlds," Merlin said. "I remember they were two bright points of light like the rest. Why?"

"It was just lights?" Alex asked. "Not... not clear round worlds? When I saw them, they were all very clear! At least, the ones close to me. I saw Earth like a photograph from space and a couple other worlds with continents and clouds and-"

"No," Morgana answered. "I only saw bright points of light."

"As did I," Merlin agreed. They were both looking at her curiously now. "Interesting. I wonder if the help of the others allowed you to see more or if it is some strange ability of the Iron Soul."

"Why?" Bran asked. He was frowning in Alex's direction now. "Why would the Iron Soul have a power like that? It exists to protect the Iron Realm. I would have thought Alex would be even weaker pushing her mind out towards the Tree of Reality."

"What did you see in the trunk?" Nicki asked, leaning forward to better see Alex.

"Bright light," Alex said. "I remember thinking they were like wells... I'm not sure if there was one or two."

"There were always two lights before," Merlin reminded her.

"Yeah, but all that light was flowing up through the Earth and then going to other worlds via some kind of connection system. That's what the branches are. That's what the pathways between worlds follow." Merlin hummed thoughtfully, but his face gave nothing away. "I'm pretty sure that what is below Earth in the Tree of Reality isn't another world. It's something else."

"Really?" Bran's voice was soft and disbelieving. "Do you- uh-"

"No clue," Alex replied. Smiling at his reaction, she shook her head. "Sorry, no idea. It was just this well of light. Most of it was traveling to the rest of the Tree of Reality."

Nicki nodded this time, her eyes bright. "So, there's something much more special about the roots of the Tree of Reality then some dark underworld."

"You thought there was an underworld?" Aiden asked.

"Seemed possible," Nicki answered defensively. "Almost every mythology has some version of the underworld."

"Those are the invention of humanity," Morgana said calmly. Her eyes were still locked on Alex. "Going into the Tree of Reality was dangerous, Alex."

"You weren't talking," Alex retorted. Morgana's eyes widened at her tone. "I needed to, Morgana. And I'll need to again. None of this conversation answers what Arthur is doing and we need to figure that out."

"It might not be a danger to us," Merlin said. "It may just be curiosity."

"Doubtful," Alex snorted. Staring at the far wall, she frowned. The voices were louder now, everyone was chiming in with their thoughts. Cuthbert was insulting her and the others so she tried to ignore him.

"No, I think Arthur is looking for something. While he may not want to help the Sídhe, he might want to know if there is a threat to him."

"Fair point," Nicki agreed. She glanced at Merlin and Morgana. "After all... we don't know if he'll have the longevity of you two. If he thinks he will then he may really want to be ahead of a potential threat."

"This Darkness..." Morgana shook her head. "I just don't see how such a thing is possible."

"Somehow the Tree of Reality links different universes," Bran said. His fingers were tracing something on the tablecloth. "We don't know why or how. We don't know how something like that formed, but it did. It really shouldn't be so difficult to believe that something is happening at the outer reaches of the tree."

No one had an answer. Merlin and Morgana were quiet, their eyes distant and both frowning. Both seemed unsettled and worried. It was a rare expression for them, and Arto whispered his worries. Tensing, Alex did her best to ignore how terrified Arto's concern left her. Merlin and Morgana were supposed to know; they weren't supposed to be confused.

"You raise some interesting questions," Morgana said slowly. How carefully she was considering her words showed in each syllable. "We have long focused on the safety of the Iron Realm, and simply kept other elements at bay the best we could. But if this Darkness is real, then we should make an effort to understand it."

Alex was grateful that she was sitting down. Trembling in relief, she exhaled slowly. Black spots flickered at the edge of her vision. Her mouth was dry and no one spoke up. They didn't know anything about the Darkness. It frightened whole worlds to the point of them invading other worlds, but beyond that they had nothing. Merlin and Morgana were looking at Alex as if expecting her to talk.

"I've got nothing," she said. "I've told you my theory. The Darkness and the poison are connected. But... honestly, I don't think I saw much of the Tree of Reality last time. I couldn't confirm that there was anything wrong."

"Perhaps you or I should take a look," Morgana said, turning to Merlin. "We'd be more likely to understand changes."

"But I see it more clearly," Alex reminded them. "I see the worlds. You don't. That has to mean something."

Morgana glared at her, narrowing her green eyes and studying her. Her worry radiated off of her, but Alex didn't take it back. An itch to look again was growing in her chest. Merlin and Morgana were finally listening. She could see more of the Tree than they could: it had to be her.

"I'm going to get dinner," Aiden said. Slowly standing up, he glanced between her and Morgana. "Bran, some help please?"

"Sure!" Bran jumped up and they both rushed into the kitchen.

Finally, Morgana blinked. "Very well, you may try again, but Merlin and I will assist as well. I dislike you taking unnecessary risks."

Smiling, Alex nodded in agreement. Her chest was lighter and she was suddenly very hungry. Merlin relaxed in his chair, but he looked down at the wrapped-up amulet. Signs of his concern and frustration still lined his eyes, but Alex was going to take this as a small victory. They needed any that they could secure.

As the first bowl of pasta came out, Merlin cleared his throat and launched into a lecture about the history of the nearby worlds that he knew thanks to his early training with Cyrridven. Morgana added where she could, but most of her knowledge was about the Sídhe branch. Alex accepted the bread bowl and focused on the words. She might be the Iron

Soul, but it seemed that the time to worry only about the Iron Realm was officially past. That was a good thing. Yet, it didn't make her happy.

15

Tracking the Fae

1 516 C.E. Rhineland

Magic flickered in Michel's hands, shifting and swirling into small bolts just waiting for his command. But he didn't move. Staying still in the shade of the trees, Michel watched the movement in the small village below. It was tucked against a long cliff, existing in the long shadows cast by the hillside that kept the small thatch homes in the shade.

It would be easy to dismiss this village. Far from the main roads and surrounded by thick orchards with a forest to the east, it was isolated. No one here ever seemed to leave and no one came here to trade. But Michel knew it was different and special. The figures walking in the village all wore hoods but every so often he caught a glimpse of pale skin and hair.

Still, there was nothing happening. Michel's grip on his magic faltered and a few stray sparks flew away. They vanished quickly, but Michel was glad that Morgana hadn't seen that loss of control. Holding back a yawn, he shifted back to lean against a tree. Then he shifted just enough to scratch his back using the rough bark. A yawn did escape him now and the magic pulsed, threatening to move away.

Turning his right hand, Michael examined the white sparks that made up his magic. When they'd first manifested, Morgana and Merlin had been both pleased and sad. He suspected that the color of his magic was similar to Arto's. The boy he had been and wasn't any longer. It was a strange thing to know was true. He had no memories of being Arto, and the occasional dreams he had seemed more likely to be the result of Morgana and Merlin's stories.

Shaking his head, Michel pulled back on his magic. Nothing was going to happen. He was becoming more and more confident of that. One of the Fae was sheering a small group of sheep in a pen just outside the village with bronze blade sheers. Bundles of wool were being taken into a nearby house. There was a limit to what he could see. They were at a safe distance and the Fae mostly worked indoors.

Letting more of his weight rest against the tree, Michel used the bark to scratch another itch. Suddenly the sounds of footfalls on the hillside made him tense. Straightening up, he summoned more magic, letting the white sparks dance across his skin. Then Merlin stepped into view, using a tall walking stick to help him navigate the steep slopes of the hill. The older mage smiled at him and then nodded his head away from the village. Michel stayed silent and followed his uncle away from the collection of houses.

Morgana was waiting for them down the hill. She had a small fire set in a ring of stone in front of a log. A small pot was hanging over the fire and a thick meaty smell reached Michel's nose. His mouth began to water and he happily sat down on the log alongside Morgana. She checked him over quickly with her eyes as Merlin handed him a waterskin. Dutifully, Michel took a long drink of the clean liquid. Having magic to clean your water supply was a blessing indeed. He had understood years ago why Merlin and Morgana never allowed him to drink the water in town without them first cleaning it.

"Anything to report?" Morgana asked. "Nothing attempted to leave the area while you were up there, and I picked up nothing on my scrying mirror." She held up the polished bronze disk that Michel knew to be very old. "So far I've seen nothing that provides any detail of what is causing the rising levels of magic."

"I found nothing out of sorts," Merlin said. "They've settled in the shadows of a cliff. I'd estimate the village is at least a few decades old given the growth of moss on some of the houses. The construction is a bit old fashioned and simple, but solid. They have some orchard trees, further indicating that they've been here for years, and sheep."

"I didn't see anything strange," Michel agreed. He tried to think of something else he could add that would show he'd been paying attention, but Merlin had covered everything already.

"They seem peaceful enough," Morgana said. Her frown betrayed her frustrations. "And yet, magic continues to build in this region."

"There may be too many of them in one area," Merlin said. Slumping forward, he held himself up with his walking stick and drummed his fingers on the wood. "In addition to this village, there is another Sídhe settlement a few miles away. There are at least three hundred of them nearby."

"I suppose that is a large population," Morgana conceded. "And they are living above ground."

"Maybe they're the farmers for an underground area," Michel offered.

The pair of older mages looked at him and then at each other. "That would make sense," Morgana said. "We've never known a great deal about their survival underground. I've always assumed mushrooms or foods like that."

"Frea's people lived above ground, in part at least," Merlin said. "So, these villages could be connected underground or be independent."

"Can't we just ask?" Michel questioned. He almost stood up to pace, a nervous energy building in his chest. The spark of magic flared, giving him a heady rush of power. "I mean, if they are peaceful then surely, they'd want to reassure us."

"Something is going to happen," Morgana said. She sounded confident, absolute in her knowledge. "Magic is building in response to something. Peaceful or not, this could be a problem."

"Why? We have magic," Michel said. "Isn't that a good thing? You've told me that sometimes you can barely use magic because there is so little of it."

"That is true," Merlin agreed. "And yes, having magic is nice, Michel, but we have an obligation to be sure that there isn't a threat to the Iron Realm. The Fae don't belong in our world, and if this is a question of the high population then it needs to be addressed."

"A high level of magic could attract more beings," Morgana said. "Wake Old Ones or potentially even draw Demons from the east. We don't need that."

"But then what do we do?" Michel asked. "If it is just a population issue? We can't just kill them!"

Morgana and Merlin didn't reply right away. Michel's stomach twisted at the idea. It was very abstract to think of magic being a problem. Surely it was better to just leave things be then kill the descendants of the Sídhe.

"Killing is hard," Merlin said. "It isn't the ideal solution. If it is a population problem then perhaps, we encourage a lower birthrate and ask them to spread out more. With the help of our magic, we could even relocate some far away through a water tunnel. There are several options, but we need to understand the problem first."

Relief welled up in Michel. Smiling, he nodded. "Okay, that sounds reasonable." Not ideal, of course, but it could work.

"I'm not sure it's that simple," Morgana said. She looked towards the village again. "I'm just not sure what to make of all this."

"I believe that Michel has the right idea," Merlin said. "We've investigated and found no signs of problems. The logical next step is to speak with them."

"Are you sure that's wise?" Morgana pressed. She nodded in his direction.

"He's not a small child any longer." Merlin smiled sadly at him. "As much as we might both wish it. He has control over his magic should they attack us."

Morgana pressed her lips together, clearly displeased, but Michel could see that she was considering the words. Then, she exhaled and nodded.

"Very well," she said. "But, Michel, you will stay close to us. Understood?"

"Of course!"

"Then let us not delay," Merlin said. He stood slowly, his back creaking a little as he stretched. "Ah... that was unpleasant. We're getting old."

"You're getting old," Morgana corrected.

"You wound me, my dear Morgana," Merlin laughed. "And let us not pretend. You are not that much younger than I and raising a child certainly adds to the years."

Holding back a smile, Michel relaxed. They weren't too worried at least. That soothed the flickers of fear that had been trying to rise in his chest. Merlin was right. He wasn't a child anymore, but it was still very easy to let the others lead the way. But he couldn't rely on them forever. In his chest, the spark of his magic quivered and Michel pulled softly on it. Power poured down his arm, warm and reassuring. It was there if he needed it.

There was a small path that led into the village. It was worn down from years of use, but still gave the impression of a small forest game trail somehow. Merlin led the way, walking tall and purposefully thudding his walking stick onto the hard ground with each step. Morgana was behind Michel, keeping him firmly between herself and Merlin. Worry and excitement radiated off of his aunt, and he wondered if she wanted to fight the Fae or not.

A young Fae was near one of the fruit trees and looked up as they approached. Their violet eyes widened and they promptly rushed off, leaving their things behind. Michel inwardly grimaced at the reaction, but he supposed they didn't have many visitors. As they drew closer to the main village, he could see some Fae vanishing into their homes while a few came out to take a look. One figure stood out. It was walking right towards them with a few others following behind.

Michel had never seen such an old Fae. All of the Sídhe creatures always seemed to carry an air of eternal youth and grace with them. This one, however, had small lines around his eyes and carried a deep furrow between its brows. The long silver hair was tied back in a braid and its pale skin shimmered in the low light filtering through the trees.

"I am Merlin," his uncle said calmly. "This is Morgana and our student Michel."

A few of them looked at him curiously, but most were fixated on Merlin and Morgana. Shades of awe and terror filled their faces. Michel swallowed. His guardians had long histories. There was so much he didn't know about them. They told him stories, but they were ancient. What stories didn't he know? What stories did the Sídhe tell of them?

"Greetings Grand Mages," the Fae replied. Their voice quivered slightly. "I am Nikola." He nodded to them both and then to Michel. "What brings you to our village?"

"The level of magic is rising," Morgana said bluntly. "Our investigations as to the source indicate that it is in this area."

"We fear that something is going to happen," Merlin inserted smoothly. "Such a buildup is likely to attract Old Ones or other beings in our world."

"I know nothing of that," the Fae said quickly. "None of ours have been able to use any kind of magic in decades. Only the Brownies have any power in this realm."

"How many of you are there in this area?" Merlin asked. "We believe that the magic build up may be a result of there being too many of you." Many of the Fae drew back. One pulled a child closer to them. "If that is the case," Merlin added quickly. "Then we'd seek to relocate some of you. We have no desire for bloodshed. Morgana and I have long allowed those descended from the Sídhe and their former slaves to live peacefully in the Iron Realm."

There was some chatter in the back and Nikola's calm expression changed. Morgana narrowed her eyes, and Michel was sure that the temperature of the air dropped. He debated speaking up for a moment. He wasn't one of the Grand Mages, but... he was still a mage.

"Has something happened?" Michel did his best to keep his voice calm. Nikola shifted again. "Some change in the population?"

"Some of the young ones have left," the older Fae said quickly.

"Left?" Merlin repeated. "Were they seeking to found a colony elsewhere?"

Now Nikola shifted uneasily. Soft whispers grew in the crowd and suddenly Michel had a very bad feeling. Morgana put a hand on his shoulder and gripped him tightly. His legs tensed, ready to run, and his fingers twitched.

"No," Nikola finally said. "No. A strange Fae came here. He spoke about pushing back some of the humans and establishing a Fae country. I said that it was madness, but some left to follow him."

"What?" Morgana asked softly. Her voice was dangerously low and even more of the Fae drew back. "What did he say? Where did he plan to establish this kingdom? Ireland? England?"

"Peace, Morgana," Merlin whispered.

"He didn't provide details," Nikola explained in a rush. "It was the eagerness and brashness of youth." Then he sighed, the motion so very human that Michel was startled. "But some of the young ones were inspired, attracted by the idea. They hurried after him when our backs were turned. I fear I don't know where they went."

"Please," a voice called. "Please don't hurt them." It was a Fae with long hair tied up in a braid whose hood was falling back. "They're young and foolish. They don't understand."

"Our desire is not for conflict," Merlin said simply. His tone was empty, betraying nothing. "I want to find this Fae before any conflict starts. What was his name?"

"Oberon, he called himself Oberon," Nickola replied quickly. Someone drew the woman who had spoken back into the crowd. Michel watched her. She was shaking. "That's all we know. I swear it to you."

"Oberon," Morgana repeated. She frowned and looked at Merlin. "That name... it's from one of those heroic songs minstrels tell."

"Yes," Merlin agreed. "A fairy king of some sort if I recall. There was more to the story...."

"We know nothing about him," Nikola said urgently. "We wish for peace, Grand Mages: this man swayed the young who left despite our pleas. I know nothing more than that."

"This is most worrying," Merlin said. "Humans are finally beginning to shift away from ideas of magic. I dislike the potential ramifications of an army of magical creatures attacking a city or starting a war."

"Chaos," Morgana said softly. She glanced towards Merlin, both of their expressions guarded. "We need to learn more about this Oberon."

"Was there any indication of where they were going next?" Merlin asked. "How many left with him?"

"About ten left with him," Nikola answered. "But he said that there were more waiting for him at his 'court'. As to where that was, he gave no indication. Please, I swear we know nothing more."

Michel held his breath, but then Merlin nodded slowly. Morgana touched his shoulder and turned away from the Fae. Turning around, Michel almost tripped over his own feet but followed Morgana back the way they came. A moment later, he heard Merlin fall into step behind them. Voices whispered back in the village, but they soon faded away. Mind whirling, Michel shivered as all sorts of horrible thoughts of what was to come started pouring through his mind.

16

Exchanging Words

His hair was almost dry now, and Aiden brushed his bangs out of his face. He was due for a haircut. Overdue honestly, given how much of his dark hair he could see. Sometimes it was tempting to just grow it all out, but his father would likely have a few words for him on that front. Nicki would either tease him or cheer him on. He wasn't sure which, and that sort of frightened him. Aiden pushed his feet into his shoes, too lazy to even untie them.

Bran was already gone from their shared room. Aiden tried to remember what his roommate had today. There was a vague memory of a project for one of his classes or maybe a lab. Dismissing it, Aiden reassured himself that Bran could take care of himself. Of them all, Bran was the most likely to know when trouble was coming.

Closing his laptop, Aiden left his desk and grabbed his bag. A quick check confirmed that even in his hazy state last night after long talks about what to do next with very few decisions, he'd managed to pack his bag properly. Unease hung over him as he headed up the stairs. Everything was still in the house. It wasn't that early, and others might already be gone like Bran, but it still seemed unnatural. There should have been some argument or negotiations over bathroom time or someone moving around. He hadn't even heard Alex leave for a jog.

Aiden stopped walking towards the front door and looked into the living room at the sound of a soft snore. Alex was sprawled awkwardly on the longest of the sofas. Her blonde hair was a tangled mess. Her phone was on the floor and her feet were up on the armrest. The scrying book was open on the coffee table next to her, telling him at once why she was there. Sighing, Aiden shrugged off his backpack and set it by the front door where he wouldn't miss it.

Walking closer, he realized that Alex was in the same t-shirt she'd been wearing last night and frowned. He paused next to her, wondering if he needed to try and move her. Upper body strength really wasn't his strong point: he worked part-time in a bookstore and was an engineering nerd. Bran was better at telekinesis than he was. Besides, waking up floating didn't sound pleasant.

Alex looked calm. Her eyelids were moving slightly, but her face was relaxed, not tense. He noted that her shoes had been kicked off and were on the floor at the edge of the couch. Glancing down at the book, he found the same words that had been there for the past two days still there. No change. Nothing new to guide them. Arthur had gone poking into the Tree of Reality. He hoped that the spell wasn't a one-time thing. Given the work that Nicki had put into it, that might be fatal to someone when she found out.

Backing off, he headed back towards the entry and the kitchen. Footfalls were the only warning he received before he almost walked into Avani. She jumped slightly, but they avoided a collision.

"Good morning, Aiden," Avani greeted. There was a steaming mug of tea in her hand and a soft smile on her face. Something must have shown on his face because she frowned. "Is everything alright?"

"Alex is on the couch."

"Oh… the book?"

"Yeah." Aiden groaned and rubbed his eyes. "I'm starting to worry."

"I understand." Avani nodded and shifted so she could see into the living room. "She isn't good at taking care of herself."

"She used to be better," Aiden said. "But… well, honestly, I think she's always been a little obsessive. Back when… well, Lance and Jenny, when that got started and Arthur was still around, she ran herself into the ground worrying about it."

"I see."

"Alex just-" Aiden ran a hand through his hair, trying to find the right words. "She's good, right. I'm not saying she isn't. She's good. She's kind and wants things to work out, but she can become a little too focused."

"Given last night's conversation, it would seem that her concerns about the Darkness may be warranted."

"Yes, yes, it can be a good thing. But… I don't know. I can't help but worry. She doesn't have anything else. The rest of us have families, but Alex doesn't anymore."

"Nicki told me what happened." Avani frowned and looked into the living room again. "Poor thing."

"That's one way to put it," Aiden grumbled. "Maybe I'm projecting."

"Given what happened to you, it would be reasonable for you to be worried," Avani said. Her voice was a little too soft, a little too gentle.

"Nicki tell you about that too?"

"It's a difficult memory for her," Avani said. "But she also felt that I needed the full story of the history with Arthur." Shaking her head, she took a quick sip of her tea. "It's hard for me to imagine a time when he was trusted."

"Arthur put on a good show." Aiden slumped against the wall. He really needed to be heading to class, but suddenly there was no motivation. "He was... attractive, smart, and seemed like a good guy. I wasn't close to him though. Once everything seemed to come together, he still spent the most time with Alex. We talked occasionally." Frowning, Aiden thought back to those days. Even now, in hindsight, there hadn't been anything that painted Arthur as a traitor. Just a few little things here and there. "Looking back now, I'd say that he knew Alex was the Iron Soul before any of us. He was the most interested in her. We thought it was just romantic. Alex's crush on him had been pretty obvious since the beginning, and they seemed to click."

"How long were they together?"

"A few months, but... but I got the sense that it was pretty serious." Aiden grimaced at the reminder. "I'm not really comfortable talking about that."

Avani nodded sagely, her eyes darkening with both anger and sorrow. He remembered that emotional combination too well after he woke up and learned what had happened. "Fair enough. You're a good friend. I'm sorry. I'm just trying to understand the history here. If I ask questions, please know that I won't take offense if you're not comfortable answering." Smiling again, she looked content. "As I said, you're a good friend. I wouldn't want to damage that."

"I try to be." Aiden wasn't sure how good a friend he really was to Alex. All he seemed to do was tiptoe around her lately. Inhaling, he straightened up and pushed himself off the wall. "Speaking of which. You hurt Nicki and I have to hurt you." Avani smiled. Aiden sort of hated that. In fact, she looked incredibly pleased with his statement. "Don't look happy about that. It's a shovel talk!"

"Yes, exactly." Avani nodded and her smile widened. "But you see us as serious enough to warrant a shovel talk." Her expression softened and she looked down into her tea. "For a while... I wasn't sure."

"Nicki may joke, but she doesn't play around with people," Aiden said quickly. "She's very serious about you. She liked you pretty much the instant she met you."

He watched Avani's expression. She wasn't looking at him now but was smiling with bright eyes. Something relaxed in his chest and he exhaled. There had been worries. Small worries that maybe Avani just wanted a mage rather than wanting Nicki, but maybe that was silly. Maybe he was just jumping at shadows.

"Nicki is very special," Avani said. "She's creative and fierce. Talking with her is an adventure. She's so passionate about knowledge and truly enjoys sharing what she knows, but not in an arrogant way. It just makes me happy to be around her."

"Good. Good, that's good." He nodded and swallowed, suddenly at a loss. "Just... be careful, okay? You may not be a mage, but you're in this with us." Aiden wasn't completely certain what he was warning her of, hurting Nicki and damaging their alliance or being hurt herself in battle. Both were potentially terrible given Nicki's temper and emotional investment.

"I thought about it before I agreed to start seeing her," Avani told him. There was now a hint of steel in her voice. "I didn't want to make things worse or complicated, but... it was nice. I love my parents, but being away from them allowed me to explore something..." She trailed off and suddenly looked at him with her teeth grit together. "Sorry. That's not... you don't need to know about that."

"Ah... yeah, that's not my business." Aiden shifted nervously, suddenly very unsure as to what he should say or avoid. "But if you want to talk, I'm good at listening. At least that's what Nicki tells me."

"I'll keep that in mind." Avani smiled and turned towards the kitchen. Aiden blinked as he heard some movement inside the room. "Let's go into the kitchen. I don't want to wake her."

Alex hadn't woken up yet and Aiden suspected that she wouldn't anytime soon. He followed Avani into the kitchen. Timothy was moving across the kitchen counter calmly. The door of the fridge was open and a carton of eggs was slowly floating up to him. There was a pot heating up with a bit of butter in it. Aiden's stomach reminded him that he hadn't had anything for breakfast yet. The eggs lowered onto the counter and came to a stop. Timothy bounced over and opened the cardboard container. With quick motions, the Brownie cracked open the tops of a couple of eggs and pulled away parts of the shells Then he hoisted them up and carried the first one over to the pan, pouring the yolk and whites into the pan.

"I don't understand Brownie magic," Avani said softly.

"I'm not sure I get it either."

"We don't either, for what it is worth," Timothy said. The Brownie smiled over at them, tossing the eggshells into the sink which was several feet away. "Our magic works in the Iron Realm, unlike most other species. It has been suggested that we were bred by the Sídhe during our years of enslavement. Perhaps my ancestors were experimented on."

"Oh, that's horrible," Avani gasped. "I'm sorry, I wasn't trying to-"

Timothy waved to her and smiled. "Don't feel bad. No offense taken. Just telling you what we think. We have magic, but it works best for helping others, not fighting. Hence, we think that we were made this way as servants."

"I suppose it would fit," Aiden admitted. "The Sídhe would have needed to be experimenting to come up with things like Changelings."

"Yes," Timothy agreed. "How many eggs?"

"Uh... two, please," Avani said. "I had a cinnamon roll earlier."

Timothy wrinkled his little gray nose. He hadn't been impressed with the box of cinnamon rolls that Nicki had picked up. Packaged food seemed to insult the Brownie, no matter how much they tried to explain that they just didn't want to burden him with doing all the cooking. So far, that was a losing battle. He hadn't liked pizza night either.

"Do you have time to eat?" Avani asked.

"Uh, yeah I've got time," Aiden agreed.

"How many eggs?" Timothy asked.

"Four please."

"Good, good," Timothy said. "Mages need to eat breakfast." He gave Avani a side look. "Not just sugary pastries."

Avani chuckled and went through the kitchen to sit at the breakfast bar. Almost stumbling over his feet, Aiden joined her. He glanced over at the coffee machine, debating getting up before Timothy bounced over to it. The bag of coffee floated out of a cabinet and filled the top of the machine. Aiden shook his head and stayed put. Timothy didn't seem in the mood for help this morning. He wondered if Merlin and Morgana being here last night had upset him, or if it was the topic of conversation last night.

"There's something in the book!" Alex's voice cut into his thoughts. He jumped; she'd been asleep last time he checked. Avani blinked and Alex shouted again. "Guys! There's something in the book!"

There was no rush of feet upstairs. Aiden realized that while loud, Alex's voice was still fairly weak and wasn't reaching very far. That thought more than anything else got him moving. Avani was faster and more graceful than him, slipping off of the stool and striding into the living room through the dining room while he was just turning around. Alex was upright now, her hair still a tangled mess and her eyes a bit too bloodshot for Aiden's comfort.

"What does it say?" Avani asked calmly.

"Arthur's in the Tree of Reality again," Alex answered. She was cradling the book and frowning down at it. Aiden wished he knew what was going through her head, but was afraid to ask. "Strange... I wonder if it can only pick him up doing that."

"Or it's the only time he lowers magical protections he may have cast on himself," Avani suggested. It was exactly what Nicki would have said, and that almost made him smile. "I obviously don't know how that works in detail or understand the limitations of mages, but I know that my ritual magic requires focus. I can't split my awareness two ways."

"That makes sense," Aiden said. He nodded to Avani and then turned his attention back to Alex. "But it doesn't help much."

"Not immediately," Alex said. "But it proves what I was worried about. Arthur really is looking for something. This isn't just... curiosity. This is something else. Something more."

A dark mood settled over Alex. With slow deliberate motions, she set the book back down on the coffee table and reached for her shoes. Without a word, she pulled her shoes on, tied them, and picked up her phone. He stayed silent as she texted someone, and a bad feeling settled into his stomach.

"Alex," he said. "Wait, before you do anything, you should eat."

"But if I try to go into the Tree now, I might find him," Alex protested. Her gray eyes were wide and wild.

"Bran isn't here," Aiden said firmly. Stepping forward, he hesitantly touched her shoulder. Alex almost flinched back, her whole body tensing. "We have to do this together. Besides... what if you do find him? What then?" She blinked, her mouth opening, but no reply coming out. "We don't know if you could kill him or what would happen if you tried fighting him in the Tree of Reality."

"But-"

"Do you think he's harming anything there?" Avani asked. Her calm voice helped Aiden's heart slow down a little.

"I... no, I don't think so," Alex admitted. "But I'm not sure."

"Eat first," Avani said firmly. Stepping forward, she pulled the phone out of Alex's hand and put it on the table next to the book. "You need your strength."

Aiden had a headache now. There was a dull ache settling into the sides of his head and tapping harshly directly on his brain. A small voice at the back of his head suggested he just go to class like he'd been planning on and not deal with this right now. But he didn't listen to it. He was a mage. For better or for worse, he wasn't going to leave this alone. Avani escorted Alex to the breakfast bar and then grabbed the first of the scrambled eggs from Timothy. The Brownie put on a few more as Aiden pulled out his phone and texted Bran. School was unofficially canceled for the day.

Avani caught his eye and nodded. Holding back a sigh, he headed upstairs to wake up Nicki and brief her on the situation. With any luck, his headache would go away by the time Alex used their magic to check on the Tree of Reality.

17

Back to the Tree

Alex tried to listen to her friends. They were right about waiting for the others to get here. She knew that, but there was an urgent need to check on the Tree of Reality clawing at her chest. At least Aiden hadn't insisted they wait for Morgana and Merlin. The two professors were decent about getting away from the university when necessary, but given the heightened state of awareness on campus, she didn't want to push it.

Coffee had helped. Avani had set her down at the counter and returned with a glorious cup of coffee. It was one of Nicki's fancy flavors, but since it came from Nicki's girlfriend, Alex felt no guilt in drinking it down. She'd felt more alert after that and had worked her way through the eggs. Avani had stayed close, a protective little angel on her shoulder. The mental image made Alex snort into her mug and got her a look of confusion from Avani. She smiled and waved it off, shaking her head.

"You are strange," Avani said.

"That is very very correct," Alex said. Giving the other woman a big grin, she kept her hands tightly clenched around her mug of coffee. "After all, I'm the only sane person I've ever heard of with voices in my head."

Someone, maybe Gobifen, laughed in her head at that. Alex inwardly sighed. Maybe it was a good thing that her parents weren't alive to become aware of just how insane her life had gotten. That stray thought darkened her mood but did nothing to stem the desire to check on the Tree of Reality.

Timothy kept cooking more and more eggs. In a house with seven humans in their twenties and a Brownie, they kept a lot of food at the ready. Jenny and Lance came down and Jenny stopped to check on Alex on her way to get coffee. It made Alex feel warm, even if Jenny couldn't really check on anything below her skin. Lance nodded to her, his eyes lingering on hers for a long moment, but he seemed satisfied. There wasn't enough room at the island for everyone so plates were loaded up with eggs and taken into the dining room.

It could have been a normal morning. Bran took some of Timothy's offered eggs and went to the dining room. Alex caught him whispering with a still tired looking Nicki and Aiden. She excused herself to go upstairs now that she was properly awake.

There wasn't time for a shower. That nagging instinct wasn't releasing her, but Alex washed her face, brushed her teeth and combed the knots out of her hair. There were bags under her eyes. Not too bad, but they betrayed how late she'd been up staring at the empty pages of the book, urging it to find something. Alex studied the faint lines starting to form at the corners of her eyes with a frown before deciding it didn't matter.

When she got downstairs, the three other mages were waiting in the living room. Jenny stopped her with a soft hand on her shoulder and gave Alex a quick, but very tight, hug.

"Be careful," Jenny told her. "Just... be careful."

"I will be," Alex promised. "But I need to check. We can't let Arthur get ahead of us."

Jenny nodded, but she didn't look too convinced. She hadn't seen the Tree of Reality. None of them had, and maybe... maybe when things calmed down a bit, Alex needed to help the others see it. Everything was there, whole worlds just floating delicately in some strange void. They were fragile and connected by mere strands of ... something. Alex didn't understand it, but she would.

Sitting down amongst the others, Alex released a small sigh of relief. A warm feeling washed over her as Nicki took her hand. Her friends were worried. She hated making them worry, but it reassured her. Their affection poured into the small pit trying to form under her heart, helping to fill it for the moment.

"We're right here," Bran said. He took her right hand and squeezed it. "Tell us what you need."

Alex didn't need Bran's gift of sight to understand that he wasn't just talking about this. Smiling, she nodded to him and watched with satisfaction as he relaxed a little. Aiden didn't look convinced. Sitting across from her, worry still filled his eyes, and Alex hated that she'd put it there. She'd clearly been disoriented this morning.

They all settled into comfortable positions and breathed slowly. She watched Nicki and Bran close their eyes. Their hands began to glow softly with the colors of her magic. Aiden watched her for another moment before he relaxed and allowed his magic to flow. For a second, Alex hesitated. A few of the voices whispered that maybe she was worrying too much and needed to calm down. Maybe it was a bad idea. But the fear and need to check didn't fade away. She made up her mind.

Closing her eyes, Alex turned her attention inward. Counting the beats of her heart, Alex eased her body back against the side of the armchair. A fuzzy sensation crept into her mind. That vague sense of falling asleep. She tried to picture the Tree of Reality. Pushing her magic into the image, she wished for her power to take her back there.

She knew the way this time. Everything… shifted around Alex, making space for her to slip away. In her gut was a strong, warm line, leading her back to her body and her friends. If she needed to, Alex knew that she could follow it back in an instant. There was more control now. More understanding of what was happening as the layers of reality peeled back. The line quivered but stayed intact. She could cut it too, Alex realized. Then she pushed the thought away.

Something was different. Something had shifted. It was small, like a tiny change in the wind. Alex opened her eyes and frowned. The colors were more vivid. For a moment, Alex's senses were overwhelmed. Around the familiar tones of green and blue that she knew well when she looked at the Earth, there were strange hints of reds and purples that didn't make sense. Yet, she understood clearly that she was looking at her home planet.

Giving herself a moment to recover from the transition, Alex searched the North American continent until she found Oregon. She couldn't be completely confident of the location of Ravenslake, but she knew it was there. Once again, she found herself wondering just what this place was. It wasn't space. That much she knew for certain. Astronauts went into space all the time and had never reported seeing glowing strands linking their world to something else.

No, this was someplace else. It wasn't physical in the normal sense. Alex wished that she could bring Nicki and Bran here. They'd have more ideas of how to describe it than she did. Her eyes traced over Earth, taking in the strange hints of color with a slight frown. That was another mystery. Maybe she was just seeing more now. Merlin and Morgana had never seen it as clearly as she had last time. Maybe this was normal.

Remembering why she had come; Alex scanned the area around her. There was no sign of Arthur. Disappointment welled in her chest before Alex reminded herself that she could not have really expected him to be here. An annoying thought finally occurred to her: this may not even really be a physical location that others could come to. Maybe it was some sort of manifestation for each person. She wrestled with the thought, not happy with how she was thinking about it, but it was enough for the time being.

Alex's eyes followed the lines connecting Earth to its neighbors in the Tree of Reality. Their colors had shifted slightly as well, but it still gave her no clues as to the state of those worlds. Alex tried to move her hands, but they were heavy and sluggish. Her eyes moved between the branches, trying to tell them apart. She had no way to know for certain which branch was which. But she turned her gaze on a lower branch with a couple of other branches off of it.

The glowing stream of power connected several worlds. It was easier to see now, sharper and clearer than before, with the extra colors providing more richness. Alex tried to move her feet, but once again she was kept planted firmly next to Earth. Groaning, she startled when the sound echoed around her. Inhaling slowly, Alex confirmed once again that she could breathe, but the sound was strange. It rattled in her head and lingered too long.

"This really is a strange place." The words formed properly and echoed, bouncing off of nothing. A nervous giggle escaped Alex and she reached up to tuck a strand of hair behind her ear. "If only I could get over there." Whatever held her in place didn't release her. "You'd better hold Arthur too and not just me," she grumbled.

Unable to move around and properly study the worlds, Alex leaned forward to inspect the lines of energy. They shimmered and illuminated the dark space around her, bathing the worlds and herself in a warm glow. This time, Alex properly noticed that the energy didn't just run through the Earth in a straight line. Instead, it poured over the surface, shimmering and forming tiny ripples that she had to squint to see. The changes in the colors made it easier with a soft purple color appearing across the Earth in tiny lines that marked the way. She stared until her eyes got sore and she had to blink.

While she couldn't move her feet, Alex did find that she was able to bend her knees. The bottoms of her feet were still glued to the spot, but she managed to awkwardly lower herself. She was off center, but Alex focused on the odd point of light below Earth. Even bent over, it was still below her, taunting her with an imperfect view. It seemed darker to her. She hoped that was just the change in color. There was only one that she could see, releasing those beams of energy that spilled up into Earth. But only to Earth.

That felt important. Alex wasn't sure why it mattered, but that fact was burning itself into the front of her mind. A rush of voices left Alex swaying. Her ankles ached with sharp pains as she nearly toppled over and the magic holding her still refused to release. She just couldn't see enough or at least didn't understand what she was seeing. The whole place was like the set of a science fiction show. Smiling at the idea, Alex tried to imagine a little spaceship zooming by. This would be some sort of pocket dimension or something like that.

Standing back up was even harder. Alex tried to touch the floor, hoping to see if there was actually something below her. There wasn't. Her feet were just stuck at that point in this strange space. Still, she was able to push against something and force her body upright. It just made the backs of her calves twinge. Alex's head spun, trying to make sense of what was around her, but she couldn't. Her brain just gave up. Its last valiant attempt at logic and order was to remind her of what she'd been so worried about.

Alex looked up. There it was. Alex couldn't move. She forgot and tried to step back. The magic holding her tightened, a silent caution to go no further and Alex released a shaky breath. The dark cloud shimmered with tiny hints of purple. Small flickers of light around it kept glowing, but their time was limited. Now that she'd seen it, Alex didn't understand how she'd missed it.

This black was different from the rest of the landscape around the Tree. There was no stillness here. Instead, thanks to the flickers of purple, Alex had the distinct impression of a storm rolling in. Dark clouds were sweeping forward. It was slow, yes, but it was there. Dropping her eyes, she looked at the next world in its path. There were two faint lines coming from the world that led into the Darkness. Proof that there had been worlds there.

"Oh, God," she breathed. The words hung around her. There was a tiny shift in the Darkness, a tiny movement that brought it a little closer. "It's real."

All the voices started talking at once. Cries of horror filled her head, drowning out her own thoughts. Shock, terror, guilt, and grief hit one after the other, piling on top of each other like bodies tossed into a bloody pit. Alex wanted to look away. Arto begged her to look away, but she didn't. She couldn't.

There were more branches leading into it. The Darkness stretched over the Tree, hanging like a low cloud on a mountain. She tried to count the strands of dying light leading into it. There were two on the first branch, three on another and one on a third. The others were lower, out of reach, but that wouldn't last forever.

Fighting for air, Alex could only stare. Above her the Darkness shifted, churning slightly, but mostly just hanging ominously. There were worlds in there. Were they all in ruins like the Sídhe homeworld, devoid of any life? Had their species managed to flee like the Sídhe had or did they die on a choking world? Her vision blurred. Alex's chest tightened. She couldn't breathe. None of the air was reaching her lungs. Magic flared off of her quivering fingertips. It wrapped around her, trying to soothe, but it didn't help. As she watched, one of the lines of energy flickered like a dying light. It held on, but the glow was faint and wavering.

There was a flash of light. It blinded her, burning her eyes. Stumbling, Alex's ankles creaked as she failed to fall or step back. The voices screamed. Everything blurred. Alex reached for her magic. Scrambled for that connection to Earth. Heat exploded in her chest, forcing her lungs to expand. Suddenly she was falling. Being pulled back.

Blinking, Alex found Aiden's face coming back into focus in front of her. Bran's warm hand on her shoulder to her right was keeping her upright, and Nicki was still tightly holding her left hand. Jenny and Lance were sitting on the sofa with Avani, all three of them wearing expressions of relief.

"I'm back," Alex said. Her voice cracked and she swallowed. Bran turned around and picked up a glass of water. He brought it forward to her. Someone had been smart enough to put a straw in it. "Thanks," she said.

They waited, all of them watching her. In her hand, the glass shook. Her hands were trembling. Tears gathered in her eyes and her heart raced. She could still see it. With every moment, the idea grew more and more terrifying. It was real. It wasn't some dream, some delusion or only affecting one world.

"I saw it," Alex said. "The Darkness. No doubt about it this time. I'm not sure how I missed it... everything was sharper. Clearer this time."

"So, it was really there?" Nicki asked.

"Yeah." Swallowing, Alex took another sip. "Yeah, it was. And...and I saw the connections between worlds, the branches, vanishing into it."

"What about Arthur?" Aiden asked.

"No sign of him," Alex admitted. Her thoughts were swirling, struggling to come into focus. "I... I realized that maybe we wouldn't ever be able to be there at the same time. Maybe it isn't actually a place... it's just." Alex shook her head. "Sorry, it's all a bit...."

"That's okay," Bran said. He was still keeping her steady. "It's okay. We'll discuss it and brainstorm later. How do you feel?"

Alex frowned. Her head was aching, but the voices had quieted. They had quieted a lot. It was almost silent. Taking another sip of water, Alex closed her eyes and focused on the soft whispers. Nothing was clear. It was all jumbled. The pounding growing at the back of her head didn't help matters.

"Fine," she said. It was an obvious lie. "Just tired."

18

Highway Fae

1 517 C.E. Rhineland

Michel hit the ground with a groan. He really didn't want to get up. Every bone in his legs was ready to snap. The muscles burned and he just really wanted to stay on the ground. Musty leaves surrounded him, filling his nose with a reassuring earthy smell. This was a much better place to be. But it wouldn't be permitted; he knew that. Even now as his ears were cleared, he could hear people moving and shouting.

"Michel!" Morgana called. Her voice cut through everything else. "On your feet."

He obeyed, pushing up his body on his weak arms. His fingers dug into the leaves, but the sounds of the battle were breaking through. He looked up. Morgana and Merlin were nearby, standing protectively against a line of Fae who were snarling at them. Both were tense from the fight to hold the Fae back.

"Let us pass!" One of the Fae snapped. "This does not concern you!"

"You seek to attack humans," Merlin replied. His voice was calm, but the green glow of magic around his hands flared. Morgana was next to him, glaring at the tall Fae that had gotten the drop on Michel. "That we cannot permit. Return to your families and let this stop before the humans notice your actions."

"We won't stop!" The Fae that shouted looked young. It was a bit shorter and had finer features than the others. Michel thought it was probably female, but wasn't sure. "We can't live in the shadows forever!"

"I am sorry," Merlin said. Shaking his head, he did look sympathetic. "But humanity's weapons of war have grown more and more dangerous. Please understand: an outright war would destroy you all and potentially lead to even worse things."

"Oberon will protect us!" Another Fae shouted.

"Where can we find this Oberon?" Merlin asked.

"So, you can kill him? We are no traitors!"

"I wish to talk," Merlin said patiently.

"If we wanted the Fae dead then they would have been dead long ago," Morgana snapped. There was soft hiss to her voice that made three Fae draw back. Several looked at her with open fear. "You are alive today because Merlin and I recognized that your ancestors... well, your first ancestors were enemies of the realm, but their children had no part in the war. If you restart that war, then you forfeit your lives."

"This is not simply a question of a home," Merlin interjected. He glanced towards Morgana, and she scowled. "Too many Fae in one area has magical ramifications. Those ramifications could change the world. It is dangerous. Please disperse and go home."

"No, no, we aren't going back into the shadows!" one of the Fae shouted.

It held up its sword and started to step forward. Morgana did not wait. Raising her hand, she released an orb of silver magic that flew into the midst of the Fae group. They shouted wildly and tried to jump away, but the orb exploded in waves of silver light. Michel flinched. Morgana's magic ripped through the Fae. For a split second he could see their waists turning to dust, separating their legs and upper bodies before the rest of them followed. Their final expressions were terrified. But they didn't flee.

Frantically he scanned the tree line, trying to count what Fae were left. More were coming out of the thick trees as others fell. Dozens of them were coming forward, far more than they'd estimated at home. He looked at Merlin and Morgana: they didn't seem worried. Michel pulled on his magic. His lungs emptied, the air rushing out of them as the heat rushed down his arms. That never stopped being strange. Amazing, but strange.

White sparks circled his hands as Michel flexed his fingers. He had to be ready. Being hit twice in a fight would be far too much. The Fae didn't pause at the sight of more magic. Their simple stone weapons and old bronze tools were ready. Some wore rough looking leather armor while one or two had more substantial bronze chest pieces. None of it fit right. Stolen, his mind provided, or made by a lousy smith.

"Stop this," Merlin snapped. "You cannot win."

"We can kill you!"

A brave Fae in leather armor lunged at Merlin, swinging a bronze axe that caught the light of the setting sun filtering through the leaves. Merlin didn't flinch. He barely seemed to notice at all. A thin green bolt erupted out of his right hand and blasted through the armor and the Fae's chest. It fell, body falling apart and fragments of ash slipping out through the openings of the armor.

The Fae spread out. There were eight left, but then one turned and fled into the trees. Michel sighed in relief, but it was short-lived. The remaining seven did not follow. They brought up their swords and clubs threateningly. Heart pounding, Michel tried to focus. There was too much movement, too much to watch and worry about. He looked back to Merlin and Morgana. They were calm. They were in control

Morgana brought up a glowing hand threateningly. Two of the Fae raised round hide shields in front of them. It did nothing to slow Morgana's attack. Silver light lashed forward like a whip, slicing through the shields and armor. One dashed out of reach of the whip, dropping its heavy axe and pulling a dagger from its belt. It rushed him. Michel threw his hands forward. A stream of white magic poured forth, shimmering and sluggish. It was enough.

The Fae screamed. The sound filled his ears and skull, shattering his concentration. Michel swallowed, limbs shaking as he watched the body turn to ash at the onslaught of his magic. He could never get used to it. Bolts of bright green sailed through the air like arrows, striking down three of the Fae at once. Two were still standing, terror on their faces.

"Leave," Merlin ordered. "Leave with your lives and cease your hostile actions on their humans traveling in this area. Return to your families. There is no outcome here that sees you victorious."

Suddenly, Merlin gasped and twisted to the right. An arrow hit the ground and Michel looked into the trees. The runner hadn't been fleeing. He was up higher on a hill with a bow. As they spotted him, the Fae struggled with another arrow and raised the bow. Morgana threw her hand forward. A bolt of magic passed the arrow in midair. A shimmer of silver appeared in front of them and the arrow smacked against it before falling uselessly to the ground. Michel looked back at the archer, but there was nothing left to see. Its clothing was already on the ground, the Fae destroyed.

Huffing, Morgana pointed her finger at one of the remaining Fae. A small bolt of silver ripped through its chest and it broke apart, leaving only one standing. The Fae's eyes were wide, the violet color impossibly bright. It trembled but didn't flee. Merlin took a step closer to it, but the Fae just raised its weapon over its head. The older mage stopped. When the Fae moved to attack, Merlin sighed and waved his hand. Bright green magic rushed forward like water and struck the Fae back against a tree. It struggled and Merlin closed his fist. The green magic circled tighter. Michel grimaced as the creature's body fell apart.

Silence took over. The trees swayed in the wind and a few colored leaves drifted to the ground. Exhaling slowly, Michel closed his eyes and recentered himself. In his veins the magic still thrummed, but it was slowly cooling. The fight was over. They'd won, which was no surprise, but he still felt sick to his stomach.

Looking over at his guardians, Michel suddenly felt very small as Morgana calmly brushed some ash off her cloak. Her triskelion pin shined in the low light. Michel focused on it as something familiar. The symbol always reassured him that things would be alright. But neither of the older mages were bothered by the fight.

Morgana moved closer to him, lifted up his chin, and examined his eyes. "Any pain?" she asked, her tone soft and concerned.

"Just...sore," he admitted.

"Yes, you need to be more aware of your surroundings," Merlin said. "But you haven't been in many battles. Let's just be grateful you can learn from the experience."

Morgana released Michel's chin and ran a hand over his head, checking it carefully. "Yes, you seem fine," she conceded. "If you still feel sore tomorrow, tell me at once. We'll heat up water for you to bathe in when we get home. That should help."

"Thank you." Michel meant it. He knew he was lucky to have the advantage of magically heated water. "That would help."

"Not tumbling down a hill would also help," Merlin teased with a smile.

Morgana had moved over to the armor, glaring down at the items scattered across the forest floor. "I'm getting tired of this," Morgana said. She kicked a pile of armor that had fallen on the ground when the Fae had been destroyed. "Look at this. Ill-fitting armor, and half of these weapons are stone."

"They can't use iron or steel," Michel reminded her weakly. She hardly needed it, but he felt he had to say something. "They have to use something."

"We'll see basic wooden gear soon at this rate," Morgana hissed. Shaking her head, she nudged a bronze axe carefully with her foot. "All they're achieving is pulling us away from the shop."

"That's not completely true," Merlin said. He was leaning on his walking stick and looking at the fallen weapons and armor. "They've managed to be rather vicious highway men thus far."

"Which will only attract more trouble," Morgana said. Shaking her head, she waved her hand and the armors began to float. "Sooner or later, someone with real authority is going to send men, and while they may not be mages, they won't have a problem killing them. They'll just see them vanish and *we'll* have the problem."

"My concern is why are they robbing people?" Merlin said. He looked up at the thick canopy of leaves. "This forest does provide their eyes with decent protection, but it has to be uncomfortable. What do they want money for?"

"Maybe better tools," Michel said. "Or... to hire mercenaries to fight for them." Both of the older mages turned towards him sharply, their expressions thoughtful and worried. Michel thought about what he'd just said. It had been an automatic response. He hadn't really considered it, but it made sense. "If… if they really are looking to conquer a city for themselves then they may need help."

"That could very well be the plan," Merlin agreed slowly. Then he visibly shuddered. "It's a horrible plan. A terrible idea, all of this."

"I don't know," Michel said. "Maybe it would be best if they had an island or a city or something."

"They have settlements across Europe," Morgana said. "It is impressive how far they have managed to spread given their dislike of direct sunlight."

"I know, but a place that humans knew was theirs," Michel said. "You've told me that in the old days people knew that the mounds marked their homes and left them alone."

"Not all the mounds," Merlin corrected. "Most of the mounds are graves. Only a few were actually Sídhe hills."

"Okay, but still. I sort of understand what they want," Michel insisted.

"As do I," Merlin agreed. He reached out and put his hand on the top of Michel's head. The familiar gesture of affection quieted Michel and he met his uncle's eyes.

"You said… that a war could lead to worse things," Michel said. "What did you mean?"

"I worry about what might happen if people came to realize, truly realize, that the Fae are real," Merlin said. Sighing, he leaned back against a tree and stared off into the distance. "It was different in the past, Michel. Humanity had barely shifted to iron from bronze. Being able to fight back at all, even with swords and arrows, changed things."

Michel frowned. Morgana and Merlin liked talking about the advancements in technology, but it was difficult to really imagine a world like that. A world without real countries and instead isolated villages and long trading routes.

"The Fae would lose," Merlin continued. "And while in some respects that might be a good thing... sooner or later, some monarch would want to have all of magic at his command. Thus far, Earth has been the place that others invade. I do not want to see humanity become the invaders. Magic... it was a given in the old days, but it was more feared. Now... I don't know. I worry about what would happen. There is so much technology, such a struggle for power, and greed. Maybe I'm worrying too much, but my instincts tell me that now that humanity is moving away from their belief in magic, we and the Fae should stay in the shadows."

Michel glanced at Morgana. She had remained silent this whole time. A small frown marred her face and she seemed thoughtful, but not in the mood to share. It was Merlin who spoke of the past the most, and sometimes, like now, Michel wondered what he didn't know about Morgana's past. He disliked the notion that he didn't know her story. She'd always been the one he'd been closest too. She had been the one to care for him when Merlin went on business trips. Yet...

He pushed the thought away. She was allowed her past, her secrets. They were old. Both of them. And if Merlin liked talking about the past more than she did then that was just fine. Instead, he considered Merlin's words. It was hard for him to say for sure if humanity really was all that different now. He'd always lived in the same world.

Merlin and Morgana used some magic around the house but had trained him to always keep it a secret. They'd told him of the Sídhe war, the Old Ones, and the various species that lived in hidden places throughout the world. He had never known anything else. They'd told people when he came into their care that he was the son of Merlin's brother and he'd always kept to that story. They blended into the city. It was home, despite the secrets.

But maybe Merlin was right. He probably was. Sometimes, the law keepers in the city weren't fair. Sometimes people cheated each other. Michel watched Merlin and Morgana, who were sharing one of those long silent conversation looks. If someone threatened them… he might use his magic to lash out at the nonmagicals.

Still, he looked at the piles of ash that were already being blown away. This made him uneasy. He didn't like fighting in battle, but didn't see what else he could do. Merlin called his name and Michel jumped. His uncle smiled warmly at him and beckoned him to follow. They collected the bronze tools and weapons, left the stone, and took Morgana's floating pile of armor back to the wagon they'd left half a mile back. As they packed everything away and Michel's stomach finally started to settle, Merlin and Morgana discussed what prices they could ask in the shop for their new inventory.

Merlin and Morgana took their places at the front of the wagon and Michel hauled himself into the back. Some of the weapons shifted around him, and he flinched. He really did not want to sit on a piece of armor that had just been worn by a now dead Fae. Sadly, he didn't have a choice, and did his best to make himself comfortable for the long trip back to Strasbourg.

19

Mirror

Staring up at her ceiling, Alex traced the faint shapes that she could see. There were faint holes and bumps from uneven drywall beneath, but at least there were no signs of water damage. Then again, Morgana seemed the sort of woman who even when she was in a hurry would carefully inspect a house before buying it. A soft knock made Alex shift her head and twist her torso so she could see the door.

"Yeah?"

"Hey," Jenny greeted, opening the door. She poked her head further into the room and gave Alex a soft smile. "What are you up to?"

"Nothing," Alex answered. "I should be doing some reading, but I can't find any motivation." She smiled a little when Jenny chuckled warmly.

"Understandable," Jenny answered. "I'm going to bake some cookies; I'll bring a couple up to you when they're done."

"Cookies?" Alex mustered enough energy to sit up on her elbows. "What sort of cookies are we talking about?"

"Chocolate chip, of course," Jenny assured her. Then she looked towards the window. "It's getting colder outside, the perfect time to have the oven on and bake something warm."

"How many cookies are we talking?" Alex asked. "We do live with a bunch of people."

"I picked up stuff for three double batches," Jenny said.

Alex's eyes widened. "Wow, you're taking this seriously."

"Everyone's been stressed lately." Jenny's smile faded a little and she leaned against the doorframe, tugging at the hem of the dark blue shirt she was wearing. "This is just... this is a way that I can help."

"You help a lot," Alex said.

"Not as much as I'd like to," Jenny said. Shaking her head, she put a smile back on her face and straightened up. "Anyway, I'll bring you some cookies when they're ready. Unless you wind up sitting at the kitchen island before then."

Alex smiled in return. That was a distinct possibility. She watched her friend and former roommate head down the hall and sat up the rest of the way. Folding her legs under herself, Alex settled in the middle of her bed and considered what to do next. Going downstairs to snag a few chocolate chips was certainly tempting, but she wasn't quite ready to be properly social.

It was quiet. Very quiet. It had been for the last three days since she went into the Tree of Reality. Her fellow mages were researching old books, mostly Norse, for any clue that might help, any old story or legend. Alex didn't think it was likely that they'd find anything that fit. Even Merlin and Morgana had been blindsided by the Darkness.

Closing her eyes, Alex waited for the voices to say something. But they were all muted. There was no soft encouragement from Arto, no snarky insult from Cuthbert, no suggestions from Lokpal. Thor wasn't shouting for battle. Gofiben wasn't trying to make her think about all the questions facing them. The other lesser-known voices were gone. It was silent. Alex licked her lips, trying not to freak out. This might be a good thing.

"Still," Alex said softly. "Some useful help in figuring this all out would be nice." Nothing came, just the same low silence. "And now I really am talking to myself." Huffing, she blew a strand of hair from her face. "This is all Arthur's fault."

Arthur. It all boiled down to Arthur. Even now, years later, it all circled back to him. Honestly, it was ridiculous. He should have been dead by now. After his betrayal, all his lies, and almost killing her and Aiden, he should have been dead. But the snake was good at slipping away, vanishing through water tunnels just beyond her reach. Even now, the book wasn't helpful.

She wanted him dead. An old anger simmered in her gut, urging her on, encouraging the hatred. Maybe it was Arto, maybe it was all her, but it was there. It should have been over a long time ago, he should never have been born, and yet here she was, still dealing with him.

Maybe it was time to reevaluate how she thought of him. The glimpses of his childhood that she'd seen were uncomfortable to this day. His thing with his mother was never going to stop being gross, but he'd survived. Arthur kept surviving. He'd outlasted the Queen and was doing something right that the Fae kept following him.

"He's doing something right," she said again, testing the words out loud. The idea was uncomfortable, but it was time to be realistic.

Swinging her legs off the bed, Alex set her feet down on the carpeted floor. It tickled her bare feet, so she reached over to her nightstand to reclaim the socks she'd taken off earlier. Standing up, Alex glanced towards the door. Jenny hadn't shut it all the way. For a moment, she considered going downstairs and distracting herself. But that wouldn't help. Instead, Alex went to her desk and picked up a notebook.

Pacing, she started writing out everything she knew about Arthur for certain. It wasn't much. She knew his age, that he'd been made with the power of the Iron Chain and possibly some power from the Iron Gate that was still linked to his and the Queen's souls. He'd been emotionally, psychologically, and mentally abused by Scáthbás, no matter what the woman had said while dying. He was a master manipulator, a good actor, and had magic despite not being allied to the Iron Realm. Her handwriting was a mess, but she wrote it all down as bullet points.

It wasn't much. It wasn't much at all. Alex grit her teeth and tossed the notebook onto her dresser. A can of dry shampoo rattled and fell over. Stomping over, Alex grabbed the spray can before it could roll off the dresser and set it back up. Then her eyes landed on her reflection in the mirror. Her image met her gaze calmly.

"Mirror, mirror," Alex sighed. "Pity you can't really tell me anything useful."

Stopping, Alex stared at her reflection. She watched a slow smile spread over her face. A terrible idea was forming. A really horrible idea. If she was smart, she'd call Nicki and talk it over. Alex waited for a voice to caution her. Waited for someone to stop her, to talk her out of it, but there was only silence.

Touching the corner of the mirror, Alex closed her eyes and pulled on her magic. It was sluggish as if sensing her hesitation to this idea, but it cooperated. Unsure of how to do this, Alex tried to picture Arthur's face. It was easy. Far easier than she would have liked. The memory of him looming over her as she collapsed to the ground, a hole torn in her body from her own sword and blood seeping through her hands. He'd been smiling, his usual boyish charm replaced by cruel satisfaction.

Her hands quivered, but the magic slid into the mirror. Opening her eyes, Alex took a fortifying breath. "Find him," she said. "Find a mirror, find a reflective surface." The glass shuddered, small ripples appearing across the surface. Beneath her fingertips, the glass quaked and Alex braced herself, worried that it was about to shatter. "Find Arthur," she repeated. "I need to see what he's doing."

The glass started to rattle in the wooden frame beneath her fingertips. The frame was light, maybe too light, and Alex braced herself for it to completely shatter. Her magic rippled around across the reflective surface, forming tiny fractals of gray. Then the magic settled into the mirror, twisting across the top like oil over water. It wouldn't hold the magic for long, but an image was forming as Alex's own visage blurred out.

It looked like some sort of hotel room. Boring but comfortable, with neutral earth tone comforters and pillows on the bed beyond the mirror. There was a duffle bag open with some clothing visible, but nothing more. Her mouth went dry. That wasn't her room. Not at all. Licking her lips, she nervously held back her glee and considered pulling away. This was too fast, too impulsive. She hadn't considered this. Morgana was going to kill her.

But there was someone moving. The sound was muffled, but there. Her heart jumped as the noise grew louder. She wanted to move her hand. It wasn't too late. She could still stop this before she had to see him. The mirror might go both ways and he'd see her. She didn't want that, but...but she needed to see him. Inhaling a deep breath, Alex did her best to calm her expression.

Arthur stepped into view. Thankfully he was dressed. He looked ordinary in a t-shirt and jeans. Rubbing the back of his neck, he looked like a completely normal twenty-something. There was nothing that gave away what he was. Then he froze in place, his eyes darting over to the mirror. Alex's stomach twisted. He could see her after all. It went both ways.

Spinning towards the mirror, Arthur drew a knife out from under his shirt. It looked like one of the ones that Merlin had made. Anger flushed in Alex's chest, but she stayed still. She kept her hand on the mirror as Arthur's eyes widened.

"Hello, Arthur." Staying calm and looking like this was on purpose was the best way forward. Alex was sure of that. But still, none of the voices offered any advice.

"Alex?" Arthur's eyebrows went up in real surprise. He took a step towards the mirror and Alex suddenly wondered if she could reach through it and attack him. The glass shook again and there was a faint crack. No, she decided. Not without more preparation for the glass to take that kind of magic. "Well, this is a surprise." Leaning forward, his eyes traced the edges of the mirror on his side. "I never considered anything like this," he said. He put the knife down on the dresser below the mirror with a soft thud and tapped the mirror. It was solid and he smirked. Slipping his hands into his pockets, he met her gaze without a flinch. "Rather fairy tale. Was it Nicki's idea? This seems like something she'd think up."

"No."

"Really? Aiden's then?" Arthur grinned and then chuckled. "You? Really? Well, then you've got more imagination then I thought, or at least you're finally taking some cues from stories."

Alex ignored the jolt of hurt his words caused. It was stupid to be upset by anything he said. He was watching her and waiting for a reaction. Instead of giving him what he wanted, Alex focused on his face. There were lines around his eyes that made him look much older than before. His blond hair was shorter now, coming just past his ears, and there were shadows beneath his eyes.

"I don't enjoy the sight of you," Alex said. "So, I'll try to make this short. The Darkness. What do you know about it?"

"The Darkness?" Arthur groaned. "Really, Alex? You're starting to sound like my mother." He leaned away from the mirror for a moment and then straightened up with an apple in hand. "I'm talking to a mirror," he said, tossing the apple in the air with a grin. "Seems appropriate."

"I know you've been peering outside the Tree of Reality," Alex said.

"Been doing that for a while now. Mother wasn't sharing what she knew. Our agreement was always very clear that she wasn't to keep secrets."

"Why?"

"Curiosity," Arthur answered. He shrugged a little, looking far too at ease.

"It's more than that," Alex said firmly. "What are you after Arthur?"

"What do you think this conversation is going to accomplish?" Arthur asked. He gestured between them and leaned forward a little. Alex struggled against the instinct to move back. "I mean really? This isn't a spy film where I tell you everything right now."

Arthur's smile widened and he leaned even closer. There was something wrong with his right eye. It wasn't the right shade of blue. A section had changed color. There was a dark green path in the upper right portion. It glimmered with a light of its own. Alex's magic churned in her chest. A sharp pain radiated across the side of her head.

"What?" Arthur snarled.

"Your eye," Alex whispered.

Glass shattered. The mirror exploded, sending shards of glass towards her. Alex threw up her hands, pulling on her magic before she even thought of it. There were soft pings as the shards hit her shield and then hit the floor. Panting, she slowly lowered her hands and looked around. A few stray pieces of the mirror were still fixed in the frame, but most were scattered around her. Turning to look behind her nervously, Alex sighed in relief when she saw that nothing had hit her laptop at least. She looked at the frame. Her head still hurt, but all she could focus on was Arthur's eye. Something had changed. Something was very wrong.

"Alex!"

There was a rush of running on the steps. Closing her eyes, Alex stayed still and breathed slowly. She flexed her fingers as her magic slowly calmed. Her door was pushed open and she turned to see Bran and Aiden in the doorway. Each of them had their hands raised and faint glows around their palms.

"Alex?" Bran asked. His eyes scanned the room and slowly, very slowly, his brow eased. "What happened?"

"I tried to make a magic mirror." Gesturing at the pieces, Alex suppressed a nervous giggle. "Didn't exactly work, but I had a chat with Arthur before it shattered."

There was a moment of heavy, disbelieving silence before Nicki pushed past the boys and grabbed Alex's sneakers. Moving carefully, she avoided the largest pieces of glass and set Alex's shoes down. Then Nicki waved her hand, sending out blue sparks of magic that swept up the nearest fragments.

"I'll get a trash can," Bran said quickly. "Alex, stay still. Let Nicki help you."

Nodding, Alex didn't try to argue. She was suddenly aware that her knees were shaking. The glass was being carried away and Nicki grabbed her hand. The redhead gave her a look and knelt down, putting Alex's hand on her shoulder before helping her put on her shoes.

"What were you thinking?" Nicki asked in a low voice.

"I... I just wanted to see him," Alex whispered. "Not- not like that. I don't know. It felt important."

"I thought you had more sense than that," Nicki growled. "He's dangerous, Alex."

"I don't think he caused this." Alex bit her lower lip. It was like she was a little girl who had been caught again. "It was the magic. It didn't mix with the mirror well."

"Maybe," Nicki said. Her friend stood up. Aiden was at her bed and a thin fog of red sparks moved over the dark comforter, removing the small flakes of glass. "Still... this isn't good. What were you thinking?" Nicki's tone hardened again.

"Nicki," Aiden said softly.

"No, I want to know what she was thinking." Nicki gripped her shoulder. "Alex, we have the book. We're making progress. I can't believe that you talked yourself into trying something like this alone without even talking to us."

"Nicki." Aiden was giving Nicki a warning look.

"I...I don't know," Alex said. "I was just trying to think about everything, trying to put it all together." She looked towards the notebook still on the dresser. "It just seemed the right thing to do."

Bran was back with a trash can. Nicki pushed Alex down onto the cleared bed with a warning look. Alex was silent as the three mages swept the room with magic, collecting the large shards, small pieces, and tiny fragments. The empty frame was still secure on the wall and Alex looked back at it, trying to understand why she had done it.

"I can't hear the voices anymore," Alex confessed.

"What?" Bran asked. He moved closer and touched her arm. "The voices?"

"Arto and the others," Alex said. Lowering her eyes, she watched a stream of blue magic sweep the glass off her desk. "They're silent. Ever since my last trip to the Tree of Reality I can't hear them."

"...Is that good or bad?" Aiden asked. His lips were a bit twisted as he held up the small trash can from the bathroom for the last of the glass.

"I don't know. It's just different." Wrapping her arms around herself, Alex pulled her feet up on the bed. Then she shook herself. "But before I forget, there was something odd with Arthur."

"What, the homicidal rage?" Aiden muttered.

"No, his eye. His right eye... it was different. There was a dark patch on it," Alex said in a rush. "When I tried to look closer, that's when the mirror exploded."

The others were exchanging looks. Worried and thoughtful looks. Nicki's frown deepened, making small furrows appear between her eyes. Aiden was lingering at the door and gently set the trash can outside. Then Bran moved closer, coming around to inspect the mirror frame. He said nothing and Alex pulled her knees up to her chest. Nicki sighed and sat down next to her.

"Why didn't you tell us about the voices?" Nicki asked quietly. "That they were gone?"

"It's a weird thing to say," Alex admitted. "Hey guys, we should be worried because I don't have voices in my head anymore." Aiden snorted and Alex smiled. "I was maybe hoping that trying something would make them come back, but... I'm not sure that having them is a good thing. I've gotten used to them sure, but still..."

"Fair enough," Nicki sighed. Putting a hand on Alex's shoulder, she squeezed. "But seriously, Alex. Don't try something like this again."

"I'm sorry," Alex said. Smiling sadly at Nicki, she nodded. "I don't know why I did. I knew it was a bad idea, but... I don't know. Sorry." But Nicki was staring at her with wide eyes. She leaned forward into Alex's personal space and when she tried to pull back, Nicki caught her chin. "Nicki, wha-"

"Bran!" Nicki barked. "Look at this!"

"What?" Alex tried to move again, but Nicki was holding her firmly with a hand on her shoulder and on her chin. "Nicki, what are you doing?"

Aiden and Bran both came closer, Bran bent over as Nicki turned her face towards him. Alex waited for a heartbeat for Bran to make a joke, but instead, he inhaled sharply with a hiss.

"What?" Alex demanded.

Bran licked his lips and hesitated, but then he answered. "Alex, your left eye has changed. You've got a dark green spot in your iris now."

20

Dark Spot

The latex gloves were cold. They felt wrong against her skin, and Alex was fighting the urge to pull away from Morgana's hand. But the older mage had an impressive grip on her jaw and was keeping Alex's face tilted just so. She flinched as a light shined into her right eye, but managed not to blink.

"Stay still," Morgana ordered. Her tone didn't leave any room for argument. Tapping her feet on the floor, Alex did her best to obey. "Now, you only just noticed this?"

"Yeah, right after I told Nicki about the change in Arthur's eye." Inhaling slowly, Alex counted the beats of her heart. Outside the door, she could hear the others whispering and lingering even if she couldn't see them. "Then Nicki noticed the same thing in my eye." Swallowing, she debated her next question, but it had to be asked. "What do you think it is?"

"I've been a doctor," Morgana said softly. "But never an eye doctor. It looks like the pigmentation of your right eye has changed. There are no signs of problems with your blood vessels. I'm tempted to take you to a proper eye doctor to see if they think it is strange or just sectoral heterochromia." Releasing Alex's jaw, Morgana lowered the light and sighed. "If not for Arthur experiencing the same thing, I might not be so concerned."

"Maybe it's just a side effect of visiting the Tree of Reality."

"Maybe." Morgana rose up from her knees and sat down on the bed beside Alex. Without Alex saying a word, Morgana wrapped an arm around her shoulder and pulled her into a hug. "That's possible. But the voices vanishing is a bit more worrying. That's a very sudden change."

"What if they're gone because I've seen what I need to?" Alex suggested. "What if they were only supposed to help me get so far and now I'm there?"

A soft chuckle escaped Morgana. "I don't have an answer for you," Morgana said. "Reincarnation is complicated. Merlin and I know it happens, but the why behind who is reborn is a mystery. Lance and Jenny seemed to have been reborn due to their guilt, but if it was somehow self-inflicted or caused by magic itself I don't know. Bran has connected with his prior life, but he doesn't have clear memories or the voice of the prior Bran in his head."

"Right." Alex licked her lips. She felt fine. The silence was still strange: funny how used to the others talking to her she'd become. "Sorry you had to come over."

"This couldn't wait for morning," Morgana said. "You know that Merlin and I are here to help you. That is truly our greatest purpose in this world, guiding and teaching the Iron Soul."

"I don't..." Alex paused and frowned. "I don't feel like the Iron Soul right now."

"What do you mean?" Morgana pulled back and frowned down at Alex. Her hand went to touch Alex's forehead. "Is something else wrong?"

"No, nothing like that. I've just gotten used to the others," Alex said.

Morgana was still. Her whole body was tense and Alex knew that she had no idea of what to say. What could a person say to that? It was almost flattering. She was the strangest thing that Morgana had come across in her long life, or at least one of the strangest things.

"Sorry I'm so weird," Alex said.

"We'll figure this out," Morgana promised. The promise didn't feel right and Alex held back a shiver. "Try not to worry. Stress won't help the situation."

"Right, I'll try."

Morgana's expression softened. The woman who had put on latex gloves to examine her eye now leaned forward and kissed her bare forehead. That gesture more than anything helped Alex calm down. Glancing towards the empty mirror frame, she shifted on the bed, wishing she could just close her eyes and call it a night.

"What does it look like?" she asked.

"Just a spot that is dark green now," Morgana said kindly. "Exactly what it sounds like. The rest of the eye isn't red and the pupil looks fine, but as I said, I wasn't an expert in eyes. And even if I had been, my education is a touch outdated at this point." Her expression softened and she went over to Alex's desk where she had tossed her purse upon her arrival. Alex stayed still as Morgana dug through the purse for a moment. When she returned, she was carrying a small compact mirror. "Here, take a look."

Slowly, Alex brought up the mirror to inspect her eye. While it wasn't a major thing, it was a startling one, and she was certain that she would have noticed it this morning when she got up to wash her face. A small part of her left iris in the upper part had turned dark green. She brought the mirror even closer. There was a strange blend of green and gray where the two colors met.

"I don't think this was here this morning," Alex said softly. "And it definitely wasn't there yesterday."

"You're sure?"

"I cleaned up my eyebrows yesterday," Alex explained. "I was right next to the mirror. I don't think I could have missed this."

"That narrows things down at least," Morgana said. She didn't sound happy about it. Her green eyes were sharp with worry, but she was trying to hide it for Alex's sake. "You went into the Tree last night, correct?"

"Yes," Alex said. Quickly reviewing her day, she couldn't think of anything else odd or magical that had occurred. "But I felt fine this morning. I went to classes, came home, Jenny was going to make cookies... uh, are there cookies downstairs?"

"I believe some more are in the oven now." Morgana rolled her eyes but smiled a little. "Well-"

A knock on the doorframe made them both turn. Merlin was standing in the hallway, a slightly sheepish expression on his face.

"About time," Morgana huffed.

"My apologies," Merlin said. He nodded deeply to Morgana, almost a bow before moving further into the room. "What are we dealing with?" Merlin asked.

"Unknown," Morgana said. Pulling out her small flashlight, she held it out to Merlin. "Take a look at her right eye."

Alex didn't groan as Merlin and Morgana switched places. Merlin knelt down in front of her and frowned as he studied her face. "You look tired," he said. "Are you not sleeping well?"

"No, I fell asleep easily last night," Alex said. "Never woke up. Maybe it was just using the magic through the mirror."

"Indeed," Merlin said. He was smiling a little at her, but it was a sharp teasing smile. "Don't think that we won't be discussing that."

"Yes, sir," Alex grumbled.

Merlin chuckled warmly, his hand coming up to touch the crown of her head. Then he turned and accepted some latex gloves from Morgana. He pulled them on quickly and then tilted Alex's head back. His gloved fingers moved around her eye, gently holding back her lid.

"It doesn't look that strange," Merlin said. Alex could tell that he was mostly speaking with Morgana. "Simply a slight discoloration."

"Yes," Morgana said. "I think it best if Alex sees an eye doctor, someone more aware of what damage to look for."

"You're seeing fine?" Merlin asked.

"Yes."

"Well, given the recent events, I daresay that this is magical in nature," Merlin said. He pulled his hands back. "But to be blunt, Alex, I've never seen a physical change like this." He glanced towards Morgana. "Though... it is possible that it might fade away."

"Possible," Morgana agreed. "But I doubt it, Ambrose. The spot is very distinctly part of the iris. It looks like natural sectoral heterochromia."

"I don't disagree," Merlin said. Standing up, he pulled off the gloves and tossed them into the trash can that was still half full of glass. "But we shouldn't panic."

"Arthur had the same sort of discoloration." Morgana crossed her arms and glared. "Alex saw it when talking to Arthur."

"So you said on the phone." Merlin was remaining calm and even smiled a little. "But you and I have never spent so much time in the Tree of Reality. We don't know what sort of side effects being there might have. We mustn't do something foolish in a panic."

Morgana raised an eyebrow, but after a few moments, she nodded slightly. It was more of a small incline of her head. Just as Alex was beginning to hope that maybe this was over, both of them turned back to her.

"Why did you want to see Arthur?" Morgana asked.

"I just- it felt important," Alex said. The words were heavy on her tongue and didn't seem exactly right. "It's hard to explain," she added uselessly.

"Alex, how did it feel important?" Merlin pressed. "Did you feel your magic activate? Was it some sort of vision?"

"No, I don't think so." Alex shook her head. "It was just an instinct. Hell, I thought it was probably a bad idea, but I did it anyway." Closing her eyes, she lowered her head. "God, it was so stupid."

"But you didn't feel forced?" Morgana asked. "You didn't sense any magic making you do it?"

"No." Alex looked up at the two mages. Both of them were studying her intently. "No, I didn't feel anything like that. And I'm sure it wasn't Arthur. He was surprised. I just felt like I needed to try and see him, since the book wasn't working well."

"The book works fine," Merlin said. "And the mirror wasn't a bad choice. After all, Morgana uses her polished bronze disk and Bran has used a mirror in the past." He glanced at the empty frame. "But that... the destruction of the mirror is strange."

"And Alex is certain that her eye only changed today," Morgana said. "I wonder if speaking with Arthur somehow triggered it."

"Triggered it?" Merlin repeated. He hummed thoughtfully, still looking at Morgana. "Yes... that might explain the mirror. There could have been more magic traveling through the mirror than Alex intended."

"Wait, what?" Alex stood up suddenly, ignoring a wave of vertigo. "How could I not know? Besides, the mirror was shaking when I first touched it."

"Really?" Merlin's frown deepened. "I do not like the sound of that. Did Arthur touch the mirror on his side?"

"Uh... yes." Alex nodded. "Yes, I remember he did at one point."

"Then he might have done something," Morgana growled. Every inch of her body was tense and all but vibrating with anger. "Tried to attack Alex through the mirror."

"Maybe, or he might not have had control any more than Alex did," Merlin countered. "Alex, do you know if his eye looked different before he touched the mirror?"

Blinking, Alex tried to remember. It was a blur. Arthur's eye had stood out when he leaned forward, but she wasn't sure. She'd asked when she'd noticed, but that had been after he touched the mirror. At least she thought so.

"I'm not sure," she said. "I noticed his eye when he leaned forward." Licking her lower lip, she shrugged. "Sorry, I'm just not sure. I was trying to pay attention to any sign of where he was."

"A valid attempt," Merlin said gently. "But you shouldn't have tried it alone. There is too much going on now that we don't understand." He shared a look with Morgana. "I fear that things have rather gotten ahead of us."

"We can only go forward," Morgana said. "Given Alex's concerns about the Darkness, we should brief the Old Ones who are allies. Shiva may face more problems in the future if the Demons find a way past the Iron Gates. They may become desperate enough to attempt what the Sídhe did. The last thing we need is diseased and corrupted Demons in the Iron Realm."

Alex waited for Thor to say something to offer context or for a memory to push through. Nothing came. Her mind was just her own again. She pushed down the fear starting to bubble up in her chest. Was this just exhaustion or had the Tree of Reality done something to her? She just... didn't know how to feel about not hearing the others. They weren't a comfort. They were annoying, but... Alex shook her head and focused on Merlin and Morgana again.

"How do we sort all of this out?" Morgana asked. "Scrying isn't helping and we can't possibly send Alex back into the Tree of Reality without understanding the side effects." Morgana reached over and squeezed Alex's hand. "And if Alex is right about the effect the Darkness has..."

"I still say it looks like the poison," Alex said firmly. The older mages looked at her, their faces blank, but their eyes dark with worry. "That really is what it looked like."

"If Cyrridven was alive then I would ask her," Merlin said softly. Mournfully, he lowered his eyes, and Alex was sharply aware of a small flutter of guilt over the Old One's death. "She probably knew more about magic than anyone."

"Odin is our best bet, then," Morgana said. "The Tree of Reality became a major part of Norse Mythology; he may have come across something."

"From what source?" Merlin asked. "Odin has never had the sort of connection to the Iron Realm that Cyrridven had."

"Where did the story of Lancelot and Guinevere come from?" Morgana countered. "Merlin, myths, and legends have emerged that are correct without us. Likely from mages we never knew about. We can't afford to discount anything at this point."

"A fair statement, Morgana." Merlin nodded and smiled at Alex. "I'll call Sif and see if she can put us in contact with her father." His smile widened and his eyes glittered for a moment. "I admit, the idea of Odin on a cell phone is amusing. But Sif has adjusted quickly."

"She always was a clever being," Morgana replied.

"Indeed, I'll see what I can learn," Merlin said. He smiled at Alex once more. "Alex, please avoid using magic for at least two days. I want to check that spot again then and make sure it isn't larger."

"We'll have to keep an eye on it," Morgana agreed sternly. "As for the Tree of Reality, I'll review my memories and see if I can scry anything useful. Check with Nicki on your way out, I'm certain that she's watching the book."

"I can tell when I'm being dismissed, Alex." Merlin huffed slightly, only to get a dismissive glance from Morgana. His smile softened and his eyes took on a worried glint. "Take care and rest. We'll do everything we can."

"I'll be more careful," Alex promised.

Merlin hesitated, just watching her for another moment. Morgana said something to him in their language. Alex was tempted to try and understand it. Her magic even started to rise in her chest, but she held back, remembering Merlin's words. Yet, she had the distinct impression that Morgana had promised to update him as soon as she left for the night. Then Merlin left the room and Alex could only review he and Morgana's conversation.

Nothing about the poison being connected to the Darkness, Alex noted. They still didn't seem willing to address that. Then again, she didn't understand how it could be connected. If Cyrridven was alive, they could have asked her. The original potion had been taught to Merlin by her. The original poison had come from the first brewing of the potion that had helped Merlin connect deeply with the Iron Realm and learn of the Iron Soul. It just seemed odd that a potion meant to help mages would also create something so dangerous. Just one more thing that she didn't understand.

It nagged at her. Alex frowned. It was like something was trying to push through. The thought was right there, but too blurry for her to see clearly. Words danced on the tip of her tongue. In her chest her heart fluttered and her magic flared up, reacting to something intangible and just out of Alex's reach.

A sharp pain jolted down the right side of Alex's head. She flinched and grabbed her head before remembering that Morgana was there. The older mage touched her shoulder.

"Alex? Are you alright?"

"Just a headache," Alex said.

"You've never been very prone to them before."

"Yeah, well, it's been a very long day at this point," Alex grumbled. "Sorry, I guess I'm just tired."

"I'll leave soon," Morgana promised. She reached into her bag and pulled out her phone. "One last thing. I need a photo of the spot. We need to keep track of if it grows."

Morgana pulled on another glove. With gentle motions, she tilted Alex's head back just enough that the light in the center of the ceiling would help illuminate the picture. She stayed as still as she could while Morgana held open her eye. There were three quick clicks from the phone and then Morgana let go of her face.

"I'll get out of your way," Morgana said. She kissed Alex's forehead again. "Please be careful. If you feel anything like that compulsion again, yell for the others." Alex said nothing and Morgana sighed. "We'll update you as soon as we hear from Sif." Morgana walked to the doorway, only to stop and turn back. "Alex, would you please leave the door open? Not just for my sake. You worried the others as well."

"I will," Alex promised softly. "I'm sorry."

"I know, sweetheart," Morgana said. "I know."

Then she headed down the stairs leaving Alex alone. Exhaling slowly, Alex rolled over and picked up Galahad. She ran her hand over the stuffed toy carefully. There was no sign of glass. The others had been thorough with their spells. Hugging him to her chest, she laid back on her bed and closed her eyes. For the first time, she tried to reach out for the voices. She called to Arto and then Thor and then Lokpal. But none of them answered her.

21

Oberon

1 518 C.E. Rhineland

It was too cold to be outside. Ice hung from the branches of trees and large drifts of snow clung to the cold earth. Michel's breath wafted on the air with every exhale. The stillness in the air was worse. He shivered under his cloak, wishing he had something a bit heavier, but it was wetter than they'd expected. Michel softly cleared his throat and looked over at Morgana and Merlin.

They were unmoving, still as statues and watching the trees with sharp, careful eyes. He wanted to pace, wanted to fidget, but stayed as still as he could manage. Michel didn't understand how Merlin and Morgana could look so calm.

"When will he be here?" he asked softly. His voice was much louder than he meant it to be.

"We'll see if he comes at all," Morgana replied.

"I'm confident that he will," Merlin said. "The Fae have gained no ground in the past few years. All Oberon has achieved is the death of many Fae."

"He's almost done us a favor," Morgana said. Michel turned to find her smiling a little. "The concentration of Fae has certainly dropped."

"Morgana," Merlin scolded. "You and I both understand their anger."

"Being angry does not excuse attempting to break the world and reveal the whole messy nature of magic to the crowns of Europe." Morgana adjusted her cloak and scanned the trees again. "You want to pity them, that is your business, Merlin. I'm too irritated with their childishness at this point to feel sympathy."

Somehow the air went even colder. Michel almost asked the question about Morgana's history with the Fae and why she was so against them. It forced itself onto the tip of his tongue. Tightening his jaw, Michel held it in and grit his teeth together. Morgana had never shared.

"I'm surprised you agreed to this," Merlin said.

"He suddenly wants to talk," Morgana sneered. "But if he tries to trap us, I will not hold back."

"I would never ask such a thing of you." Merlin's tone was light and his presence was reassuring, but it did nothing to cut the tension.

Every sound was amplified. The wind rustled the wet, dead leaves that were exposed here and there. Tree branches creaked, and something moved on the hillside. Michel's heart was racing. He was too old to be so frightened, so worried. They'd faced Fae on many occasions. He wasn't a child anymore, but Oberon was their leader. The Fae adored him, and now Michel was going to meet him.

If this wasn't a trap.

Then a figure appeared on the distant hillside, wearing a long cloak with the hood up. It was a thin but tall figure, walking with its head lowered to protect its face from the sun. Michel inhaled slowly to calm his beating heart. This had to be a Fae. And they were alone. Tearing his eyes from the figure, he looked up at Merlin and Morgana. They were watching the newcomer intently.

No one spoke until the figure stopped a few feet away from them. Now, in the shade of a group of trees, they looked up and exposed their face. He gave them all a small, calm nod of greeting. Michel stared. The being's face was startling. Like the rest of the Fae, this one had smooth pale skin, but also a faint glow that highlighted his high cheekbones and made his violet eyes stand out vividly. Michel had the nagging sense that he was missing something, but he wasn't sure what. Instead, he focused on the leader of the Fae Rebellion in front of him.

"Greetings, Mages of the Iron Realm," he said. "I am Oberon."

"We suspected as much," Morgana said. "You have no guards?"

"My invitation to talk did promise that I would come alone. Some of my men are waiting a mile back." Oberon gestured behind him, turning away from them for a moment. Michel was stunned that he was so relaxed. "They will no doubt come looking for me if I fail to return, but I trust we can have a peaceful discussion."

Merlin cleared his throat. "We were surprised to receive your message."

"I thank you for not slaying my messenger," Oberon replied.

"He left it on the counter and fled." Morgana smiled dangerously. "So, what is it that you wanted to discuss? You were very vague."

"The situation as it stands is not positive for anyone in this realm," Oberon began. "The Fae are eager for change."

Merlin shook his head. "I'm sorry, but we do not have the ability to change the natural order of the Iron Realm. Your people come from other worlds very different from this one. Two natural orders are clashing every moment you are here."

"Your little war is going nowhere," Morgana added. Merlin's shoulders tightened at her words, and Michel could tell he wanted to sigh. "Your people are getting out of control."

"I only seek to build a better world," Oberon said. His tone was measured. "I am aware of where you live. You are the Iron Soul Michel, raised by Merlin and Morgana and currently thirteen years old." Oberon's arrogant smile softened. "Like our own Fae children, you have had to grow up very fast." Then he looked back at Merlin and Morgana. "Yet, we have not attacked you at your home. Things are not as out of control as you may believe. The highway robbery situation is unpleasant, but it is allowing us to raise funds."

"For what end?" Merlin pressed. "Hire an army to help you take a city?"

"Nothing so violent." Oberon sounded surprised at the suggestion. "No, my goal is to raise funds in order to purchase land. A place where we can build a city for ourselves. The Americas are ripe for colonization. Purchasing a ship and supplies would be an ideal way for us to escape the shadows of Europe and create something for ourselves."

Michel looked at Merlin and Morgana hopefully, but they were both staring at Oberon in shock. "That won't work," Merlin said. "It doesn't deal with the problem of people noticing you, or the rise in magic that so many of you being together causes."

"Surely that isn't a bad thing," Oberon countered. "Magic being plentiful makes you more powerful."

"Yes, but that power comes with responsibility," Merlin nearly growled. "Magic is the world trying to fight back. If you create a situation that makes the very world fight back, then don't you think we are obligated to step in?"

"You've left the communities alone for hundreds of years." Oberon was frowning, a furrow of frustration and confusion between his eyes. "Why is this so different?"

"They weren't a problem," Morgana insisted. Her hands were clutching her cloak tightly. "They were small communities that didn't cause problems. We left them alone as an act of mercy, and at the moment you are making me regret it. A large number of Fae all together is dangerous, and I will not ignore it even if your intentions are well-meaning! Things could too easily turn dangerous to the Iron Realm and humanity, who are my concern!"

Shaking himself, Merlin gave Oberon an imploring look. "We have no idea what the potential ramifications of a large population in one place would be. It could unravel part of the natural order due to too many of you enforcing yours in an area. We just don't know, and we can't gamble with the world."

"Oberon, this needs to stop," Michel said. His tongue felt heavy. He wasn't sure what he should say. It was Merlin who had a gift of speech. "I don't want to fight any of you."

"I don't wish to fight either, Michel," Oberon said. Something in his voice shifted. It became sad and lighter for a moment, but then deepened once again. "But surely you can understand why we are willing to fight."

Michel wasn't sure how to respond. Oberon was just watching him, an expression of patience and calm on his face. Yet, once again, something seemed off. The soft glow taunted Michel, and his magic churned. Maybe it was just something about Oberon.

"As peaceful as you may want your army to be," Merlin said. "We've had to kill dozens of them in the past year. They've killed humans and even raided a small town. If rumors start spreading then they will start hunting you down."

"Yes... that was unfortunate," Oberon said. "They were told to avoid violence. I am sorry that they failed to listen to my instructions."

"You aren't listening!" Morgana huffed. "Disperse your army. Send them home!"

"I can't." Oberon's voice wavered for a moment and he looked at the ground, his shoulders dropping an inch. "It is too late for such a thing. When I found them, they were already seeking blood and violence, their frustrations boiling over. I sought to direct that energy into something productive. If I end the plan now then I have no doubt that they will attack the nearest city in a vain attempt to get what they want." Oberon straightened up, his features determined. "No, they will follow me, and I can build a future without shadows or fighting."

Michel wanted to believe him. It twisted in his chest when he saw the light in Oberon's eyes, but an instinct warned him that Oberon was wrong. Merlin's word about the natural order rang loudly in his head. What they wanted didn't matter: there was only the cold reality of the Iron Realm and those who weren't supposed to be here.

"Oberon, I wish you could," Merlin said gently. "But I doubt you can."

Oberon's eyes flashed, the light fading into anger. Without a word, Oberon raised his right hand and held it palm up. Golden sparks flared around his hand, creating a brilliant glow all around him. There was a sharp, almost pained cry from both Merlin and Morgana.

"You have magic?" Morgana gasped.

"I do," Oberon replied. Magic crackled around his fingertips creating flashes of light. "Stand down mages. I do not wish to fight you."

"Never!"

Morgana threw her arms forward. Silver light flooded the space between her and Oberon. Michel flinched, drawing back from fear at the sudden release of power. But a wall of golden light held Morgana's attack back. Oberon's calm expression was gone. Instead, the Fae's face was tight with concentration, but there was still the hint of a smile around his mouth. Like he was enjoying this. The light changed and Oberon suddenly stepped to the side. The silver light blasted past him, crashing through two trees, felling them both.

"You really should be more careful," Oberon scolded Morgana. "Anger will not help you."

"What are you?" Morgana demanded. "The Sídhe haven't had magic in centuries!'

"I do not consider myself a Sídhe. None of my people do," Oberon said. "We have been here for centuries. We are born here. We grow up here and live our lives. We find our mates and raise our children here. Sídhean is a long way away. It is closed to us, sealed behind gates of iron and your magic. Why would I consider myself a Sídhe?" Oberon's smile changed again, and his eyes glittered with amusement.

"That does not explain your magic," Merlin said. He put a hand on Morgana's shoulder and studied Oberon carefully. "Or is this some sort of trick?"

Oberon smoothed his expression to calm and neutral. For a moment, Michel thought that he was going to reveal something, but the Fae shook his head and stepped back.

"This is necessary," Oberon said. "The Fae want this. They need this. They need to build a home, a real home in this world." The amusement was gone, instead there was now an undercurrent of anger that made Michel shiver.

"We have told your followers of the danger," Merlin said. "These robberies, these crimes need to stop before you draw the attention of the army. If they find you and realize that you aren't human, it could mean the destruction of the Fae across all of Europe. The paranoia and panic would be devastating. I don't know how old you are and I doubt you'll tell us, but Morgana and I have seen what happens when cities panic. We lived through the plagues and the blame and the terror. You do not want to inflict that on your people."

"No," Oberon said. "No, I do not, but what else can we do?"

"Live quietly," Merlin said. "That's all you can do. I know it isn't fair, but it is the best option for everyone. This is the Iron Realm. It belongs to humans, not to the Fae or the Old Ones or the Demons or any other beings that have slipped into the world. You being here makes the very realm itself fight back. Wanting it to be otherwise will not make it so."

For a moment Michel feared that Oberon would lash out. His calm mask cracked, his teeth clashed together and his fingers tightened into fists. Michel braced himself for a tantrum. It was odd. One more thing that didn't seem to fit, but he had no idea what to make of it.

"I don't think we have anything more to discuss," Oberon said. There was a flicker of hesitation in his eyes, but then he took a step back. "I hope that we meet again under better circumstances."

Staying perfectly still, Michel watched him go. Around them, the area remained silent and still. There was no sign of Fae charging in to attack them. No sign of Oberon about to turn back and use his magic. Birds chirped in the distance, and he heard soft dripping nearby as melting snow hit the ground. Oberon walked up the far hill and in a few more moments vanished from their sight. Licking his lips, Michel flexed his fingers just in case. But nothing came. There was no attack.

"He's in over his head," Merlin said. A deep sigh escaped him and he shook his head. "He has no idea what is happening."

"Started a movement that's spiraling out of his control," Morgana agreed. "He won't be able to keep control of them, Merlin. They've already proven they're an old barn full of dried hay. All it needs is a spark to explode."

"I know." Merlin put a hand on Morgana's shoulder. "I know, but we have to be careful. We attack him and they will absolutely attack the city." His voice softened and he leaned closer to her. Michel could barely hear his next words. "He has magical abilities. I can't imagine that his followers don't look at that as a sign that it's time for them to change the world." Merlin released Morgana's shoulder and rubbed his eyes. "I wish that were possible."

"His magic could be a side effect of the large population," Morgana said.

"Maybe," Merlin agreed softly. "But before we start attacking the Fae in hopes of stopping this and urge more to take up arms, let us try building more Iron Gates. It is possible that a weak point has opened in the area."

"I doubt it," Morgana said. "Last time we checked-"

'That was ten years ago," Merlin said gently. Turning to Michel, he reached over and placed his hand on the top of his head. "Besides... it be will be good magic practice for Michel. He's old enough to be learning a trade. Blacksmithing isn't a bad choice."

Morgana was eying the hill, her whole body tense. She and Merlin exchanged a long look and Merlin shook his head. Then the old mage gently pushed Michel towards their wagon, urging him to move. Twisting to watch Morgana, Michel stumbled a little, but saw her sigh and start to follow them back towards the wagon. It seemed they were done here.

22

Splintered

Tapping the end of his pencil against the scarred wood of the table, Aiden just stared at the whiteboard on the far wall of the study room. It was quiet. In the corner of his eye, he could see people walking past the small room in the library. Things weren't busy yet. Midterms were still a week away, and panic hadn't settled in.

That was fine with him: it meant that there wasn't competition for the rooms and he could have some privacy. His laptop sat open, but it had long since gone to sleep. Guilt crept up on Aiden. He should be at home. Either with his friends or his family. But Morgana had shown up last night after Nicki's frantic call and was hovering around Alex. They'd had conversations with Nicki about making bracelets or something similar for Alex to wear to suppress her magic, though Merlin had expressed concerns.

They'd spoken of the Iron Trishula and contacting Shiva only for Merlin and Morgana to shoot down that idea for the time being. Officially, they had concerns about Shiva leaving an area still dealing with a recent Demon invasion, but Aiden couldn't help but wonder if there was something else. He didn't blame the Grand Mages for their hesitation. Everyone was worried and no one wanted to make things worse.

Knowing that the spot in Alex's eye was mirrored by one in Arthur's was terrifying as it was.

Aiden should be at home, but he didn't want to be right now. He wasn't in the mood for fruitless worry induced research. Aiden was pretty confident that nothing in mythology books or online was going to answer this question. It was new and terrifying territory.

Eyes were important. Maybe that was what they needed to focus on. Some kind of magic that entered through the eye. Again, he wasn't sure where to look. Internet searches hadn't turned up anything that looked relevant. And New Age stores and forums weren't Aiden's idea of a good source.

Something was going on. Aiden bit his lower lip and pushed the tip of the pencil down against the wood. The thin tip snapped off and he brushed it to the ground. Alex wasn't hearing the voices anymore. On the surface that should be good, but such a sudden change was freaking him out. There was an ugly little suspicion, that Alex was infected with some sort of magical curse thanks to Arthur, bubbling at the back of his mind. Yet Aiden doubted Arthur's ability to come up with such a thing on his own.

Then again, he'd created those damn amulets. Aiden broke some more pencil lead and glared at his laptop. The screen was dark. Not that he had any idea of what to try to research. This was all new, and there wasn't any precedent to help them. Aiden hated it. Suddenly, the door to the study room swung open and someone came in.

"Go away," he grumbled without looking up. "There are still lots of rooms open. I don't want company."

"I'm sorry to hear that, Aiden," a familiar female voice said.

It was Robin. She was dressed in an oversized Ravenslake hoodie with her hair in cornrows. It was a different look for her, but Aiden recovered from his surprise quickly. Shaking himself, he sat up a bit straighter in his chair.

"Hi, Robin. Sorry, I was a million miles away."

"I can leave if you like." Robin's voice was gentle, and she was smiling softly. He took that as a good sign that she hadn't taken it personally. "I think you were more than distracted."

"No," he said quickly. "I mean, you're right, but no, you don't need to leave. Maybe company is what I need." He gestured to the chair across from him. "Sorry about snapping."

"It's okay."

"No, it really isn't." Aiden shook his head. "I really am sorry."

"Again, it really is okay." Robin sat down, putting her bag on the chair next to her. "Are you alright, Aiden?"

"Me? I'm fine."

"But?" Robin pressed.

"But one of my roommates is having a rough time," Aiden said. "Last night we found something... uh, it could be a bad sign."

"Like cancer or something?" Robin asked.

"Hopefully nothing that bad," Aiden said. "We just don't have answers yet."

"Ah, the scary phase of a problem," Robin said. "I'm sorry, Aiden."

"Scared... maybe," he admitted. It was a touch embarrassing to say, but Robin didn't seem ready to judge him. "She's been... acting weird, I guess. She's been a bit different for a while now, but lately it's like she's either obsessed or staring off into space."

"She must be thinking of something very deeply," Robin said.

"Maybe, I don't know. A lot has happened recently. Alex lost her... her whole family." Robin's eyes widened and her smile vanished before she nodded with sympathy. "We're all she has now. Her personality has just been uneven lately."

"Grief is a powerful thing."

"I'm not sure that this is grief," Aiden said. "Then again... she never really grieved properly either." He frowned, disliking the idea. "I'm not sure. But... I want ..."

"You want to help but don't know how," Robin suggested gently. Her expression was sad and understanding. "You're trying to figure out something you can do or say that will make things better, but don't even know where to start."

"Yeah." Aiden exhaled. "Yeah, that sounds right. I know that something is wrong, but I can't put my finger on it and don't know what I can do."

"Do your other roommates have thoughts?"

"They're... working on something," Aiden said. "But it doesn't feel like the right direction to me." Shaking his head, he struggled for the words to explain it without revealing the big secrets. "But I don't want to sit there and sulk. I hoped that my homework would at least distract me."

"You're not going to get anything done tonight," Robin said. "Maybe you should go home and rest."

"Sorry I'm such bad company."

"You're not." Robin grinned at him with bright eyes. "I find you very pleasant, Aiden. You're just struggling with what to do right now." Robin lowered her eyes for a moment, a shadow falling over her features. "I've been there and done that. My attempt was something of a disaster."

"What happened?" Aiden asked. He wished he could take back the question as soon as it left his lips. "I mean, if you want to talk about it."

"Maybe some other time," Robin replied. But she didn't look as sad now. "I was younger then, and too arrogant and too reckless."

"Sounds like your teenage years were wild."

A grin took over Robin's face as her eyes lit up with real amusement. "Yeah, they were."

"You're probably right about going home," Aiden said.

"If you'd like to stay, I certainly don't mind the company," Robin said. "I still don't know many people yet."

"I suppose it is a bit hard coming to a new school," Aiden said. "Uh, I didn't ask before, but are you a freshman?"

"Yes," Robin agreed. Aiden scanned her face, trying to decide her age. She looked a bit older than the usual freshman and didn't talk like she was fresh out of her parents' house. "I'm afraid that I had to spend the last two years or so playing catch up." Robin's expression was calm and maybe a touch wistful. "I'm afraid my education was spotty at best."

"Sorry to hear you had trouble," Aiden said carefully. "But good for you for getting into college and not giving up." Holding back a flinch, Aiden considered smacking himself. He sounded like an idiot, but Robin just looked amused. "Uh…"

"It's fine," Robin said. "I know you meant it as a compliment, and thank you. It was a lot of work and I'm not embarrassed by the need for it." She pulled another book out of her bag and grinned, her whole face lighting up. "I'm just happy to have a chance to learn so much. There's so much knowledge at your fingertips now. It's an exciting time to be able to focus on learning."

"I understand that," Aiden agreed.

"Oh, I've been meaning to ask, any relation to Professor Bosco?"

"He's my father. Are you in one of his classes?"

"Chemistry 101," Robin replied. "He's a very good teacher. Do you plan on being a professor?"

"No, I don't think I have the temperament for it," Aiden said. "I'd like to use my degree to work on electrical projects. Designing, troubleshooting, that sort of thing. It depends on what sort of job I can find after school, I suppose."

"Fair enough."

Robin gave him another smile and opened her book. Aiden watched her for a long moment, but she didn't look up at him. Finally, he swallowed and tried to focus on his own work. Nothing jumped off the page and he just kept rereading the same sentence over and over. He knew that he had a project to work on, but there was no drive. Aiden glanced at his laptop but made no move to use it. On the wall above them, the clock kept ticking softly.

"Are you sure this is where you want to be?" Robin asked without taking her eyes off her book.

"Not sure."

"Go home, Aiden," Robin said. This time she raised her eyes to meet his. They were twinkling a little in the fluorescent lights. "But how about coffee tomorrow morning? I have a free block at 8."

"Yeah!" Aiden swallowed when Robin's smile widened. "Coffee sounds nice." He stood up so fast that he banged his knee on the underside of the table. Sheepishly, he rubbed the back of his neck. "Uh... you're probably right about me heading home."

"It's not that late," Robin added. "Plenty of time to try and clear the air a little."

It was hard not to grin like an idiot despite the pain radiating through his knee. A dozen questions for Robin danced on the tip of his tongue, but he decided quickly not to push it. As weird as it seemed, he had a date of some sort in the morning. Grabbing his things, he packed them up while trying not to make a fool of himself. Robin smiled at her book, making a point of not watching him.

"Thank you," he said. He stopped at the door of the room. "Thanks for listening and, well, thanks."

"You're welcome," Robin said. "Bookend Coffee tomorrow at 8?"

"Bookend," he repeated, realizing that they hadn't said where earlier. "Got it, I'll see you in the morning."

His knee still ached a bit as he headed out. Excitement fluttered in his chest and he really wanted to go back and talk more with Robin, but she was right. He wouldn't settle until he'd checked on the others. Sulking wasn't going to help, especially not if he couldn't even manage to get any homework done. Working to straighten out his thoughts, Aiden stepped out into the darkness of the night. He almost cursed himself. It was autumn now: he had to be mindful of when the sun went down. Arthur already had Fae attacking them during the late hours of the day, but longer nights would only make things easier for them.

It was a long walk to the parking lot where his car waited. With every step, his mind whirled and tried to figure out the solution to their current problem. The urge to fix it battered at his skull, but Aiden had no idea what to do. Letting the cool air wash over his face, he tried to take a step back and consider the situation as an outsider would.

Alex wasn't hearing the voices anymore. She hadn't always heard them, so they weren't a critical part of who she was. Yet, they'd been with her ever since they finally finished Arto's burial at Stonehenge. Tradition stated that the soul resided in the head. They'd been operating under the assumption that something had lingered in Arto, some fragment of soul that had finally been transferred to Alex.

But that was a very mystical assumption. He was a mage, but magic had rules. It had a reason for being and he couldn't lose sight of that. Maybe contact with another creature like itself had completed a circuit, or merely switched something on inside of Alex? If that was the case, then the question of what turned it back off took on even more importance. Aiden unlocked his truck, his mind turning over this new idea. It was worth more consideration.

There wasn't much traffic in the parking lot and he quickly pulled out into the street. Aiden's fingers tapped on the steering wheel. He did feel a bit better now. Smiling, he wondered what it was about Robin that made her so easy to talk to. Maybe he'd really just needed to talk to someone who wasn't a mage.

The porch light was on when he pulled into the driveway. He could see the shadow of a figure moving through the living room window against the closed curtains. They were pacing, by the looks of it. That probably wasn't a good sign, but he tightened his grip on the strap of his backpack and headed inside. Setting his bag down on the bench by the door, he called out a quick hello. He inhaled the scent of brownies and his mouth started watering.

Nicki poked her head into the entry and smiled at him. "Hey, welcome home. Jenny's baking again. I approve of this development."

"I don't," Jenny shouted from the kitchen. "I don't spend enough time in the gym to have this many baked goods around."

"Everything okay?" Aiden asked Nicki.

Her lips curled up on one side into a knowing smirk. "Yeah, no new disasters to report. You?"

"Had some thoughts. Didn't get any work done. I have a date tomorrow though. I think it's a date."

"Oh?" Nicki's face lit up and he felt a hundred times better. "Is she cute?"

"Yeah, and nice. I don't know her well yet, but she's really nice."

"I'll expect details."

"It's coffee in the morning, so you won't get them right away."

"Texting," Nicki said. "It's a wonderful thing." Stepping forward, she kissed his cheek. "I'm glad you're back."

Nicki gave him a look, one that silently warned him to not go sulking off alone again. She knew exactly what he'd been doing. Then she vanished into the living room. He could hear the TV and walked over slowly to see what was going on. Nicki and Avani were making themselves comfortable on the sofa and an unfamiliar show was starting to play onscreen. Aiden's lips quirked into a smile and he headed for the kitchen.

Lance was leaning against the counter, smiling softly at Jenny. There was a hint of flour on her cheeks and her hair was piled up on her head in a messy bun. Without warning, Lance leaned forward and kissed Jenny's far cheek. She grinned but glanced Aiden's way sheepishly. That was a good sign and he started to relax.

There was no sign of Alex, but everyone was calm. The house was peaceful so he told himself to relax. Books were piled up on the dining room table. A notebook lay empty and two tablets were discarded to the side. Apparently their attempts at research had gone no better than his attempt at school work. Not wanting to disturb the others, Aiden headed downstairs after snagging a fresh brownie.

Bran was seated in his desk chair, staring at nothing. Only one of the ceiling lamps was on. Bran's computer was off and there was an open mythology book lying on his bed. Bran's frown consumed his whole face. He was glaring down at the floor pensively, his chin resting against his right hand. Sparks of yellow magic were faint around his left, which tapped against his thigh. They were faint, but there. Aiden hesitated, wondering if he should just leave his friend alone with his thoughts. Yet he stepped closer. Robin hadn't left him alone despite his dark mood, and he barely knew her, so he certainly owed his friends more than that.

"Hey," he greeted softly. Aiden thumped his feet a little as he walked over to his bed, giving Bran extra warning. "You look ready to set something on fire."

"That's your thing," Bran replied.

"I suppose so." Aiden slowly unpacked his bag, watching Bran all the while. "Where's Alex?"

"Working on homework in her room. We tried to research for a bit but didn't get anywhere. I think it just made Alex uncomfortable."

"I can see that. Sorry you didn't have any luck."

"We're missing something," Bran said. "It's there. I know it is, but it's just out of my reach."

"Have you tried scrying?"

Bran flinched, guilt flashing across his face and Aiden's stomach tightened. "Yes," Bran said. "I tried scrying to see if I could find out what was wrong with Alex. To see what she saw in the Tree of Reality... The magic pushed back against me. It didn't just not show me, it pushed me away."

"Oh... did Alex-"

"No, that's the thing." Bran's eyes were wide as he flung his hands around. "She didn't notice! Her magic reacted; I'm sure it was hers, but she didn't notice. I'm not sure what to make of it. Maybe some sort of magical defense system for the Iron Soul." Bran shivered. "I haven't had a vision, but I've got a bad feeling about this. I know that the voices are... strange, but I can't shake this bad feeling I have. It's all got to be connected: Alex's eye, Arthur's eye, and the muted voices. It has to be connected."

"I... I had a thought too," Aiden said. His good mood was quickly vanishing. "About what you guys said happened at Stonehenge. That's when the voices started, right?"

"That's the assumption."

"What if... what if there was some kind of circuit that got flipped on then?" Aiden said. It was hard to find the right words. "When you think about it, having an important reincarnation system like the Iron Soul without memories seems weird. Merlin and Morgana help, but they aren't always around."

"It is odd," Bran agreed. "But I don't have memories of the other Bran. Lance and Jenny don't have theirs either. I'd hate to think that having memories was the way it was supposed to be and it only now started working. It makes the fact that it's gone now all the worse."

"If it's true though, then it means that something has flipped the switch off," Aiden said. "Some kind of magic that Alex was exposed to in the Tree of Reality."

Bran didn't say anything. He pressed his lips together tightly and resumed glaring at the floor. Aiden swallowed and slumped onto his bed. Helplessness was the worst. The idea at the back of his head was still trying to form. Pulling on his magic, he waved his hand and sent the bright red sparks to Bran's bed. They swept up the book and brought it to him. Checking the cover quickly, he ignored Bran's gaze. It was a book on Irish mythology. With a sigh, he laid out on his bed and started to flip through the pages in search of something that would help his strange ideas come together. They needed an explanation, and they needed it soon.

23

Dreamscape

This was a dream. Or at least something similar. Alex told herself that as the wide field opened before her. Overhead a storm was churning. The smell of rain filled the air, along with a hint of ozone. Pausing, Alex flexed her toes in her shoes and raised a hand to touch her face. It felt real. Her skin was warm and a touch clammy beneath her fingertips. But this was all still in her head; she had to remember that.

The last thing she remembered was going to bed after an evening jog and a shower. It had been a quiet day in classes, and somehow, she'd managed a good grade on a recent paper. Jenny and Lance had been out on a date. Avani and Nicki had been outside playing in the autumn leaves by the light of the porch lamp. Bran and Aiden had been downstairs in their geek cave and Timothy had already turned in for the night. She hadn't gone anywhere. This had to be a dream, but the tickle of the wind against her cheek felt very real.

Staying where she was, Alex looked around and took in the landscape. The light breeze was rustling the tall grass. It ran through her hair, which was hanging loosely around her shoulders. A roll of thunder made her look up. The dark clouds were churning and threatening rain. Alex didn't mind. A soft haze surrounded her, cradling and protecting her. She was safe here.

Tension rolled out of Alex's body. She stretched out her arms and inhaled the sharp, fresh air. Ozone tingled on her tongue, and Alex made herself take her first step. Her footfalls were cushioned by the thick grass. Finally, she looked down at herself. She was in jeans, simple sneakers, and a Ravenslake t-shirt. Her hands were her own, and Alex flexed her fingers.

Looking around again, Alex shrugged and started walking. Standing still wouldn't do her any good, and at least it wasn't that damn boat. Cuthbert's ship still showed up in far more nightmares than Alex ever wanted to admit to having. Some thunder rumbled overhead, and Alex wondered what rain would feel like in a dream.

So, she walked. The landscape had some shape to it as she headed down a slight slope. The long grass tickled at her fingertips and palms as she held out her hands. It was peaceful

Inhaling and exhaling with slow measured breaths, Alex let herself slip into a near meditative state. She'd been neglecting letting her mind rest over the past few weeks. Then she caught sight of something, or rather someone. Standing in the distance was a cloaked figure. Alex sped up and walked towards them.

"Hello, Alex." His voice was achingly familiar. To her surprise, she knew him at once.

"Arto." There was no doubt who he was as she stepped up next to him.

Arto was taller than Alex had envisioned, and older than he sounded when Merlin and Morgana spoke of him. He had a kind face, with warm eyes that were similar in shape to Morgana's and brown hair that was tied out of his face. His clothing was strange and yet familiar at the same time, with the simple tunic and cloak barely gaining a glance from Alex. On his back was a sword with a golden hilt in a leather scabbard.

"Cathanáil," she whispered.

"Yes," Arto agreed. Smiling at her, he raised his right hand and pulled the sword free. "I created this sword in my youth. It was a turning point in my life."

"It is amazing," Alex replied. Her voice was soft, barely above a whisper, but Arto heard her.

"Thank you." He kept the sword free, but Alex didn't worry. Alex knew he'd never harm her. "I'm glad that you were able to recover her. It is best that she is in trustworthy hands." Arto's smile faded and he turned his gaze back to her. "Why are you here, Alexandra Adams?"

"Something... something is in my head. Something that doesn't belong."

Arto stopped, his eyes turning to a point on the horizon. Alex followed his gaze. The storm was growing worse, but there was something out there. A point of light no larger than a star in the midnight sky.

"Yes," Arto said. "There is."

"Didn't you know?"

Arto didn't answer. He frowned at the question, almost as if he was confused. Fear radiated up Alex's chest. How could he be surprised? This was all in her head. They were just... echoes... collections of memories. She pushed that thought away. She didn't know. Alex had no words for what they were other than the voices of her past.

"Are you all here?" Alex asked softly.

"Yes: all those you know, and many more you don't," Arto said softly. "I was the first."

"And I'm the latest," Alex sighed.

"You are the last."

"Seriously?" Alex scoffed. "This isn't a movie. We don't have to be cryptic."

"We are blocked," Arto said. "There is a wall forming. We can't go past it." He shook his head and frowned. "Something is wrong, Alex. You need to hear us. We need to be with you."

"I know." The whisper escaped her as tears tried to well up in her eyes.

Arto sheathed Cathanáil and stepped forward. Her prior life pulled her into a tight hug, wrapping his arms around her. Holding back a whimper, Alex buried her face in the rough fabric of his tunic. It smelled of smoke. Thunder rolled and Alex shuddered. Releasing her, Arto stepped back from her and vanished in the blink of an eye. She looked around, searching for him, but he was gone, leaving her alone in the field while the storm grew overhead. Lightning flashed through the sky in the distance, branching out through the dark clouds like a tree.

Closing her eyes, Alex wrinkled up her nose and tried to change the dream. This wasn't fun anymore. She wanted to do something else. Magic fluttered in her chest, but a vice tightened around her lungs a moment later. It hurt. She tensed and opened her eyes. Arto was gone. There was no sign he'd been there. Everything was darker now. The clouds were thicker overhead and the wind was stronger. Licking her lips, Alex started walking in the direction that Arto had been looking. Emotions churned in her chest, but she didn't want to examine them. Never sounded like a good time to unravel this new knot.

She didn't see anything. This plain of grass went on forever. It reminded her of a road trip as a child through the Midwest. There'd been nothing to see for miles, and she and her brothers had wound up all sleeping slumped against each other in the back seat. The memory brought a pang to Alex's chest, but nothing around her changed. Her magic fluttered again and Alex quietly admitted that maybe this wasn't a standard dream.

Waiting, Alex watched the clouds churn overhead and listened to the deep rumble of thunder. Nothing happened. Alex gave up and started walking again, heading in the same direction as before. She kept her hands closer now, not playing with the tall grass. Her earlier calm was gone. Another figure came into view, but they were on the ground and much closer. Cautiously, she approached.

The man was lounging on the ground, sprawled on the grass and staring up into the dark cloud. His long hair was bleached blond with a faint hint of red at the roots. A familiar hammer was on the ground next to him, within easy reach. He was younger than he should be. Alex knew that he'd been a life that had died of old age.

"Hello, Thor," she greeted.

"Hello, Alex." Thor didn't look at her and just breathed in. "Storm is coming."

"Pretty sure that's it's already here." Curiosity tugged at Alex along with the sense that something wasn't right. "What's going on?"

"You came looking for something," Thor replied. He shrugged a little, but still didn't move from his spot. "Even if you didn't mean to."

"You're too young," Alex said. "You died old."

"I did," Thor agreed. "But this was me when my magic was at its peak. In my later years, I didn't use much magic. I just kept the peace. It's a pity that the Dvegers are gone. They were a good lot."

"Yeah, but there's too many species here as it is," Alex said. Frowning, she did her best to follow that thought. "It changes the world."

"It does," Thor agreed. "Probably for the best that only males came through. Still, I liked them."

"Do you know what I came looking for?"

"Something else is in your head," Thor reminded her. "Something came through from the Tree."

"That's right," Alex said. Lightning flashed across the sky in the distance. Thunder followed a moment later, and Thor smiled. "That's why I came here... wherever here is."

"Inward," Thor said simply. "You're inside yourself. Deeper than you've ever gone. We're all here. We're with you."

"I know."

"I'm sorry you haven't heard us," Thor said. His voice was gentle and soothing. "I'm sorry you couldn't hear us. What came through from the Tree drowns us out. We couldn't warn you."

"Warn me... is it dangerous?"

"It's in your head. It's pulling strings that only the Iron Soul is meant to pull." Thor stared at the horizon. "Sounds dangerous to me."

But Thor began to fade before she could ask for clarification. He glared at his own hand as it vanished. Then he was gone, and Alex was alone. Biting her lower lip, she felt her heart beginning to beat faster and faster. Thor's words about danger and something else being in her head rattled around. In the distance, she could now see a cliff. There was nothing beyond it but a haze of storm clouds where the field of grass ended. Another crack of lightning lit up the sky above, and the answering thunder forced her to move.

Alex kept walking. There was no pain, no aches, in her legs. Grass rustled around her and the thunder boomed overhead. With every step, the air grew sharper with the smell of ozone, but Alex found it comforting. When a new figure appeared, she huffed but hurried over to them.

This man was unfamiliar to Alex. She strained her memory and found only a flash of his face. No memories sprang to mind and she frowned, displeased with being at such a loss. His skin was a warm shade of copper, and long, black hair was tied in a simple braid that hung between his shoulders. His clothing was fairly simple, made of leather with small designs worked into it. He was sitting cross-legged on the ground. Beside him was a strange metal jar with a sealed metal top. As she approached, he shifted his right hand and rested it over the top of the jar.

"Hello," Alex greeted.

"Hello." He didn't look at her, his eyes still staring off into the distance.

Alex studied him. Familiarity tugged at her enough to make her relax. He was her. Another aspect even if an unknown one.

"Uh... hello."

His lips shifted into a smile, though he still didn't look at her. "Yes, I heard you the first time."

"Who are you?"

"Another incarnation of the Iron Soul," he answered. Alex looked down at the jar curiously. "You're correct about the Darkness, Alex. It is coming: it follows the lines between the worlds, seeking the root of the tree. The very heart of creation."

"You know about it?" Alex was near breathless. "Really?"

"I do. There is much I wish I could tell you, but there isn't time. Be careful and trust your instincts. They have served us well thus far."

"But can't you-"

"I do not know the source of the Darkness," he said. "But it did slip into our world once, centuries ago. I fought it back and sealed it away the best I could. I never knew the Grand Mages," he said bluntly. "I was alone." His grip on the jar tightened and he nodded forward. "What you seek is over there. Be mindful. Things are about to change."

Alex looked at the jar again. Something tried to stir at the back of her mind. A memory tried to form. It tried to push its way forward, but it was blocked. Lightning flashed in the corner of her eye. Frustration welled up in Alex, replacing the fear from Arto and Thor's words. Turning her attention to where he was looking, Alex readied herself to ask him more about his own life and the Darkness, but he was already gone when she glanced back towards him.

Her head ached more and more with every step. Every so often something flickered up ahead and Alex braced herself for another incarnation to appear. There were many others, but only a few vague forms briefly appeared. Twice, she thought she heard her name being called on the wind, but nothing more reached her. Around her, the world grew darker and darker.

A raindrop hit her cheek with a sudden splash of cold. The world turned hazy, but it wasn't enough to wake her. Another drop hit her face and a dull drizzle began to fall from the sky. Wet grass hit her jeans, soaking her legs and weighing her down. Ahead, the cliff loomed, and Alex kept pushing forward.

Then she saw it. A light above the cliff, just hanging in the air like an orb of magic. Yet it wasn't her magic. It wasn't even really magic. It was something more, something else. Against the dark clouds beyond it, the light shone like a beacon, calling her closer and closer. Alex strained her memory. This was different. This wasn't familiar to her, but it had to come from somewhere in her memory. Dark waves churned and a rumble in the sky promised that things would only get worse. Taking a step closer to the edge, Alex admired the glitter of light at the tips of the waves. It was beautiful how they caught the last of the sunlight.

Around her, the air vibrated. Thunder crashed, louder than before, and shook the dream world. Alex's heart jumped and she looked up fearfully. The light didn't move. It did nothing. Licking her lips, Alex reached towards it. Her hand heated up as it moved closer to the light.

Cheerful pop music exploded around her. Blinking her eyes rapidly, Alex was suddenly aware of her pillow against the side of her face. On her nightstand, her phone was flashing as a pop ringtone played on a loop. Groaning, Alex reached for the phone to turn off the alarm, trying to hold onto the dream as it started to slip away. She scrambled out of the bed and grabbed the small notebook and pencil on the nightstand. Before the thought slipped away, she wrote:

Something is in my head.

24

The Dance Begins

1 518 C.E. Strasbourg, Rhineland

The shop was far too hot, and Michel was very tempted to use his magic to cool himself down. Merlin grumbled in the back, something about making a talisman that would help keep him cool. Michel really hoped that if the old man made one for himself, he'd make one for him as well. It was tempting to open the door, but the shop smelled pleasant and the streets of Strasbourg did not.

Shelves of spices and exotic wines and ales lined one wall of the shop behind the counter. Bolts of cloth were carefully packed into cabinets and shelves on the right wall of the shop. Small trinkets from far off cities and markets were displayed on tables near the door, but not so close as to make theft easy. Not that they'd ever really had a problem with that. While Merlin and Morgana were careful using their magic in the city, they did have a few spells around the shop to deter anyone looking to cheat them.

Michel navigated the broom around the legs of one table, mindful of the glassware on display. It had been quiet so far that day. though yesterday had seen several special purchases and pickups. Usually, Merlin dealt with the customers while Morgana kept herself in the back room or upstairs.

He chased down some dust clumps in a corner and swept them towards the door. Once he was sure that he had most of the dirt, he opened the door and quickly swept everything out into the street. The July sun beat down on the city, with the buildings casting long shadows. There were people hurrying down the street and movement around the different shops and businesses. The strong smell of the butcher's shop down the way hit his nose and Michel quickly shut the door.

Michel moved around the shop, tidying up anything out of order while his mind wandered. There was so much to think and worry about. They hadn't seen or heard from Oberon throughout spring. Merlin was hopeful that they'd gotten through to the Fae or at least cut off his magic with the creation of a new Iron Gate, but Morgana didn't share his optimism. Michel wasn't sure what to think.

The door opened behind him and Michel quickly turned around with a smile. It widened into a much more real expression when he saw the lanky young man with brown hair who was about his own age.

"Hi, Klaus," he greeted. "Good to see you." Extending his hand, Michel gripped Klaus' hand in welcome and they beamed at each other. "I haven't seen you in weeks."

"I know, sorry about that," Klaus apologized. "Honestly, I only offered to pick up my father's order so I could see you. I can't stay long."

"Well, I'm still glad to see you. One second and I'll get your package."

Klaus nodded and released his hand. Michel grabbed the broom and took it behind the counter. In the shelves built below the countertop were a few bundles. Small scraps of paper had names written on them and Michel quickly found the right one.

"Looks like some fabric."

"For a dress for my sister," Klaus explained with a shrug. "Probably a wedding gift." He didn't seem very interested, but leaned against the counter and pulled out the proper amount of coinage to pay for it. "Oh, did you hear about the dancing?"

"Dancing?"

"Mrs. Troffea is dancing in the street," Klaus said. "My mother heard that she won't stop. People keep trying to give her water, but it's like she's in a trance."

Michel stared at the other boy, trying to wrap his head around the words. He didn't really know Mrs. Troffea, but Morgana dealt with her from time to time. Strasbourg was much too large a city for everyone to know everyone.

"How long has this been happening?"

Klaus shrugged, but the gleam in his eye hadn't decreased. "I'm not sure. I heard some guards talking: they said she started three days ago."

"And she hasn't stopped to sleep?" Horror curled in Michel's stomach. Surely she had to stop at some point.

"No, she hasn't. A priest is praying over her and trying to get her to stop." Klaus's eyes were bright with interest.

"Don't sound so excited," Michel scolded. "She could die if she doesn't rest soon."

Klaus had the decency to flinch a little. "You're right. How haven't you heard? Have your aunt and uncle been keeping you locked up in the shop?"

"Something like that," Michel said. "There are always chores to do." Swallowing, he leaned the broom against the wall and dusted off his hands. "How is the new apprenticeship?"

"It's alright," Klaus said. "It's hard work and I don't get to work on anything interesting. Master makes the most beautiful woodwork, but I'm just sweeping up the wood scraps."

"I'm sure you have to learn a lot before you can do what he does."

"Yeah." Klaus shrugged again. "I'm learning the tools. That's something, I guess. It's just sinking in how long I'm going to be his apprentice." Then Klaus glanced around the shop. "So are you going to become an apprentice?"

"I'm not sure." Merlin had begun to teach him blacksmithing with iron, but that wasn't a true apprenticeship.

"Probably not. Since your aunt and uncle don't have children you'll inherit the shop," Klaus said. "Course, your uncle has had you helping out for years, so I suppose that's a kind of apprenticeship."

"I suppose so." Michel frowned a little. He'd never thought about it. Staying with Merlin and Morgana had always been the course of his life. He'd never considered that it might change someday. "We'll just have to see."

"They'll die someday."

Michel didn't know what to say to that. He nodded awkwardly and hoped that Klaus wouldn't dwell on it. He didn't, and started talking more about the workshop he now lived and worked in. Apparently, he still had a day off every other week to visit his mother, which was a treat. Michel nodded here and there but wasn't truly listening.

Merlin and Morgana wouldn't die someday. They had already lived for centuries. They'd never hidden that from him. Even now, they already looked younger than other people who had children his age. How long would it take for someone to ask questions about how old they were? Would they simply use magic to keep people from noticing, or would they vanish in the night? What would happen to him?

A weight settled in Michel's stomach at the thought. He loved them. They were the only parents he'd ever known, but they'd still be living long after he was gone. Did they care about him as much? There was affection to be sure. Swallowing, he reached under the counter and found his water sack. Klaus just kept babbling as he took a drink.

What would happen once Oberon was defeated? Would he keep living and working in the shop? Would Merlin and Morgana just vanish once their task was done and go back east? Would they leave the shop to him, and he'd stay, or would he go with them? Such things had never crossed his mind before, but now he ached with the weight of the questions.

"Are you listening to me?" Klaus demanded. "I only have one day every other week and I came to see you." He truly sounded hurt.

"Sorry," Michel said quickly. "I heard part of it, I promise. I just keep wondering about the dancers," he lied quickly with a sheepish smile.

Klaus' hurt melted away. "It is pretty crazy, isn't' it," he agreed. "I didn't believe Mother when she told me. I'm surprised that everyone in the city hasn't heard yet. Maybe the guards are trying to keep it quiet so there isn't a panic."

"That would make sense," Michel agreed. "But I am glad that you like your position."

"It's okay, but someday I'll make a masterpiece and have a workshop of my own," Klaus said. "You'll see."

Michel nodded, but he wasn't so sure of that. Klaus liked talking more than working. He might end up a journeyman working in someone else's workshop for the rest of his life. Then again, maybe his master would teach him how to focus. He smiled and nodded again to show his support. Klaus looked pleased, but then he picked up the bundle of cloth.

"Sorry, Michel. I should get back to my mother's. I just wanted to stop by."

"I'm glad you did." Michel smiled. "It was good to see you. Be careful on your way home."

"Don't worry so much."

Then Klaus was out the door and the shop was quiet again. Michel walked to the window and peered out at the street. Things looked normal enough, but then again, what did he expect? Even with strange things happening, life had to go on. Behind him, Michel heard a thump from the back room. He closed the shutters and put the board across to keep them shut. Then he secured the front door. Hopefully, no one else would come by, but he needed to speak with Merlin and Morgana right away.

He heard voices as he approached, low and worried, but he didn't let that stop him. In the back room, Morgana was sitting on a crate and Merlin was organizing small bottles onto shelves. This small packed room had no windows and was where the most valuable things were kept, far from the door and potential thieves. Both mages looked over at him as he entered.

"You look excited about something," Morgana said.

"Morgana, Klaus was just here and he was telling me about people dancing-"

"We've heard," Morgana said. She began pacing in the room, using the narrow aisle between the shelves. "The nobles and the priests are already talking."

"As far as anyone can tell it all started with Mrs. Troffea," Merlin said. He finished putting up the jars and bottles and turned to Michel. "But others have joined her."

"It's July," Morgana said. She came to a stop and gestured towards the door. "I can't believe that this is intentional. No one in their right mind spends that much time out in the summer sun and forgoes water, food, and sleep."

"Some sort of mania," Merlin suggested. He didn't sound convinced, and Morgana gave him a withering frown. "Yes, yes, I know. That's unlikely given the number of Fae nearby."

"This has to be Oberon's doing." Morgana shook her head and stalked out of the room. Merlin and Michel followed her. She grabbed a cloth and began wiping down the counter and shelves angrily. "His magic, whatever twisted source it is coming from caused this."

"But we made another Iron Gate," Michel protested. Then he shrank into himself, slumping his shoulders, and looking at Merlin. "Did I do it wrong?"

"No," Merlin assured him. The older mage moved closer to him and put a hand on his head, smiling sadly. "You're getting too tall for this."

"Focus, Merlin," Morgana said. Her eyes softened a touch as she glanced their way. "If it wasn't a weak point in the shields and a connection to the Sídhe Empire powering Oberon, then where is he getting his magic from? We all saw it, and now this dancing plague is taking root."

"We don't know for certain that this is Oberon's doing," Merlin said. He didn't sound convinced, and Morgana scoffed. Sighing, Merlin just shrugged.

"How many people are there?" Michel asked. He couldn't imagine people just dancing in the streets. "There can't be that many. I would have heard about it before."

"Morgana and I only learned of it yesterday," Merlin said. When Michel frowned, Merlin offered him a small smile. "We wanted to know more before we told you. I saw no reason to make you worry."

"It's hard to get details," Morgana admitted. "I've considered going over to check myself... but until we know what is going on it seems like an unnecessary risk."

"I agree." Merlin's tone was firm and clear. "This is likely a trap or an attempt to use humans as hostages."

"What about... uh, are people blaming magic yet? Is this going to trigger that war you were afraid of?"

Merlin and Morgana exchanged one of their heavy looks. He often wondered if they were using magic to speak to each other's minds, but Morgana had assured him that they merely knew each other very well. He braced himself for the answer, telling himself not to panic. There was no place for panic in a mage's heart.

"Hard to say," Merlin said. "Physicians are trying to answer the question of what is happening, but I've no doubt that anyone local who claims to know some magic is being consulted. With luck, they'll blame it on the heat or something else equally foolish."

"We can hope," Morgana said. "But clearly it is spreading. We can't just talk to the guards, Merlin. We need more information, and quickly before people truly start panicking."

"Panic isn't our only problem," Merlin said. "If it is a spell then more and more people could be pulled into it if they go too close. Human curiosity is sometimes even stronger than their survival instinct."

"So what is the plan?" Michel asked eagerly. "Can I help?"

"Tomorrow, I think I'll pay a visit to city hall." A small smile graced Merlin's face. "See what I can learn."

"I'll check the gossip with the women," Morgana added.

"And me?" They both looked at him.

"It would be best if you remained here," Merlin said. "We don't want to make it too obvious that we're investigating." He walked over to the front door and unbolted it. "If this is the work of Oberon then he'll have Fae in the city keeping an eye on things."

"But I could help."

"You will be helping," Morgana said. "If customers come in then see what they've heard. Soon it will be all anyone is talking about. Be on guard against Fae and be ready to protect yourself so we don't have to worry."

Michel wanted to protest. Oberon was active in their home city. This wasn't highwaymen miles away attacking travelers. This was home. He'd grown up here, even if he'd been born in a small village a day and a half away. Yet he didn't argue. The lines around Merlin and Morgana's eyes warned him not to. They were worried, scared even.

It took him a moment, but he realized why they were concerned. If something did happen that made the population panic about magic and they were exposed, they didn't want him with them. Swallowing, Michel nodded that he understood, and saw some of the tension leave his parents. He almost asked what they wanted him to do if something did happen, but he couldn't bring himself to ask.

This was going to change everything. He knew that much. His instincts and his magic insisted that something was going to be different very soon. Michel just hoped that it was for the best.

25

Consulting the Chalice

Steam curled out of her teacup. It was warm and solid between Alex's hands. That was good, she could focus on that. She glanced up as Morgana entered the room, taking off her scarf and coat in one smooth motion. Merlin was already there and was helping Timothy in the kitchen. She snuggled back into the couch and adjusted the blanket laying across her lap. Her feet were warm in her slippers and her pajamas were cozy. By rights, she should have felt comfortable, but a chill lingered along her spine. Alex recognized it as foreboding and wondered just what they'd find when this was all over.

She looked up at the television. The smooth black surface carried a reflection of the room, but thankfully it wasn't clear enough that she could see her eye. When Nicki had found her asleep in the living room this morning and woke her up, she'd announced that the spot was larger. Alex hadn't looked at herself yet, and didn't want to.

"I've sorted out classes for the day," Morgana said. She put her purse next to the sofa and moved closer to Alex. Leaning down, she put a hand over Alex's. "We'll sort this out."

"Indeed," Merlin added. He entered the living room with a fresh pot of tea. "Do you need more, Alex?"

"No," she replied. "I'm fine. Thanks."

"Well then," Merlin said as he sat down in an armchair. "We'll begin once Morgana reassures herself that you're not in immediate danger."

Morgana scowled, but she gently tilted Alex's chin up to inspect her eye. Holding her breath, Alex stayed as still as she could and kept her eyes open. Morgana's hands were warm despite the autumn chill outside. The exhaustion that had made her nap on the sofa had already returned with a vengeance, and she just wanted to curl up around that warmth and go back to sleep.

"Alex?" Morgana called gently.

"Just tired," Alex murmured. "Only managed a nap after the dream."

Morgana pressed her lips together tightly, a shadow in her own eyes. "The spot is larger."

Alex said nothing. She could barely swallow as Morgana's eyes bored into her own. Merlin cleared his throat and Morgana stood and moved around the sofa to lean against its back. Judging from Merlin's expression, Morgana had given him some sort of sour look.

"Tell us what happened," Merlin said gently. "Nicki's message this morning was a bit... panicked. I believe we should all be on the same page."

"Sorry," Alex said. "I fell back to sleep waiting for a reasonable hour."

"Don't wait," Morgana ordered with stern eyes. "Alert us at once."

"It was like two in the morning when I woke up," Alex protested. "And I... I don't know. I was kind of in shock, I guess."

"That's fair." Merlin smiled, but he gave Morgana a stern look.

The others took seats around the room, Aiden bringing a couple chairs from the dining room into the living room. It gave her a few moments to gather her thoughts. Still a bit dazed, Alex licked her lips and tried to find the right place to start.

"Look," Alex said. Doing her best to stay calm, she folded her hands in her lap. "I'm not sure what is going on, but I know that something is in my mind. The dream is a little hazy now, but I was definitely communicating with my other selves... some of them, at least. It was weird; like, none of them could speak freely, but there was this light and..." She trailed off and furrowed her brow. "It's hazy," she said again. "But I know it was real. Something jumped into me when I was in the Tree of Reality, using me as an escape path from the Darkness."

"We believe you," Morgana assured her smoothly. Alex wasn't sure if she believed that or not. "The question is how to deal with this. Do you think it means you harm?"

"I don't know," Alex admitted. A vague memory of the light pushed forward. Her other selves had kept their distance. "But even if it doesn't, it's drowning out my other lives. That can't be good."

"Indeed," Merlin agreed. He was very still in the armchair, gripping the armrests tightly. "This is unlike anything we've seen before, though there are many tales of possession."

"We can't assume it's the same thing," Morgana said sharply. Alex flinched at the idea. The silence in her head was worse now. The others should be there, giving commentary both good and bad on these events, but they weren't. "The eye doctor didn't notice anything in Alex's eye. He didn't think anything was strange, so it isn't physical."

"But the spot in her eye is larger today," Bran said. His shoulder brushed against hers as he shifted on the sofa. "So even if the physical impact is limited, it is there."

"You're not wrong," Morgana agreed. She stood up and paced around the back of the sofa, her fingers drumming on the back cushion. "Provided that the dream was real and not merely a manifestation of your magic trying to warn you, then we know that the other selves are intact, even if they are silenced."

"Do we think the silence is intentional?" Avani asked. Her expression was thoughtful, and Nicki made a small noise of alarm next to her. "Is this passenger trying to divide and conquer, or is Alex's magic isolating her other selves in order to protect them?"

"An interesting question," Morgana observed. "And one we don't have an answer to. Alex, do you remember anything from the dream that would be of use?'

"I don't think so," Alex said softly. Struggling to remember what her other selves had said, all she got were vague words and a sense of worry. "They were worried about me not hearing them." Something did tug at her memory. "There was a jar... one of the men had a jar."

"A jar?" Merlin repeated.

"He said something about the Darkness...." Groaning, Alex rubbed her eyes. "I'm sorry, I don't remember. I just woke up sure that something was wrong. I wrote down that something was inside my head."

Bran grabbed her hand when she lowered it and squeezed. "It's okay," he insisted. "We believe you. If your magic is trying to help you find out what's wrong then we'd be fools not to listen." He looked up at Morgana. "So, what do we do? Wait it out: see if Alex has another dream, or try to communicate with it?"

"I'm not sure," Morgana admitted. "The spot in Alex's eye is larger. That could be due to her using magic in the dream."

The question of what would happen if her eye was completely changed went unsaid, but it hung in the air. Squeezing Bran's hand, Alex fought to control her breathing. Panic was gathering in her chest and the edges of her vision were blurring. She wasn't sure if she was going to cry or have a panic attack, but both were possible. Bran turned slightly on the sofa and covered her joined hands with his free one.

"We're here to help," he whispered. "We'll figure it out." Then he cleared his throat. "Why don't we try to scry with the Iron Chalice? It's connected to Alex's magic, so it might let us learn more about what is happening."

"What are you looking for?" Alex asked softly.

"What it looks like? Any hints that magic can offer about what we should do," Bran said. His voice was soft and he patted her hand. It was grounding and comforting. The blurriness was easing a little. "How does that sound?" Bran asked. "I want you to be comfortable."

"That... that sounds like a start," Alex said. "I don't want to attack it, even if we knew how just yet. If it was fleeing the Darkness then it might not mean any harm."

Merlin's face closed for a moment, his eyes darkening and his features freezing in place. He didn't believe that. Alex was sure of that much. She didn't have to turn around to know that Morgana was frowning, but she didn't want to cause more harm than she already had.

"I'll go and get the Chalice then," Nicki said. Her voice was calm, and she gave Alex a soft smile.

Affection rolled over Alex. Her eyes scanned the room, taking in the worried faces of those present. They all had lives outside of this house. Everyone was missing classes, and yet they were all still here with her. Tears pricked in her eyes. Bran's hand was warm and solid against hers. The fear eased a little. Jenny passed her a warm smile before pulling the curtains closed. At least Jenny was on top of things.

"How was lunch with Robin yesterday?" Bran asked Aiden as they waited.

"It was fine," Aiden replied quickly. His body tensed up and Bran smiled.

"Just fine? You two have been seeing each other pretty frequently over the last two weeks."

"We haven't talked about if we're dating yet," Aiden admitted. "But I like her."

"I saw them at lunch the other day," Lance offered. A mischievous smile tugged at his lips. "She's pretty."

"Sooner or later, we'll all have to meet her." Nicki breezed back into the room; the Iron Chalice gently clasped in her hands. She smiled at Aiden and winked. "I need to be sure that she's good enough for you."

Aiden made a face, wrinkling his nose while Nicki grinned and Avani smiled warmly. Alex held back a laugh while Bran chuckled. He winked at her and released her hands before standing up. Bran inhaled slowly and reached for the Chalice. Nicki carefully handed it to him. Morgana touched Bran's shoulder.

"You scry first," Morgana said. "You have the strongest link to the Chalice apart from Alex. I don't want her using magic."

"Fair enough," Bran agreed. He went to the middle of the floor and sat down, crossing his legs. "I'll see what I can find."

Alex didn't move from the sofa. No one made any move to leave the room. Lance and Jenny were lingering in the doorway of the kitchen and Timothy was perched on Lance's shoulder. There was the faint rumble of a car on the road outside, but a heavy silence had taken hold. Bran's hands began to glow yellow.

The glow spread across the metal of the Chalice but didn't sink into the iron. It glistened, casting a soft, almost comforting glow. Itching to reach out with her magic, Alex sternly reminded herself to be careful. Morgana didn't want her to use magic, and the spot in her eye was supposedly larger. Making a fist with her hand, Alex tensed her muscles and didn't dare blink.

Alex watched Bran's face intently. There were small flutters in some of the muscles, but for the most part, he remained calm and still. In his hands the Iron Chalice glowed softly, a faint light pouring out of the metal. Alex tightened her grip on the armrest. It felt wrong to watch someone else use the Chalice. It was good that the others could use it, but something twisted in her unpleasantly at the sight. Wetting her lips, she took another sip of her tea to refresh her suddenly dry mouth. It helped, but only a little.

"Stay calm," Morgana whispered.

"I am calm."

A humorless chuckle escaped Morgana. Oddly, that made Alex feel better. At least she wasn't the only one worried. Her eyes swept across the others. They were all worried. Apprehension colored everyone's faces as they watched. Yellow sparks swirled around Bran in thin streams of light. It looked wrong and Alex leaned forward. Morgana's grip tightened.

Bran's face twitched. He tilted his head. The yellow glow around his hands intensified. The Iron Chalice shuddered in his hands, shaking despite Bran's steady grip. Alex started to move, but Morgana grabbed her shoulder and fought to keep her in place.

"Don't," Morgana warned.

Merlin leapt forward, kneeling beside Bran. The old mage reached out a hand and steadied Bran's arms. The Chalice kept shaking. Looking at Morgana with an unreadable expression, Merlin began to call Bran's name.

"I see-" Bran's voice was gravelly and broken. "It's-"

"Bran, let go," Merlin ordered. "Let go!"

Convulsing, Bran flinched and groaned. His magic flared around him, creating a halo of heat and sparks that rolled through the living room. Aiden and Nicki flinched back, but Alex tried to pull forward. A few sparks hit her hand and faded harmlessly into her skin. Then with a soft grunt, Bran fell against the floor, his legs still crossed. The Chalice tilted, spilling water over Bran's chest, but he didn't react at all.

Merlin tugged the Chalice out of Bran's hands and set it on the floor. Struggling to breathe, Alex waited and watched Bran's own breathing even out. He grumbled something softly. Then his eyes opened and a collective sigh of relief went through the room. Jenny's hand went over her heart and she shared a look with Lance, who put an arm around her. Nicki closed her eyes and Avani touched her shoulder. Aiden looked ready to fall over.

"Bran." Alex pushed Morgana away and knelt down beside Bran. Her long hair slipped out of her ponytail as she leaned over him. "Are you okay?"

"Yeah... what hit me?" He blinked a few times, his eyes moving between Alex and Merlin. "Uh..."

"You were using the Chalice as a scrying tool," Merlin explained. He still had a hand on Bran's shoulder. "You began to convulse."

"Oh." Bran looked up at the ceiling, a dazed expression on his face. "That doesn't sound good."

"I take it you didn't see anything," Merlin said. "Bran, if you did then you need to tell us. Clearly, it was dangerous for you."

"There was a light... no, I saw two lights. But they were.... It felt wrong." Bran spoke slowly with deliberate words, seeming to struggle with what to say. "It's hard to explain. But I saw the lights."

"Lights," Alex repeated. "I only saw one in the dream. At least, I think there was only one."

The others moved closer and Merlin finally moved his hand, allowing Bran to sit up. Jenny knelt down next to him with a glass of water complete with a straw. Giving her a grateful look, Bran sucked down several long slurps.

"It was hard to get through," he said a moment later. "There was a strong resistance. My magic was sluggish, but I could feel the Iron Chalice trying to help." A small smile appeared on his face and he turned back to Alex. "I think I saw the lines of magic. Like you do."

Smiling a little, Alex nodded. She wasn't sure what she should say. Two lights. Her mind kept repeating that, but it stirred no memory. There had been a cliff. She remembered that much: she'd been walking towards it and her other selves had been looking at it. But she only had a vague memory of one light.

Aiden and Lance helped Bran to his feet and Alex quietly returned to her seat. Morgana sat on the arm of the sofa and put her hand back on Alex's shoulder. Bran swayed, but Lance took on his weight without protest. Aiden patted Bran's back and the pair helped him over to the sofa. He still looked dazed but managed to stay sitting upright.

"Sorry I wasn't of more help," Bran said. Grimacing, he looked at the Chalice. "Whatever it is pushed back."

"That's alarming," Merlin said. He hummed thoughtfully, meeting Morgana's gaze. "It must have some sort of magic then."

"Or it is using Alex's," Morgana suggested.

The temperature of the room dropped. Staring at Morgana in horror, Alex waited for her to say something else. But the older mage just looked thoughtful. No one said anything against Morgana's suggestion. Then Bran nodded, his Adam's apple bobbing.

"Yeah," he said. "That...that seems right."

"Great," Alex groaned. "So, what now?" No one answered her. Slumping onto the sofa next to Bran, Alex shivered and grabbed the blanket. "Merlin? Morgana?"

"I don't know," Merlin said slowly. "I hesitate to call Shiva here given the recent situation with the Demons, but we may need to consider trying to use the Iron Trishula on Alex." Merlin offered her a small smile. "We'll figure this out, Alex. Don't worry."

His words sounded hollow. Holding back a scoff, Alex nodded and pulled the blanket up to hide her trembling hands. Next to her, Bran leaned back and touched their shoulders together. It didn't help. The memory of the light on the cliff was brighter than before. Morgana was beside her. It should have been comforting, but Alex's stomach turned. Bile burned her throat. Everyone was watching her.

Keeping hold of the blanket, Alex stood up and swung it around her shoulders as she strode towards the bathroom. She heard Nicki say something behind her, but her chest muscles were clenching. Throwing open the door of the small downstairs bathroom, she gave up the pretense and dashed to the toilet. Dark spots were creeping in along the edge of her vision. Falling to her knees, she started to heave.

Aching all the way down to her bones, Alex clutched at the toilet bowl and tried not to think. She couldn't help it. Flashes of the light kept forcing their way forward. Arto's voice echoed in her head, but as a memory rather than a supportive presence. Her stomach emptied itself. Alex coughed and choked. Tears were running down her face. When that had started, she didn't know.

Then someone was pulling her hair back, holding it out of her face and away from her mouth. A warm hand on her back somehow penetrated both the blanket and her pajamas. The smell of the ocean filled Alex's nose. It was subtle, but it told her exactly who was behind her.

"Easy," Morgana whispered. "Easy."

The black spots were getting worse. More tears were mixing with vomit. Alex's stomach was empty of everything she'd eaten at dinner the night before, but she kept heaving. Morgana rubbed circles on her back. A flare of memory hit Alex. They'd done this before. Morgana had cared for her when she'd been ill before. She was almost happy at the memory, but the ache of being ill clouded over everything else.

Then she coughed and the heaving eased. A sink turned on and she heard someone else moving in the room. Sucking in a deep breath, Alex closed her eyes. The stink of the vomit hit her. Morgana pulled her back from the toilet. It was flushed and a damp washcloth was gently moved around her mouth.

"Thank you, Jenny," Morgana said gently.

"I- I'll give you a minute," Jenny said softly. Alex didn't open her eyes. "If you need anything."

Morgana shifted Alex, letting her lean back against Morgana's chest. "Yes," Morgana agreed. "I'll call."

Alex kept her eyes shut and listened to the bathroom door close. The washcloth was tossed up into the sink with a splat.

"Alex? Can you hear me?" Morgana asked. Her voice was controlled, but Alex could hear the worry.

"Yeah." Alex inhaled and exhaled slowly, counting her own heartbeats. The panic attack was there, ready to blow in like a storm.

"Just breathe," Morgana said. "That's it. I know it is scary, but you have Merlin and I and all your friends. You're not alone."

The words did nothing to comfort Alex. She didn't voice that but focused on holding back the panic attack. Too many thoughts were spinning through her brain. She ached and now her mouth tasted horrible. Alex finally opened her eyes. The only light in the room was coming through the curtain, so there were no bright lights to torment her. Pushing away from Morgana, she leveraged herself up with the sink and started rinsing out her mouth.

A glance into the mirror told Alex Morgana was standing behind her. It also let her see how much the spot had grown. It covered roughly half of her iris now. Alex felt sick again and quickly lowered her eyes.

"I can avoid using magic when I'm awake," Alex said hoarsely. "But when I'm asleep..." She trailed off and swallowed, turning to look at Morgana. "What are we going to do?"

She prayed silently for the woman to suddenly have a new idea, but Morgana's expression remained sorrowful. "We can watch you," Morgana said gently. She shifted Alex back and they sank to the floor once again. Sighing, Alex leaned her head against Morgana's shoulder, letting the woman hold her close. "If you start talking or we see signs that you're dreaming, we'll wake you up. It isn't ideal, but hopefully we can hold this off until we can find a solution."

"Is there a way to bind magic?" Alex asked softly. "Any way to stop me from using any magic?"

"No," Morgana admitted. "I'm afraid not." Morgana's fingers smoothed Alex's hair gently. "We're with you. I'm not going to let anything happen. Nicki may have some ideas. You know how clever she is. Try not to worry."

Alex wished that the words reassured her. They didn't. Her chest tightened and her heart jumped painfully. Sitting up straight, she grabbed her knees and closed her eyes. Fear, panic, and anger crashed down. Tears sprang from her eyes again. Nausea churned in her gut as she grew dizzy. Morgana's voice grew distant as Alex started to sob.

26

Rejection

The soft hum of Alex's heater did little to dispel the silence settling into the house. Outside her bedroom window, the world was dark and cold. The dark blue curtain hung over the window, but Alex knew if she pulled it back there would be swirls of frost on the glass. She was propped up in her bed, leaning against a stack of pillows with a bedside lamp on.

It was all very comfy and restful. At least, it should have been. Her door opened slowly and Nicki stepped inside. The redhead frowned at the sight of her reading in bed but didn't say anything. Nicki was dressed in her own pajamas, fluffy, colorful things that looked way too warm to Alex, and carrying her phone and a tablet.

"Jenny said you were still asleep," Nicki said. "Sorry I'm late." Alex tilted her head and raised an eyebrow. "No need to use the 'Morgana eyebrow', Alex," Nicki said. "We all know you don't like this."

"Anytime you people want to stop and get a full night's sleep again is fine with me," Alex said. Then she shrugged and sighed a little. "I was asleep, but Jenny woke me up about midnight."

"So, you decided sitting up to read was better."

"Hard to fall asleep with someone staring at you every few minutes," Alex said. "Even reading doesn't distract you guys for long."

"We're doing this to protect you." Nicki gently closed the door and walked over to Alex's desk chair. "*The Tenant of Wildfell Hall*?" Nicki read aloud. "Brontë? I'm not familiar with that one."

"Most people aren't," Alex said. Putting her bookmark in place, she closed the book and studied the cover with a small smile. "It was... a bit radical. Anne Brontë wrote this one. She tends to be the overlooked Brontë sister. She died only a year after publishing this one."

"Radical, huh?" Nicki was making herself comfortable in the desk chair. "I'll bite, why?"

"It's now considered the first feminist novel," Alex explained. She set the book on her nightstand and turned around to adjust her pillows. "The main character, a woman named Helen, leaves her husband and supports herself. At the time that was against the law."

"And they printed it?"

"It outsold *Wuthering Heights* by her sister Emily." Then Alex sighed and leaned back against her fluffed pillows. "But like I said, Anne died not long after. Her sister Charlotte kept it from being republished."

"Oh, jealousy or something?"

"There's debate on that reason. But she said that she thought the novel was a poor reflection of her sister's character."

"Translation, her sister wasn't afraid to break social convention."

Alex shrugged and stared up at the ceiling. "Do you think this is still necessary?"

Nicki sighed. "I know you hate it, Alex, but so far it seems to be working."

"Three weeks," Alex grumbled. "Three weeks, Nicki, and nothing has happened. We had midterms and Halloween without any problems."

"Yeah well, that's because we've been waking you up if you start show-ing signs of distress." Nicki sounded far too calm about this. Alex turned her head to find Nicki scrolling through something on her phone."

"And you aren't tired of having a 'watch Alex sleep shift' each night."

"Oh, I'm tired of it," Nicki agreed. "But I'm not going to risk letting something bad happen to my friend. I know it sucks, but Merlin and Morgana just need time."

"They haven't found anything," Alex said. "Honestly, if they've never encountered something like this why do you think that they'll suddenly figure it out?"

Nicki sighed, the loud, labored sigh of someone who had been a part of this conversation before. A twinge of guilt echoed in Alex's chest. This was just venting, and it wasn't fair to the others. This wasn't their fault. If anything, it was hers for going into the Tree of Reality. She didn't regret it exactly, but the after effects made her insides churn with frustration.

"Please just lay back and try to sleep," Nicki said. "For me?"

"I'm becoming immune to that plea," Alex said. She smiled a little, hoping that Nicki would understand she was trying to tease. "I get it every night from all of you."

"Staying awake all the time won't help," Nicki replied. Her voice remained stern and serious. "And yes, the afternoon naps help but Tim-othy worries about not being able to wake you up if need be. So be a good girl and lay down."

Sticking out her tongue, Alex made a show of grumbling, but she'd already started adjusting her pillows. She gave them one more fluff and adjusted the angle. Putting a pillow between her legs, she rolled onto her side so she was facing Nicki. It would be a lot easier to sleep facing the other direction, but Alex had promised to cooperate with their task of watching her face and eyes for signs of dreams. She was starting to really miss deep nights of sleep.

"Good night," Nicki said more gently.

Closing her eyes, Alex tried to relax. As with every other night, she was sharply aware of Nicki's presence in the room. Her friend wasn't really making any noise. There was a soft occasional tap as she touched her phone, but the chair didn't squeak and she didn't hum. Alex mentally reviewed her homework and promised herself to give an essay one more look in the morning. Merlin had been going very easy on her in classes and she'd done remarkably well on her midterms. There wasn't anything to worry about there. Turning to counting sheep, Alex giggled to herself as she tried to imagine fluffy sheep bouncing over a fence. Sadly, she'd never really seen sheep up close. Not in this life at least. There was a soft pull, and the world started to fade away as her exhaustion weighed down on her.

An alarm blared throughout the house. Alex sat up sharply, eyes wide and her sleepiness completely gone. It blasted again and Alex's mind caught up with what it was. Their magical alarm against the Fae. Nicki was on her feet, putting her phone on Alex's desk and frowning. She pulled open the door and Alex saw the hall light turn on. Unable to see the other's doors, she nonetheless could hear the sudden burst of activity throughout the house.

Lance and a frazzled looking Jenny appeared in the hallway with Avani right behind them. Lance came into her room and nodded to Nicki. She glanced at Alex and frowned. "Stay here," Nicki said firmly. "Don't use any magic."

Then Nicki was out the door, rushing downstairs to join Aiden and Bran. Jenny came in and took Nicki's place beside Alex's bed. Avani glanced into her room and nodded before following Nicki. Alex swallowed, hoping that nothing would happen to the magician. Three mages should be enough to handle whatever was here, but she couldn't ignore the icy pulse of worry in her gut. Glaring at the doorway, Alex tossed back her covers and stood up.

"They can handle it," Lance said firmly. Jenny nodded in agreement.

"This is the first attack in a month," Alex said. She ignored her friends and went to the window. Pulling back the curtain, she pressed herself against the window frame. "Why now?"

"Well, it is a surprise," Jenny said. "We were expecting them at Halloween." She pouted a little and huffed. "We didn't even go to any parties."

"None of us have social lives anymore," Alex said.

Red light flared brilliantly outside, making Alex blink. It was too dark and she was at the wrong angle to see anything clearly, but when she turned her head, she could see flashes of yellow, red, and blue down below. There was a brilliant blast of blue that quickly dimmed. Alex grit her teeth. She glanced back at the doorway, but Lance shook his head at her. Without magic, she doubted she'd get past him.

"Let your friends help you," Jenny said firmly. Her dark eyes were stern and she was watching Alex like she was a troublesome child. "It's not that bad."

"I don't use a lot of magic in my day-to-day life," Alex said. Tapping her fingers nervously against the window frame, she could barely contain her anxiousness. "But I used it more than I realized. Right now... I hate this."

"I know, honey." Jenny's expression softened.

Alex's breath had fogged up the window and she used her sleeve to wipe it away. A shout from outside made Lance straighten up. A moment later there was a crash downstairs. Jenny squeaked and fumbled with the pockets of her robe before pulling out a dagger. Alex was surprised that she had it with her now, but she was more than a little pleased.

Something slammed into a wall downstairs. Alex crossed the room and reached up to where Cathanáil was hanging over her bed. She didn't bother grabbing the scabbard leaned against her nightstand. Her fingers touched the hilt and a shock traveled up her arm. Surprised and pained, Alex yelped and pulled her hand back, staring at the sword in stunned silence.

"Alex?"

"It- it shocked me." Alex shook herself and reached out to try again. It was probably just normal static. But a line of magic met her finger when she touched the hilt and sent pain radiating up her side. "Oh god-"

She heard something in the hallway. Jenny made a sound of alarm. There was shouting downstairs and she looked over. A Fae in jeans and a black hoodie was running towards them. Its violet eyes were wide with glee. An amulet was dangling around its neck and it held a long, wicked knife in its right hand. Alex froze. Her heart beat faster and she started to move her hand to summon her magic. Yet, fear held her still. She couldn't use magic. If Morgana was right.

Lance reached past her. His hand wrapped around Cathanáil and he pulled it from the stand without a sound. He shouted for Jenny to get back. The Fae lunged towards Lance, slashing at his bare chest. Lance leaned back enough to avoid the attack. When the Fae started to draw back, Lance brought up a knee, striking it in the leg. It twisted back with a grunt of pain.

Cathanáil glinted in the artificial light of the lamps as it sailed through the air. There was a squishing sound followed by a crack as the sword collided with the Fae's neck. Jenny turned away and Lance made a small sound of surprise and disgust. Silver blood ran down the Fae's black clothing, but only for a moment. There was a muffled gurgle right before the body began to vanish in small wisps of dust.

No one moved. Lance's eyes dropped to the sword in his hand. Eyes wide, his jaw went slack and his breathing turned uneven. Alex's fingertips ached and disbelief and anger welled up in her chest. Then Jenny was beside her, a hand on her shoulder and serving as a grounding presence. Lance stepped towards the doorway, Cathanáil still in hand.

"Avani?" he called. "You okay?"

"I'm fine," Avani answered. "Are you? One got past me."

"Yeah, we got it." Lance sounded too calm. He raised Cathanáil up a little more, gripping it with two hands and holding it at the ready.

An order to put down her sword burned at the tip of Alex's tongue. She held it back, letting it try to choke her, and strained her ears listening to the battle outside. The sounds were lessening, and she moved over to the window. It was easier to breathe when she couldn't see her sword in someone else's hands. Alex shivered. She told herself it was the chill coming in through the glass. It wasn't just seeing someone else with her sword. Nicki had handled it when working on the scabbard. That had never bothered her.

Cathanáil had shocked her. The magic inside Cathanáil had attacked her, not once, but twice. The last bursts of color outside were gone. Holding her breath, Alex waited for more. They didn't come, and it remained dark. The sudden silence and stillness took away her distraction. Turning back to Jenny and Lance she found them watching her.

"Alex?" Jenny called. She started to reach for Alex but pulled her hand back nervously as Alex approached. "Are you okay?"

"The sword," Alex whispered. Lance swallowed and gently laid it on her bed, treating it reverently as he stepped back. That didn't help the ache in her chest. "...I couldn't even touch it."

"When did you touch it last?" Jenny asked softly.

"Uh... a few days ago, I think," Alex said. "I've just been keeping it in the scabbard." Glancing between the scabbard and the wall holder, she shivered. "Nicki put it up there on Friday night. Said she was tired of seeing it always in the scabbard."

"Calm down," Lance said. His eyes darted between her and the sword. "This is probably just a side effect of whatever..."

"Whatever is in my head and screwing with my magic," Alex snapped. "Yeah, I got that thanks."

Jenny walked over and put her hands on Alex's shoulders. The warmth of her hands sank into Alex's flesh and soothed her. Without prompting she inhaled slowly and closed her eyes, holding the breath. Her heart slowed a little, though Alex's mind still raced. A slight sting of pain lingered in her hand.

"It may be trying to protect you," Jenny said softly. "You absorb magic so easily."

"I'm not sure it is aware enough to try and protect me," Alex said. Swallowing, she exhaled and opened her eyes. Forcing a smile, she gave Lance an apologetic look. "Sorry."

"It's fine," Lance assured her. Then he looked towards the hallway. "Sounds like the fight is done."

"Yeah."

There was a burst of noise downstairs. The alarm had gone silent. Alex wanted to go downstairs, but instead, she sank down on her bed. Her eyes were fixed on her sword. She didn't touch it, but she couldn't bring herself to move too far away. Lance coughed lightly and excused himself. Alex heard his heavy footfalls down the hall and then downstairs. Relief that she wouldn't have to hear the explanation washed over her.

But then she heard people on the stairs. Of course, they were coming up here. She braced herself and shifted back a bit on her bed so she didn't look quite so dejected. Everyone was in their pajamas, though Bran had at least thrown on a robe before running outside.

"So," Bran said slowly. He stepped into the room first, cautiously. It made Alex feel like a wild animal. "Lance said what happened. Did you... were you aware of anything?"

"There was no vision," Alex said. "It just shocked me."

"Can I check your eye?" Bran asked. Frowning, Alex nodded slowly and tilted her chin up as Bran approached. He leaned forward, and everyone waited. Then Alex heard him sigh in relief. "No change," he said.

"Well that's good," Jenny said. "But it doesn't explain what just happened."

"Maybe the Sword was trying to protect Alex," Aiden said. When everyone looked at him, he shrugged. "Not like a completely sentient thing obviously, but it is in tune with your magic. Maybe the stored magic recognized that something was off."

"That would make sense," Nicki agreed.

"Plus, with your ability to absorb magic, it could have made things worse," Bran offered. His voice was the softest. "If whatever is in your head is using your magic to grow stronger."

Closing her eyes, Alex resisted the urge to scream. Weeks. She'd been waiting weeks for some kind of answer, but it was always just beyond her reach. Bran took a step back, giving her some space. Taking several slow breaths, Alex struggled not to start cursing even if the idea was attractive.

"Fuck," she hissed. It slipped out before she could stop it. "Just fucking great."

Bran chuckled and smiled at her as she opened her eyes. Without prompting, he picked up Cathanáil and put it into its stand. The others were still lingering in the doorway. Alex's mind was a mess, but her exhaustion from weeks of poor nights of sleep was returning.

"Nicki, will you let Merlin and Morgana know what happened?" she asked.

"Course," Nicki replied.

"Great, thanks." Alex shifted in her bed, laying down and pulling the blankets over her head. "Alex doesn't want to deal with anything more tonight."

"Fair enough," Bran said.

There was noise as the others shuffled away. Through the comforter, Alex couldn't see anything, but there was a change in the light as the hall light was shut off. A chorus of voices wished her goodnight and Alex muttered into the fabric. Someone shook her shoulder.

"Alex," Nicki called. "Come on, I need to be able to see your eyes."

Alex pushed back the blankets and glared at Nicki. The redhead didn't flinch at the expression. Sighing, Alex rolled onto her side and made herself comfortable for another long and awkward night.

27

Oberon's Trick

1 518 C.E. Strasbourg, Rhineland

Michel barely recognized the old grain market. Cleared away were the boxes and bags. Gone were the merchants and farmers and travelers. The guilds had constructed a large stage in the middle of the square which was crowded with convulsing bodies. Overhead the late August sun beat down on everyone and everything.

The throng of dancers just kept moving. Some were dancing frantically with large and fast motions. Others were barely moving, their weak bodies merely swaying as the strongmen held them up. Their expressions were all over the place. One nearby woman looked frightened, almost ready to cry while the man next to her was all but glowing with glee. Others were happy, others were calm, some were manic and some had blank, empty faces.

Music was flowing across the crowd from the assembled pipers and drummers. It was a fast tune, meant to urge those moving and burn through their heated blood. Bile rose in Michel's chest as he watched. One woman fainted and was carried off the stage by one of the strongmen the councilors had hired. Onlookers were watching with fascination and a few joined in with the dancing. Michel just hoped that whatever web was being cast didn't catch them as well.

Through the crowd of spectators, he spotted Morgana glaring at the stage as if willing it to burst into flames. He hoped that she'd keep her temper and her magic in check as he hurried over to her. She glanced at him and then sighed. It was too noisy to speak properly and she nodded towards the road. It took them some time to make their way out of the grain market, but as they stepped into a shadowed side road, Michel breathed in the cooler air with relief.

"They are fools," Morgana said. "This is no solution."

"They don't know better," Michel said.

Morgana shook her head in disgust but didn't correct him. They hurried along the road, keeping to the shadows. People were milling about. Some were working but others were heading towards the grain market, no doubt to see for themselves just how many dancers there were now.

Staying quiet, Michel ignored the curiosity and excitement of the people they passed. His stomach turned at the idea of them going to cheer on or laugh at the dancers. Rumors had filled the city in the past weeks. Some dancers had been stopped by tying them up, but more joined the crowd every day. No one knew how many had died, but with the heat and no rest, some collapsed every day.

Morgana was walking faster and faster with each passing moment. A low growl escaped her as more people passed them on their way to the market. Michel stayed silent, not daring to anger his aunt. They finally made it back to their home street and hurried for the shop. It was open but there were no customers. Merlin was behind the counter and looked up with a smile which faded upon seeing their grave faces.

"I take it that you don't like what you found."

"It's magic," Morgana said. She started pacing across the floor of the store, not at all concerned for the more valuable items on display. "It has to be."

"Indeed." Merlin was moving around her, picking up the imported glass pieces and carrying them to the cabinets. "Magic does seem to be the most likely option. But the victims are from different neighborhoods."

"People are dying," Morgana growled. Tension filled her shoulders. "There are almost 400 dancers now."

"The stage was a horrible idea," Merlin said. Morgana glared at Merlin and he shook his head. "Don't glare at me, Morgana. It wasn't my plan."

"I can't believe they honestly thought that giving them a stage and music would make things better! There were people joining in now. If that's the magic spreading or their own minds giving in to the mania this blasted situation has created, I don't know, but it's getting worse."

"At least they've decided that it is a natural disease," Merlin said. "Let's be grateful for that."

"I am grateful," Morgana hissed. "But my gratitude won't help anything."

"Nor will your anger," Merlin said. "We need to find a way to unweave this magic."

"It's too strong," Morgana said. The words almost sounded like they hurt her to say. "I tried at the grain market, Merlin. But the spell... it isn't just a manifestation of will and power. There's something else here. It's like it has become tangled up."

"We know little about Sídhe magic," Merlin said. "I hate to ask, Morgana, but-"

"No." The word was sharp and heavy. "I don't remember ever hearing of anything like this. Even during the war, the Sídhe warriors with magic were able to do only basic spells. Even shields were beyond their power in our realm. I still don't understand how something like this is even possible."

Merlin hummed thoughtfully and put away the last of the glass. Michel waited for the older mage to say something useful. Watching the pair of them struggle for answers was painful. It was wrong, on every level. Neither Morgana nor Merlin spoke. Each of them had pensive expressions and were clearly deep in thought, so Michel stayed quiet. The shop was hot, but he didn't want to open the windows and run the risk of being overheard. Unsure of what to do, he fetched the broom and started cleaning up the corners where all the dust usually settled. Merlin gave him a look and a small smile that didn't reach his eyes.

A knock on the door drew their attention. Michel glanced at Merlin, who nodded. "Let them in," Merlin said. "Business would at least make this a productive day."

Nodding, Michel obeyed and unbolted the front door. When he pulled it open, he noted that the heat outside was even worse than it was inside as it hit his face like a wall. Then he turned his attention to the figure waiting on their doorstep. They were wearing a long cloak despite the summer heat. As it lowered its hand, Michel saw the too pale skin and tensed.

"Peace," the figure said. "I mean no harm. Please, may I enter?"

His jaw dropped a little. The figure made no move to push past him or harm him. Still stunned, Michel slowly stepped out of the way and allowed them to walk into the shop. Merlin and Morgana had positioned themselves in the shop but froze as soon as they saw the figure. Morgana brought up a hand, palm towards the figure who quickly held up their hands.

"Peace," they repeated.

Moving quickly, Michel shut and bolted the door. With the windows closed, they were alone with the Fae. Silver magic appeared around Morgana's hand and she glared at the figure, making no move to back down. Merlin came around the counter and stood next to her.

"Come here, Michel," Merlin ordered.

Nodding, he walked slowly around the figure. Their guest stayed completely still, though their hands clutched at their robes nervously. It was a very human gesture, and it hit Michel right in the chest. Once he was beside Merlin, the older mage relaxed a tiny bit.

"Morgana," Merlin said. "Please calm down. Stay at the ready if you must, but I think we best hear our guest out."

Morgana lowered her arm though the silver sparks continued to circle her hands. She said nothing and her glare didn't lessen at all. But the Fae didn't run for the door which Michel found impressive.

"Thank you," the figure said. Pulling back the hood, Oberon revealed himself, but he was different. His features were softened, almost blurry and he looked exhausted. Morgana grabbed Michel and harshly pulled him back behind her. He almost stumbled over a table but managed not to fall over.

"What are you doing here?" Merlin demanded. Glaring at the Fae, Merlin's fingers flexed and green sparks burst from his fingertips. "This city is suffering enough under your magic."

"Yes," Oberon said. "I know." Pausing, Oberon looked over his shoulder at the doorway. "I've seen it firsthand. Things have gone out of control. I fear... I don't know where to begin."

Something shifted in Merlin. His tension visibly eased and his frown became more quizzical and curious than angry. Morgana glanced at him before returning her eyes to the Fae and shaking her head slightly. Clearing his throat, Merlin stepped forward a little bit and let his hands hang loosely at his side.

"Start at the beginning, Oberon. Given the conflict between us, we are surprised just to see you here."

Oberon's lips thinned. His violet eyes darted nervously between Merlin and Morgana. The change was so dramatic that Michel doubted it was truly the same Fae. It just didn't seem possible. Shrugging off his cloak, Oberon draped it over one of his arms, buying him another moment of silence. In the corner of Michel's eye, he saw Morgana shifting. She was done waiting, her suspicions no doubt teetering on the edge.

"I am not a Fae," Oberon said. With a deep sigh, he closed his eyes and his skin started to glow. The light blinded Michel and he turned away even as Merlin stepped forward.

Blinking, Michel recovered quickly and raised his eyes back to Oberon only to gasp in surprise. The face was older than he felt it should be, but it was familiar. Michel didn't have the best memory. He was a human being, but he did remember the young Old One he'd played with long ago. In all the years since he'd never met another Old One. Numerous things clicked into place in his head and he almost cursed his own silliness.

"An Old One," Merlin said. "Who are you?"

"Puck," Michel said softly.

Puck's broken expression mended a little and he smiled. It reached his eyes and brightened them a little. "You remember me?"

"Yes," Michel said. Excitement crept into his voice before he realized it. Morgana was glaring at Puck and he swallowed. "Uh, yes, I remember you, but what is going on here?"

"I wanted to make things better," Puck explained. His expression fell again. Tossing the cloak to the side, he rolled his shoulders and shuddered. "Us Old Ones...we look like what we want to look like. Usually human, but I came across a group of Fae and thought, why not? As an Old One, I had the ability to use some of my own energy to impact your world, a kind of magic all its own."

"So, you tricked them," Morgana said. There was the hint of a sneer on her face. "Toyed with them."

"The plan was real," Puck snapped. "It was." Suddenly his voice was petulant and higher than before. The change from the deep tones of Oberon was startling, and even Morgana jumped a bit in surprise. "The goal was to create a homeland for the Fae, and maybe even for the Old Ones. We blend in better... but we still don't belong. Why do you think some of us live in family groups?"

"To be worshipped," Morgana snarked.

"To not be alone," Puck corrected. "My mother went into the waters not long ago, but..." He swallowed thickly.

"But- but you're just a child," Michel said. The words came out before he thought of them. "Like me," he added to soften the statement.

"I'm a lot older than you," Puck protested. He wrinkled his nose and glared. "I only look young by choice. It made my mother happy."

"Puck," Merlin said sharply. "What possessed you to lead the Fae? Was this some sort of sick joke to you?"

"It wasn't a joke!" Puck protested. "They were angry! We lived near some of them and I'd hear them talking, the young ones who were look-ing at a future stuck in the shadows. It wasn't hard to understand their anger." Shaking his head, Puck stepped back and took a deep breath. "I understand the plight of the Fae. Better than you could. But you're correct that there are magical ramifications. At first, the spell seemed to work, but then something went wrong. My power... it twisted up with the magic being created by so many Fae in the area and... and I can't stop it.
"

"Do you understand what you've done?" Merlin asked. His tone was low and dangerous.

"I'm sorry!" Puck shouted. "I am! I just thought that leading the more violent Fae on for a bit was better than them actually starting a war." He managed to smirk at Morgana. "If you're honest, I've done a good job keeping them in line."

"By deceiving them," Merlin said. He was glowering at the Old One while Michel bit his lower lip nervously. "It was a vile thing for you to do, Puck. You would have been better served staying amongst your own kind."

"Fine, fine," Puck grumbled. "You don't like me."

"I'm deciding how to destroy you," Morgana said. Michel didn't like the smile on her face. "You've caused a lot of problems. This dancing plague is simply the latest one." She took a step forward, her magic flaring up her arm and around her body like flames. "Give me one reason-"

"I'm sorry!"

Puck stumbled back from her, shifting closer and closer to the door. His eyes were distant and he was panting. Michel stepped closer to him and Puck sprang back from him. Searching his brain, Michel tried to remember how long all of this had been going on.

"The Dancing Plague was just supposed to be a simple thing," Puck said. "I only meant it to distract some people. It was supposed to manifest as a jinx, a trick, and make people dance for a bit. No one was supposed to die. The goal was just to scare the city and maybe the Holy Roman Empire enough that they handed over some territory. I was shocked when it turned into this. Even more shocked when the humans decided it was natural!"

"Similar events have happened," Morgana said.

"I know… that's where I got the idea. I want to stop this," Puck insisted. "Before it gets any worse. If it keeps growing stronger and building then it could even spread outside the city. I don't know enough about magic to anticipate it."

"Listen to him," Michel said. Turning back to Morgana and Merlin, he gave them his best pleading look. "I understand him wanting to help. This just went wrong, and killing him won't help."

"It might," Morgana said.

"Doubtful," Merlin said. Staring hard at the Old One, he huffed but nodded. "Very well, Puck. You will tell us exactly how you cast this spell and what you were trying to do."

"Are you going to kill me?" Puck asked softly.

"What about the Fae?" Morgana asked. "Are they so easily leaving behind their plans?"

"The spell trapped them too," Puck said. "As I said, the magic of the Iron Realm twisted with my power and… followed me home. I'm not sure how, but over a dozen of the Fae were infected. I was able to remove the spell from them, but it frightened them. Magic was well and good as long as I could control it."

"So, you've lost their faith," Merlin said. "Should we worry about them attacking?"

"No." Puck shook his head. "No, they all ran back home." The words were tainted with bitterness, and Michel suspected the parting hadn't been that peaceful. "You don't need to worry about them."

Morgana finally lowered her hands and walked right up to Puck. They were now the same height, but Puck wilted under her stare. A small smirk appeared on Morgana's face, but it was an unpleasant expression. Pity for Puck welled up in Michel's chest. It was foolish and overly sentimental, but it was there.

"Your power is tied up in this," Morgana said slowly. "Your life force. No wonder you are desperate to stop the plague. Every victim drains your life force."

"Of course," Merlin said with dawning realization.

"No, I really do want to help," Puck said. "I didn't want this."

Lashing out, Morgana wrapped her hand around the Old One's neck. A faint silver glow radiated from her hand and Puck gasped. Merlin made a small sound of protest. Michel jumped forward before he thought of it and grabbed Morgana's arm. He tried to tug her away and Morgana looked at him in surprise. Opening his mouth, he tried to say something but was at a loss. Then Morgana dropped her hand from Puck's neck, letting her magic fade, and sighed.

"Fine then," she said. "He can help, but if you double cross us-"

"I won't," Puck said quickly. "I swear it."

"Then tell us how you stopped the spell on the Fae," Merlin said. "We'll work from there. When this is over, we will decide what is to be done with you, little trickster."

Puck nodded in agreement, fear still lingering in their eyes, but Michel thought he saw a small spark of hope.

28

Raging Storm

The storm was in full effect when she opened her eyes. Raindrops pelted her face and arms, stinging her skin as a cold wind howled around her. Thunder rolled overhead constantly as bolt after bolt of lightning flashed across the dark sky. The brilliant electric blue burned itself into Alex's eyes. She stared up into the churning clouds, trying to catch her breath and reassure herself that it was only a dream.

A crash of metal made her jump. Her eyes scanned the landscape nervously, finally remembering the presence of her past selves in the last dream. Tall grasses formed wild waves in the wind, but did nothing to hide the crowd of people in the distance and the blinding point of light floating amongst them. They were running and jumping, shouting and screaming chaotically, all the people circling the Light.

Running towards them, Alex nearly lost her tennis shoes in the mud. Suction pulled her down, but she fought to keep moving forward. Ahead of her the Light pulsed, making the air shimmer around it. Something was wrong. Unease was turning into worry and fear in Alex's gut. Beams of light were ripping apart the landscape, leaving deep scars scattered around the Light, which shimmered with tones of gold and blue.

Her eyes scanned the people. She knew them, but her eyes were drawn to one in particular. Arto grunted, raising an iron-banded shield in front of him with his left hand. The twisting beam of golden light struck the shield, pushing Arto back several feet. Stumbling, he tried to recover his footing, but his whole body swayed. In his right hand, Cathanáil glowed, but he failed to lift the sword and attack.

Alex started. The Light pulsed and moved towards Arto. Another figure moved and Alex turned to watch them. Thor swung Mjǫllnir through the air, a vicious roar escaping him as he approached the Light. The Iron Hammer collided with the Light. There was an explosion of gold and white. Thor was thrown back against the ground and Mjǫllnir hit the dirt with a metallic thud a few feet away.

Arrows flew through the air, striking the Light, but there were only tiny bursts of gold and dark blue. The shining orb was clearer now to Alex. It was about two feet across all told, with a shining halo around it. More thunder rolled overhead as another flash of lightning did more to illuminate the broken landscape than the Light itself did.

Thor pulled himself to his feet and magic sparked off his hand, forming a stream of power that surrounded Mjǫllnir and pulled the Hammer back to him. A Korean man dressed in a simple long tunic and pants rushed forward and swung a curved sword at the Light. He was thrown back just as Thor had been.

Gasping, Alex stumbled back, clutching her hands to her chest. Alex closed her eyes and urged herself to wake, but the sound of thunder and shouting stayed with her. The smell of the storm and the wet earth filled her nose. It was all too real. There was a scream. Opening her eyes, Alex found a man dressed in a thick fur parka being pinned against the ground by a beam of light. His face was distorted in pain, and a sharp ache radiated through Alex's limbs, nearly knocking her to the ground.

Arto leapt forward, shoving his shield into the beam. The iron started to crumble, but the Korean man pulled the man back to his feet, and they retreated.

Spinning around, Alex tried to take them all in. There were at least thirty men running around the Light. Most were armed, but a few were dressed in cloth and carried no weapons. All their faces were familiar, and as she inspected each face in the low light, she named them. They rolled through her mind like raindrops down a windowpane, there but quick to vanish.

Lokpal moved slowly, keeping to the shadows as another beam of light was released. It struck Thor in the chest, throwing the ancient Norseman back onto the ground. Another man rushed over, helping him to his feet. There was no sign of any change in the Light. Gottfried raised his service pistol, still dressed in his SS uniform, and opened fire on the Light. The bang of the bullets echoed across the plain, yet the bullet sailed harmlessly through the Light. Its glow increased, and the assembled men fell back.

The air shuddered before exploding in waves of light. Alex's skin burned. Someone pulled her down onto the ground. It was a tall man with coal-dark skin and sharp brown eyes. His face was familiar, and the name Josfa sprang to the tip of her tongue. Memories of green hills, a high plateau, and short trees hit her fast. There were huts with small statues crafted from terracotta and the smell of a forge. There was no context, but she knew that place.

"Stay down," he ordered. His accent was musical, but she had no difficulty understanding him.

"Josfa, what is happening?" she asked softly.

"We fight for our soul." He didn't react with surprise to her speaking his name. "It is trying to force us back. It does not belong here."

"Wait, what?"

The man leapt up without answering her questions. Grabbing a spear from the ground, he rushed forward. More joined him in an advancing line, all armed with different weapons. None of them glowed to Alex's eyes like Cathanáil, the Trishula, or Mjǫllnir. Lokpal jumped forward, thrusting the Trishula into the Light. For a moment, the battlefield froze. Alex's chest went hot. The Trishula glowed. Then the Light moved.

It zipped away as a bolt of lightning, a strange electrical sound making Alex's skin crawl. It flashed and flared, sending out several streams of gold and blue energy that tore into the landscape. Her different lifetimes scattered, jumping to avoid the beams before returning to form a line.

Cuthbert cursed and aimed an antique firearm at the Light. It went off with a bang but had no effect. Leugio had a spear and shield, but fear filled his eyes as he watched the others move around him. Dobiemir had a rough club and was beside Thor, talking with the other man too softly for Alex to hear. It was surreal. None of it felt real.

"What is going on?" Alex shouted.

Arto appeared at her side and grabbed her arm. He said nothing but started pulling her away from the Light, which had begun to glow brighter. Alex didn't fight him, but kept her eyes on the Light.

"It needs to get to you. We're trying to hold it back, but you have to go," Arto ordered.

Finally taking her eyes off the Light, Alex twisted around and straightened up. She was only an inch shorter than Arto. He glanced nervously at the Light, but the others were closing in again, trying to attack it.

"Seems like only the Trishula worries it," Alex said.

"Yes. The Trishula purifies, but we are manifestations of memory. The real items are in the world, not here."

Those words resonated through Alex, settling into her brain and sparking something in her mind. But there was no time to dwell on it.

Arto kept her moving. She saw Josfa throwing a spear through the Light. Lokpal was behind Thor, who was holding the Hammer up toward the sky. Lightning crashed down, bouncing from the glowing metal of Mjǫllnir towards the Light. Once again, the air shifted as a strange sound radiated out from the Light. Lokpal leapt forward and tried to use the Trishula once again. He was pushed back by a violent blast of golden light that threw him several feet away.

Gofiben appeared and grabbed the Trishula off the ground, running towards Lokpal. More men rushed in with shields, forming a temporary barrier between the Light and Lokpal. Another group attacked with bows in a fresh shower of arrows. Scanning them, Alex found men of different ages, most seemingly in their thirties, all dressed from different periods. The variety of materials and styles made her head spin. Names came too quickly, leaving her dazed.

Waves of attacks hit the Light, but nothing seemed to phase it. In her chest, Alex's magic fluttered like an impatient bird that was eager to test its wings. Remembering Morgana's words and the fear that overtook her every time she saw that the spot in her eye was forced down.

"Stay down," Arto hissed. "We don't know what it'll do with you."

Thor took another swing at the Light. As it blasted him, Lokpal tried to use the Trishula once again. A young man with long brown hair tied back and what looked like 17th-century clothing rushed forward to help hold the Trishula steady. It glowed, but then the magical glow of the artifact was overcome by a brilliant golden light.

"Back!" Gofiben shouted.

The men drew back, giving the Light distance. As she stared at it and waited, Alex's lungs constricted tightly. The storm was churning more violently and raging above them. More flashes of lightning illuminated the scene. Scanning the faces again, Alex named them one after the other, moving her lips as she whispered them.

"Do you know what it wants?"

"It keeps digging into your magic," Arto said. "We... we're worried about what will happen."

"My magic?" Alex asked.

A strange little smile appeared on Arto's face, making a dimple appear on his cheek. Morgana had never mentioned that. For a moment, he looked amused before gesturing around them.

"What do you think this is? This is a manifestation of you, and by extension your magic."

"What?" Alex took in the plain of grass and the storm overhead. How could this be her? Yet, something about it tugged at her memory beyond just dreams. Something one of the others mages had said about her Connection. "Oh."

"The damage it is doing..." Arto shook his head. "We're holding it, but Morgana needs to find a way to help you."

Suddenly waves of golden light crashed across the landscape. Plants were ripped from the ground at their roots. Rocks were exposed as the layer of dirt was thrown into the distance. The clouds shifted colors above Alex's head, losing their dark gray tone and being stained with vivid gold. Yet, she wasn't moved. She heard her other selves shouting as they were thrown back, but she was stuck fast. Alex tried to run, panic ripping at her chest. Her hairs were on end; her magic was weakly flaring, fighting against her knowledge that she shouldn't call it and her survival instinct.

Arto dashed forward to pull one of the men caught in the wave back. Low moans filled the area. Aches spread across Alex's body. How much of this was real? How much of it would affect her? None of her past selves were able to jump back up. The Light hovered in the air, a faint hum coming from it. Alex pinched her arm in an attempt to wake up. She listened, hoping for a distant sound of someone calling her. There was nothing.

The Light's hum changed. It didn't move, nothing about it changed, and yet Alex suddenly had the distinct impression that it was aware of her. Around her, the others were trying to stand. Arto was shaking his head at her. Josfa was helping Lokpal to his feet.

Everything was still. Even the storm overhead had fallen silent, though raindrops continued to bombard Alex's face. It was hard to breathe. The air was too thick, too charged with electricity and magic. In her chest, Alex's magic was pulsing through her body even as her lungs struggled to expand and contract.

"Hold," Alex ordered.

Arto made an abortive move, but a short, elderly looking man whose name came forth as Timur grabbed his arm. There were flickers of memory, but the images of high snow-covered mountains and a small village weren't important right now. Gofiben was retreating while Thor was eying the Light with a tight grip on Mjǫllnir. But the fighting wasn't helping anything. Alex waited a moment, hoping once again to wake, but she didn't. Licking her lips, she swallowed and focused all of her attention on the Light.

"What are you?" Alex asked.

The sphere of light hummed again. In her chest, Alex's magic twisted and flared to life. Closing her eyes, she breathed in and out slowly, urging the magic to help her. Tiny flickers wound up through her veins, settling high in her cheekbones, making them itch, and reached for her ears. She felt it all. Every tiny movement of the energy in her body.

"What are you?" Alex repeated.

"Lost," came a soft whisper. It echoed in her head. "Running. Afraid."

"Afraid of the Darkness?"

"Yes, the Darkness. The End. The Death."

She studied the Light, trying to understand what it was. Other beings were familiar from mythology. There was something familiar about them, but this... this was different in a new way.

"You need to stop this," Alex said gently. She tried to smile, but her muscles didn't want to work properly. "I'm trying to learn about the Darkness. I want to stop it. Right now, you're hurting me. I can't help anyone like this."

For a moment Alex was hopeful. The Light was humming softly, and she had the distinct impression that it was thinking. She gestured to the others, hoping that they'd stay back.

"We must escape," the Light said. "You cannot stop the Darkness. We will not go into the Darkness."

Alex tensed. The tone was hostile, angry and the halo around the Light darkened. She heard a shout of warning. A beam of twisting golden and blue light struck Alex in the chest. It burned. Her magic pushed back. Around her the air turned hot, burning her skin and hairs. Her back hit the ground, whatever had been holding her, finally releasing her body. A roar echoed in her ears and the sound of the Light's hum turned high pitched. It echoed in her ears, burrowing into her skull. Screaming, Alex tried to move, but she was pinned down. Light filled her eyes.

Then she heard the others. Thor gave a war cry and the others echoed it. The Light's hold weakened and Alex sat up. All the others, over thirty of them, were rushing in towards the Light, forming a violent mob. Pulling herself up, she stumbled to her feet. Heart racing, she gave up on talking and turned to action. Gritting her teeth, Alex summoned her magic, as much of it as she could. Around her the landscape shimmered and the storm grew stronger.

Thunder rolled. Ozone filled the air, and the hairs on the back of her neck stood on end. Her magic shifted and tugged like a racehorse just waiting for the gate to open. Alex's hair flew in all directions, and she stared at the Light, waiting for it to make a move. The world trembled beneath her feet, reminding her that all of this was just a manifestation of her mind, memory, and magic. How fragile it was she didn't know.

Arrows were released, shots were fired, spears were thrown, and those with melee weapons rushed forward. A beam of light began to gather. Alex saw a faint rippling across the surface of the Light as the attack began. She raised her hand and aimed there. Bolts of dark gray collided with the Light. Its beam snuffed out as it moved, actually drawing back.

She watched. She waited for it to recoil or vanish. Alex's magic drained away, and the landscape flickered. Heat burned her muscles as the ache of exhaustion settled into her bones. The Light's glow intensified, and the lightning faded, dissipating into the air. Arto shouted something and the others attacked with renewed desperation. Off to her right, the landscape flickered and began to fade. Blackness started creeping into the edges of her vision. Was that because she was running low on magic, or was it another panic attack?

Not now. Not now. This was a dream. It was real, but it was also a dream. She wasn't in some distant place. This was her body. Her mind. That was the problem. That thing was in her head, and it wouldn't leave. It was as desperate as her. She couldn't breathe. Couldn't move. Everything was wrong.

More magic flared to life, summoned by the panic. Alex shoved it forward against the Light. Lokpal pushed the Trishula forward. It glowed. The color of the Light changed, its golden glow shifting towards a dark blue. Power exploded in a wave of blue that rippled through the air like waves on the surface of a lake. It was wrong, and Alex shouted out a warning. Her other selves hit the dirt.

They needed more magic. Her attacks were helping, but it wasn't enough. Alex was about to shout for the others to use their powers when it hit her. She was the only one with magic. All the others were relying on swords, spears, shields, and guns. Another blast ripped another hole in the landscape. Alex flinched, a headache growing on the right side of her head and pounding in time with her heartbeat.

Straightening herself up, Alex inhaled slowly and let the magic build up in her chest. It wasn't flowing as smoothly as usual. She wasn't pulling it in from the ground and the world around her. It was finite, and she was burning through it fast. Letting the energy build up, Alex raised both of her hands. Small arcs of lightning bounced between her palms, warming her hands and building up power. She trembled, the magic trying to break free. Her own thoughts, her will was scattered as fear took on more and more power. Putting all of her focus into one thought, she imagined the Light being broken apart, ripped apart by her lightning and dissipating.

The Light dodged, sweeping up and spinning away from their attacks. Rage boiled in Alex's chest. Thor struck the Light with his Hammer. There was a reaction. The orb shifted a tiny bit. The sound it was giving off changed, but it didn't fall. Two arrows struck it before bursting into flames and turning to ash. Heat rolled off the Light and Thor had to retreat. Gofiben took his place, swinging a normal iron sword through the Light. It didn't react at all.

Alex released a barrage of magical bolts. Three hit the Light, but it started to move, its shape elongating and thinning as it dodged the bolts. It was like an Old One, some part of her brain suggested: it could change its energy's shape. She pushed the thought away and tried again. It dodged them all.

Two more men rushed in, but a wave of energy knocked them back and sent a blast of dirt into the air. The soil swirled like a dust devil. Another beam blasted a group of her past selves back. They hit the ground with a hard thump. Alex watched them, but they didn't spring back up. Pain jolted down her arms. She trembled, suddenly weaker than before.

Tears stung her eyes. It was stupid. She hated it. The blackness was creeping in. Breathing was hard. Surely, they'd wake her soon. Her friends were watching over her. They'd wake her soon. They had to wake her soon. That thought repeated over and over again. Desperately.

Another beam of light rattled the world around them. Alex's chest burned as another scar was cut deep into the ground. Pain beat through her body in time with her heartbeat. It cut deep, finding every weak point, every nerve and applying pressure. Her head pounded. The others were screaming. More were falling to battle and not rising. Was her soul being torn to shreds? Were they gone forever? Would she be gone forever?

Alex's mind raced, trying to find a solution and avoid the dark fears creeping in. Her foe was desperate and already had the advantage. Even if Aiden or Nicki or Bran were able to wake her now, it was already in her head.

The Trishula. Her eyes darted over to Lokpal, who was still trying to attack with it. If she could wake up, then she could tell the others to seek it out. She should have thought of it before. They all should have. The Trishula was a weapon, but at its core, it purified and saved those who needed it. Like Shiva. She swallowed her frustration. Anger at herself wouldn't help now. Using magic on herself might be dangerous, but it was better than this.

She jumped to the right, barely avoiding a beam of light blasting where she'd been standing. Alex's eyes widened. Distantly she heard someone call her name. It echoed through the sky, which shuddered in response. Dull pain radiated through her shoulder. Someone was trying to wake her.

"The Trishula," she shouted. Maybe if she started talking, they'd hear her. "Get the Trishula!"

Her words echoed across the landscape. Alex's throat was raw. The Light was spinning towards her. Scrambling to her feet, Alex gave up shouting. Now she just had to hope that whoever had been trying to wake her was still there and that she'd talked out loud. It was a frail hope, but she clung to it. She couldn't let go of it.

A beam of twisting light raced toward her. The gold and the blue were coiled around each other like braided hairs. Releasing her magic, Alex threw up a shield and concentrated all of her might on holding it. The beam crashed across the surface in a rainbow of colors. Gritting her teeth, Alex pulled on all the magic she had left. The world dimmed and flickered at the far edges. Around her, the shades of her past selves were beginning to fade. Alex didn't know what that meant. She didn't want to know right now. Her heartbeat echoed in her ears. Raindrops and tears stained her cheeks. Beneath her hands, the shield wavered. Lokpal and the Trishula vanished, and with them, her hope that it wasn't too late.

The shield cracked. An opening burst apart as her magic dissipated. There wasn't even time to scream. The beam struck her. Alex was thrown back harder than before to the ground. Heat crawled over her arms. She screamed, but couldn't move her legs. Pinned beneath the beam, Alex thrashed and pulled frantically on her magic. It tried to respond but was burning away in the heat.

Around her, the world crumbled. The storm stopped. There was nothing in the distance; just a blackness taking hold. She heard screaming from her other selves, but it was too late. The Light burrowed forward, shrinking smaller and smaller while its brightness intensified. Thrashing her legs, Alex screamed in pain. It dug into her skin, burning it. The smell of cooking flesh filled her nose. It dug deeper. Overhead the clouds vanished, leaving only pitch blackness.

Her eyes were still open. Alex struggled to breathe in the dark. She was floating in nothingness, her feet kicking uselessly, and her hands grappling at empty air. Around her, the darkness shifted. A tiny hint of light revealed a purple shine. She gasped. A world hung ahead of her. A small, shimmering pearl of pale gold, with hints of blue scattered across its surface. Nothing like Earth, but a world nonetheless. The thick mass of the Darkness was moving, shifting closer and closer to it, like lava running down a hillside.

"No." The word was rough and cold in her mouth, falling off her tongue and hanging in the air.

The Darkness just kept creeping forward, inching closer and closer to the world. Her anger faded but didn't disappear. She understood the Light's fear. Her magic built up in her chest. Alex summoned every last shred of power and strength in her body. Her hands lit up, bright in the blackness around her.

"You have to let me go," she ordered. "I can help."

"No," that strange voice whispered back. "You can't. No one can. All we can do is run."

"Please," Alex begged. "Please, let me go."

"I'm sorry." She almost believed it. "But I will not surrender to death."

"Please." The heat was growing. The Light was moving. Alex tried to move. She'd even head towards the Darkness. "Please, don't. Please."

She couldn't move from her spot. Her legs kicked uselessly. Pain filled her chest. Her limbs trembled as her fine motor skills deserted her. The Light appeared in a brilliant flash of light beside her. Its glow burned. Hints of gold swirled around it like thin wisps of fog. Alex hated it even as her eyes were drawn to it. She tried to swim through the air. It didn't work.

"Please." The plea slipped out. "Please, stop. Don't. Please. I need to-Arthur, he's a danger. There's something- please stop."

"I am sorry."

It wasn't the Darkness that swept over her. It was light. Closing her eyes, Alex turned her face away from the blinding glow. Heat washed across her skin, shifting from pleasant to painful in seconds. A hum filled her eyes, rising higher and higher. Her mouth fell open to scream as the noise echoed in her skull, carving a place for itself.

Then she fell silent. There was no breath. There was no energy to scream. There was nothing as the Light dug into her bones, seeped into her muscles. Alex's eyes opened, and she stared out into the Darkness. The Light was fading, but not away. It was just crawling inside, burrowing into her gut now. Her eyes traced the shimmer of purple on the Darkness' surface. It moved a little closer to a dying world as Alex lost.

They had failed. She had failed.

29

Loss

There are limited words to describe watching a person sleep. One is creepy: very, very creepy. Two is boring. Maybe a glance at a person while they curled up their nose or something might be cute, but sustained observation was just dull. Alex didn't move much in her sleep. She tended to find a position and burrow in for the night, a bit like a hibernating bear.

Aiden looked down at his phone and reread the latest text from Robin. He was trying not to get too excited about it, but they weren't doing coffee or lunch this Friday. No, he had an invitation to dinner. Nicki might tease him, but he was excited by it. Enough time had passed that he needed to move on from Sarah. She'd been friendly and great, but their relationship just hadn't survived being apart. He'd taken that harder than she had, but he was ready to really try to build something with someone new. Shaking his head, he knew he had a dopey smile on his face and put his phone away. He needed to keep an eye on Alex.

She looked asleep. Aiden leaned forward, watching Alex's eyes carefully. They'd all gotten lectures on what to watch for when this whole creepy 'watching Alex sleep' business had started. Her eyelashes were fluttering softly, and her eyelids were twitching. Sighing, he stood up.

She was definitely dreaming. Her foot suddenly moved, knocking her stuffed dog off the foot of her bed. It hit the floor with a soft thump.

Aiden gingerly picked up Galahad and smiled a little at the stuffed dog before he placed it on the desk. He knew how fond of the old toy Alex was. Stepping forward, he called Alex's name. She groaned a little but didn't wake up. He tried again with no response. Rolling over, Alex stretched out her legs and muttered something in her sleep. That was a bad sign.

"Alex!" He raised his voice, and this time he reached out to touch her shoulder. It was hot. Her skin was burning, even through the long sleeves of her pajamas. Pulling his hand back, he hissed at a sharp lingering pain and looked at his palm. It was red, redder than it should have been. "Alex!"

There was no response. Stumbling across the room, he turned on the main light. It flooded the room and made some of his fear retreat. Alex groaned softly and started to stir. Relief swept up Aiden's body, and he slumped against the wall. Through the wall, he heard someone moving.

"Aiden?" Nicki asked. She sounded tired and disoriented. He looked into the hall to find her stumbling out of her room. "Everything okay?"

"I'm not sure." He looked back at Alex. Her eyes were still closed. "Alex! Wake up!"

Another groan was his only answer.

"Aiden?" Nicki asked. "What's wrong?"

"The Trishula!" Alex screamed. Her voice split the air and made them both jump. Her eyes were still closed, and she wasn't moving. "Get the Trishula!"

"Alex!" Aiden shouted. He ran back to the bed and shook her shoulder. "She's not waking up! Nicki, call Morgana! Call her now!"

"Keep the others back," Bran added, appearing in the hallway. "Aiden, stay with her. I'll check the defenses."

Nodding, Aiden took a few steps back. Alex began to thrash, twisting her body around into unnatural positions. Clawing at the sheets and blankets, Alex begged something to stop. His fingers itched to reach for her, but she was moving too violently now. Calling her again, he desperately hoped that maybe this time she'd wake up. Nothing was working, and he swallowed. Alex's skin started to shimmer with magic. Maybe it was her in control, but he wasn't sure. He couldn't be sure of anything.

He backed away to the door as the air thickened. Ozone began to fill the room. Eyeing the laptop and lamp on Alex's desk, Aiden fought the urge to run. Alex's power was destructive against their enemies, but right now... he didn't think she had any idea who was with her.

"Morgana is on her way!" Nicki called.

Aiden nodded. The others weren't next to him, but it felt right to react that way. He took a deep breath. He couldn't panic. This was the wrong time to panic. His magic flashed to life in his gut, and he flexed the fingers of his right hand. A moment later, he felt the warm heat of a small flame grasped in his palm.

A low groan escaped Alex. Aiden tensed, holding his breath, waiting for Alex to say or do something. Her eyes didn't open dramatically: they fluttered open slowly, disturbed by the light overhead.

"Alex?" Aiden called gently. "Alex, you okay?"

On the bed, Alex sat up slowly, swinging her legs onto the floor. Alex's eyes swung over to them, but they were wrong. Staring at her, Aiden couldn't move as he tried to understand what he was seeing. Then Alex took a step toward him, and he saw it. The dark spot was larger than before, covering the whole of both her irises.

"Alex?" Aiden called. She didn't understand. "Alex? Can you hear me?"

Then Alex tilted her head, like a bird studying something it had never seen before. A shudder shook Alex's body. The hairs on the back of Aiden's head and arms were standing on edge. His mouth went dry. Magic flared in his chest, sending shocks of heat into his arms. Instinct warred with the image of his friend.

"Alex, if you can hear me, I need you to say something now."

Nothing came out of her mouth. Alex's breathing seemed labored, but was starting to recover. A slight smile tugged at her lips for a moment before it turned into a wide grin. Yet the expression only worried him more. It wasn't right. It wasn't Alex's smile.

Holding up a hand, Aiden pulled on his magic. It rushed down his arms in an instant, illuminating his fingers with a bright red glow as the flame grew in strength. Through his shoes, he could sense a sudden rapid pulse as more magic was all but shoved at him. Panic filled his chest at the sensation. It had never been like this before. The magic of the Iron Realm aided Alex the most; it had the strongest connection to her.

"Guys!" His scream echoed through the house. "It's Alex!" he shouted. "I think she's possessed!"

There was no cry of alarm or shout of surprise. No one thought he was joking. Behind him were rapid footfalls on the staircase. Alex took a step towards him. Her knees shook, and her eyes shifted to look at them in surprise. Then she adjusted her stance and stood more naturally. That wasn't good. Whatever this was, it was learning quickly. The dark eye settled on the glow surrounding his hand.

"What now?" Bran asked. He was next to Aiden in the doorway. "Alex?"

"She won't answer," Aiden said urgently. "Look at her eyes. They've completely changed."

Alex took a step toward them. She swayed, but quickly recovered her balance and adjusted her body. Whatever had control was learning fast. Aiden couldn't breathe. Terror held him in place as his mind raced over the horrifying implications. Alex's body shifted. She looked behind her at the weapons on the wall.

Bran's yellow magic flooded past him, but it didn't strike Alex. Instead, it snaked behind her and surrounded the sword mounted on her wall. A small gasp escaped Aiden, but he understood. Summoning his magic, he pushed the bright red sparks at Alex. They struck her chest, knocking her back onto the bed. Yellow sparks swept around the Iron Hammer, and a moment later, both items were sailing over to them. Nicki pushed past him, holding up her glowing blue hand and grabbed the backpack near the edge of Alex's bed.

"Got the Chalice!"

Cathanáil and Mjǫllnir reached Bran, who took one in each hand and stepped back. Nicki shifted behind him and dug into the backpack. Keeping a tight grip on his magic, Aiden watched Alex as she stood up again. Her movements were more natural now.

"Do you mean harm?" Aiden asked. His mouth was dry. It was hard not to panic. "You have taken over the body of a friend of ours."

It didn't speak. Whatever had control observed them with those strange dark eyes that were so different from Alex's pale gray eyes. Nicki made a small sound beside him. Maybe he should tell them to leave with the Iron Artifacts, but his mouth didn't want to work. The being was still looking at them, adjusting Alex's body to stand more naturally. Then dark gray sparks flashed around its hands. Inhaling sharply, Aiden summoned more of his magic.

"What's going on?" Lance asked behind them.

"Lance," Nicki said sternly. "You, Jenny, and Avani need to head to Morgana's house right now."

"Aiden said that Alex was-"

"Yes," Aiden snapped. "Go."

Thankfully, Lance didn't ask any more questions. There was noise on the stairs a moment later. Aiden heard a rush of voices and then the door. That made it a little easier to relax, but the creature had lifted Alex's hands and was inspecting the magic flowing around them. It had the body of a mage, and any hope he'd held that it wouldn't have Alex's magic was brutally crushed.

"What do you want?" Nicki asked. She almost sounded calm.

"To escape," it answered. The words were sharp and clear. It was looking at them again, though its hands were still up. "We must flee the Darkness."

"We?" Nicki repeated. "How many of you are in there?"

"This body holds only one of my kind, but many minds. They fought back."

"What did you do to them?" Bran asked. "Did you destroy them? Is Alex still alive?"

The creature didn't answer. A slow smile appeared on its face as it tilted its head to look past Aiden. He didn't know which of the artifacts she was looking at, but his gut twisted. He heard the others move back. The gray magic around Alex's hands grew darker, illuminating the creature's hands. It looked like Alex, but as the smell of ozone intensified his fear skyrocketed.

"Move!" Nicki yelled. She grabbed his arm and pulled.

They dashed to the stairs. Aiden's head was pounding. Shock weighed him down. His limbs weren't working right. Nicki was talking, but he didn't really hear her. Bran ran ahead of them, still carrying the Sword and the Hammer. Turning around at the bottom of the stairs, Aiden set his feet and pulled on his magic. Alex was at the top of the stairs, gray magic swirling around her.

"Don't," Nicki hissed. "We can't hurt Alex."

"We can't just run," Aiden snapped.

Gray magic swirled around the creature. Lightning arced off of Alex's fingertips. The flames around his own hands grew, but Aiden didn't throw the fireballs. His heartbeat echoed in his head. He needed to use another spell. He needed to bind her, but nothing came to mind. What was he supposed to do against his friend?

Alex's hand snapped forward. Nicki grabbed his arm and pulled. A bolt of lightning blasted past him. Around them, the air shuddered. Shifting the Chalice into her left hand, Nicki raised her right hand. Lines of blue magic burst forth. The thing's eyes widened, and it drew back. Gray magic flared and pushed back the blue lines.

"Outside," Bran said. "We need to get her in the open!"

Aiden didn't understand, but he followed. The cold air outside hit his skin, making him shiver and suck in a sharp breath. Lance's truck was gone. Nicki ran to her car, digging into her pocket for her keys. Bran followed her, and they shoved the iron artifacts into the front seat.

They spread out. Aiden shook himself and focused on the front door. Using his magic, he warmed his bare arms and waited for Alex to appear. Lights were still on the house. He realized with a jolt of horror that Timothy might still be inside. Then again, with the yelling, hopefully he had slipped out the back. Tensing, Aiden glanced around nervously. What if the thing had gone out the back? Did it have Alex's memories?

"What if she went out the back?" Aiden asked.

Nicki had enough time to flinch before the front door banged open. A gray aura surrounded Alex as she stepped out onto the front porch. Her dark eyes looked black and sunken in. Behind her, light from the living room poured out. Aiden didn't remember turning on the light. It must have been Lance and Jenny. Then the creature stepped forward, the gray magic swirling dangerously like a storm.

"Talk to us," Bran ordered. "Let us help you."

"The girl wanted to help," the creature replied. It was Alex's voice, but the inflection was all wrong. "You can't."

"You've enslaved the mind and body of the Iron Soul," Bran said. He stepped forward, the yellow magic around his hands disappearing as he raised them in front of them. "This isn't going to go well. Work with us. We don't want to fight you."

The thing smiled, Alex's lips twisted into a strange and wide grin. She hadn't smiled like that in forever. Out of the corner of his eye, Aiden saw Nicki flinch at the expression, but she didn't move back. His mind raced. They needed to stall her. Morgana and Merlin would be able to bind her. They had enough understanding of the capabilities of their magic to stop her. Fire licked up his arms, his nervousness feeding his magic. The smile changed as the being looked down at Alex's hands. Around her, the gray magic thickened. Dark eyes jumped up to them. Aiden stepped towards Nicki just before the creature raised Alex's hands.

The storm of gray magic rushed forward. It crashed into his chest. Lightning flashed in the air and intense pain jolted down his side. His back hit the gravel of the driveway. Opening his eyes, Aiden gasped for air and looked up. There was a hint of light in the dark sky, but his gaze was drawn to the sparks of gray dancing in the air.

"What do we do?" he asked. "Nicki?"

Suddenly Alex's body stopped. In the low light, Aiden couldn't see much of her expression, but she was looking off in the distance. The glow around her hands dimmed. Aiden groaned, sitting up slowly, minding his aching side. His vision cleared just enough to see Alex's form running into the woods. On instinct, he called out to her. She was barefoot and without a coat. Then the magic crashed down on him. A roar of pain ripped from his throat. Something was pressing him down.

Looking up, he found a large gray mass of magic was lowering towards them. Lightning flashed inside the cloud of sparks, filling his nose with the smell of a storm. The air was getting thin. His chest ached and his limbs were heavy. Familiar; this was so familiar. His mind jumped back to a shoreline and his body collapsing from using too much magic. He struggled to push himself up onto his elbows only for a bolt of lightning to lash out. His chest burned. Gasping, he slumped back on the ground. Turning his head to the right, he found Nicki and Bran trapped just like him.

"Shit," Nicki groaned. Her eyes were bright with fear. "What the hell?"

"She's getting away," Bran said. He started to sit up only to be zapped. "What the-"

"It knows Alex's magic," Nicki hissed. "How?"

"Alex sounded…" Aiden shivered as he remembered the pleading. "I think they were fighting in her head."

Nicki nodded and slowly raised her hands. "Brace yourselves."

Her hands glowed a brilliant blue. The sparks of magic swept up into the air, forming a shield over them. Pushing it up, Nicki groaned as the gray and blue sparks flared off of each other. It suddenly got easier to breathe, and the ozone smell faded a little. Over their heads, the gray magic thickened. Throwing his arms up, Aiden focused all his energy on pushing the magic away. Red sparks blasted up, joining Nicki's magic in creating a dome. Moments later, yellow magic blended with theirs and they all pushed. Fresh air brushed over his face.

"We need-" Nicki started to say. "We need to stop her!"

"Focus on not getting crushed," Bran shouted. "What is this spell?"

"I don't know," Bran snapped. "Just push!"

They were winning. The gray color was fading, but the pressure wasn't. Heat filled his limbs, but it ached. It hurt. It wasn't like his fire. Fatigue weighed down his hands. Black crept into the corners of his eyes. This was just like before. Alex was in trouble, and he was running out of magic.

"Aiden," Nicki called. "Don't panic. Just push."

"I can't-"

"You can," Nicki said. Her voice was gentle now. "Morgana will be here soon. We just have to hold on. Stay with me."

He pushed. Biting his lower lip, Aiden kept pushing. Slowly, inch by inch, the gray was fading. Beneath him the cold ground was solid and cooling to the burning in his arms, but it wasn't enough. Aiden's throat tried to close up. His lungs didn't want to work correctly. Fear. He remembered this fear. It was just as bad as last time. Strange how even after several years of this, a coma, and dozens of fights, he still hadn't fully learned how to live with it.

Fear was manageable. Fear was a natural reaction to something that could hurt you; nature's way of trying to make you back off before you got yourself killed. It was useful and necessary. Panic was something else completely. Panic threatened to shut you down. Aiden's limbs were burning and shaking, but he couldn't stop pushing more magic up at the mass of Alex's magic. It didn't make sense. She'd never unleashed that much magic all at once before. Then again, Alex wasn't in control, and he'd never been on the receiving end of her powers before. They didn't use magic on each other.

Nicki was cursing next to him, her voice chanting frantically while Bran was horribly silent. Alex was long gone now; they had no clue where she'd run to and panic was tearing at Aiden's chest. It compressed his lungs; it made his vision blurry and was clawing like an animal desperate to rip its way out of his chest.

The sound of tires on gravel was heavenly. Aiden trembled with relief but didn't release his magic. How much time had passed? It felt like forever, but maybe it was only moments. There was a chance they could catch Alex. A car door opened and someone was running closer.

Silver light drew his attention away from the gray cloud. Aiden strained his neck trying to look back up the driveway. Then silver magic swept into the gray cloud itself, pushing the magic apart. Time lengthened as the dark gray magic was torn apart spark by spark. Suddenly the last of the pressure was gone and Aiden's arms fell to his side.

"Are you alright?" Morgana asked. Rushing forward, she reached for Bran's arm and helped him up. "Are any of you hurt?"

"No," Bran replied. "Tired, but we're not hurt." He turned and helped Nicki up while Morgana moved to Aiden and helped him to his feet.

"Where is Alex?" Morgana looked around, her green eyes wide and nearly frantic. "Alex!"

"She's gone," Aiden said. Catching his breath, he looked towards the house. The door was open, but there didn't seem to be any damage. "Whatever it was she was scared of took over. I tried to wake her, but she didn't respond. When she woke up, it wasn't Alex anymore."

"Where did she go?"

"Into the woods," Aiden said. He pointed into the trees. "She stopped at one point and lost interest in us and then just took off."

Shaking her head, Morgana waved her hand at the front door. It slammed closed, and she nodded towards the cars. "Come on." She took the first step with Nicki hurrying after her. "Why didn't you contain her?" Morgana asked sharply. She started to move for her car.

"We don't know how!" Nicki shouted.

"You have your magic-"

"We have never contained someone!" Nicki stomped forward in front of Morgana, who halted. "Think about it! We kill, Morgana! That's what we mostly use our magic to do." Silence fell around them save for Nicki's soft breathing. "We don't capture. We kill. That's what we've been taught. What we've been trained to do, so we hesitated. We tried to avoid using our magic on Alex's body because she's our friend, and we have no experience using our magic for anything but hurting a target. I'm sorry that she ran off, but I'm not sorry that I didn't accidentally kill my friend because I was panicking!"

Aiden swallowed. His own hesitation to fight suddenly made more sense, even if he didn't have the words to explain it. On the other side of Nicki, Bran shifted uncomfortably and looked off into the trees. Staring at them, Morgana sighed softly, and her shoulders slumped. The lines around her eyes were more intense in the headlights of her car. She closed her eyes for a moment and just inhaled slowly before pulling out her phone. Without saying a word to them, she texted someone, probably Merlin, and then headed for her car.

"Come on," Morgana said. Her tone was even and neutral. "We need to find Alex and quickly."

Nicki glared but followed, though she veered towards her car. Aiden frowned. Whatever that thing was, it didn't seem interested in the magical objects. His train of thought was cut off when a burst of light filled the sky. Spinning around, he sucked in a sharp breath. A massive column of light stood in the distance. It was glowing a familiar dark gray color.

30

Undoing the Damage

1 518 C.E. Strasbourg, Rhineland

Puck was a brave Old One. Fear all but radiated off of him whenever Merlin or Morgana looked his way, but he hadn't run yet. He kept walking down the streets beside Michel without any argument. Michel was impressed. Even knowing that Merlin and Morgana would never harm him, he'd shied away from them many times in his life after making them angry.

Oberon was gone. The calm pride of the Fae leader had faded into Puck's determination and guilt. The Old One had given up the form of the Fae leader and the personality he had created for the character. His brown eyes occasionally flickered with a shade of violet when he looked around at people they passed. Michel wondered just how long it had been since Puck was in his Puck shape. It was worrying, and almost worth admiring. Michel had never believed in anything that strongly. There'd never been an ideal that he had surrendered himself to. He'd always fought for the cause of the Iron Realm as Merlin and Morgana told him to. Pity had taken hold in his chest: it was tragic that it had come to this.

His thoughts were scattered. Puck was a fascinating creature. It wasn't that he was an Old One: Merlin and Morgana had told him a lot about many of the Old Ones in the past. One of his past lives had even married one and lived with her until dying of old age. Puck wasn't like any of the others in those stories. There was a vibrance to him even while he was downcast with defeat. Maybe it was seeing an Old One who had tried something new, and something that Michel found himself wishing had worked.

Keeping that thought to himself, he focused on their surroundings more diligently. They were approaching the grain market, and he could hear the music. It must be terrible for those who lived nearby.

"How many are there now?" Puck asked.

"Several hundred," Morgana answered. She gave him a searching look as his shoulders slumped. "What is it?"

"I... I won't be able to free them all at once. It'll take some time."

"How much time?"

"I don't know... I'll stay out your way and work on undoing the magic every day, but it won't be all at once. I'm sorry."

Morgana looked like she wanted to say something harsh, but Merlin nodded in understanding and touched her arm. He wasn't happy. Disapproval radiated off of the old man, but at least he wasn't running the risk of driving Puck off. They'd had no luck on their own trying to fix this, which now made sense.

"Are you certain?" Merlin asked.

"I can try, but I did the Fae one at a time to avoid causing them injury."

"People are dying every day of exhaustion," Merlin reminded Puck. There was an oddly gentle and patient tone to the man's voice.

"You know that there are worse things than death," Puck responded. His eyes were downcast. "I don't want to change dancing into something more destructive to those around them."

Morgana's expression changed. There was a hint of shock in her eyes, and Michel tried to imagine what idea had struck her that left her suddenly shaken. A few thoughts raced through his mind, and he shuddered.

"Keep to the edges of the stage," Morgana ordered. "We don't need anyone seeing anything unusual."

"Of course," Puck answered. He nodded obediently, but Morgana still gave him a doubtful look. "It'll be easier if it's just me-"

"No," Morgana said firmly.

"I came to you, remember?" Puck pointed out. His nose wrinkled a little as he glared at Morgana. "I'm trying to clean up my mess."

"Fixing this now won't restore those who died to life," Morgana said.

"I'll stay with him," Michel said.

"Absolutely not-"

"You and Merlin need to keep an eye out," Michel pointed out. "Keep everyone from panicking when people suddenly stop dancing. I can't do magic on the mind."

"It will be alright, Morgana," Merlin said. "I doubt that Puck wants us to hunt him for the rest of his days for harming Michel."

"I'm not going to hurt him," Puck said firmly.

Merlin and Morgana eyed the Old One again. Puck didn't shrink at their gaze, and Morgana finally nodded. With a small, relieved expression, Merlin nodded and gently led Morgana into the crowd towards the guards and nobles. They'd be the worst people to have notice something. The town seemed ready to move on, and Michel was in no hurry to bring their fears back.

"I hope it's not necessary," Michel said softly.

"Shouldn't be," Puck said. "But better to play it safe until we know for sure."

Michel waited for Puck to say more, but the Old One was eager to get to work and get away from Merlin and Morgana. They walked towards the stage. Music kept pounding through the grain market, and the onlookers were cheering and squirming in equal measure. There were fewer now than there had been weeks ago when the stage was first established. A few were watching their loved ones hopefully, while others were staring with horrid fascination at anyone who looked ready to topple over. Some were swaying along as before, and Michel eyed them carefully lest the spell take hold of them.

"What do we do?" he asked.

"You do nothing," Puck said. "This is my power."

"But you said it's tangled up in magic."

"It is, but I undid the spell on the Fae myself. I know how to."

Nodding, Michel gave Puck some space. Looking around, he scanned the crowd to make sure that no one was watching them. They weren't. Compared with the dancers on the stage, they didn't stand out at all. He was confident that there were more people than before both watching and dancing. If he hadn't had to be here, Michel knew he'd be in the shop rather than watching these poor souls.

Michel watched in open fascination as wisps of power spun off of Puck's skin. It looked a lot like magic, but now up close he could feel a difference. The air nearby tasted a little differently. The light it gave off wasn't exactly like the soft shine of the magic of a mage. His magic stirred in his chest. Curiosity made him lean forward.

"Careful," Puck cautioned. "I don't know what my energy would do to a mage."

"So, this is your... life force?"

"Close, but not exactly," Puck said. "My real form is just energy, like a ball of light. My mother helped me take a human form soon after she made me. I can eat and rest to help my body restore energy that I use up doing things." He smiled a little, making small dimples appear on his cheeks. "Mother always said that I was very talented at using my energy."

"Who is your mother? You've never said."

"Her name is Brigid. She used to live in England a long time ago, but came south because of all the magical wars there."

"And do you have a father? You've never mentioned one."

Puck looked at him, raising an eyebrow, and then he laughed. It was an abrupt sound, and Puck looked surprised that it had come from him. His eyes watered a little and brightened. For an instant, Michel forgot about the bad things happening in Strasbourg. It was just nice to talk with someone who wasn't Merlin or Morgana.

"Three different Old Ones made me," Puck explained. "Only Brigid stayed with me. Beings like me aren't born from sexual intercourse like humans." Michel blushed a little, but Puck continued. "Or the Fae for that matter. We're energy. Each Old One who wants to reproduce has to give up part of their energy and merge it with the energy of another Old One. It takes at least two for the process to work. The energy sparks to life, and you get a new Old One. Since your world doesn't like us, most don't' reproduce often, but Brigid was able to convince a couple of others to help her have a child."

"She must have really wanted you."

"She wanted a child." Puck's expression turned wistful. "But I'm not sure she wanted me. I'm always getting into trouble. This time is the worst."

There were so many questions that Michel wanted to ask. Things he wanted to say danced at the tip of his tongue. He wasn't sure how old

Puck was, but he had the distinct impression that Puck was a young man like him. An excitement that was inappropriate for the situation they were in stirred in his chest. This was someone he could talk to about magic and growing up with mages and everything else that he could never breathe a word of to anyone else.

Puck's energy swirled through the air. Michel strained his eyes trying to follow the thin line of gold. Suddenly his magic flared, and the world dimmed a little while the gold brightened. Colors washed away, leaving a gray scene, but Michel wasn't scared as his magic thrummed in his chest. Fascination pushed everything else to the side as he watched the tiny stream of Puck's power go for a nearby woman who was stumbling as she danced. Her exhaustion was apparent, and Michel was grateful that Puck had picked her first.

As he watched her, the faded gray color of the world changed around her. There was a line of gold spun around her that perfectly matched Puck's power. Magic was tangled around the thread of Puck's energy around the woman. It was dark gray in color, unlike his, Merlin, or Morgana's magic. It shimmered softly, and Michel was unsure of what to do. Puck was hissing in frustration as he reached out and pointed a finger at the magic. It wasn't his, so he didn't expect anything, but it slowly began to untangle from Puck's energy.

Sweat trickled into his eyes, stinging them and making Michel hiss. He blinked rapidly as the colors came back into the world. It was so strange. His arms ached, and Michel was confused. Maybe he had been using his magic. He just wasn't sure what he'd been using it for. Maybe to help him focus or perhaps to help Puck.

The woman stopped dancing. Her arms dropped to her sides, and she stumbled. From the side of the stage, two strongmen hurried over to help her off the stage. They seemed mildly confused but didn't ask her any questions. Michel and Puck were both still as she sat down on top of a barrel and drank some offered water. A small sigh of relief escaped Puck.

"It works, good." Then he looked at Michel. "What did you do? That was easier than with the Fae."

"I'm not sure," Michel answered. "I saw your magic and just tried to help it detangle."

"Well, it helped." Puck's expression brightened a little. "With your help, this will go a lot faster."

"How much faster? How many do you think we can do in a day?"

Puck grimaced and glanced up at the sun. Michel followed suit only to swallow when he realized how far it had moved. Just that one woman had taken over an hour. Looking out at the stage, he groaned out loud, and Puck sighed.

"It's going to take a while," Puck said. "I may be an Old One, but even I need to rest." Shaking his head, Puck turned his eyes towards the next dancer, this time an older woman. "Come on, let's focus on the eldest first and go from there."

"This is going to take weeks," Michel whispered.

"I know. I'm sorry," Puck said softly. "I never meant for it to get this bad. But I promise you that I won't leave until this task is done. The spell is my mess, and I'll clean it up."

Michel smiled and nodded. Something in Puck's voice resonated. It wasn't exactly like how he'd been when playing Oberon, but it rang of truth and determination. Turning his attention to the same old woman that Puck had been paying attention to, Michel did his best to focus on Puck's power again and help him pull it back. If nothing else, this would get him out of working in the shop for the next few weeks.

"We saw," Merlin said. Michel jumped. He hadn't realized that the man had returned. Spinning around, he found Merlin and Morgana right behind them. "The nobles saw nothing. It was very discreet."

"But this will take some time," Morgana said. Her disapproval radiated off of her, reminding Michel once again of her frustration. "We can't stay here for weeks on end."

"I'll stay and help Puck," Michel said.

"It is easier with the help of a mage," Puck said. "It's like the power of the Iron Realm is cooperating more because he wants the people released."

"Oh," Michel breathed. "That's what that was."

"That's not-" Merlin started to say.

"Puck isn't going to hurt me," Michel said. "And I want to help. I'll do more good here then I will back at the shop." Frustration built in his chest and Michel did his best to keep his tone even. "It'll raise questions if the shop is closed too long. You two should stay there and keep our normal lives going. I'll help Puck, come home every night, and report on progress."

"I'm not sure I like you spending that much time with him," Morgana said stiffly.

"I'm not a child anymore," Michel said. "My friends are all becoming apprentices now and working on their future lives. I'm still just working in the shop."

"The shop will be yours one day," Morgana replied. Michel hoped his surprise didn't show. They'd never discussed this before and Morgana stated it like it was obvious. She sounded a little hurt. "Michel, we're not trying to oppress you, we want you safe. That's our job in this world. Train and protect you."

"And I want to do my job. You say that I'm the Iron Soul. So, let me help Puck help the people trapped in the spell. Let me be the mage you trained me to be. I can handle it, and if he tries anything, I'm capable of dealing with him and alerting you."

"Very well," Merlin said, before Morgana had a chance to gather her thoughts. "We'll expect you at home every evening. Be sure to rest if you need it. If you allow yourself to become too fatigued, then the spell may take you as well." Merlin's eyes went to Puck. "I trust that you can take care of yourself for as long as this takes."

"I'll be fine, Merlin," Puck replied quickly. "I just want to focus on fixing my mistake."

His guardians were torn. They exchanged an uneasy look and Morgana leaned closer to Merlin, saying a few words in their native language. Michel's magic buzzed softly, but he didn't bother trying to use it to translate. Then Merlin nodded.

"Alright, Michel. We trust you. Be careful and if you need help-"

"I'll tell you right away," Michel promised. It was an easy promise to make. He wanted to say more, but someone knocked into him, reminding Michel of just how public they were. The music and dancing meant no one was paying attention to them. "I'll see you at home."

He held his breath, his back tight as he waited to see if Morgana or Merlin would argue further. To his surprise, Morgana's gaze softened, and she nodded. Before he could stop her, Morgana leaned forward and kissed his forehead. He was tall enough now that she had to stand tall and tilt her face up. Merlin gave Puck one more look, and then they departed, maneuvering through the crowd and vanishing onto a side street. A soft exhale escaped Michel, and behind him, Puck chuckled.

Turning back, he found the Old One watching him with a slight smile. His earlier fear and worry were gone. The pair stared at each other, both forgetting about the people still around them and the urgency of their task.

"I take it you've wanted to say that for a while," Puck teased.

"Maybe a little," Michel admitted. "I love them. I'm grateful to them for raising me and training me and apparently planning to give me a business, but... they can be very frustrating."

"That's my mother too," Puck agreed. He nodded towards the stage. "Come on, let's get back to work. You having a good report each day is probably the only thing that's going to keep Morgana from hunting me down."

It shouldn't have been that funny, but Michel laughed anyway. The drums kept pounding around them as they moved back to the stage. Puck looked over at him with a grin and glittering eyes. Apparently, he wasn't the only one who found it a bit funny. His new potential friend took a deep breath, straightened his shoulders and pointed to an older man near the center of the stage who was moving sluggishly. Michel nodded and let his magic build up in his chest. After a quick glance around to make sure that they weren't being noticed, the pair got to work.

31

Beacon

Aiden's grip tightened around the hilt of Cathanáil as he stared out the front of the car. The beam of light was still there, bright as a beacon, right in the middle of Morgana's windshield. Overhead the sky had opened up and rain was pouring down as thick, dark clouds rolled in from out of nowhere. The moon had vanished behind clouds and the dark sky obscured the rising sun, making the beam of light all the more visible. His stomach tightened painfully. There was no way that they'd be able to hide this occurrence.

Glancing at the digital clock on Morgana's dashboard, he noted that it was almost five. People would start waking up soon, if they weren't already. His fingers drummed against the iron blade of Cathanáil, barely aware that it could cut him easily without the scabbard.

"What is that?" Nicki asked from the front seat of the car. She was leaning forward to stare ahead. "We're already close to the lake. It doesn't seem far enough away to be at the school."

"We need to stop whatever this is before it uses Alex's magic to do something dangerous," Morgana said. "Well done, grabbing Mjǫllnir and Cathanáil before she reached them."

"I'm not sure whatever has control was aware of their importance just yet," Bran said. He was next to Aiden and holding the Chalice in his lap. Mjǫllnir was on the seat between them. It was ridiculous. All of this was ridiculous. "But Cathanáil didn't let Alex touch it earlier, so maybe it wouldn't have been a problem. The Sword must have been aware that something was trying to take over the Iron Soul."

Aiden wasn't sure of that. He wasn't sure of anything. A dull pounding was taking hold in the back of his head. His shift watching Alex had almost been over, and he was tired. The ache in his muscles wasn't helping, but every slow inhale was easing the pain. Lightning cracked across the sky, making him grimace. So far this thing almost seemed better with Alex's power than Alex was, and that was a terrifying thought.

"I think it's coming from the north island," Nicki suddenly said.

"I agreed," Morgana said. "That's good. No one lives on the islands."

"There's nothing there," Aiden said. He leaned forward and looked out towards the lake. "I mean, yeah, I think you're right, but why would it go there?"

"Doesn't matter." Morgana turned the wheel sharply, and they turned onto the road beside the lake. The beam was out in the middle of the water. "Let's go." The car came to a sudden stop, and Morgana opened her door.

Keeping a tight hold on Cathanáil, Aiden clamored out the car and almost fell onto the ground. His knees were still shaking. The beam of light, while dark gray, gave off enough illumination that he could see it was coming from one of the small islands in Raven's Lake. There was nothing out there, not even a cabin.

"We need to get out there," Morgana said. She glanced at the artifacts and frowned. "Keep them with you. Nicki, you take Mjǫllnir. The last thing we need is them being stolen."

"How are we getting out there?" Aiden asked. "And we're almost out of magic. Fighting the spell took a lot out of us."

"I'll freeze the water," Morgana answered. She climbed over the guardrail, leaving her car parked along the side of the road, and headed for the shore.

They hurried after her once Nicki had claimed the Hammer from the back seat. While it seemed natural for Alex to hold it, Mjǫllnir looked too large and heavy in Nicki's hands, but she was able to carry it without any problem.

"I hate to ask this," Aiden said. "I really hate to ask this, but what's the plan for after?" Morgana stopped and looked his way, but stayed silent. "Do we think the Iron Chalice can fix this? Or is Merlin going to have to go into her head to... I don't know, exorcize the thing?"

"I don't know," Morgana answered. "None of us know for sure what has caused this, Aiden, but we can't allow the Iron Soul to be running amok."

"What happens if we can't stop her?" Nicki asked. Her hands trembled, but her face was stone.

"We may have to consider alternatives," Morgana flatly stated.

"Like what?" Bran asked. He closed his eyes, his body quivering for a moment. "We kill her? Then we lose the Iron Soul." The last words were almost a whisper, they were so forced out.

"Not completely," Morgana said. "We've... Merlin and I forced the reincarnation of the Iron Soul once before. If we had to, we could do it again. It isn't ideal." Aiden stared at her in shock, understanding what she was saying even as his mind rebelled against the idea. Only Alex had known before this. Shaking her head, Morgana swallowed. "And enough talk about that. We're going to pin her down and stop this thing before it hurts anyone."

"She was asleep," Aiden said. He shuddered at the memory. "She screamed for us to get the Trishula."

They had reached the beach of the lake. Morgana's hands glowed brightly silver as she summoned her magic, but the glow only exposed the sorrowful expression on her face.

"Morgana?" Bran asked. "It's the best option. I get that you and Merlin-"

"You're right. We can't delay any longer." Morgana shook her head. "We hoped to have a better idea of what we were dealing with before exposing this creature to the power of the Iron Trishula, but we have no choice now." Aiden opened his mouth, but Morgana hushed him. The ripples of the lake froze at the touch of Morgana's silver magic. "Hurry, and try to stay quiet."

Without another word Morgana stepped out onto the ice and walked forward in a determined stride. Bran hurried after her, almost losing his footing in his sneakers. Nicki huffed, but followed her a moment later, clutching Mjǫllnir to her chest to keep her balance. It was slow going. Aiden tried to remember how far out the island was. He couldn't remember; he couldn't even focus on anything substantial. The pillar of magic loomed over them, growing larger and larger the closer they got. Beneath his feet the ice creaked, but it held. He heard rather than saw the waves of water splashing over their makeshift bridge. Aiden's heart raced in his chest. His mother would be getting up soon.

Then his feet found the shore of the island. It was small, less than the size of a football field, but there were over a dozen trees on the hilly mound of land. His feet sank into the small pebbles that made up the beach, and he followed Nicki, Morgana, and Bran toward the pillar. His hair stood on end. A high little whine rippled through the air. Instinct screamed to run, but he took another step and then another, drawing closer to Alex, standing in the middle of the pillar.

Alex, or rather the thing controlling her, was staring out towards the campus. Around her body, the brilliant pillar of light pulsed with magic, but it wasn't solid like Aiden had feared. Aiden waited for her to move. She had to know they were there. Yet she didn't move. Her bare feet were caked with mud, and there were hints of red around her ankles that made Aiden grimace.

"Look at the ground," Nicki whispered.

He focused on the ground beneath her feet only to hiss in shock. Everything was dead. The last hints of life in the grasses and ferns were gone, leaving dried, twisted black husks. The nearest trees were ashen gray, and their trunks were cracking. The gray glow only intensified with each moment. Then it hit him. The creature was using Alex's power to draw magic to her. The pillar was a vast store of energy, but she'd taken it from the living things around her. Aiden shook his head. He didn't want to think about that. He didn't want to consider the ramifications of that right now.

Alex's hair was a mess. Strands were flying loose from her braid, and there were leaves and twigs caught in tangles. Her gray eyes were glazed over and wild. When it saw them, Alex's body shifted. Straightening up, her body was loose, and her expression fell to a completely neutral and vacant state. Her eyes scanned over all of them.

"Alex?" Morgana called. Stepping towards the creature, she held her hands up. Her voice wavered. Holding his breath, Aiden held back the fear that inspired in him. "Can you hear me?"

The creature said nothing, its eyes settled on Morgana, but there was no spark of recognition. No flash at the affectionate nickname. He wanted to look at Morgana, wanted to check on her and see her face, but he didn't dare look away.

"What do you want here?" Morgana asked after a long pause. "What is it that you seek?"

"A way out," it replied. The tone was dismissive and stern, unlike Alex in every regard. "Leave me be."

"I can't do that," Morgana said. "You are holding a mage captive and using her powers to the detriment of the Iron Realm."

"I will not allow your world to rip me apart." The thing touched Alex's head. "I learned what it does to beings from other worlds."

There was a pause the length of a heartbeat, then Morgana and the creature both moved. With a shout, the creature threw its arms forward and released numerous bolts of lightning. Morgana unleashed a whip of silver that the creature jumped to avoid. Throwing himself to the right, Aiden heard the air crack. It rang in his ears, and the scent of ozone choked him. In the light of the pillar, the island was bright and navigable. Yellow magic erupted from Bran's hands in a flurry of sparks that looked more like a roman candle going off than a controlled assault. The creature raised Alex's hands; the pillar dimmed a little and a shield appeared in front of her.

Anger flashed across Alex's features, twisting them into an ugly expression before the creature snarled. The dark eyes somehow grew darker, and the rain worsened. Aiden shivered as the wind howled around his soaked form. His shoes were being pulled into the mud every time he tried to move. Beside him, an evergreen tree was turning brown, its needles falling to the ground.

Beneath Alex's feet, the ground rumbled before exploding up. With a cry of surprise, the creature stumbled back, losing its footing. Merlin's green magic flared around her and vines burst up from the soil to tie it down. A veil of yellow washed over Alex's body, holding the creature down while the vines entangled all of her limbs. Nicki's blue magic rushed forward, and more vines sprang up, tightening the earth's hold on Alex. Turning, Aiden found Merlin running up the rugged terrain of the island, one hand outstretched and absolute rage on his face.

Twisting up around Alex's body, the vines pulled the creature down and pulled Alex's hands behind her back. For a moment, Aiden was hopeful, but the creature glared, and the pillar shuddered. More magic poured down from the sky in a rain of dark gray bolts. Ducking beneath the wilted branches of an evergreen tree, Aiden choked back a shout of terror. Merlin and Morgana were shoulder to shoulder with a shield over them, both glaring at the creature.

The vines shredded as the dark gray magic tore through them. Pulling on his magic, Aiden ignored the burn from his exhaustion even as it reminded him to be careful. They couldn't afford anyone collapsing. In his right hand, Cathanáil was heavy and useless. He couldn't use a sword on Alex, but he couldn't just let it go. Moving in the shadows of the trees, he watched the creature as the last of the vines fell off and waited for inspiration. It didn't come easily. Above them, the pillar of dark gray light remained, though it was dimmer than before. A terrible idea came to Aiden.

"We need to exhaust it," Aiden shouted. Nicki looked his way, her nose wrinkled up as the rain-soaked her. "Throw everything you've got!"

"We could hurt Alex!" Nicki shouted.

Bran clutched the Chalice to his chest and nodded. Shifting the Chalice to his left hand, he raised his right, and yellow magic sprang forth, illuminating the tree he was huddled under. Merlin and Morgana didn't argue, and both launched attacks towards the creature. A dark gray shield blocked the spells, so Aiden raced around the side to flank it. As soon as he was past the bright line of the shield, he pulled on his magic and released a single bright red missile.

More attacks came. The storm rumbled overhead and the pillar slowly, very slowly, dimmed. It was still a bright beacon though, and Aiden knew that people had to be seeing it. Swallowing, he did his best to put that out of his head. If his mother saw it, then she'd start calling him to see if he was safe. His chest burned as he called on more magic. Black flickered at the edges of his vision, but he launched the fireballs anyway.

The creature dodged them. Panting, Aiden kept them coming. It threw up a shield, pulling more magic from the pillar. Its glow was dull now, and the creature looked up with a frown. It had a purpose to the creature. He didn't know what it was. Aiden couldn't focus on it. They were wearing the creature down.

Everyone was moving all at once. The shapes of his friends ran across the island, ducking and dodging behind trees between slinging spells. Nicki's bright blue illuminated the island as long spears of ice were launched at the creature. It threw up another shield of dark gray to block the attack. Opening his hand, Aiden stepped out from behind the tree and released a stream of fire that licked across the shield. His heartbeat was pounding in his ears, hints of shouts and screams penetrating from time to time. The assault continued. The pillar kept dimming as the creature used more and more magic. Alex's body couldn't take much more of this.

Suddenly the gray magical aura around Alex's body changed, shifted and darkened. The wind died down, and the rain eased, but the sudden stillness horrified Aiden. A whip of silver dissolved as it came too close, and the sparks were pulled into the cloud. The creature had finally figured out how to draw in their magic. With trembling hands, Aiden stumbled back, and his hope withered.

Golden beams struck Alex's body from the right. A new figure was rushing up the hill, golden light spilling from their hands. His eyes jumped to the others. Morgana, Merlin, Bran, and Nicki were already here. Avani's magic didn't work that fast. The creature spun towards the newcomer, gray magic flaring around them.

Nicki screamed something. A stream of blue magic swept around the shield, coiling around Alex's arms and pinning them. Yellow magic cracked the shield and encircled the creature in a glowing halo. Vines surrounded by a bright green glow burst from the ground and entangled Alex's legs. Visualizing bindings, Aiden threw his magic into the fray. His red magic joined Bran's in forming a shield that this time trapped the creature. Golden lines wrapped around Alex's torso and pulled.

The creature went still, Alex's body collapsing against the ground, completely still. No one moved. All their magic kept swirling around Alex in a kaleidoscope of colors. Bile hit his tongue, and Aiden slowly exhaled. The smell of ozone was fading, and his heart was slowing down. Then he looked at the new figure who had intervened. It was Robin, his maybe-girlfriend, but they hadn't had the conversation yet.

The golden lines of power swirled tighter around Alex's body. Robin's hands were glowing, her feet sinking into the mud as the rain poured down, and her whole body tensed. But she held the power around Alex's body. Then she looked towards him.

"Aiden, are you hurt?"

"What?"

"Are you hurt?" Robin glanced at Alex's body before she walked towards him. She kept one hand up, and the golden bindings around the creature stayed secure. When Robin was right in front of him, she reached towards his face. On instinct, Aiden twisted away as best he

could. Sighing, Robin dropped her hand. "Oh, okay then. I won't touch y
ou."

"What are you?" Aiden asked. The words were rough and barely above
a whisper. "Are you a mage? How did you learn? Or are you a magician...
no, magicians can't do that..."

"Aiden, you're rambling," Robin said. The right corner of her mouth
lifted in a tiny pleased smirk. "I'll explain everything. I promise."

"Uh, okay." Aiden was fumbling for words. Unkind thoughts and
worries sprang forth, but he tightened his jaw to hold them in. This
wasn't the time for accusations. "Okay."

"Morgana," Robin called, turning to look at the older mage. "What is
happening?"

"Which Old One are you?" Morgana demanded. Then her eyes narrowed, and she looked back at Alex. "What did you do?"

"It's just holding her. It won't last long," Robin said. "What is your
plan?"

"Help is coming," Morgana said sharply. "Who are you?"

Robin didn't have a chance to answer. Even in the midst of the layers
of magic, the creature was making Alex's body move. The pillar was
fading fast, but the dark gray aura around Alex's body was still intense.
It was fighting back. Merlin's bright green layer of magic was rapidly
disappearing. Aiden swallowed. He had no more magic to give. Staring
at Robin, Aiden couldn't think. Everything was on a messy loop of
confusion. But then, he heard water churning; not just the waves on the
beach, but splashing and fierce movement.

"That would be Shiva," Merlin announced. The older mage's shoulders relaxed, and he almost smiled. "He's coming with the Trishula."

Except, as the water tunnel formed and Morgana tossed an orb to
illuminate it, the being that stepped out onto the shore wasn't Shiva.

It was Arthur. Their enemy's eyes widened, and in the light of the orb, Aiden could see that one of them was a solid dark color. Then, with a shout, the creature ripped through their magical layers. Robin's golden lines snapped, and gray magic blasted around them as Arthur rushed to its side.

32

Battle on Raven's Island

Black magic rolled across the island from Arthur's outstretched hands. Hitting the dirt, Aiden checked on the others and fought to catch his breath. A roll of thunder punctuated the sudden silence. Then Merlin moved, sending a stream of green magic at both Arthur and the creature holding Alex's body. The creature flinched back behind Arthur while the traitor put up a shield. Seeing Alex looking to Arthur for protection made Aiden's stomach turn.

"Into the tunnel!" Arthur shouted.

They began to retreat. Aiden blinked, trying to process this sudden and strange turn of events. Robin ran forward, golden energy flashing around her as she waved her right hand. Arthur twisted away, but the energy kept going past him. Tearing into the water tunnel, Robin's power made the water turn bright gold before it collapsed onto the surface of the lake with a splash.

Arthur snarled, his features twisting, and black sparks swirled around his hands. While the creature in Alex fell back, Arthur launched an attack at Robin. A silver shield appeared in front of her, blocking the attack as Morgana charged forward. Aiden looked around, trying to find Nicki.

He didn't see her. An orb of light was launched into the air by someone, casting a bright glow across the island and creating long shadows.

Wind ripped through his hair. Everyone was moving. Magic flew back and forth as Arthur and the creature dodged their attacks and Robin retreated. They were all tired while Arthur was fresh. His blond hair was plastered to his forehead as the rain sputtered. Merlin and Morgana stepped forward, and a wall of earth rose up behind Arthur, blocking his escape to the water. The ground turned to pure mud beneath his feet, and he sank in. Arthur reacted quickly, pulling his feet loose and unleashing a wave of magic on the ground. Aiden tried to pull on more magic. His nerves were raw. The corners of his vision flickered black, and he collapsed back against the trunk of the nearest tree.

"Aiden?" Robin called. Her wet hands touched his face. Focusing on her, he met a pair of worried brown eyes. "Are you alright?"

"Tired," he said. "Feels like before." Shaking his head, he tried to stand up.

"Before? What happened-" Robin cut herself off. "Never mind - you stay down. Stay behind me. You mages are out of magic. You're only going to hurt yourselves."

Aiden inhaled slowly, counting softly in his head, and willing his heart to slow down. His magic was slipping away, the last vestiges sinking into his bones and trying to soothe the aches. It was silly, he decided, to have mages feel pain when they'd pushed too much energy through their bodies. Then again, it was an effective warning system that you were about to burn your body out.

Robin took point, staying in front of him and creating more golden light from her hands. It looked a lot like Bran's yellow magic, but there was something different about it. Something that he couldn't put his finger on. Robin's hands shimmered and, for a split second, he thought that they flickered out of existence. Despite his exhaustion, his brain tried to put it together. He was missing something. This wasn't the time, but he couldn't help his curiosity.

"Robin?" he called.

"Just stay behind me."

Movement caught Aiden's attention before he could ask the questions pounding in his head. Emotions churned in his gut, unsure of what to make of Robin's sudden appearance, but they were all muted as his eyes found Nicki charging Arthur. With a scream, Nicki swung Mjǫllnir at Arthur's head. Her balance tipped though, and Nicki stumbled as Arthur darted out of the way. Lightning flashed, revealing Nicki's narrowed, wild eyes. Whatever Arthur saw made him back up quickly and draw a dagger from his belt. It was the same one that Alex had given him, and new rage filled Aiden's chest. A flicker of magic tried to spark forth from him, but then Arthur's right fist glowed, and he brought it up to punch Nicki.

Silver magic pulled Nicki back, coiling around her waist and tugging her away from Arthur. Keeping a grip on Mjǫllnir, Nicki waved her arms angrily and screamed curses that were lost on the wind. Running forward, Aiden caught her free hand as Morgana's magic dropped her and pulled her back. Her hand was cold and wet thanks to the rain, but he could feel her pulse when he shifted his grip a little higher. She was alright.

"This is our chance!" Nicki shouted. She didn't look at him. Rage poured off of her. "We can finally kill him!"

"Don't get yourself killed!" Aiden yelled back. Looking towards Merlin, Aiden found Bran still holding the Chalice and now in a more defensive position. "We have to protect the artifacts."

That thought was solid. Arthur wanted Cathanáil, and he couldn't let him have it. Having the artifacts here was suddenly a much more dangerous idea. Pulling Nicki's arm, he led her back behind Merlin and Morgana to let the older mages take a defensive position. Robin moved with them, standing near Morgana and Merlin, but still giving them space. Morgana cast a strange look in Robin's direction but didn't ask any questions.

The assault on Arthur continued, with Merlin and Morgana throwing spell after spell to batter the black translucent shield. Glaring out at them, Arthur kept slowly moving back. Aiden's eyes jumped to the water. If Arthur could get another water tunnel working, then he and the creature could escape.

A black bolt shot past his ear. Nicki pulled him closer to her, and he raised Cathanáil. It caught the light of the magical spells and gleamed. In the distance, Aiden thought he heard shouting. The beam of light was gone, but maybe people were seeing the flashes of light.

"Give up, Arthur," Morgana said, voice strong and proud. "We outnumber you."

Arthur straightened up, his shield still in place, but more transparent than before. Hopefully that meant he was stretched thin. Both of his hands were pushed forward, touching the shield with open palms. Studying Arthur, Aiden searched for any clues about what was going on. Arthur looked almost the same. His hair was a bit longer and pushed out of his face. Dressed in jeans and an old t-shirt, nothing about him stood out until you looked at his eyes. One remained bright blue, but the other was dark, just like Alex's.

"Arthur," he called. "Are you possessed?"

The question sounded stupid. Merlin looked towards him, but Morgana didn't take her eyes off of Arthur. Slowly, Arthur smiled at them, his eyes sweeping across their line of defense. Behind him, the creature in Alex's body took a few steps back.

"Let's go," the creature ordered. "We don't need to stay here."

"They'll never stop hunting you," Arthur said. He took a few steps towards them.

Slowly, Morgana turned her left hand. The silver glow brightened. Arthur tilted his head and pulled his left hand away from the shield. No one else moved. Silver sparks swarmed up Morgana's arm. A strange black halo surrounded Arthur, dimming the world. Merlin hissed and threw an arm forward. Plants ripped up from the ground below Arthur's feet, trying to catch him and forcing the man to stumble to the left.

The battle began again, the brief calm over. Nicki lunged at Arthur, closing the distant in mere moments, swinging Mjǫllnir. Lightning flashed off the end of the Hammer and collided with the shield. It flickered; a large crack forming for a moment before more magic filled the void. It was enough to pull a cry of satisfaction from Nicki. Arthur grunted, nearly falling to his knees. His left hand reached for the water. The creature stepped closer to him, taking his hand. Gray magic blended with black. Aiden's stomach twisted. It was wrong.

Water struck the shoreline. The wind was picking up again. Aiden could barely see the opposite shoreline, and to his surprise, there were only a few lights on. With the pillar gone, maybe, just maybe, this could all be written off. More splashing followed. Morgana unleashed a wave of silver magic that knocked Alex's body and Arthur back. They both stumbled, but their blended magic remained. It grew thicker and thicker, like a gathering storm cloud. The crashing of the waves increased, and Aiden's eyes searched the dim shoreline.

"They're trying to escape!" he shouted.

Merlin's bright green magic continued to crawl towards Arthur as vines. The creature waved her free hand and dark gray magic coiled around them, choking the life out of them. Her eyes glowed with a strange light. The vines withered.

"Stop it!" Morgana called. "She's pulling your magic out of them!"

Nicki blasted several bolts at them which twisted around the shield and slammed into Arthur's side. He fell to the left, releasing Alex's hand and grasping at his side. Waving Alex's hands, the creature reached out towards them. There were no dark gray sparks, nothing came out, but the hints of color that lingered in the air spun towards her. The creature was harvesting their magic now. It smiled as the red, blue, yellow, and gold sparks turned a deep gray color.

A wave swept up into the air. Aiden gasped, fixing his eyes on it and waiting. Arthur was going to take the creature and run. They were about to lose Alex. Beneath his feet there was a faint pulse of magic, a tiny spark of energy that raced up his body, leaving a fiery, burning trail behind it. Common sense told him to fall back with the artifacts. The memory of his mother's face when he woke from his coma pushed forward. The hints of black toyed at the edges of his vision.

"Stop them!" Morgana screamed. Desperation, rage, and fear colored her voice. "Stop them now!"

The creature released a wave of magic that rolled across the island. When it struck Aiden's chest, he stepped back and gasped for air. His ears were ringing; his vision blurred. Distantly, he thought that he heard someone shouting. There were flashes of color that slowly became clearer as he blinked. Focusing on Arthur, Aiden swallowed and shook his head, trying to clear the fog. He found himself moving towards Arthur, moving towards the creature that held his friend captive.

More water spiraled up into the air. Aiden just barely caught a look of confusion and surprise on Arthur's face. He didn't understand it. Nicki's bolts continued to find weak points, but they weren't enough to take him down. Arthur grit his teeth, his eyes glaring at them all. The creature had her hand extended. The magic around her was growing, their attacks weakening as they approached. It wasn't enough.

Running forward, Aiden was raising Cathanáil before the thought processed. He was out of magic, but Cathanáil's hilt was warm in his hand. At the motion, it pulsed in his grip, sending a jolt of energy into his fingers. The black faded a little from his vision. He was upon Arthur in only a few seconds. Swinging Cathanáil, Aiden felt it hit the shield with a thud, but sparks of magic jumped up the blade and across his flesh. The shield vanished, the wall of black shattering. Arthur's eyes widened. He reached for the hilt. Aiden started to fall over, his grip loosening.

Bran caught him, hoisting him up by throwing his right arm around his shoulders. Cathanáil threatened to slip from his hand, but somehow, he found the strength to tighten his grip. Around him, the world was hazy and darkening fast.

"Stay with us!" Bran shouted. "I know it's been too much, but just stay with us!"

"The Artifacts," Aiden groaned. "We need to get them out of here."

"We will, but we have to keep them here," Bran said. "Shiva is coming. It'll be alright." Aiden didn't think he sounded all that confident.

"Robin..."

"I don't know," Bran said. "I think she's an Old One. That's not important right now."

Aiden wanted to protest, but his tongue was heavy. Blinking, he struggled to clear his vision. Nicki stepped forward, her stance defensive and her eyes jumping between him and the creature. Bran grabbed his arm and pulled him further back and away from Arthur.

Magic exploded behind him. A silver whip reached out and lashed Arthur's chest, sending him collapsing to the ground. Then it coiled around Alex's arm and dragged her away from the water. The creature screamed in shock, but green magic spun around her, binding her arms once again. A golden stream from Robin wrapped around the creature's chest, encasing it in a golden glow. It tried to twist its hands and closed its eyes. Aiden hoped they had a plan; they were just feeding it magic.

Behind the creature and Arthur, the water kept spinning. It was high and wide now, large enough to pass through. Arthur was climbing to his feet. Aiden fell back, holding onto Cathanáil like their lives all depended on it. They probably did. Then the water shifted. Light spilled out of it. Arthur and the creature looked at the tunnel and then at each other. Something was off.

"Get ready!" Merlin called.

A figure leapt out of the water. They hit the ground of the beach with a thud and straightened up. Aiden heard a cheer erupt from the mages. Shiva extended his six arms, armed with swords, a bow, and most importantly the Trishula. The creature tried to pull back, but the gold, silver, and green magical bindings held it fast. Shiva stepped forward, his dark eyes fixed on Alex's body, but lacking all the fondness that had filled them in India.

Shiva pushed the Trishula forward. Two of his arms moved, notching an arrow on his bow and firing at Arthur. The traitor retreated, throwing up another, much smaller shield in front of himself. Shiva's water tunnel collapsed, and Arthur cursed, glancing frantically between them and the shore. The creature pulled back from the Trishula, twisted away from the metal as it began to glow softly.

"Do not fight," Shiva ordered. His voice filled the air, echoing in Aiden's head. "You cannot take the Iron Soul."

Robin jumped forward and grabbed Alex's hand. Bringing it up, she forced the creature to touch the metal of the Trishula. It lit up like the sky at dawn as a scream ripped from Alex's throat. Pulses of light traveled up Alex's arm. Robin held her there.

Black bolts flashed through the air. Arthur's dark eye caught the light at just the right angle to make it look black. His attacks met a glowing blue wall that Nicki's hand was extended towards. She was panting, her limbs trembling. Aiden leaned against a tree as Bran finally let him go. His friend turned and waved his hands, summoning faint flickers of yellow magic.

The color of Alex's eyes were shifting: with each second, they faded to a lighter and lighter color. Her body trembled, but the light from the Trishula continued. Throwing its head back, the creature screamed and twisted, desperately fighting to free itself. Shiva didn't flinch. Robin kept a tight hold of her, preventing it from fleeing. Merlin and Morgana's magic shined even brighter than before, keeping the creature pinned.

"No, please," it begged in Alex's voice. "Please, don't. I'll die. I can't survive here. Please, I need to get away. I won't hurt you! I don't want to hurt you! Please let me go!"

"Stop it!" Arthur roared. His black magic darkened, forming a thicker aura around him. "Stop! Attack! Attack!"

"Fae!" Merlin called in warning. "Morgana! Your bridge!"

"Damnit!"

A dozen Fae came racing up the hillside, waving weapons including firearms. Pressing his back against the tree, Aiden gripped Cathanáil with two hands and brought the Sword up to protect himself. Alex's screams continued. He wanted to look, but one of the Fae was closing on him. He couldn't. He had to focus. Arthur had planned this. Somehow. Maybe he'd just had them waiting quietly in town, ready to strike when they saw the beacon. Aiden's mind couldn't settle on an explanation, but it didn't matter.

Nicki roared with rage. Swinging Mjǫllnir, she caught a Fae in the chest. Lightning flashed off of the blunt weapon and struck the next Fae. The Trishula flashed, blinding everyone on the island for a moment. Alex fell to the ground, suddenly silent and still; her long blonde hair spread across the muddy ground. More Fae rushed in. Out of the corner of his eye, Aiden saw Arthur staggering towards Alex while three of the Fae closed rank around him.

Two Fae grabbed Robin, one pulling on her hair to expose her neck while another brought up a dagger. Shiva was on his in seconds, slashing at the Fae with his swords. They backed off and circled the Old One and Robin. Arthur waved his hands towards the water, and it began to rise and swirl once again. A Fae charged Aiden while two more engaged Bran. Aiden couldn't keep track of everything. There were only hints of magic in the air. No one had anything left. Even Merlin had drawn a dagger.

The water spun up into the air, splashing violently as a rough whirlpool formed. Arthur lunged forward and grabbed Alex's collapsed body. Twisting around, Aiden tried to summon his magic, but there was nothing left. Beneath his feet the ground quaked, and Arthur pulled Alex up and slung her over his shoulder. She moved a little, but not enough to reassure him of who was in control. Shiva reached for them, but a group of Fae pushed forward, slashing at him with their weapons. Firearms went off. The sound of wood exploding rang in the night. Someone screamed. Another shouted. Shiva blocked the path of the bullets and struck down Fae in a whirl of limbs. Alex moved, lifted her head, and looked around weakly. Her eyes were gray. Dazed and distant, but gray.

"Alex!" Merlin shouted. "Fight! Don't let him take you!"

A second Fae rushed up on Aiden, and he flinched back. The closest one swung a short sword at him. A few feet away, he heard the click of a firearm. There was a blast of green light. More were coming. Arthur released a wave of magic that crashed over everything around him. A nearby tree split with a thunderous crack. Aiden lifted Cathanáil and swung the Sword at the nearest Fae. It tried to move back as it brought its sword up, but it was too late. The magic blade sliced into the flesh and Aiden flinched. It was too easy, and he hated it. Somehow, he lifted his arms and slammed the edge of the blade into the gut of the second Fae. They both dissolved into dust, leaving amulets, pistols, and clothing on the ground.

Cathanáil slipped from Aiden's hand at long last and hit the ground with a heavy thud as he slumped against the tree. Nicki raced past him, bending down and sweeping up Cathanáil. The Hammer fell to the ground, sinking into the mud. Aiden mustered the energy to look up, opening his mouth to call out to her. Nicki kept moving, raising Cathanáil. The blade gleamed in the light of Morgana's orb. Arthur started to run, letting Alex slip off his shoulder and fall to the ground. Arthur's feet hit the water. Aiden watched as he waded into the cold lake.

The water iced over. Shouting in pain, Arthur stopped, his fingers clawing at the surface of the ice. He was thigh high in ice. Then an icicle jutted out of the surface of the lake, slamming into Arthur's chest. Another followed and thrust into his side. Then another and another, pinning him in Nicki's ice. Blood flowed down the icicles, coloring them bright red. Nicki was upon him. Cathanáil flashed just before it was shoved into Arthur's gut. Arthur's hands came up, trying to stop Nicki and the Sword, but it was too late.

Everything was silent and still. No one spoke or cheered. Nicki withdrew Cathanáil and stepped back onto the shore, her body shaking. She crumbled to her knees. Arthur's mouth was open, gasping and stunned. The icicles that had stabbed him crumbled, turning back into water. A moment later, Nicki fainted, and the ice vanished. Arthur fell into the water face down, the waves pushing him further onto the shore.

33

Farewell

1 518 C.E. Strasbourg, Rhineland

Three months of nonstop dancing mania, and it was finally coming to close along with the heat of the summer. Michel almost didn't believe it. Months of worry, many deaths, and a general unease was finally rolling off the shoulders of the city. It didn't seem real. But the cool temperatures of the coming autumn were beginning to appear and the nights were growing longer each day.

Leaning against the wall of a small bakery, Michel closed his eyes and inhaled the warm smells wafting out of the shop. He wasn't hungry, but the scents were pleasant. A calm had descended on the city. The usual underlying fears of a bad harvest, political strife, or illness were still present, but at least the bizarre event had concluded. Compared to the near frantic state of things in August when the city had finally recognized that the stage was a horrible idea, Michel's life was almost normal.

Watching people in the street, Michel held back a sigh. He shouldn't be sad that the trouble was almost past. The Fae had gone home to their villages and, according to Merlin, one of the villages was going to relocate to prevent too much magic from building up. The business was fine, his friends were all settling into their apprenticeships, and no one was dying from the dancing plague. He should have been happy, or at least content, but he wasn't.

He didn't name the feelings storming in his chest. They created a peculiar ache that he hadn't experienced before. Suddenly he was frustrated and sad, and a little angry all at once, but the danger was past. The spell was almost completely unraveled, and the locals had dismissed claims of magic. The age of reason and science that Merlin and Morgana hoped for did truly seem to be dawning.

So, he should be happy and relieved. Life would return to normal. Sooner or later, he'd gain control of a solid merchant business with lines of trade already established thanks to Merlin and Morgana's connections. Yet, the churning emotions remained. Nothing had been resolved properly. There were still Fae in the world who were angry at the status quo, and he could do nothing. Hundreds had died in the dancing plague which had been an accident, so justice was complicated at best. It just left him uncertain and frustrated. What was he supposed to do with himself next? Kicking at the street, Michel huffed and looked around for any sign of Puck.

The Old One appeared in the distance a few moments later. Dressed in his usual dirty clothes, he swaggered down the street completely at ease. He was a being from another world, and yet he seemed more at home with humans than Michel was. It was one of those strange mysteries of Puck, along with his charm and talent with magic despite the rejection of the Iron Realm.

"Morning," Puck greeted as he got close. The bag slung over his shoulder made Michel's mouth dry out. "Thanks for meeting me, Michel. I appreciate it."

"Of course," he replied. "I wasn't going to send you off without a goodbye."

"Well, thank you. I know it wasn't under good circumstances, but it's been nice working with you over the last few weeks." Puck's smile widened, and his eyes were bright. Michel felt his cheeks heating up. "I'll miss you."

"Really?" Michel inwardly grimaced at how excited he sounded. "I mean, you could come back when the dancing plague is over."

"I'll visit," Puck said. "But I don't want to risk angering Morgana and Merlin by coming around too often."

Nodding, Michel licked his lips. It was hard not to look at the bag and be aware of the finality of this conversation. His feet tapped on the cobblestones as he waited for Puck to say more. The Old One didn't and merely adjusted his bag, seeming as uncertain as he was.

"I've heard that things like this have happened in other places." Michel leaned against the wall, using the rough wood to scratch an itch on his back. "Not as bad though. It's helped people accept it and move on."

"No, the other incidents weren't as bad," Puck said. "Those were just manias, I think. Or something that people ate." Puck's smile turned a touch sheepish. "It is where I got the idea, to be honest. Though I didn't mean for it to get so bad."

Michel knew that he should be mad. People had died. Not as many as the rumors proclaimed, though. If those numbers had been real, then more people would have fled the city rather than treating the whole thing as entertainment. Then again, people were strange creatures. One more reason why he was uneasy around them.

"At least they got rid of the stage quickly," Michel said. "That only made it worse."

"True," Puck agreed. "Honestly, I'm glad that they're sending the last dancers to the monastery. Ever since they barred them from dancing in public spaces it's been too difficult to find them."

"Still... we didn't do badly."

"No, we made a good team," Puck agreed.

"I'm sorry I'm not going with you," Michel said.

"I don't think that the Shrine of Saint Vitus is going to be that interesting." Puck shrugged lazily, but Michel thought that his friend was disappointed too. "We've unraveled enough of the spell that I think it's ending on its own. Even the first victim was fine once she was removed from the city. I can sort it out by myself. You've done more than enough."

Michel nodded. He didn't know Frau Troffea at all, but the news of her recovery at the shrine had been tremendous. Puck's theory was that getting away from the epicenter of the spell had helped weaken it. He wasn't about to give any credit to a Christian saint on the matter.

"Almost done then," Michel said. "Are you sure you even want to bother going to the shrine?"

"Seems like a good idea," Puck replied. He didn't meet Michel's eyes. "Just to be sure. The spell is falling apart here, and the last of the dancers are being sent to the monastery. The last thing we want is the lingering magic to grow stronger again. Besides... Morgana is losing patience with me."

"I won't let her hurt you," Michel promised.

Puck's smile widened though his eyes dimmed. "They're immortal you know, or near to it. My kind lives much much longer than humans. Even if she doesn't hurt me while you're alive, there's no promise that she won't come after me later."

"She's not that terrible."

"You're her student, and she helped raise you," Puck said. He tilted his head a touch. "I'm not sure if she sees you as a son or not, but she cares about you, Michel. You're safe from her wrath either way."

"I suppose so." Michel swallowed and fell silent.

"What?" Puck pressed.

"They're talking about leaving soon," Michel said. "Not immediately, but Merlin is talking about teaching me how to keep the books. He and Morgana were talking the other night about needing to leave before people ask about their ages. They came here because of the high level of magic, and it's starting to fade now. That was almost fifteen years ago now, and they haven't changed."

"They do look too young for a nephew your age." Puck glanced around and then leaned closer. "Why do you call them aunt and uncle, not mother and father?"

"I don't know," Michel admitted. "I suppose that people knew Morgana wasn't pregnant or maybe they weren't comfortable with it. All I know about my birth family is that when I was born, Merlin paid them gold to turn me over and they took it." He ignored the small pang of hurt that the idea caused. "We don't talk about them. I suppose it doesn't matter. It was better for Merlin and Morgana to take care of me."

"So, will you stay here after they go?"

"Probably... it's the only home I've ever known." Michel's eyes traced the nearby buildings. "I'm not sure what to do with myself now. Honestly, you're one of the first people I've ever been able to talk to."

Puck swallowed, his Adam's apple bobbing. His eyes softened, and they stared at each other with soft, sad smiles.

"I'll come to visit," Puck said finally. "Once I'm done at the monastery, I'll swing through to let you mages know that all is well."

"Then what?"

"I can't stay here," Puck said. "Too many of the Fae... they're angry. They don't know the full truth, but they know that everything fell apart. Many of them died, and it achieved nothing." Guilt filled Puck's eyes, though his expression stayed tight and neutral. "There were some who were thrilled at the plague, who wanted humans to die in the area." Shaking his head, Puck allowed himself a deep sigh. "So much happened, and it fixed nothing."

"I think... I think that's how it works, sometimes," Michel offered softly. The words were too little, but they were all that came to mind. "If there were a solution then I'm sure that one of my previous lives would have tried to fix it. I know that Merlin and Morgana don't like it. They spared the descendants of the first warriors and the free slaves who started this." Michel looked at the ground, watching a small insect crawl between the stones that made up the road. "I'm not sure there's a solution. We can only do what we can."

"Seems like compassion is useless then," Puck grumbled. "I was trying to help."

"I know." Michel reached out and touched Puck's shoulder. Heat radiated off of the Old One's body. "I know that, Puck. And I think Morgana and Merlin understand that too. That's why-" He stopped himself, but Puck snorted in understanding.

"Why they haven't killed me," he finished. "Sometimes they seem too soft and other times too hard. They're strange."

"They've lived a long time. Merlin told me once that you have to be careful to live a life that you can live with."

"Good advice."

"...What are your plans for after this is done?"

"My mother is going back to England," Puck said. "With Morgana and Merlin living on the continent, she wants some distance after this. I figure that I'll join her there, at least for a while."

"You will stay out of trouble, right?"

"Well..."

"Puck."

"Mostly," Puck said. "Mostly." Smiling mischievously, a faint dimple appeared on his cheek and Puck's eyes lit up. "I'll have a bit of fun, but I'll be careful," he promised.

"Just keep in mind that Merlin and Morgana won't be inclined to forget you."

"Won't be inclined to forget me," Puck repeated. "That is an impressive warning."

"I just don't want you getting into too much trouble," Michel said.

"I'm more worried about you," Puck said.

"Why?"

"You're sweet," Puck answered. He wasn't looking at him and instead was watching a cat leap between barrels across the street. "That can be dangerous. You care a lot. That compassion issue again."

"Maybe, but I'd rather care than not."

"Then I just hope it doesn't trick you into doing something horrible like it did me." Puck's tone was soft and distant, his sorrow thick in the air. "A lot of people died because of me."

"I'm sorry. I wish I could take that pain away."

"Compassion," Puck said again wistfully. Then he shook his head and straightened up. "Enough of that. We're just going in circles. The wagons are leaving soon, so I should get a move on."

"How are you getting there?"

"Walking," Puck answered. He didn't seem concerned. "Weather is still fine, so it shouldn't be an issue. I'll be a little behind the wagons, but not too much."

"Are you sure? We could probably arrange-"

"I'll be fine," Puck assured him. His smile was fond. "I'll miss you. It's been nice for me too, having someone to talk to. Mother was always very protective. She didn't like me talking with other children."

A wagon rolled past filled with boxes and barrels. The driver glanced their way, but his gaze didn't linger. They were just two young men. Holding back a laugh, Michel wondered what they would all think if they knew the truth. He sobered quickly. They'd try to kill Puck. He was sure that it was possible to kill an Old One, based on Merlin and Morgana's stories of his past lives, but he doubted any normal human would manage the feat.

"It'll be boring without you," Michel said. "But thank you, Puck. I mean it. Thank you for wanting to help. Thank you for coming to us and telling us what had happened. You could have fled, but you didn't. I'm grateful for that."

"You're welcome." Puck's cheeks didn't redden, but Michel had the impression that he was embarrassed. "Thank you for having faith in me. When I reached the shop, I almost turned around. I almost didn't come in. I was so sure that Morgana and Merlin would attack me."

Another wagon rolled past. In the distance, a bell rang. Puck sighed. They were just dragging this out now, and Michel had no idea what to say now. He was flattered and happy now, in addition to every other messy emotion he was feeling.

"At least things are calm now," Michel finally said. "It's not- not a good ending exactly, but at least it is some kind of ending."

"Yes," Puck agreed. "But I still worry."

"Me too; someday it's not going to be enough to just hold the status quo," Michel said. The sun vanished behind a cloud, dropping the temperature in the street. "I know I probably won't be around to see it, but... I will be, in some form."

"I don't know what'll happen," Puck said. "But if things get bad and I'm still around, I'll come and help you. In whatever form you're in then."

"Even if Merlin and Morgana are still around?" Michel smiled a little as he asked the question.

Puck made a face but nodded. "Even then. I may hide behind you from then on to keep her from killing me."

"I'm sure she'll move on."

"It's nice that you believe that. I don't, but you should."

"If you're going to be mean then maybe you should go!" Michel huffed. He couldn't help his smile from widening. "Before I decide to take you out."

"Nah, you won't. You like me too much."

"I might like you a little, but only a little."

Puck's answering smile could have lit up the street. Adjusting his bag, he glanced around the road before leaning forward and kissing Michel's cheek. "I'll be back to visit," he promised. "Especially once the Grand Mages are gone."

Opening his mouth, Michel's brain tried to catch up with what was happening and respond. Then he just gave up and smiled. Puck's smile turned more easy going. He gave a little wave and turned to start walking away. Puck stopped and looked over his shoulder again. Michel smiled, ignoring the way that his heart was pounding and nodded.

"I'll see you soon," Michel promised. "Just be careful."

"I promise," Puck said. "Uh... don't tell Morgana I just did that."

"Don't worry," Michel laughed. "I won't."

Puck winked. His eyes gleamed with mischief, but Michel wasn't worried that Puck didn't mean his promise. The Old One nodded once more to him and headed down the road. Exhaling slowly, Michel shook his head and gave up on trying to gather his thoughts. Life, it seemed for the Iron Soul, was simply strange, and there was nothing he could do about it. At least, for now, the darker thoughts and questions were silenced. He wasn't going to discover the solution to the Iron Realm eroding the foreign beings in it today.

34

Awakening

Groaning, Alex struggled in vain to open her eyes. The last vestiges of a nightmare slipped away, but she was troubled. The dream lacked an ending, leaving only fear and a horrible sense of dread in its wake. Her eyelids were heavy, and pain pulsed through her body despite the warm, soft surface beneath her. Awareness came slowly, but Alex identified the weight across her chest as blankets.

Content that she was safe for the time being and tentatively dismissing her dread as merely the leftovers of her nightmare, Alex wrestled her eyes open. Lights were on, and the ceiling lamp was her own. Lowering her eyes away from the brightness, Alex blinked a few times before her eyes found something to settle on.

Galahad was on top of her chest, looking right at her with those dark plastic stuffed animal eyes. Her lips quirked into a smile, and the fondness billowing through her chased away the lingering dread. But it was not enough to dispel the pain. Alex tried to remember why she hurt. Shuddering, she recalled the battle against the Light. The scents and sounds returned with brutal force, stabbing her with a sharp knife of panic and twisting until she gasped for air.

"Easy, Alex," Morgana's voice said. "You're alright. It's alright. You're safe." The older woman suddenly appeared beside her, sitting on the edge of Alex's bed.

"What?" Alex finally recognized the dull burning ache that had settled into her bones as the indicator of overuse of magic. That wasn't good, and it instantly brought back an image of that horrible Light and battle. "What happened?"

"What do you remember?" Morgana asked cautiously.

"The Light," Alex whispered. Sitting up, she looked around nervously and clutched Galahad with one hand. Her desk was intact, Galahad wasn't damaged, and the room seemed as she'd left it. Twisting around, she noted that the Sword and the Hammer were missing. "It was in my head, and I was- It took over. It defeated me."

'Us,' a soft inner whisper said. 'We all lost.' It was Arto's voice, faint, but there. Alex's shoulders slumped in relief. 'Safe now.'

"Alex?"

"The voices are back," Alex said softly. "At least, Arto is back."

Morgana's expression fluttered through several different emotions before returning to neutral at the mention of her brother. Alex's chest tightened. It hadn't been that long, but already she struggled to recall the faces of her brothers. She couldn't imagine holding onto affection for three thousand years, but Morgana had.

"What happened?" Alex asked softly.

"You shouted for the Trishula," Morgana said. "Aiden had the others alerted us, and we kept the creature from hurting you or leaving town."

"Is everyone alright?" Alex asked. Her fingers dug into Galahad's soft fur. "I didn't hurt them, did I?"

"Everyone is exhausted," Morgana admitted. "A few injuries, I'm afraid. Nicki was shot in the shoulder and Merlin in the thigh." She held up a hand before Alex could freak out. "They're fine now with the help of the Iron Chalice. Thankfully, Shiva took most of the bullets. You might not remember, but he kept physically blocking the Fae who were using firearms. Due to being an energy being, he was able to fix himself up within a few hours." Alex couldn't remember any of that, but just hearing about it made her feel sick. Morgana hesitated, a strangely pleased and worried expression overtaking her features. "A great deal happened, Alex. I'm not sure where to start."

Alex glanced towards the window. Light brightened the fabric of the curtains in a way that told her it was later in the morning. Morgana followed her gaze and nodded.

"We were lucky," Morgana said to start with. "The creature wasn't interested in the mages or the magical items. It went out to an island on the lake and created a beacon. We're not sure why, but it drew Arthur and some Fae he must have had spying in town."

"It was calling him," Alex whispered. "His eye... it was like mine. Maybe he was possessed too, and they were trying to meet up."

Morgana inclined her head thoughtfully, but then she smiled. "It doesn't matter now. He's dead. Nicki gutted Arthur," Morgana explained, with apparent glee in her voice. "He was trying to flee after you were freed."

"...He's dead?" Alex repeated. "Are you sure?"

Merlin suddenly spoke up from the doorway, "Really most sincerely dead." He was smiling and leaning against the doorframe. He looked younger than he had yesterday, with the furrow on his brow gone and his eyes brighter. "The body is in the back of my SUV. I'll destroy it at my home just to be sure."

Telling herself to keep breathing, Alex tried to remember it, or at least imagine it. But there was nothing after the burning heat of the Light.

Not even a vague impression. Time had stopped and then restarted when she woke up. Swallowing, she tried to find some words, but nothing came to mind. Arthur dead. Nicki had killed him. That part wasn't a surprise. Alex had always figured that Arthur should fear Nicki. As angry as Jenny was over their history, she lacked an instinct for violence. Nicki did not.

"Wow," Alex finally whispered. "That's...it's a lot to take in."

"Without his leadership and magical abilities to help them, we expect the Fae to scatter," Morgana was glowing with satisfaction.

"That's good," Alex said. She brought Galahad closer so she could hold him with both hands. "I'm sorry about all of this. If I hadn't tried to look into the Tree of Reality-" Alex cut off her apology. While she was sorry that this had happened, there was a small part of her that didn't regret it. Her trips had confirmed the danger. "We still have the Darkness to worry about."

'Yes,' one of the voices whispered. 'The Darkness is spreading. Branches dead, only roots remain healthy.' Alex knew that voice. The image of an iron jar came to mind, and she remembered a man firing at the Light with a bow. 'Must be ready.'

"Alex?" Merlin called. "Are you alright?"

"Yes." Alex shook herself. "Arthur dead. That's good. Really good. Uh, is Timothy okay?"

"He is, and Jenny, Avani, and Lance evacuated quickly," Merlin answered. He glanced at Morgana and gently said. "Aiden said that his *friend* will be here soon. She just called and reported that the clean up on the island is complete."

The way he said friend made Alex frown. Morgana's smile faded, and she looked towards the window. Something ticked at Alex's memory, but nothing solid manifested. She was lost.

"Now?"

"She did keep her distance when we commanded it," Merlin reminded Morgana. "And while I don't like to admit it, she was very helpful in that battle. That creature made perfect use of Alex's powers."

Alex wasn't sure that she wanted to know what that meant and didn't ask. Nodding, Morgana climbed to her feet and brushed a speck of dust off her green sweater.

"Fine. Alex, stay here."

"No," Alex said. Shaking her head, she swung her feet out of bed and stood up, ignoring the lingering pains throughout her body. "I'm confused as it is, Morgana. I don't want to stay here and wonder what is going on."

She couldn't stay here. Alex shifted away from the bed and looked down at herself. She was dressed in an old t-shirt and shorts that she hadn't worn to bed. Again, she tried to remember what had happened but nothing came forth. Merlin and Morgana were looking at each other in another silent conversation that Alex ignored.

"Alex-" Merlin started to say.

"No," Alex said firmly. "I remember nothing that happened. My body was taken over. I'm not going to sit in my room with no control or knowledge of what is happening now."

Morgana's expression turned pained. She quickly moved around the bed as Alex pulled on her robe. Sighing softly, Merlin nodded in agreement. He reached out his hand and put it on her head. The familiar gesture made Alex pause and inhale slowly. Some of the aches eased, and there were a few warm, happy whispers in response.

The pair of older mages didn't make a fuss about her going downstairs. Each of them watched her carefully as she brushed out her hair and pulled on her slippers. It wasn't anything fancy, and in truth, Alex knew she should get dressed, but she didn't have the energy. Stubbornness alone was keeping her upright.

Downstairs in the living room, Aiden was waiting with a pretty dark-skinned woman who was wearing jeans caked with mud. Aiden was fidgeting and jumped to his feet when he caught sight of Alex.

"How are you feeling?"

"I'm okay," Alex said. "I'm sorry I scared you."

Swallowing, Aiden nodded and stepped forward, opening his arms. Alex accepted the hug gratefully, enjoying Aiden's body heat as she watched the woman over his shoulder. She was smiling a little at them, but her expression faltered a little as she caught sight of Merlin and Morgana.

"You arrived quickly," Merlin said. He walked forward, staying close to Alex.

"Cleanup was done," the woman answered. "All the clothing is picked up, and I took care of the blood on the beach. If people go out there, they'll see lots of footprints and some evidence of a boat."

"A boat?" Morgana repeated.

"College party made sense," the woman replied. "And we don't want them believing that an ice bridge was used, do we?"

Again, Alex was left dazed at how much she had missed. Tonight, she'd try to sit down with the others and get a complete recap. The woman's eyes met hers, and she stood from the armchair, giving Alex a slight bow and a mischievous smile. Something about the smile was very familiar.

"Who are you?" Morgana asked sternly.

"You know me," Robin said delicately. "We've met many times over the centuries, though I usually do my best to avoid you. I saw you last about two hundred years ago."

'Puck,' a voice whispered. Alex identified it as Michel.

"Puck," she said out loud. A dozen images flashed through her head as the word left her lips. "Uh, you're Puck, aren't you?"

"Yes."

"Puck," Morgana spat. "What dirty swamp did you crawl out of?"

"Lovely to see you too, Morgana," Puck replied. There was no anger in her eyes, and instead, she simply gave Morgana a charming smile. "I woke about a year ago. I've been keeping busy learning about the modern world. I'm sorry for the way modern culture remembers you: that's got to be uncomfortable." Morgana's glare increased, but Puck kept on talking. "Once I was confident in my ability to pass for a human, I came to the convergence point of magic and decided to investigate the mages a little."

"You were spying on us," Bran said. He tensed next to Alex, and she reached for his hand. Alex squeezed it quickly, hoping he'd understand to remain calm.

Puck actually frowned, looking hurt. Tossing her head, she made her thick hair bounce and fixed a smile back on her face. "Spied would be too strong a word. I've never broken into your home; I've never used my power to see anything unusual. I merely became a college student and talked to one of you while keeping my ear to the ground about what was going on."

"Why are you here at all, Puck?" Merlin asked. He put a hand on Morgana's shoulder and gave Puck a slight smile. "We've not seen you for some time."

"No, you haven't." Puck glanced at Morgana. "I made mistakes long ago. I know that, and you helped me fix what I had done. Since then, I've avoided trouble." Morgana snorted. "Too much trouble at least," Puck amended. "Things don't look good, Merlin. Old Ones waking all over the world, Demons breaking through the defenses, the Sídhe trying to invade again and the Fae rallying behind a new leader. That's a lot going wrong at once." Puck's eyes jumped between the mages. "No wonder there are so many of them now. Usually, there weren't."

Aiden tensed, and Puck seemed to make a point not to look too closely at him. Alex's thoughts were drawn back to Puck's words as several of her past selves agreed with the statement. In their references to the past, Merlin and Morgana would mention a couple of mages, but never such a large group. There were faint memories of a few other mages, but most of the time it had been herself, Merlin, and Morgana.

"It's easier for people to travel now and medicine is far improved," Morgana replied. "I suspect that there were always meant to be more mages, but they either died too young or never found the way to where they were needed. After all, only one of the mages was born here. All the others moved here at different times."

"And the leader of the Fae is now dead," Merlin added. "And the Demon's portal has been closed."

"But something is happening to trigger all those events," Puck said firmly. "Too much has happened in too short a time. It bears investigating."

"What are you?" Aiden asked suddenly.

"I'm an Old One," Robin-Puck said carefully. "We're beings of energy. I may have been born in this world, but that's still true for me. I can look like whatever I want." Shrugging, Puck shifted a little nervously, but that smile didn't disappear from their face. "I decided to try something new."

"Something new," Aiden repeated. His voice was thin, shifting towards panic. Alex flinched, wishing she had the strength to go to her room. "A girl?"

"I've been female before," Puck replied. This time they did roll their eyes. "Honestly, you humans and your fixation on genitals. It's weird; I hope you understand that. No, I decided when I woke up last year that I needed to learn a bit more about the modern mages. I got myself caught up and decided to play human on hard mode." Puck gestured to their face and down their body. "Black woman with natural hair. Human life on hard mode. Granted, things are a bit easier on a college campus."

"So, this whole time, you've been studying us?" Aiden's tone didn't give away much.

"Yes and no, I was curious about you, but I am truly a student and doing all the work." Puck's smile widened, and their eyes gleamed with delight. "The things that humans can build now... it really is amazing. I was awake for a bit during the space race, and I'll tell you, that was a hell of a time to be paying attention to science."

"I'll take your word for it."

"I'm sorry," Puck said suddenly. Their happiness faded, and they sighed. "I've freaked you out, haven't I? Is it the gender thing? Cause' I've got to say, Aiden, I was expecting better than that from you."

"No!" Aiden shook his head. "It's not that at all. I just... you're an Old One. We haven't had the best of luck with them. They either seem to be allies or crazy."

"Well, I'm a little crazy," Puck admitted. "But not corrupted, being torn apart crazy." Puck's expression changed again, turning wistful. "I learned my lesson a long time ago."

Morgana made a sound of displeasure but didn't add anything to it. In Alex's head, Michel sighed, but there was a ripple of fondness through her mind. Arto grumbled about Morgana's stubbornness while many of the others were simply fascinated by Puck. Alex's mind jumped back to when Merlin had taught them about Shakespeare's play *A Midsummer Night's Dream* in class. He would have known Puck then. At least he was calmer than Morgana about this.

"I'm here to help," Puck said solemnly. "I give you my word. You may recall that I also owed a debt to the Iron Soul." Robin inclined her head toward Alex, a soft, affectionate smile on her face. "I confess, learning that you had a female form was part of my inspiration. To think that I once assumed that your cycle of reincarnation would get boring."

"Puck," Morgana scolded. "Now is not the time to toy with Alex."

Alex glanced at Aiden. He was pale, his mouth pinched. In any other circumstances, she would have thought Aiden was about to be sick. He still might be, but then he groaned and rubbed the back of his neck. Puck's gaze jumped over to him, but he didn't meet her eyes. In a low voice, Aiden excused himself and hurried off to shower, leaving Alex in her chair and Morgana watching Puck disdainfully. The Old One merely sighed, nodded deeply to Alex, and headed for the front door.

"We'll be in touch," Merlin added. "Thank you for your help."

Puck stopped and looked back at them. She inclined her head again before adding, "You best deal with the body in your car, Merlin." Then she was out the door, letting it slam behind her.

"Body?" Alex repeated. Then it hit her, and she swallowed. "Arthur."

"Yes," Merlin admitted. "I wanted... I wanted to check on a few things before destroying his body. He was made with the Iron Chain. I don't want to risk something backfiring."

"He's outside," Alex said.

Walking to the front door, she opened it again and looked out. Robin, or rather Puck, had climbed into a small white sedan and was pulling out. Alex only watched her for a moment before her eyes went to Merlin's SUV. The dark windows in the back hid anything from view. He was in there. Arthur, the man who had killed her parents, tried to kill her, and been the source of so much suffering. He was dead, and in a car, waiting for his final destruction.

"Alex?" Morgana called. Gently, she put her hands on Alex's shoulders, standing right behind her. "It's alright. It's over now."

"There's still the Darkness," Alex said.

"Yes, and we will deal with that," Morgana promised.

"What about me? Are you sure that thing in my head is gone?" She still didn't look away from the SUV.

"We believe so," Merlin answered.

Belief was not certainty. Alex nodded to herself and pushed open the screen door. Morgana's hands fell off her shoulders, but Alex could feel the woman follow her outside. Behind her, Alex heard the crunch of Merlin and Morgana on the gravel. Some of the stones were sharp enough to poke the bottom of her feet through her slippers. Alex noted that her feet felt more tender than before, but wasn't sure why.

The SUV was unlocked. Pulling on the handle, Alex leaned back to allow the rear door to swing open. A blanket had been tossed over the body, but part of a boot was sticking out on the far side. His head was right in front of her.

"Alex," Merlin said gently. "It's him. We're sure. Nicki spat on him when it was all said and done."

"That doesn't surprise me," Alex said softly. She was suddenly happy that the others were occupied. "I need to see him."

"Alex-"

"Leave her, Merlin," Morgana said. "Remember his wrongs. She needs to know that he's really gone."

With that blessing, Alex pulled back the blanket to reveal Arthur's face. His eyes were closed, and Alex almost wanted to open them and check his irises. His skin lacked color. Memories of her parents in their coffins sprang to mind. Other beloved faces caught by death pushed their way forward in her mind, threatening to overwhelm her. Shaking herself like a dog trying to rid itself of cold water, Alex reached out and touched Arthur's neck.

A spark of magic jumped from her fingers, sending a painful shock up her arm. Like a static shock but a dozen times worse. Morgana pulled her back as Alex waved her hand, trying to cool the sudden burn. Arthur remained still, and Alex sighed in relief. The voices in her head grew louder and clearer. She frowned and studied Arthur's face.

"That's that," Merlin said. "But there might still be some magic in his system. We don't know much about those creatures. Judging from his eye, I'd say that he was carrying one too."

"Be careful with the body," Morgana said. "Just to be on the safe side."

"I will be," Merlin promised. His lips were pressed, and he was eying the body with renewed worry.

Alex flexed her fingers. Strangely, despite the aftermath of the shock, she felt a bit better. More alert, her thoughts a bit clearer, and the voices were more distinct. Names and small facts flowed over her surface awareness and started to organize themselves.

Then Arthur's hand moved. Morgana tugged her back, shoved Alex behind her, and raised a hand to summon some silver sparks. Arthur's eyes flew open, and he gasped for air, his back arching. Merlin raised his hand, green sparks encircling his fist, and Arthur tilted his head to catch sight of the mages. His eyes were dark, almost black. They glowed bright white for a moment. Merlin and Morgana both released their magic, but a sharp light encircled Arthur's body. He vanished.

35

Hollow Victory

The sun was high in the sky now, and normal life in Ravenslake had resumed. Cars were zipping across the bridge, and Alex almost thought that she could hear the noise of the campus, even across the lake. She couldn't of course, but her senses were raw. Every sound was a little too loud. Even the faint breeze on her skin was heightened in sensation.

Alex rolled her shoulders and inhaled slowly. Her lungs expanded, and she paid close attention to the beat of her heart. It was all so much more distinct. The memory of her failure, of the Light burning into her, pushed itself forward. Shivering, Alex tried to push it away, but it was impossible to ignore.

She'd been possessed. Something from another world had taken over her. It had been frightened and desperate, but it had decided to use her and risk her survival for its own. There was no getting around that. Alex didn't remember anything. Just the Darkness and the Light burning her. Then she'd woken up in her bed, gasping for air and confused, but so grateful to see the others. At least it hadn't been for long. They'd been there for her, and they kept Arthur from leaving with the being.

It was fortunate that the Light didn't know how to make water tunnels. If it had... well, Alex didn't want to think about that. Exhaling, she watched the water ripple onto the beach. There were a dozen things she should be doing. Classes were in session, but today wasn't the day to attend them. She had homework waiting and all those little things that made up the rest of her life.

She didn't move. Alex made no effort to leave the beach. All the heat had burned away with the Light, leaving an aching cold that Alex didn't know how to deal with. It was for the best, but as she tightened her coat around her, Alex almost regretted it. She shouldn't. Maybe it was some sort of Stockholm syndrome, feeling sympathy for the thing possessing you, or maybe she was just too terrified of what it all meant now.

Was Arthur dead? She thought so. Yet something had happened. Flexing her fingers, Alex felt the phantom of the sting that had occurred when that spark had jumped from her to his corpse. Merlin and Morgana couldn't explain it or where he'd gone. Alex hoped that he'd been burned up by whatever that Light was, but doubted it. Those last moments near him, he'd felt different. Some of the magic, some of the scent and presence that she'd gotten used to were gone. Replaced with something else. Swallowing, Alex searched the beach and found a large smooth rock. She sat down on it, grimacing at the chill. Even the sun hadn't been able to warm it up much.

Stretching out her jean-clad legs, Alex let the sunshine sink into her flesh and bones. Maybe she needed a nap on the couch in the living room with the curtains open. Curled up in a sunbeam like a cat. The mental image helped. Her lips curved into a small smile. Maybe that would be enough to dispel the last of the cold that she couldn't shake. Of course, sleeping meant dreams. While the Light was gone, her memory was scarred. The peaceful plain had reformed, but deep gorges marred its surface. Though the voices had returned, they were hesitant. They were all trying to recover, trying to find a way forward, but unsure what it looked like. Even Cuthbert had stopped his usual dark and insulting rumblings. It should have been a relief, but it wasn't. They were scared. Even the memories of her soul had been shaken by the effort, and she didn't know if they could recover. That Light, that spark of life from another world, had hurt her, maybe more than even Arthur had ever managed.

That Arthur was gone. Alex was sure of that. All attempts to scry for Arthur as they knew him had been a dead end. It was an instinct, a gut reaction that told Alex that Arthur was dead. But it did not answer the question of what would happen now.

Groaning, Alex tried to shut her brain off and just focus on the pretty scenery. Couldn't she have a day of peace and quiet without having to worry about what came next?

'No,' Leugio whispered. 'You can't.'

'Sorry,' Thor added. 'But you're the Iron Soul.'

"Thank you for clearing that up," Alex grumbled. "It's not that helpful."

Low chuckles rolled over the surface of her mind. Then she heard the gravel shift behind her.

'Someone's here,'

'It's Puck,' Michel said.

Turning around on her rock, Alex kept her body relaxed and smiled a little. Robin or Puck was walking towards her, carefully navigating the slope of the hill with a warm, autumn red scarf trying to fall off her shoulders. Puck offered her a slight smile and quickly fixed the scarf.

"Hello, Alex."

"Morning, Puck," Alex said. "Or do you prefer Robin?" Another thought occurred to Alex. "Which pronouns?"

She could hear Cuthbert grumbling at her but ignored his comments about Robin's chosen race. His voice became a touch muffled, and she wondered if the others were able to shut him up.

"The name Robin has grown on me over the years," Robin replied. "And she and her pronouns are fine." She gave Alex a warm smile. "How are you?"

"A bit dazed," Alex replied honestly. "But I hear the others again." She frowned as one of the voices pushed forward. It was familiar, and she easily placed the name as Michel. A few memories flashed across her eyes, but she lacked context. "Uh... Michel says hello."

Robin's face lit up, and her smile widened into a grin. "Hello back, Michel." She waved a little and adjusted her stance to stand more comfortably. "That's a bit odd for you, isn't it?"

"A bit," Alex said. "But it's not the first-time a past life has wanted to interact with an old friend or loved one."

"Sif might have mentioned something about Thor showing up when I spoke with her," Robin agreed. Then she came a little closer, slipping her hands into the pockets of her coat. "So... do you remember me?"

"There's bits and pieces," Alex said. "Flashes, but I don't know how it fits together."

"Well, Michel helped me clean up a mess I'd made. When that was done, I jumped over to live in England where I became a beloved figure in folklore." Alex gave Robin a look, but the Old One just smiled and shrugged. "After Merlin and Morgana moved on a few years later, leaving Michel with the shop they ran in Strasbourg, I made a point of coming to visit every so often. He was a sweet man, kind, and generous, but he also knew how to have fun." Robin sighed wistfully and shook her head. "Morgana was right. I was a bad influence on him."

"Did he marry?"

"No: Michel's childhood with Merlin and Morgana left him with some difficulty in trusting others. He could never bring himself to tell people he was a mage, and Michel didn't want to marry with that kind of secret. He took in a few orphans here and there and did a lot of charity work. He had a lot of friends, and of course me. I think he was content when he passed on." Robin's smile shifted to something a bit more mischievous, but she didn't explain.

"That's good," Alex said. "I've got too many tragedies as it is."

"Yes, I suppose you do."

"Are you staying?" Alex asked. "As Robin." She glanced over the female form. It wasn't bad, but a part of her brain was rather confused. It wasn't just Michel either; she'd grown up with culture always making Puck male.

"I think so," Robin said. "I'm mostly caught up on the modern world, and from what your fellow mages have told me, it sounds like you could use the help."

"Yeah, the Darkness is- I'm not sure what to do there."

"Well, I don't know how much I can help," Robin said. "But I'm here to help however I can."

"What about Aiden?" Alex asked. Ignoring Michel's voice, Alex straightened up and tried to look intimidating. "Were you seeing him just to study us?"

"No, I wasn't. As for what happens next, that's up to Aiden. He's a bit thrown at the moment, but in my defense, I wanted to learn a bit more about all of you before jumping in."

"Do you really like him?"

"I do. He's funny and sweet. Nicki's a bit terrifying, but I think she'll warm up to me if Aiden decides that he wants to give this a try." Robin's gaze shifted to the lake. "Being in a relationship with an Old One is hard.

I wouldn't blame him if he's not interested. It's tough balancing the different natures."

"Have you been in a relationship with a human before?"

"Several," Puck answered. Her eyes darted towards Alex, and that mischievous smile was back again. "Let's also just say that there were other reasons that Michel never married."

Michel's reaction was immediate in her head, but Alex left him to his freak out. She didn't care, and his embarrassment was the last thing she needed. Though, Michel was also radiating fond exasperation which amused Alex. They must have had an interesting relationship.

"So," Puck said. "Have Merlin and Morgana learned anything?"

"No," Alex said. "No luck scrying and Morgana isn't sure what to look for. Bran even tried his tarot deck."

"That's not surprising," Puck admitted. "I've been thinking about these 'Lights,' and it seems likely that they're from the same branch as the Old Ones. They seem to be similar beings, but have less ability to adjust to this world."

"So?"

"Well, one was able to possess you. I think it's likely that Arthur is dead given the damage your friend inflicted."

"So, you think another Light is just possessing his corpse?"

"Possible," Robin said.

"Then why didn't it work right away?" Alex asked. "Why wait until I touched him?"

"Maybe it needed a bit more power. Maybe the remnant of the other Light in you transferred to it. I'm afraid I can't answer for sure. I was born in this world. I lack an understanding of what the homeworld was like."

A car door slammed, and Alex lowered her head at the rush of voices. They'd found her. She wasn't surprised. Now that they lived on this side of the lake, she wasn't even very far from home. And at the worst of times, she often found herself here watching the light dance off the waves. She didn't move, didn't run away as she listened to the crunch of shoes against the gravel that formed most of the lake's beach.

"Hello, Bran," Robin said behind her. "Any news?"

"I'm afraid not," Bran answered. "Other than that, the lights on the island have been dismissed as college kids partying. You did a good job with the cleanup."

"Thank you," Robin said. "Though leaving plastic cups there would have been more convincing."

Alex finally turned around. Bran was dressed against the autumn chill in a long coat with the labels turned up. His eyes brightened when she looked at him, and some tension drained out of his shoulders. She felt a little guilty for her distance the last few days.

"How are you feeling, Alex?" Bran asked. "No headaches?"

"Nope," Alex answered. She popped the p sound at the end of the word more than necessary. "I feel fine. The voices are back in their usual annoying glory." A few of them grumbled at that statement, but the underlying sense of victory and relief was still strong in all of them. "I'm okay." Looking over at Bran, she took in his doubtful look. "I will be. But we need to rethink some things."

"How so?"

"The Darkness. It's just going to keep pushing things towards us. Desperate and frightened beings. They aren't trying to invade: they are just running for their lives."

"So, you want to stop the Darkness."

"That's my thought."

"Any ideas?"

"Not yet," Alex said. Looking at the water again, she remembered watching the Darkness move clearly. "But I'm certain that it's happened before. Been to Earth before, I mean."

"I'm pretty sure that Morgana and Merlin would have remembered that."

One of the voices, one that had long been in the background, spoke up. He gave a warning, a simple, but clear warning. She was right. The Darkness was spreading through the Tree of Reality, and somehow, at some point, it had gotten close to Earth. She just needed to learn more about that mysterious metal jar.

"Alex?" Robin asked.

"I've seen it before," Alex said. "Another life. There's something I need to find. Memories and a metal jar," she explained. It was difficult to string the right words together. "I think one of my past selves fought the Darkness. He was Indigenous, I think. If he had a way to stop the Darkness, then I need to find it."

"Then what?" Robin pressed. "And what about that creature with Arthur's body? Do you think it's friend or foe?"

That was a good question, but it was only the first question. What was the right answer to all of this? Alex stared across the lake, watching the water ripple softly in the wind. She didn't know. Even now, with more of her memories and things clearer than they had ever been before, she still had no idea of what was coming. The Darkness was forcing beings to run for their lives. Of course, they reacted with fear and violence when the place they ran to wasn't the safe haven they sought. Alex could understand that.

And yet, it changed nothing. It felt like it should. Resentment tried to bubble up in her gut, but Alex was too tired for it. She couldn't change the very structure of the universe, and neither could they. Apparently, some things were just not meant to meet. Still, she couldn't help the sympathy in her heart for the Fae, and the Old Ones like Robin. Now she could understand why Shiva left any Demons who didn't cause trouble a lone.

But where would it all lead? She flexed her fingers. The voices whispered to her. Michel's voice was soft but determined. He felt the strongest sympathy for those who fled here. Arto was less generous, but he was understanding. Those who had experience with beings from other worlds were understanding and kind, but they didn't have any solutions either.

The wind tickled the back of her neck, tugging gently at the short hairs that wouldn't go into her ponytail. Tightening her jacket around herself, Alex watched a golden leaf be pulled from a tree. It was carried on the wind and landed on the surface of the lake. Beautiful, but not helpful.

Those fleeing creatures needed help. Their fear drove them to do horrible things like possession just for a chance to survive. She was supposed to help them, wasn't she? Alex liked to think that she was the hero, but she wasn't helping them. Did that make her a monster? Did it make all the mages more evil than good? Or was this beyond the terms of morality, and instead truly just down to the cold, hard facts of nature? Gravity was a brutal fact. It pulled on everyone and everything, even if it meant someone falling to their deaths. Magic was created even if those from other worlds intended no harm. They didn't belong. Her heart ached, but Alex told herself to accept it.

The real issue wasn't about them coming here; it was about the Darkness coming here. It all went back to whatever the Darkness was. She frowned, remembering the pitch-black mass with the strange shimmers of purple as it moved. So much like the poison. She still didn't understand how that was possible. The poison had been in the Iron Realm even before her soul had been born for the first time. And if they weren't careful, it was going to be here in the form of the Darkness very soon.

So, if she wanted a way out of her current moral debate, then the question to ask had nothing to do with what was right and what was wrong. She instead needed to ask the question of how did a mage in the Iron Realm fight back the Darkness in the Tree of Reality. So far, the only clue she had was that strange jar. Closing her eyes, Alex inhaled slowly and relaxed her shoulders. That was the place that they'd have to start. It was time to learn what another version of her had known that Merlin and Morgana didn't.

Standing up, Alex dusted off her knees and the backside of her jeans. She stepped over to Bran, entwining their arms.

"How is Jenny this morning? The hangover finally gone?"

"Seems to be," Bran agreed. "She and Nicki did go a bit hard at it."

"Jenny's still insisting that Nicki needs to find a way to share the memory?" Alex said.

"That's dark," Robin said, following along behind them.

Bran chuckled warmly, shifting a little closer to Alex. "Nah, Jenny's decided that she probably doesn't need to see his death, but she and Lance are a little freaked out by the idea of a zombie Arthur."

"I'm pretty sure it isn't a zombie," Robin said. "Then again, we'll see if the Light can hold back decomposition."

Shuddering, Alex twisted her head around to glare at Robin. The Old One just shrugged and Bran shook his head fondly. Alex sighed and rolled her eyes. She could wrestle with her ethical concerns later once she had some kind of plan. None of their team had died, and they had a new ally. This was enough of a victory for now.